**Praise for *New York Times* bestselling author
Lori Foster**

"Count on Lori Foster for sexy, edgy romance."

—Jayne Ann Krentz, *New York Times*
bestselling author, on *No Limits*

"A sexy, heartwarming, down-home tale that features
two captivating love stories... A funny and engaging
addition to the series that skillfully walks the line
between romance and women's fiction."

—*Library Journal* on *Sisters of Summer's End*

"Foster fills her scenes with plenty of banter and
sizzling chemistry."

—*Publishers Weekly* on *Driven to Distraction*

**Praise for *USA TODAY* bestselling author
Joanne Rock**

"Joanne Rock's sweet and sexy story pulled my
heartstrings and pushed my hot buttons from the
start... Multileveled and fast paced... Delivers the
couple to a well-deserved HEA."

—*Smart Bitches, Trashy Books* on
Dances Under the Harvest Moon

"The characters have a huge range, the story has a
great flow and will keep you on the edge of your seat
and yes it is hot. *Up Close and Personal* is definitely
another must read from Ms. Rock."

—*Harlequin Junkie*

JORDAN

NEW YORK TIMES BESTSELLING AUTHOR

LORI FOSTER

HARLEQUIN® SELECTS™

Recycling programs for this product may not exist in your area.

ISBN-13: 978-1-335-40668-2

Jordan
First published in 2000. This edition published in 2022.
Copyright © 2000 by Lori Foster

His Secretary's Surprise Fiancé
First published in 2016. This edition published in 2022.
Copyright © 2016 by Joanne Rock

For questions and comments about the quality of this book, please contact us at CustomerService@Harlequin.com.

Harlequin Enterprises ULC
22 Adelaide St. West, 41st Floor
Toronto, Ontario M5H 4E3, Canada
www.Harlequin.com

Printed in U.S.A.

CONTENTS

Lori Foster is a *New York Times* and *USA TODAY* bestselling author of more than one hundred titles. Lori has been a recipient of the prestigious *RT Book Reviews* Career Achievement Award for Series Romantic Fantasy and for Contemporary Romance. For more about Lori, visit her website at lorifoster.com.

Books by Lori Foster

HQN

Road to Love

Driven to Distraction
Slow Ride
All Fired Up

The Summer Resort

Cooper's Charm
Sisters of Summer's End

Body Armor

Under Pressure
Hard Justice
Close Contact
Fast Burn

The Ultimate series

Hard Knocks (prequel ebook novella)
No Limits
Holding Strong
Tough Love
Fighting Dirty

Visit the Author Profile page at
Harlequin.com for more titles.

JORDAN

Lori Foster

Chapter 1

The swine.

Jordan Sommerville stared at the hand-painted sign positioned crookedly over the ramshackle building. Visible from the roadway, the sign boasted some of the worst penmanship he'd ever seen. The bright red letters seemed to leap right out at him.

He cursed as another icy trickle of rain slid down the back of his neck. He could hear the others behind him, murmuring in subdued awe as they took in the sights and sounds of the bar. It was late, it was dark, and for September, it was unseasonably cool. Surely there didn't exist a more idiotic way to spend a Friday night.

The idea of trying to convince a bar owner to institute a drink limit, especially a bar owner who had thus far allowed quite a few men to overimbibe, seemed futile. Jordan started forward, anxious to get it over with.

Somehow he'd become the designated leader of the five-man troop, a dubious honor he'd regretfully accepted. The men had been organized by Zenny, a retired farmer who was best described as cantankerous—on his good days. Then there was Walt and Newton, who claimed to be semiretired from their small-town shops, though they still spent every day there. And Howard and Jesse, the town gossips who volunteered for every project, just to make sure they got to stick their noses into anything that was going on.

Jordan stopped at the neon-lighted doorway to the seedy saloon and turned to face the men. A strobing beer sign in the front window illuminated their rapt faces. Jordan had to shout to be heard over the loud music and laughter blaring from inside the establishment.

"Now remember," he said, and though he used his customary calm tone, he infused enough command to hold all their attention, "we're going to *talk*. That's all. There'll be no accusations, no threats and absolutely, under no circumstances, will there be any violence. Understood?"

Five heads bobbed in agreement even as they looked anxiously beyond Jordan to the rambunctious partying inside. Jordan sighed.

Buckhorn County was dry, which meant anyone who drank had the good sense to stay indoors and keep it private. There'd been too many accidents on the lake, mostly from vacationers who thought water sports and alcohol went hand in hand, for the citizens to want it any other way.

But this new bar, a renovated old barn, had opened just over the county line, so the same restriction didn't apply. Lately, some of its customers had tried joyriding through Buckhorn in the dead of the night, hitting fences, tearing up cornfields, terrorizing the farm animals, and generally making minor mayhem. No one had been seriously injured, yet, but in the face of such moronic amusements, it was only a matter of time.

So the good citizens of Buckhorn had rallied together and, at the suggestion of the Town Advisory Board, decided to try talking to the owner of the bar. They hoped he would be reasonable and agree to restrict drinks to the rowdier customers, or perhaps institute a drink limit for those that leaned toward nefarious tendencies and overindulgence.

Jordan already knew what a waste of time that would be. He had his own very personal reasons for loathing drunks. He would have gently refused to take part in the futile endeavor tonight, except that he and his brothers were considered leading citizens of Buckhorn, and right now, due to a nasty flu that had swept through the town, Jordan was the only brother available to lead.

With a sigh, he walked through the scarred wooden doors and stepped inside. The smoke immediately made his lungs hurt. Mixed with the smells of sweat and the sickening sweet odor of liquor, it was enough to cause the strongest stomach to lurch.

The dank, dark night worked as a seal, enclosing the bar in a sultry cocoon. The walls were covered with dull gray paint. Long fluorescent lights hung down from the exposed ceiling beams, adding a dim illumination to an otherwise gloomy scene.

Men piled up behind Jordan, looking over his shoulder, breathing on his neck, tsking at what they saw as salacious activity. Which didn't, of course, stop them from ogling the scene in deep fascination. Jordan could almost feel their anticipation and knew the evening was not destined to end well.

Hoping to locate someone in charge, Jordan looked around. A heavy, sloping counter seated several men, all of them hanging over their beers while a painfully skinny, balding man refilled drinks with the quickness of long practice. At the end of the bar stood a massive, menacing bouncer, the look on his face deliberately intimidating. Jordan snorted, seeing the ploy for what it was; a way to keep the peace in a place that cultivated disagreements by virtue of what it was and the purpose it served.

There were booths lining the walls and a few round tables cluttering up the middle of the floor. Overall, the place seemed crowded and loud, but not lively. An atmosphere of depression hung in the air despite the bawdy laughter.

Then suddenly the noise of conversation, clinking glasses and rowdy music died away. In its place a heavy, expectant hush filled the air. Jordan felt the hair on his arms tingle with a subtle awareness. Everyone stared at a low stage to the left of the front door, almost in the center of the bar. It couldn't have been more than eight feet wide and ten feet long. A faded, threadbare curtain at the back of the stage rustled but didn't open.

Jordan stared, feeling as mesmerized as everyone else, though he had no idea why. Behind him, old man Zenny coughed. Walt eased closer. Newton bumped into his left side.

Slowly, so slowly Jordan hardly noticed it at first, music from a hidden stereo began to filter into the quiet. It crackled a bit, as if the speakers had been subjected to excessive volume. It started out low and easy and grad-ually built to a rousing tempo that made him think of the *Lone Ranger* series. All the men who'd previously been loud were now subdued and waiting.

The curtain parted just as the music grabbed a bouncing beat and took off like a horse given his lead. Jordan caught his breath.

A woman, slight in build except for her truly excep-tional breasts, burst onto the stage in what appeared to be an aerobic display except that she moved with the music…and looked seductive as hell.

He'd seen his three sisters-in-law do similar steps while exercising, but then, his sisters-in-law didn't have breasts like this woman, and they were always dressed in sweats when they worked out.

And they sure as certain didn't perform for drunks.

Nearly spellbound, Jordan couldn't pull his gaze away. His mouth opened on a deep breath, his hands curled into fists and his body tightened. The reaction surprised him and kept him off guard.

As he stared he realized the woman wasn't exactly doing a seductive dance. But the way she moved, fluid and graceful and fast, each turn or twist or high kick keeping time to the throbbing beat, had every man in the bar—including Jordan—holding his breath, bal-anced on a keen edge of anticipation.

She wore a revealing costume of black lace, strategi-cally placed fringe, and little else. The fringe glittered with jet beads that moved as she moved, drawing at-tention to her bouncing breasts and rotating hips. Her legs were slender, sleekly muscled. She turned her back to the bar, and the fringe on her behind did a little *flip-*

flip-flip. Jordan's right hand twitched, just imagining what that bottom would feel like.

He cursed under his breath. The costume covered her, and yet it didn't. He'd seen women at the lake wearing bikinis that were much more revealing, but none that were sexier. She kept perfect time with the heavy pulsing of the music and within two minutes her shoulders and upper chest gleamed with a fine mist of sweat, making her glow. Her full breasts, revealed almost to her nipples, somehow managed to stay inside her skimpy costume, but the thought that they might not kept Jordan rigid and enrapt.

Next to him, Newton whispered, "Lord have mercy," and the same awe Jordan felt was revealed in the older man's voice. Jordan scowled, wishing he could send the men back outside, wishing he could somehow cover the woman up.

He didn't want others looking at her. But he could have looked at her all night long.

His possessive urges toward a complete stranger were absurd, so he buried them away behind a dose of contempt while ignoring the punching beat of his heart.

The audience cheered, screamed, banged their thick beer mugs on the counter and on the tabletops. Yet the woman's expression never changed. She didn't smile, though her overly lush, wide mouth trembled slightly with her exertions. She had a mouth made for kissing, for devouring. Her lips looked soft and Jordan knew with a man's intuition exactly how sweet they'd feel against his own mouth, his skin. Every now and then she turned in such a way that the lighting reflected in her pale gray eyes, which stared straight ahead, never once focusing on any one man.

In fact, her complete and utter disregard for her all-male audience was somehow arousing. She looked to be the epitome of sexual temptation, but didn't care. She might have been dancing alone, in the privacy of her bedroom, for all the attention she gave to the shouting, leering spectators.

Feigning nonchalance, Jordan crossed his arms over his chest and decided to wait until her show ended before finding the proprietor. Not because she interested him. Of course not. But because right now it would be useless to start his search, being that everyone was caught up in the show.

Despite his attempt at indifference, Jordan's gaze never left her, and every so often it seemed his heartbeat mirrored her rhythm. Beneath his skin, a strange warmth expanded, pulsed. Something about her, something elusive yet intrinsically female, called to him. He ignored the call. He was not a man drawn in by flagrant sexuality. No, when a woman caught his attention, it was because of her gentleness, her intelligence, her morals. Unlike his brothers—who were the finest men he knew—he'd never been a slave to his libido. They'd often teased him about his staid personality, his lack of fire, because he'd made a point of keeping his composure in all things. *At least most of the time.*

His eyes narrowed.

Short, golden brown curls framed her face and were beginning to darken with sweat, clinging to her temples and her throat. It was an earthy look, dredging up basic primal appetites. Jordan wondered what those damp curls would feel like in his fingers, what her heated skin would taste like to his tongue. How her warmed body would feel under his, moving as smoothly to his sexual demands as it moved to the music.

As the rhythmic beat began to fade, she dropped smoothly to her knees, then her stomach. Palms flat on the floor, arms extended, she arched her body in a parody of a woman in the throes of pleasure. The move was blatantly sexual, deliberately seducing, causing the crowd to almost riot and making Jordan catch his breath.

Her face was exquisite at that moment, eyes closed, mouth slightly parted, nostrils flaring. Jordan locked his jaw against the mental images filling his brain— images of him holding her hips while she rode him in just that way, taking him deep inside her body.

He wanted to banish the thoughts, but they wouldn't budge. Anger at himself and at the woman conflicted with his growing tension.

He knew every damn man in the place was imagining the same thing and it enraged him.

In that instant her eyes slowly opened and her glittering gray gaze locked on his. Jordan sucked in a breath, feeling as though she'd just touched him in all the right places. They were connected as surely as any lovers, despite the space between them, the surroundings and the lack of prior knowledge. Her eyes turned hot and a bit frightened as they filled with awareness.

Then she caught herself and with a lift of her chin, she swung her legs around and came effortlessly to her feet.

Scowling at the unexpected effect of her, Jordan tried, without success, to pull his gaze away. There was nothing about a mostly naked vamp dancing in a sleazy bar for the delectation of drunks that should appeal to him.

So why was he so aroused?

He hadn't had such a staggering reaction to a female since his teens when puberty had made him more interested in sex than just about anything else. But he'd grown up since then. He was a mature, responsible man now. He was…

The music died away to utter silence. The hush in the room was rich and hungry.

She wasn't beautiful, Jordan insisted to himself, attempting to argue away his racing heartbeat, his clenched muscles and his swelling sex. In fact, she was barely pretty. But she was as sexy as the original temptation, her appeal basic and erotic.

Over the silence, Jordan detected the sound of her heavy breathing with the force of a thunderclap. A roar of approval started the massive applause, and within seconds the room rocked with the sounds of masculine appreciation and entreaties for more. Jordan continued to watch her, not smiling, not about to encourage her. He waited for her to meet his gaze again, but she didn't. She looked straight ahead, deliberately ignoring him.

Anger simmered inside him, warring with lust.

Slowly, still struggling for breath, she took a bow. He hadn't noticed until that moment that she wore high heels. Amazing, he thought, remembering how she'd moved, the gracefulness of her every step. Her legs looked especially long in the spiked heels.

She tottered slightly as if in exhaustion, appearing young and vulnerable for the space of a heartbeat. Money was thrown onstage, some of it hitting the open urn positioned at the edge, most of it landing around her feet. She didn't bend to pick it up or acknowledge the money in any way. She merely stood there, as proud and imperious as a queen while the men payed homage, begging her for more, emptying their pockets.

If Jordan hadn't been watching her so closely, he wouldn't have seen her hands curl into fists, or the way her soft mouth tightened. With one last nod of her head, she turned to leave the stage. That's when the trouble started.

Two men reached for her, one catching her wrist, the other stroking her knee and thigh.

A wave of rage hit Jordan with such force, it nearly took him to his knees.

He couldn't dispute his own reaction, and started toward her. At almost the same time, the bouncer pushed himself away from the back wall, but Jordan barely noticed him. He kept his gaze on the woman's face as she tried to pull her hand free, but the drunken men had other plans. One of them attempted to press money into her hand while he suggested several lecherous possibilities, egged on by his buddy.

Others seconded the drunks' suggestions, throwing more money, making catcalls and urging her to another dance…and more.

She firmly refused, and again tried to step away. Her gaze sought out the bouncer, but he'd been detained by a table full of younger men who were insisting the woman should continue.

Jordan reached the edge of the stage just as she said, "Go on home to your wife, Larry. The show's over."

Her deep throaty voice was filled with loathing and exhaustion. It affected Jordan almost as strongly as the sight of the drunk's rough hand wrapped around her slender wrist. He barely restrained himself from attacking the man, and that alone was an aberration. Jordan had never considered himself a violent or overly aggressive person.

"Let the lady go."

Reacting to the command in Jordan's tone, the man released her automatically, only to turn on Jordan with a growl.

"Who the hell are you?" As he asked it, Larry took a threatening step forward.

Jordan gave him a stark look of contempt. In as reasonable a voice as he could muster, considering his mood and the obstreperous noise of the bar, he said, "You're drunk and I'm not. I'm bigger in every way. And right now, I'd like to tear you in two." Jordan watched him, his gaze unwavering. "Does it really matter who I am?"

Larry reeked of alcohol, as if he'd been at the bar all day. Perhaps that accounted for his loss of good sense. But for whatever reason, he disregarded Jordan's warning and attempted a clumsy punch. Jordan leaned back two inches so that Larry's limp fist whipped right past his jaw, then he stuck his foot out, gave the smaller man a shove, and sent him sprawling. Larry screeched like a wet hen, but when he hit the dusty barn floor he landed hard, and he didn't look sober enough to get back up.

"Oh, for heaven's sake…" The dancer's words were muttered low, but Jordan heard her. He glanced up. The other man stepped back quickly at the look of menace in Jordan's eyes. Unfortunately, he still had his hand hooked around the woman's knee and his sudden retreat pulled her off balance. With a loud gasp, she stumbled right off the edge of the low stage and would have landed next to Larry if Jordan hadn't caught her.

The impact of her small, lush body caused Jordan to stumble, too, but he easily regained his balance and, acting on pure male instinct, wrapped his arms tightly around her bottom. Her belly landed flush against his lower chest, her ripe breasts pressed to his face. Jordan stood, for a single instant, stunned.

Her small hands felt cool on his burning skin, the contrast maddening. Braced against his shoulders, she pushed back and Jordan was able to see her angry face.

"Are you *insane?*" she demanded.

"At this moment?" Jordan asked, unable to concentrate on anything of import, not with those incredible breasts a mere breath away. "I believe so."

He held very still, feeling trapped by her nearness, by the deep timbre of her voice, her warm, gentle weight, her seductive movements. Her body was lithe and supple, soft, despite her determination to push away from him. Acutely aware of one firm breast pressing into his jaw, he could see far too much cleavage to allow for divided attention.

Her black lace bodysuit dipped low in front, displaying the paleness and lush roundness of her breasts; the material was so sheer he could plainly make out the outline of her puckered nipples, thrusting noticeably against the material. His mouth went dry. He was so hard he hurt.

He wanted to taste her.

Contrary to all reason, to the situation, to the crowd around them, *to his own basic nature,* he wanted to draw her into the heat of his mouth, lick her, taste her, hear her husky moans. He'd only need to turn his head a scant two inches and…

His breath came faster, his stomach cramped.

Her naked thighs were sleek and smooth and warm against his forearms, which he had crossed beneath her bottom. Up close, her overdone makeup was even more apparent—but then, so was her allure. Jordan met her gaze and they each stalled.

Her pale skin was tinged pink from exertion and embarrassment. Her nose was narrow, tilted up on the end like an innocent pixie's, her mouth so full and soft he could almost feel the effect of it against his skin, making his body throb. Her face was a perfect oval, her cheeks a little too round, her chin a little too stubborn. But those arctic gray eyes…

He'd never seen any like them.

Her breath caught sharply as he studied her mouth. With a burst of near panic, she began her struggles anew. Her efforts to free herself from his hold set them off-kilter and Jordan fell back a step.

A rickety table overturned as he bumped into it, spilling several drinks. Jordan, feeling a little drunk himself as he breathed in the smell of her musky, heated skin, especially strong between her soft breasts, attempted to regain his balance and apologize at the same time.

He wasn't given a chance. This time the man swinging his meaty fist had better aim. Jordan quickly tried to set the dancer on her feet even as he ducked. He wasn't fast enough to do either.

His head snapped back from a solid clip in the jaw. Pain exploded, but Jordan didn't lose his hold on the woman. In fact, his arms felt locked, unable to open even when he wanted them to.

Ears ringing from the blow, Jordan allowed his anger to erupt. Because of how he held her, that fist had come entirely too close to touching a woman.

His head now clearer, Jordan gently released his feminine bundle and moved her behind his back, keeping her there when she attempted to stall the fight. He eyed the man who'd struck him, and with a sharp, lightning-fast reflex that was more automatic than not, Jordan used the backward sweep of his bent arm to slam his elbow into the man's jaw. His blow was far more powerful than the one he'd received, and the man sank like a brick in water. Other than his arm, Jordan hadn't moved—and his mood was deadly.

All hell broke loose.

The bouncer who'd just witnessed Jordan's retaliation came charging forward. Jordan sighed. He wasn't a regular, which he supposed meant he was automatically tagged as the troublemaker.

Looking quickly around for the older men who'd come with him, Jordan found them safely ensconced in the far corner near the front door where they could watch while staying unharmed. He didn't have time to breathe a sigh of relief.

The bouncer grabbed Jordan's arm and jerked him forward. Normally Jordan would have attempted to talk his way out of the confrontation. He wasn't, in the usual course of things, a combative man. But the bar had opened up to a free-for-all. Chairs flew around him, bottles and glasses were thrown. Men were shouting and punching and cursing.

Jordan locked his jaw. He needed to get the woman out of harm's way, and he needed to take his cohorts back to Buckhorn. Before he had time to really think about what he would do, he ducked under the bouncer's meaty arm and came up behind him. The guy was huge, easily four inches taller than Jordan's six foot one, with a neck the size of a tree trunk. Jordan gripped the man's fingers and applied just enough negative pressure for the big guy to issue a moan of pain. Jordan wrapped his free arm around the bouncer's throat and squeezed.

"Just hold still," Jordan said in disgust, wondering what the hell he should do now. He ducked a body that came staggering past, inadvertently hurting the bouncer further. Damn, things had gotten out of hand.

Jordan wasn't a fighter, but he had grown up with two older brothers and one younger. Being the pacifist in a family full of physical aggressors, he'd been taught to give as well as take. Not that he and his brothers had ever had any serious fistfights. But his brothers played as hard as they fought, so Jordan had learned how to hold his own.

Morgan, his second oldest brother, was built like a solid brick wall and Jordan had practiced up on him most of his life. There were few things that Morgan enjoyed more than a good skirmish. And though he was beyond fair, Morgan always finished as the victor.

Jordan knew how to handle the big ones. Morgan had generously seen to that.

Sirens sounded outside, adding to the confusion. In strangled tones, the bouncer demanded to be released, but Jordan ignored him, maintaining his awkward hold and refusing to lose the upper hand. Using the large man as a shield, Jordan turned to the woman and shouted, "Get away from here."

She hesitated for only a moment, sending a regretful look at the money scattered across the stage. Then her

gray eyes met his and she nodded her agreement. But
before she could go, her eyes widened and she looked
beyond Jordan. He twisted just in time to avoid getting hit from behind. The bouncer ended up taking the
brunt of the blow, which left him cursing and very disgruntled, but still very alert. Jordan raised his brows.
It was a good thing he'd immobilized the big bruiser,
because he wasn't at all certain he could have bested
him face-to-face.

He turned back in time to see the woman scrambling
up onto the stage. In her retreat, she gave Jordan a delectable view of her bottom in the skimpy costume. Despite
his precarious position—having his arms filled with an
outraged bouncer—Jordan felt his heartbeat accelerate
at the luscious sight of her. She was almost to the curtain when several policemen charged through the doors.

With a feeling of dread, Jordan saw the officers draw
their guns as they issued the clichéd order of *"every-
body freeze."*

Zenny, Walt, Newton and the others were nowhere
in sight, having evidently made a run for it when they
heard the sirens. At least they'd managed to avoid this
situation, Jordan thought. In fact, he'd be willing to bet
they were already halfway back to Buckhorn, anxious
to begin spreading tales of his night of debauchery.
This was likely more excitement than any of the older
citizens had experienced in many years, and the only
thing that might compare would be the joy of telling
others about it.

Jordan's thoughts were interrupted when a young officer climbed onto the stage and approached the dancer.
She looked like she wanted to run, but instead she faced
him with a defiant pose and began arguing. Dressed as

she was, her attitude was more ludicrous than not. A mostly naked woman could hardly be taken seriously.

Jordan started toward her, bustling the bouncer along with him, meaning to intervene. But before he'd taken two steps another officer stepped in front of him. All around them, men were shouting curses and arguing, which did them no good at all. Having no choice, Jordan released the bouncer, who began shaking his hand and cursing and promising dire consequences. He was quickly handcuffed and urged into the crowd of men being corralled outside. The officer turned to Jordan with a frown.

Knowing there was no hope for it, Jordan merely held out his hands and suffered the unique experience of being handcuffed. Beside him, men attempted to argue their circumstances, and were shoved roughly out the door for their efforts. Jordan shook his head at the demeaning display while still keeping one eye on the woman. Someone, he thought, should at least offer to let her get dressed.

"You're not from around here, are you?" the officer asked Jordan.

"No, I'm from Buckhorn." He gave the admission grudgingly, but he already knew there was no way to keep this stupid contretemps from his brothers. They'd rib him about this for the rest of eternity.

The officer lifted a brow and grinned with a good deal of satisfaction. "That's a break. You can just wait in my car while I notify the sheriff of Buckhorn. He can deal with you himself and save me the trouble."

When the officer started to pull him away, Jordan asked, "The woman…?"

"I'd worry about my own hide if I was you," he said,

then added, "That Buckhorn sheriff is one mean son of a bitch."

Since the sheriff was none other than his brother Morgan, Jordan was already well aware of that fact. He lost sight of the woman as he was escorted outside through the rain and into the back seat of a cruiser where he cursed his fate, his libido and his damned temper, which had chosen a hell of a bad time to display itself. The car he'd arrived in was long gone, proving his supposition that the others had headed home.

The car door opened again and an officer helped the woman inside. She faltered when she saw Jordan sitting there, staring at her in blank surprise. "Oh, Lord," she whispered with heartfelt distress. She dropped back into the seat and covered her face with her hands. "Just when I think the night can't get any worse…."

Jordan breathed in the scent of her rain-damp skin and hair, acutely aware of her frustration, her exhaustion. He settled into his seat and realized that despite how she felt, the night had just taken a dramatic turn for the better as far as he was concerned.

Chapter 2

"You live in Buckhorn?" he asked, which was the only conclusion he could come up with for why she was now in the car with him.

When she didn't answer, the officer gave him a man-to-man look and said, "According to her license, she does."

Jordan leaned forward to see her face, but with her hands still covering it, that wasn't possible. He gently caught her wrists and tugged them down. Their handcuffs clinked together.

Softly, attempting to put her at ease, he asked, "Whereabouts? I've never seen you before." And he sure as certain would have remembered if he ever had. Even if she'd been fully clothed and doing something as mundane as shopping for groceries, he felt certain he'd have paid special attention to her. There was something about her that hit him on a gut level.

Just being this close to her now had his muscles cramping in a decidedly erotic way. Like the effects of prolonged foreplay, the sensation was pleasurable yet somewhat painful at the same time, because of the imposed restraint.

Their gazes met, his curious, hers wary and antagonistic. She looked away. "Where I live," she said under her breath, "is no concern of yours."

The officer answered again, disregarding her wishes for privacy. "You know that old farmhouse, out by the water tower? She moved in there."

The woman glared at the officer, who did manage to look a bit sheepish over his quick tongue. He leaned farther into the car to remove her handcuffs and place her purse in her lap. Jordan stared at her narrow wrists while she rubbed them, feeling his temper prick at the thought that she might have been hurt.

She wore no jewelry—no wedding band.

The officer spared him a glance. "If I remove your handcuffs, too, do you think you can behave yourself?"

It rankled, being treated like an unruly child, but Jordan was too busy staring at the woman to take too much offense. He silently held up his hands and waited to have them unlocked. The woman stared out her window past the officer, ignoring Jordan completely.

"What are we waiting for?" Jordan asked, before the officer could walk away.

"The chief agrees that Sheriff Hudson can deal with the both of you. Our jail is overcrowded as it is, and it's going to be a late night getting everyone's phone calls out of the way. Just sit tight. Hudson's already been called."

Jordan groaned softly. Morgan had his hands full taking care of Misty tonight. She was laid low with the nastiest case of flu Jordan had ever seen, and with their baby daughter to contend with, Morgan wouldn't appreciate being called out. Of course, his brother Gabe or one of his sisters-in-law, Honey or Elizabeth, would gladly give a helping hand. But that meant they then ran the risk of getting the flu, too.

Jordan forced his gaze away from the woman and dropped his head back against the seat. "I'm never going to hear the end of this."

She shifted slightly away from him, though she was already pressed up against the door. Jordan swiveled his head just a bit to see her. The night was dark with no stars visible, no moonlight. Shadows played over her features and exaggerated her guarded frown. She looked quietly, disturbingly miserable. And she was shivering.

No wonder, he thought, calling himself three kinds of fool. The outfit she wore offered no protection at all from the rainy night air. Though it was September, a cool wet spell had rolled into Kentucky forcing everyone into slightly warmer clothes. Jordan studied her bare shoulders and slim naked limbs as he removed his jacket. It was damp around the collar, but still dry on the inside, and warm from his own body heat.

Aware of her efforts to ignore him, he held it out to her, his gaze intent. "Put this on," he told her, using his most cajoling tone. "You're shivering."

Very slowly, she turned her head and looked at him with the most distant, skeptical expression he'd ever seen on a female face. "Why are you talking like that?"

Jordan started in surprise. "Like what?" he asked, not quite so softly or cajoling.

Her frown was filled with distrust...and accusation.

"Like you're trying to seduce me. Like a man talks to a woman when they're alone together in bed."

Jordan couldn't have been more floored by her direct attack if she'd clobbered him. Totally bemused, he opened his mouth, but nothing came out.

She made a sound of disgust. "You can stop wasting your time. I'm not interested. And no, I don't want your jacket."

Taken off guard, Jordan frowned. All his life, women had told him he had the most compelling voice. He could lull a wounded bear to sleep or talk grown men out of a fistfight. At the ripe old age of thirty-three, he'd garnered a half dozen wedding proposals from women who said they loved to just listen to him talk, especially in bed.

But right then, at this particular moment, he didn't even think about trying to be persuasive. He even forgot that he *could* be persuasive.

"Don't be a fool," he growled. "You'll end up catching your death running around near naked like that."

Her arms crossed over her middle and her neck stiffened at his exasperated tone. A heavy beat of silence passed before she rounded on him. Her eyes weren't cool now. They were bright and hot with anger.

"I can't believe you got me into this fix," she nearly shouted, "then have the nerve to try to seduce me and—"

"I wasn't trying to seduce you, damn it!"

"—and to criticize me!"

Distracted by the way her crossed arms hefted her breasts a little higher, Jordan was slow to respond. He managed to drag his gaze up to her very angry face again, and he scowled. "*I* got you into this fix? Honey, I'm the one who was trying to help you out!"

She thrust her jaw toward him in clear challenge. She was so close, her sweet hot breath pelted his face. "I'm not your damn *honey,* mister, and I didn't need your help. I deal with Larry in one way or another nearly every night. He's a regular at the bar—a regular drunk and a regular pain in the butt. But I know how to handle him." Her lip curled, and she added with contempt, "Obviously, you don't."

Jordan let his hand holding the jacket drop to the seat between them. Never in his life had he been at such a loss for words. He rubbed his chin, scrutinizing her until she squirmed. Good. Her discomfort, in the face of her hostility, gave him a heady dose of satisfaction.

"Ah." He cocked one brow. "I think I understand now."

"I seriously doubt that."

He shrugged. "I suppose any woman with enough guts to display herself as you did tonight must know how to handle the pathetic drunks who want to grope her. I'm sorry I interfered. Would Larry have given you a bigger tip?"

She choked on an outraged breath. "You hypocrite! I had you pegged from the start. You sit there and condemn me, yet you were at the bar, weren't you? You'll gladly watch, even as you look down your nose at the entertainment."

Jordan leaned closer, too, drawn to her like a magnet, wishing he could lift her into his lap and hold her close and feel all that angry passion flush against his body. She practically vibrated with her fury, and for some fool reason it turned him on like the most potent aphrodisiac.

"I was there," Jordan said, "to protest the place, not to support your little display."

Her eyes widened and her chest heaved; Jordan couldn't help it, he stared at her breasts. They were more than a handful, shimmering with her frustration, creamy pale and looking so soft. His palms itched with the need to scoop those luscious breasts out of her bodice and weigh them in his hands, to flick her nipples with his thumbs until they stiffened, until she moaned.

He swallowed hard and met her gaze, knowing his look was covetous, knowing that she knew it, too.

"So," she said, and to his interest, she sounded a bit breathless despite her efforts at acerbity, "you're a vigilante? One of those crazy people who protests all the sinners, people who drink or dance or have fun of any kind?"

"Not at all." They were both so close now, a mere inch separated them. She wasn't backing off any more than he was, and her bravado served as another source of excitement. He'd never met a woman like her.

Jordan felt the clash of wills and the draw of sensual interest. "My only concern," he murmured, distracted by her warmth, her scent, "is the inebriated men who leave the bar and enter my county. *Your* county. They've caused a few problems which I'd like to see taken care of before someone ends up hurt or even killed."

Her gaze dropped to his mouth. Jordan drew a deep breath, trying to remember what it was he had to say. "I had intended to talk to the owner, nothing more. But then, I didn't realize you liked being felt up by Larry."

Her gaze jerked back to his. Her bottom lip quivered before she stilled it, making Jordan wonder if it was caused by upset at his nasty words—*why* was he being nasty, damn it?—or from the distinct chill of the night. He felt the first nigglings of shame for baiting her. In the normal course of things, he never intentionally insulted women. He was gentle and understanding. But this wasn't a normal night, she wasn't the average woman, and his reactions to her were as far from the expected as he could get.

"He touched my leg," she said succinctly, "and before he would have touched anything else, Gus would have stopped him."

"Gus?" A tiny flare of jealousy took him by surprise.

"The bouncer. The one you…"

"Ah." Jordan saw a hint of color sweep over her face and touched her cheek with his fingertips, gently smoothing a damp curl aside. "The big bruiser I stopped from knocking me out. Why the hell was he attacking me, anyway?"

She didn't protest his touch. They were both breathing too hard, too fast. She lifted one delicate shoulder in a way that made her breasts shift, teasing him with the possibility of gaining a peek at her taut nipples. He was disappointed to see she stayed securely inside the bodice. Jordan shook his head and tried to force himself to concentrate on their conversation, impossible as that seemed.

"He doesn't know you," she said. "And you looked—" She peeked up at him, a slight frown marring her brown. "Well, you looked furious."

"I was furious." His voice dropped to a whisper, making her eyes, shadowed and cautious, widen on his face. "I thought someone was going to hurt you."

Her lips parted.

Outside the car, one man struggling against being arrested fetched up against the door closest to the woman. She jumped, letting out a startled gasp. Without even thinking about it, Jordan clasped her shoulder, offering comfort and reassurance. Her soft skin tempted him and it was all he could do to keep the touch impersonal, to keep from caressing her. But she also felt cool against the warmth of his hand, making him frown.

A lot of activity was going on around them, though he hadn't been aware of it moments before. Above the din of complaints and drunken shouts, Jordan heard the sheriff arguing that he'd been called one time too many to the bar, and now he was forced to actually do something, just so he could get some peace.

Apparently that *something* was a series of arrests, and it didn't matter that Jordan hadn't been drinking, that he hadn't started the fight, and that he'd had nothing to do with the other numerous times the disgruntled sheriff had been summoned.

"Nice place you work at." Jordan continued to smooth his fingers over her skin, unable to force himself to move away from her.

"It pays the bills," was her straightforward reply, then she suddenly seemed to realize his touch and turned to glare at him.

Jordan again held up the coat. "Do you really want my brother to see you looking like that?"

"Your brother?"

"The Buckhorn sheriff. If I know Morgan, he's liable to be here any minute. I'm sure I'll get the brunt of his anger, but believe me, there'll be a heady dose for you, too, since he'd had his evening all planned and it didn't include a jaunt out into the rainy night. Wouldn't you rather be wearing a little more armor than lace and fringe?"

Her hands knotted together in her lap. "Do you think he'll keep us for the night?"

She looked so fragile and delicate, so damn young, Jordan had a hard time reconciling the confident, aloof vamp she'd been on the stage with the concerned, shivering woman she was now. She simply didn't strike him as a person hardened to life, a woman brazen enough to be comfortable with her earlier display.

It was Jordan's turn to shrug. "Who knows? He has no tolerance for ignorance, regardless of the fact we're related. But then again, he's very fair and you and I weren't to blame for what happened in there."

Her glare said differently. Jordan smiled. "Okay, so you think I was to blame. Is that any reason to sit there freezing?" He traced the line of her throat with one fingertip. "Your skin is like ice."

A slight shudder ran through her and her eyes closed. Jordan stared, feeling what she felt, the connection, the instantaneous sexual charge. Like a touch of lightning, it sizzled along his every nerve ending, making him so acutely aware of her he hurt. He'd never known anything like it and he had no idea how to deal with it. He wanted, quite frankly, to pull her down into the seat and strip off her costume and cover her with his body. He wanted to warm her with his heat. He wanted to take her, right now, right here, to brand her with his touch.

There were no gentle words of admiration in his mind, no thoughts of cautious seduction. He felt savage, and it shook him.

After a shuddering breath, she moved away from his caressing fingers and accepted his coat. He helped her to slip it on, watching her contortions in the limited space of the back seat, seeing the thrust of her breasts as she slipped first one arm though, then the other. She lifted slightly to settle it behind her, and Jordan petted the material down her narrow back, all the way to the base of her spine. She felt supple and firm and he relished the sound of her quickened breath.

He smiled at how the sleeves completely hid her hands, curiously satisfied at seeing her in his coat and feeling somewhat barbaric because of it. She trembled so badly she couldn't quite manage the buttons. Jordan brushed her small, chilled hands away and did them up for her. In a voice affected by being so close to her, he whispered, "Better?"

"Yes, thank you."

Her voice, too, sounded huskier than usual, proving to Jordan that he wasn't sinking alone. No. Whatever strange affliction he felt, she felt it, too.

The urge to touch her again was strong, and he gave into it, tucking a damp curl behind her ear. Her hair was as soft as her skin, baby fine, intriguing. It was cut into various-length curls that moved and bounced when she turned her head. Along her nape, the hair had pulled into adorable little ringlets. He lifted those small curls out of the collar of his coat. "I'm Jordan Sommerville," he said, and heard the increasing rush of her breath.

Staring down at her hands, she replied, "Georgia Barnes."

"Georgia? As in a Georgia peach?"

"Don't start." Then she blinked and looked up at him. "Sommerville? I thought you said Sheriff Hudson was your brother?"

"Half brother," Jordan explained. He felt the old bitterness rise up, nearly choking him.

Her head tilted in a curious way. "The sheriff is your younger brother?"

"No. Morgan is the second oldest, right behind Sawyer." Jordan didn't feel like explaining. If he was in Buckhorn, he wouldn't have to, because everyone there knew everyone else's business. In fact, he decided she must either be very new to the area or very isolated, not to have already heard the stories herself.

There was no disapproval in her tone when she asked, "Your mother has been married twice?"

Jordan sighed, seeing no hope for it. At least Georgia—what a name, probably just used as a stage name—was talking to him. "My mother's first husband died in the service after giving her two sons, Sawyer and Morgan. She married my father, but not for long because he became a miserable drunk shortly after the wedding."

He saw her eyes glittering in surprise, saw her soft mouth open. Jordan cupped her chin and touched her bottom lip with his thumb, hungry for the taste of her, as unlikely as that seemed. He barely knew her, and for the most part he didn't like what he did know, but he felt as though he'd wanted her forever.

Without meaning to, without even wanting to reveal so much, he added, "By all accounts, my father was the type of man who would have loved this bar—as well as that little show of yours." Slowly, he looked her over in his too large coat, her honey-brown hair wispy and curled with perspiration and rain, her flamboyant makeup smudged.

Her slender bare thigh rested only a few inches beside his, taunting him with its nearness. His hand was large enough that he could cover the entire front of her thigh with his splayed fingers. He could caress her skin, parting her legs as he inched higher and higher until he cupped her, felt her heat, her softness. The material of her bodysuit would offer no obstruction at all. He could...

He muttered a low curse. With the drizzling rain outside sealing them in, her musky scent seemed to permeate his brain. It filled him with lust so strong he felt it in his heartbeat, tasted it on his tongue. He'd never been thrown so off balance in his entire life.

"My father," Jordan said in a raw voice, "would have been right up there with the others, sweetheart, throwing money on the stage, urging you on, and doing his damndest to buy your favors. But seeing you tonight..." He hesitated and his hand opened on the back of her head as he thrust his fingers through her silky hair, urging her closer, watching her pupils expand wildly. "... I can almost forgive him for that."

Jordan's words trailed off into a whisper as her eyes slowly closed, her lips parting on a hungry breath. Her invitation was clear, and he leaned toward her, already growing hard in anticipation of taking her mouth. He couldn't believe this was happening, and he couldn't stop it.

She gave a soft moan as he kissed the very corner of her lips, and another when he tilted his head and brushed his mouth over hers. Her lips parted on the third moan and Jordan took her, his tongue immediately sinking deep, his mind shutting down on everything except the hot taste of her, the wild, savage way she made him feel.

A loud rapping on the window jarred him out of his lust-fogged stupor.

Georgia jumped back, gasping, one hand at her throat as her face drained of color. It didn't take a rocket scientist to know she was mortified, that she'd been as carried away as Jordan. He leaned past her to see his largest brother scowling through the window.

Morgan's hair was plastered to his skull, his face was unshaven and he wore a plain T-shirt and jeans, testimony to the fact that he'd been at home, not on call. He must have driven at top speed, Jordan realized, to have gotten to the bar so quickly.

Morgan's requisite badass look was firmly in place, the one that had kept Buckhorn citizens in line for some time now—the same look that made them all respect him as a man fully capable of handling any situation.

Not in the least daunted by that black expression, Jordan shoved his door open and stepped out of the car, addressing Morgan over the roof. "You've got about the lousiest damn timing of any man I've ever known!"

Morgan, red-eyed and looking mean, made a sound reminiscent of a snarl. "I'm leaving that distinction to you, Jordan. And you better have one helluva good excuse for this, otherwise I'm liable to kick your ass all the way home—where my sick wife and fussing baby girl are waiting."

Jordan prepared to blast him with his own ire, made hotter out of unreasoning sexual frustration. But he'd barely gotten two sputtering words out before Georgia shoved her door open, making Morgan back up a pace. She climbed out of the police car, faced him with a serene expression fit for a queen, and said, "You can handle this little family squabble later. I, for one, would like to get this over with so I can get home."

It was all Georgia could do to keep herself from trembling. The man staring down at her had the most ferocious demeanor she'd ever witnessed on man or rabid dog. Besides being enormous, he was dark and so layered in thick muscle she felt dwarfed beside him.

And here she'd thought Jordan was huge.

Actually, the two men were of a similar height, but where Jordan appeared athletic, lean and toned, this man looked like he could eat gravel for breakfast.

Despite her resolve, she began quaking like a wet Chihuahua. And then suddenly Jordan was at her side.

"Knock it off, Morgan. You're scaring her."

When Jordan's hands settled on her shoulders, she didn't move away. She should have, being that Jordan had the power to turn her knees to jelly and her insides to fire. *She'd let him kiss her.* The reality of that wasn't to be borne.

The man had the most sinfully seductive voice she'd ever heard, even when insulting and baiting her. She'd done the unthinkable, all because his voice had softened her, melting away her will and her resolve. She scowled at herself, feeling the shame claw at her. She didn't like men—not at all. Not for friends, certainly not for lovers.

Most definitely not for a one-night stand, which from what she could deduce, was what Jordan Sommerville was after. He'd made no pretense of liking her or approving of her in any way. The arrogant jerk.

She forced herself to meet the sheriff's gaze. "Actually, you're not. Scaring me, that is." The lie sounded credible even to her own ears, though neither man seemed to believe her. "So if it's all the same to you I'd just as soon get out of this rain and get going."

Morgan snorted, eyeing her with a mix of clear annoyance, and perhaps a touch of approval. "So anxious to spend a night in jail, are you?"

She nearly staggered. "Jail? But…" Her stomach suddenly felt queasy, her knees weak. She couldn't, absolutely couldn't stay away all night. Swallowing hard, and hating what she had to say even before the words left her mouth, she forced herself to meet the sheriff's gaze. "I have to go home. Tonight."

Morgan's eyes narrowed. "Got a husband waiting for you?"

She shook her head and felt a raindrop slither down her nose. "Two children."

Jordan's hands bit reflexively into her shoulders. *"What?"*

Georgia felt hemmed in by testosterone. The sheriff looked too grim by half, and she could feel the tension radiating off Jordan. She shifted her shoulders slightly at the pressure of his fingers and he loosened his hold, then turned her around to face him.

"You have kids?" His eyes were like green fire.

She lifted her chin. "Yes."

The shock on his face was replaced with disgust. "Where the hell is your husband?"

She owed him nothing, certainly no explanations. "Ex-husband. And I have no idea." Jordan's brows smoothed out, and she added, "But wherever he is, I hope he stays there. Now, are you done with your interrogation?"

The sheriff snorted. "Maybe you should ask me that."

Jordan, no longer looking like a thundercloud, pulled her behind his back. Georgia couldn't see around him, but she heard him plain enough as he addressed his brother.

"You're not going to arrest her, Morgan, and you know it, so quit taking your bad temper out on her."

The sheriff seemed to be spoiling for a fight. "Or what?"

"Or I'll tell Misty."

Georgia had no idea who Misty was or why her name would make the sheriff relent, but that's exactly what happened. Sheriff Hudson still sounded annoyed, but no longer so angry. "It's a lousy night for you to do this to me, Jordan."

"Yeah, well, it wasn't my idea for you to be called, you know."

"No? What was your idea? To start an all out brawl? I thought you came along to see that there was no trouble, not to insure that there was."

"I didn't cause the trouble. I was only…"

His words trailed off as Georgia stepped around him and headed for the bar. If the fool men wanted to stand around in the rain and discuss the situation to death, that was fine with her. But now that she felt certain she wouldn't be locked up, she had a better way to spend her time.

Before she'd gone five feet, Jordan's hand closed around her elbow. "Where do you think you're going?"

With a sigh, she drew up short and turned to face him. She shook back one of the long sleeves of his jacket to free a hand, and then shoved her hair out of her face. Her makeup, she knew, was a disaster.

Not that she cared.

Jordan's hold on her arm was gentle. His light brown hair hung over his brow, now more wet than otherwise, and his eyes reflected the bar lights, appearing almost… hungry. She looked quickly away. "I've got money on the stage. If I don't get it now, Bill will abscond with it and I'll have wasted the night for nothing. Since you two don't seem in a big hurry to rush off, and the other sheriff is apparently done inside—"

"Bill?"

He did seem to get hung up on every male name she mentioned. "The owner of the bar. The man you came to see before you got...sidetracked." She tried to pull away but Jordan wasn't letting go.

He turned to Morgan. "Can you give us just a moment?"

"Just." Morgan didn't look happy over the concession, but then, she doubted that this one ever looked happy. "Malone will only stay in bed when I'm there to force her to it. Otherwise, you know how she is. She'll be up and running around, making herself feverish again...."

"We'll be quick. Why don't you go warm up the car?"

With a shrug, the sheriff turned away. Georgia watched him go with relief. "Who's Malone?"

"His wife, Misty."

So it was his wife that Jordan had threatened him with? That seemed curious to Georgia.

"Why does he call her Malone...never mind." Disgusted with herself, Georgia turned away. She didn't care about these men or their strange ways. She walked briskly into the bar, doing her best to ignore the warm touch of Jordan's hand on her arm as he kept pace with her. Even through his coat sleeve, she could feel his strength, his heat. And for some absurd reason, she reacted to it. He had her thinking things she hadn't thought in years, contemplating pleasures she was certain didn't even exist.

Bill was just scooping up the money off the stage when they walked in. Jordan released her and she marched forward, saying sweetly, "Why thank you, Bill. I so appreciate you looking after my money for me."

Bill had the kind of slick good looks that he assumed would get him anything he wanted from women. To Georgia, his perfectly styled blond hair, dark blue eyes, and capped teeth only emphasized what a fraud he was. She didn't trust him one iota and never would.

Bill flashed her a surprised look. "Georgia! I thought you were gone."

"Almost." She stuck out her hand expectantly and Bill tucked the money closer to his chest. "I'm waiting," she said, well used to having to deal with Bill and his miserly ways. Like most men, he had a self-serving streak a mile wide, a selfish attitude whenever it came to money and he didn't hesitate to screw someone when he thought he could get away with it.

"What about the damages to my bar?" he blustered, and cast a nasty look at Jordan Sommerville.

Georgia glanced at Jordan, too, and saw that he had an expression almost as fierce as his brother's. It was the same look he'd worn earlier, when Larry had held on to her wrist. He'd said he was furious…because he thought she might be hurt.

She turned away. "That wasn't my doing, Bill, and you know it. Take up your grievances with the boys locked away. But give me my money." When Bill still dithered, looking undecided as to whether or not he had to obey, she narrowed her eyes and said, "You know I can dance anywhere, Bill. Don't push me. I need the money."

With a foul curse that would have embarrassed her as little as a month ago, Bill thrust the wad of bills into her hands. Most of them were ones, but altogether, it should amount up to a hundred dollars or more, money she needed to make repairs to the house she'd recently bought. With a sugary sweet, utterly false smile, she muttered, "Thank you."

She turned to Jordan, saw his look of contempt, and sniffed. Sanctimonious jerk. "I'm ready if you are."

Jordan held the saloon door open for her and kept stride with her on the way to the large black sport utility vehicle his brother drove. Some official car, she thought, eyeing the shiny black four-wheel-drive Bronco.

The two sheriffs had been talking, but as she and Jordan neared the vehicle, they parted ways. Sheriff Hudson got behind the wheel.

The rain had almost let up, but a chill had settled in that seemed to seep into her bones. Her bare legs were freezing and she'd somehow managed to step into a puddle, getting both feet soaked. She would have changed clothes, but the sheriff was in an obvious hurry to get going and she didn't want to push her luck. The quicker she got this over with, the quicker she could get home. She was so weary she ached all the way down to her toes and more than anything she needed a good night's sleep.

But once she got home, there would be chores to do. If she didn't get some of the laundry taken care of, they'd all be running around naked. She had no doubt the sink was full of dishes, and there were bills that had to be paid before she lost her utilities.

She was so drawn into her thoughts, she nearly tripped over Jordan when he held the front door of the Bronco open for her. Belatedly, she realized he expected her to ride to the sheriff's station sandwiched between two overwhelmingly male bodies.

"I'll sit in back," she offered, hoping she sounded merely casual, not concerned.

Jordan narrowed his gaze on her. "You'll ride up front. I want to talk to you."

He appeared determined and unrelenting, so she looked past him to see the sheriff. "Excuse me," she said, and Morgan Hudson turned his head to look at her, then lifted one black brow. "I'd prefer to ride in the back like any other criminal being arrested."

Morgan opened his mouth to say something, but snapped it shut when she yelped. Jordan's hands were secure on her waist as he literally tossed her into the front seat and climbed in beside her too quickly for her to do anything about it. He looked at his brother and said, "Drive," and with a slight, barely suppressed chuckle, the good sheriff did just that.

Chapter 3

Georgia steamed she was so angry. At herself as much as at the two outrageous, oversized men. They'd driven a few minutes in silence when she finally couldn't hold it in any longer and growled, "I don't like you."

Jordan started, evidently surprised that she'd spoken after being quiet for so long. And Morgan grinned. She'd already decided that the sheriff was either frowning or grinning—there wasn't much middle ground.

"Which of us are you talking to?" Morgan asked.

She was just disgruntled enough to bark, "Both." Unfortunately, Jordan seemed unfazed by her pique and Morgan was amused.

She was still pondering what to do and how to get everything done tonight when Jordan gave Morgan directions to her home, telling her without words that he was indeed familiar with the old farmhouse she'd bought.

But more important than that, she realized they were taking her straight home, rather than to the station.

"Excuse me," she said, giving her attention to the sheriff while doing her best to ignore Jordan pressed up against her side, "but if you're only going to take me home, why did I just leave my car at the bar? Do you realize what a nuisance this will be now for me to get it?"

Morgan shrugged. "Don't worry about your car. We'll take care of it in the morning. Isn't that right, Jordan?"

Jordan made a noncommittal sound that she wasn't interested in deciphering. "I don't *want* you to take care of it!"

Jordan stared out his window. Morgan glanced at her, then back to the road. "Not much choice, now. There was a lot going on. I figured it'd be easier this way, rather than hassling with the arresting sheriff. He wanted you two taken off, so I took you off. And as to that, I suppose I should give you a ticket or something." She watched the sheriff rub his thick neck, as if pondering a difficult predicament. "You see, the thing is, Jordan said you weren't to blame and I've never known him to tell me a pickle. But I gotta say, I am curious as hell as to why you were picked up, why you were there in the first place, and why you're dressed that way."

He leaned around to see Jordan, and added, "And what the hell you've got to do with it."

Though she knew the sheriff was only trying to distract her, Georgia stiffened. "He has nothing to do with me! But he did attempt to intervene…well, sort of…"

Jordan made another exasperated sound and interrupted. "I don't need you to explain for me, Georgia."

She shrugged, stung by his biting tone. "Fine." Crossing her arms, she leaned back in the seat, silent again.

Morgan began to whistle. After a moment, he said thoughtfully, "I think I have it figured out."

"Morgan," Jordan said by way of warning.

"You're a dancer at the bar, right?" At her stiff nod, he continued. "And Jordan here got a little too enthused over your…skill. Understandable. Although Jordan is a little slow on the uptake sometimes, at least where women are concerned—"

"Oh, for God's sake."

Georgia listened, fascinated despite herself.

"You see," Morgan said in something of a whisper, leaning toward Georgia, "in the last few years my brothers and I have all tied the knot. All except Jordan, and that leaves him sort of vulnerable to all the hungry single ladies looking to get hitched. He's so busy trying to fend them off, he's forgotten just how pleasant a nice, warm woman can be."

Georgia blinked. "I really don't think—"

"It's obvious to me that old Jordan here has lost his finesse. I'd be willing to bet he tried to defend your honor or something like that, is that right?"

Jordan growled, but Georgia paid him and his nasty temper no mind. This night had been endless and she'd had just about enough. "You think, perhaps, that I don't have any honor to defend just because I work for a living?"

Morgan surprised her by shaking his head. "Not at all. I don't make those type of assumptions about ladies. Malone'd have my head if I did, seeing as I once made a horrid assumption about her."

Before she could ponder that particular scenario too long, Jordan slapped one hand down on the dash and twisted in his seat to face them both. "You want the nitty-gritty details, Morgan? Is that it?"

"Of course."

Jordan glared at his brother, and Georgia could feel his hot breath as he leaned around her. Being stuck between these two big oafs was not her idea of fun. She pressed farther back in her seat.

"All right, fine." The words were ground out from between clenched teeth. "She finished dancing and some bozo started groping her leg. He wouldn't quit when she asked him to and I stepped in. Unnecessarily, it would seem, at least according to Ms. Barnes."

Slowly, Georgia turned toward him. She heard his brother mutter, *"uh-oh"* under his breath, yet all her attention was now on Jordan.

"For your information," she said in a slow, precise tone, "I work all week in the bar as a waitress. I deal with those bozos day in and day out. I know them, and I know just how to get them to back off. *Without* throwing any punches or starting any riots."

"Uh…" Morgan said, attempting to intervene, "Jordan actually punched someone?"

"Several someones!"

"Only two."

Morgan cleared his throat. "You dress like that to serve drinks? You must make some hellacious tips."

Contrary to what she'd just said, Georgia felt like throwing her own punch. "I dress like this to dance on the weekends because it pays a lot better than serving drinks through the week, and unlike some people—" she fried Jordan a look "—I have obligations, and have to do whatever I can to make ends meet."

The car slowed as Morgan pulled into her driveway. Even as angry as she was, a curious peace settled over her at being home. She'd loved the big old house on sight and dreamed of renovating it into a home her kids could finally be proud of, a home that would last them forever.

It needed work, no denying that. But the yard was spacious, giving the kids plenty of room to play. And the air out here in the country was clean, fresh, putting new color in her mother's cheeks. The house represented everything Georgia had ever wanted or needed for her family.

Her fist curled around the strap of her purse, now filled with the money that had been thrown onstage. With a little luck, a lot of determination, and enough fortitude, she *could* make everything right. She had to. Her options were sorely limited.

Morgan turned the car off and Georgia, pulled from her thoughts, realized Jordan was staring at her mouth. Again. Heat rushed through her like a tidal wave, stealing her breath until she nearly choked.

How did he keep doing this to her? He'd made it clear he didn't approve of her, yet he wanted her. And if she was honest with herself, she was far too aware of him as a man. *Absurd.* She'd sworn off men!

"It looks to me," Morgan said softly, "as if a couple of small obligations have been waiting for you."

"What?" Georgia twisted around at the considering tone of the sheriff's voice, only to see her son and daughter standing anxiously in the open doorway of the house, their noses practically pressed to the storm door. She knew in an instant that something was very wrong. They should have been long in bed. Her mother never let them to the door without her.

In a single heartbeat her distraction with Jordan disappeared, as did her exhaustion. All that remained was mind-numbing fear.

"Oh, God." Georgia practically climbed over Jordan, who did his best to get the door open for her and to get out of her way. He didn't even complain when her elbow clipped him in the nose and she stepped on his foot.

"Georgia, wait!"

She heard his alarmed tone as he followed her from the car, heard Morgan talking low, his words concerned. And then her daughter Lisa, only six years old, threw the front door open and dashed across the yard in her long nightgown. Georgia forgot all about the men.

"Mommy!"

Jordan nearly slipped on the wet grass. Knowing she was a mother and seeing a little girl address her as such were two entirely different things. His heart punched hard against his ribs when Georgia dropped to her knees, unconcerned with the soggy ground, and caught her daughter up to her.

"Lisa, what is it, honey? What's wrong?"

The little girl was crying too hard to make sense. A queer feeling of resentment—she'd left the child to dance in a bar, for God's sake—and tenderness, seeing her now, holding the child so closely, made Jordan almost breathless. He stepped closer and with a hiccup, the little girl looked up at him. She had huge brown eyes with spiked wet lashes and was about the cutest thing he'd ever seen.

Keeping a wary gaze on him, the little girl mumbled, "Grandma is sick. She won't wake up."

"Oh, my God!"

Just that quick, Georgia was back on her feet. She'd picked up the little girl and was running hell-bent across the lawn. Her high heels sank into the ground, hindering her a bit, but in no way holding her back.

Jordan rushed after her, aware of Morgan right behind him. He followed her down a short hall as she called out, "Mom!" in a heart-wrenching panicked voice.

Lisa clung to Georgia's shoulders and said in a wavering voice, "She's in her room."

They passed a family room with a television playing and every light on, toys all over the floor, then a dining room that held only one rickety table—still covered with dishes.

At the end of the hall, to the right, was a kitchen, and to the left, Georgia threw open a door then halted. Jordan could see her heaving, see the rigidity of her shoulders. Slowly, she set the girl on her feet and moved forward. "Mom?"

Jordan watched the little girl move to a corner, trying to make herself invisible. Beyond Georgia, lying in a rumpled bed, a slender woman of about sixty rested on her back, her eyes closed, her chest barely moving—until she started coughing.

Lisa cried. Jordan didn't know what the hell to do. Then Morgan was there and he went down on one knee in front of Lisa. "Hi, there. I'm the sheriff and a friend of your mom's. Are you okay?"

Lisa covered her face with her hands, hiding, and then she nodded. Seeing that Morgan had things under control there, at least as much as was possible, Jordan stepped close to Georgia and knelt by the bed. She was busy checking her mother over, her movements efficient and quick.

She glanced at Jordan. "We have to get her to the hospital. She has weak lungs and it looks like she's gotten a bad cold or something."

Jordan frowned in concern. "A cold can do this to her?"

"Yes." Georgia's voice was clipped as she moved to a portable oxygen tank and dragged it to her mother's bedside. As she sat beside her mother and pulled her into a sitting position, the older woman's eyes opened. Again, she started coughing.

"It's all right now, Mom. I'm going to take you to the hospital."

"I'm sorry, honey—"

"Hey, none of that! I love you, remember?" She glanced at Jordan. "You're going to have to take us since you left my car behind." Then, as if just realizing it, her eyes widened in alarm and she said, "Lisa, where's Adam?"

A small towheaded child peeked around the doorframe.

"They're not used to men in the house," Georgia explained, then gave her son a small smile. "Come here, sweetie. It's okay. Grandma's going to be fine."

With the oxygen over her face, the older woman did seem to be breathing easier. She kept dozing off, which alarmed Jordan, but Georgia was holding it all together. The little boy inched his way in the door. He looked to be around four and clung to his mother's knee, hiding his face in her lap.

Jordan felt thunderstruck, and at that moment, he almost hated himself.

With renewed purpose, he stood. "I can carry her out to the Bronco. Morgan—"

"I'll call it in," Morgan said before Jordan could finish. He smiled at the little girl and smoothed a large hand over her head. "Can you find some shoes and a jacket for you and your brother?"

She peeked between her fingers, then nodded.

"Good girl."

Georgia smiled an absent thanks at Morgan. "Hang on, Mom. We'll have you there in no time."

Jordan knelt beside her and added his own arm to support her mother. "Why don't you get her coat and shoes for her? I'll do this."

Georgia hesitated, her eyes on her mother's face. "Her lungs are weak from emphysema. Sometimes, if she overdoes it, she needs the oxygen so we always keep it handy. She knows—" Her voice broke and frustrated tears filled her eyes. Angrily, she swiped them away. "She knows that any kind of illness for her is serious. But…she never complains."

Jordan watched her struggle to pull herself together. He covered her hand on the oxygen mask and asked, "Are you all right?"

Lips tightly pressed together, she nodded, then pushed to her feet. She found her mother's slippers beneath the bed. When she started looking around the room, Jordan changed his mind on the coat.

"Let's just wrap her in a blanket. It'll be easier for her, and the hospital will put her in a gown when she gets there anyway." Jordan didn't say it out loud, but judging by the difficulty her mother had breathing, he thought she might have pneumonia. With his own brother being a doctor, he'd seen enough cases of it. Plus her skin was pale and dry and too warm, indicating a high fever.

Georgia took a deep breath and wrapped her mother

in a pretty quilt. Jordan saw the tears glisten in her eyes again and knew he'd made a horrible mistake.

It hadn't taken long for them to be on their way. With the combined efforts of Morgan and Jordan, things had just fallen into place. They were obviously men accustomed to taking charge. Georgia didn't know how she felt about that, but she did know she was glad not to be alone.

Lisa and Adam were buckled into the front seat with Morgan, thoroughly distracted from any worries as Morgan let them play with his radio and turn on his lights. It amazed her that a man so large, so commanding, could summon up such a gentle tone for children. Right now, as he smiled at Adam, he looked like a big pushover, when her first impression of him would never have allowed for such a possibility.

He'd already spoken with the hospital and they were ready and waiting for them to arrive. The flashing lights, which amused her kids, were necessary; Morgan drove well past the speed limit. But at this time of night, the streets were almost clear of traffic.

"It's usually about an hour's drive to the hospital." Jordan watched her closely as he spoke, but then, he'd hardly taken his gaze off her since she'd first noticed him at the bar. "At least from our house. But I'd say you're fifteen minutes closer, and with Morgan driving and no cars on the road, it shouldn't take much longer."

Georgia realized he was trying to put her at ease. She appreciated his efforts. Morgan's, too. The kids, after their initial bout of shyness and upset, had taken to him with hardly any reserve. He had an easy way about him that would naturally draw kids.

She had a feeling Jordan would be the same when he wasn't busy tending to her mother's care. She'd seen how he'd looked at her children, the softness in his eyes. He was a man of contradictions—harsh one minute, soft the next. Always strong and confident.

At the moment, with her knees shaking and her heart beating too fast, she resented his strength even as she relied on it. *She* had to be strong. And she never wanted to depend on another man for anything.

They sat in the back, her mother propped between them on the carpeted floor of the storage area. Georgia supported her mother with an arm around her waist, offering her shoulder to lean on.

Streetlamps glowed, their lights flashing into the moving car with a strobe effect. They cast dark, shifting shadows over Jordan's profile, but in no way detracted from his look of genuine concern. He was an incredibly handsome man, Georgia decided, and obviously very caring.

"Almost there," he said with a reassuring smile. "Just hang on." His mesmerizing voice soothed her as nothing else could. Even her mother, dozing and waking every few minutes, wasn't immune to it. Georgia held her close, but it was Jordan's hand she gripped like a lifeline, his voice that occasionally coerced her eyes open.

Georgia leaned close and kissed her mother's cheek. Everything would be all right. She had to believe that.

Jordan kept hold of the woman's limp hand while watching her closely for any signs of distress. Her breathing was still ragged, occasionally racked by harsh coughing, but the oxygen had helped. That, and the fact that she knew she was almost at the hospital.

Georgia looked like hell. Though she tried to hide it, her own distress far outweighed her mother's. At that moment, Jordan wanted so badly to hold her close, to protect her. There seemed to be so much he hadn't understood. Her house was a shambles, inside and out. It had potential, but it would take a lot of sweat and money to make it what it could be.

Her children, adorable little moppets who had taken a cautious liking to Morgan, had her look about them. Lisa had the same golden-brown hair, though long enough to be in a braid, and Adam's hair was pale blond. They both had brown eyes, not Georgia's gray-blue, but the intensity in their gazes was the same as hers.

How the hell did she keep it all together? Between being a single parent of two young children, and her mother's health, not to mention the work needed on her house, she had her hands full.

He couldn't keep his gaze off her and glanced at her again just as she rubbed one tear-filled eye with a fist. She'd done that several times, refusing to let the tears fall, never mind that she had good reason, that most women would have bowed under the stress of the night. Her makeup was an absolute mess, leaving dark smudges on her cheeks and all around her eyes. Jordan reached into his pocket and retrieved a hanky.

"Hey," he said softly, and Georgia pulled her gaze away from her mother long enough to send him a questioning look.

He reached over and used the edge of the cotton hanky to wipe her eyes. "You look like a Halloween cat," he teased, and she gave him the first sincere smile he'd seen. It about stopped his heart. In that moment, with smeared makeup, rain-frazzled hair and a red nose, she was the most beautiful woman he'd ever seen.

Taking the hanky from him, she scrubbed at her face, removing the worst of the smudges. "I hate this stupid makeup, but Bill insists." She grinned at her mother and added, "She gives me heck about it all the time. According to Mom, I look like a call girl. But then, I suppose that's Bill's intent."

Jordan glanced at the front seat. Luckily, her kids were oblivious to the conversation. "What do you tell them?"

Almost immediately her expression turned carefully blank. She adjusted the quilt over her mother's shoulder, refusing to meet his gaze. "That I have to work. That I'm a dancer. They've seen *Muppets On Ice* and think it's something like that."

She shrugged and Jordan suddenly realized she was still wearing only his coat over a very revealing, enticing costume. He wanted to curse his own stupidity. Why the hell hadn't he thought to grab her some decent clothes before they'd left the house? Everyone in the hospital would be staring at her.

As if she'd read his thoughts, she said, "It doesn't matter." She leaned over her mother, saw that her eyes were open and alert and smiled. "Does it, Mom?"

The older woman tried for her own smile beneath the oxygen mask, and gave one slight, negative shake of her head.

Georgia sighed. "What am I going to do with you, Mom? You're just too darn good to me."

Her mother gave her a ferocious frown, and Georgia's eyes filled with new tears. She laughed to cover them up. "No, don't yell at me. Just save your breath."

Jordan couldn't bear to see her pain. "It'll be all right, Georgia."

"Yes, of course it will." She looked up at him. "I just thought of something. You two haven't been introduced. Mom, this is Jordan Sommerville, White Knight extraordinaire. And that hulk driving—don't know if you got a good look at him, but he *is* a hulk—he's Morgan Hudson, Jordan's half brother and the sheriff of Buckhorn. Jordan, this is Ruth Samson."

Jordan nodded his head formally. "Glad to make your acquaintance, Ms. Samson." He didn't bother to tell Georgia that she needn't have explained his relationship to Morgan quite so precisely. They'd all been raised together, and were as close as any full-blooded brothers could be.

"Speaking of brothers," Morgan said from the front seat as he handed a cell phone over his shoulder to Jordan, "call Gabe and tell him to go sit on Malone. I don't want her up running around."

Jordan took the phone, and then noticed the look of guilt on Georgia's face. Their eyes met and she winced. "I'm sorry you got pulled away from your wife, sheriff."

Morgan blared his sirens for a second as he rolled through a red light, alerting any traffic and making the kids squeal. He said to Georgia, "Don't worry about it. Gabe can handle things. And Malone will understand. She's stubborn, but she has an enormous heart."

"He's madly in love," Jordan said dryly, explaining away his brother's description of his wife. He dialed the phone and Gabe immediately answered. Jordan skipped the niceties and asked, "Who's with Misty?"

"Lizzy's looking after her," Gabe said, then: "We've been waiting to hear from you."

Jordan covered the phone and said to Morgan, "Elizabeth's with her."

"Not good enough. Malone can bulldoze her. Tell Gabe to go."

Jordan rolled his eyes. "Morgan wants you to go sit on Misty and make certain she stays in bed."

"I will. But do you need anything? Misty said you were brawling at a bar or something."

There was an undertone of laughter in his youngest brother's voice. "No, I was not brawling."

He'd thought Georgia was distracted, but at his words, one slim brow went up. Jordan shook his head and explained as briefly as possible what they were doing. "We'll be at the hospital in just a few minutes."

Gabe whistled low. "Damn. You want me to send Casey over there? He just got home from a date. His car is still warm."

Jordan thought about it for two seconds. "Yeah, that might not be a bad idea." He eyed Georgia's mostly naked legs and exposed cleavage. Turning slightly away from her, he muttered, "Have Casey bring a change of clothes, okay? From one of the women." Then he re-thought that and added, "Make it a big shirt, maybe one of yours or Sawyer's."

"Chesty, is she?"

"Yeah."

Through an undertone of laughter, Gabe said, "I'll see what I can do."

"Thanks. I imagine we'll be at the hospital for a spell, and I know Morgan would like to head home."

Morgan heard him and said, "Hey, I'm in no rush."

But Jordan knew that he was, that he wanted to be with Misty and Amber. A more doting father and husband had never been created.

"Will do," Gabe said. "Tell Morgan not to worry— and if you need me just give a buzz."

"Thanks, Gabe." He closed the phone and turned to Georgia as Morgan pulled into the hospital lot.

She tilted her head. "Another brother?"

"The youngest, and most recently married. With only one anniversary to his credit, Gabe still considers himself a newlywed. He's sending my nephew, Casey, here. I hope you don't mind, but I thought he could bring you—"

"Clothes. I heard."

She hadn't quite looked at him and it frustrated him. "Look, Georgia, I don't mean to criticize exactly—"

She interrupted his awkward explanation. "Believe me, I'll be grateful to get into something different." She glanced down at her own breasts and made a sound of disgust. "I don't wear this stuff by choice."

Jordan nodded, uncertain what he could say to that. She looked hot enough to tempt a saint, and he supposed that was the main reason for wearing the outfit on stage.

To his surprise, she said, "Thanks for thinking of it."

"No problem." With her sitting so close to him, and having so much skin exposed, it was a wonder he'd been able to think of anything else. "Unfortunately, it'll take Case a little while to get here."

Morgan pulled right up to the emergency entrance, and what with his flashing lights and the earlier call, it only took about fifteen seconds before a stretcher was rolled out to the Bronco and Ruth was being taken inside.

Georgia looked overwhelmed by the speed at which

things were happening. She rushed to get her kids out of the car, trying to reassure them and keep sight of her mother as she was being whisked away.

Jordan touched her arm as she started to lift Adam from the front seat. "Go on, Georgia." She glanced up at him, clearly distracted. "Get your mother settled and appease the hospital officials with all the paperwork they'll need. The kids and I will meet you in the waiting room when you're done."

She looked at him as though he was insane, cuddling her children closer in a protective gesture and attempting to walk around him. Jordan moved to her side and kept pace with her hurried stride. Both kids stumbled along while staring up at him.

Just as the automatic entry doors opened with a swoosh, he heard Morgan call out that he'd park and be right in. Jordan waved him off.

"Georgia…"

Her high heels clicked on the tiled floor. "Come on, kids. We have to hurry."

There was a note of brittle urgency in her voice that tortured him. No woman should ever be put in such a position. Jordan again took her arm, this time pulling her to a stop. The children seemed fascinated. "Georgia, listen to me."

Utter exasperation, exhaustion, and near panic filled her face. *"What?"*

Well aware of the kids' engrossed attention, and at how close Georgia was to losing it, Jordan spoke softly, giving her a very direct look. "You can trust me, sweetheart. I swear it."

She shook her head, her face pale.

"We'll be in the waiting room," he added, ignoring

her refusal, "just around the corner, drinking hot chocolate and watching television and talking." He reached out for Lisa's hand, praying she wouldn't shy away from him, and let out a breath when she released her mother and moved to his side. Her shy smile showed one missing front tooth.

Jordan enclosed her tiny hand in his own. To Georgia, he said, "Did I tell you my oldest brother is a doctor? Well he is. Everyone at the hospital knows Sawyer, though he's always chosen to work from home, treating the people of Buckhorn. He has an office at the back of the house. His son, Casey, is the one who's bringing you some clothes."

She looked around and bit her lip when she saw her mother being wheeled beyond a thick white door. A nurse stood there, papers in hand, waiting for Georgia.

Jordan felt something against his side and looked down. Adam, chewing on the edge of his coat collar and staring up with big brown eyes, leaned trustingly against Jordan's thigh. His heart swelled with an indefinable affection. He put his hand on the boy's downy head and said again, "You can trust me, Georgia."

She wavered, probably aware she had few choices, then dropped to her knees. Pulling the coat collar from Adam's mouth, she said, "If you have to use the bathroom, or get hungry, tell Mr. Sommerville, okay?"

Adam nodded, then gave her a huge hug. Lisa was next. "We'll drink hot chocolate," she said, mimicking Jordan.

Georgia's smile was misty. "Okay, sweetie, but not too much. It'll keep you awake."

Adam tilted his head. "But we can't sleep here, huh?"

"Sure you can." Georgia grinned, kissed him again,

then stood. "There's probably a nice soft couch for you to get comfy on. If you get tired, just close your eyes and pretend you're at home. And before you know it, I'll be right back."

Jordan watched her stride quickly to the desk, her legs looking absurdly long in the high heels. Her shoulders were stiff beneath his jacket, her hands fisted on the strap of her purse. Every line of her body bespoke tension and exhaustion and fear.

A nurse, repeatedly looking Georgia over in her sexy costume, waited for her behind the desk. After Georgia had seated herself and began digging through her purse, no doubt hunting up an insurance card for her mother, Jordan looked down at the kids. Adam raised his arms and, without thinking about it, Jordan lifted the boy. He was stocky, more compact than his sister who looked almost fey she was so slight. Small arms wrapped around his neck.

"Hot chocolate," Adam said, trying for an adolescent dose of subtlety, "sure sounds good." Jordan bit back a smile. It didn't make any sense and he knew he must be losing his mind, but despite all the chaos, despite the horrid situation and his worry for Georgia and his disapproval of where she worked, he felt good, from the inside out.

Probably better than he had in months.

Oh, hell.

Chapter 4

Casey pulled in the hospital parking lot and turned off the engine. He'd driven his father's car, a spacious sedan, rather than the truck he usually favored. As he understood it, Jordan was with a woman and her two children—too many people to fit into the truck. He was anxious to hear what story his uncle Jordan told to explain all this.

But for the moment he was more concerned with how to handle Emma Clark.

The truck, being a stick shift, would have guaranteed some space between them. But the car had bench seats, and Emma scooted much too close. She smelled nice, damp from the outdoors and sweet like a female. He was far from immune. She reached for his knee before he could open his door.

"Just a second, Case." Her voice was low, throaty. "Why're you in such a hurry?"

Very calmly, Casey took her wrist and lifted her hand away. She was the most brazen girl he knew, and the most insecure. It was something in her big brown eyes, something she tried real hard to hide.

Twining his fingers with hers, he couldn't help but notice how small boned she was, how her hand felt tiny in his own. "It's almost one in the morning, Emma." The parking lot was well lit, sending slashes of light across her features, making her eyes look even bigger than usual. "What were you doing out on the road alone?"

She rolled one shoulder beneath the shirt he'd insisted she put on. He'd been left in nothing more than an undershirt, but that was better than seeing her traipse around half-naked. He still couldn't believe she'd been moseying down the damn highway so late, wearing her short white shorts, sandals, and a hot-pink halter top that left more bare than it covered. He'd recognized her world-class behind the moment his headlights had hit her. Of course he'd offered her a ride.

Of course she'd accepted. Emma had been after him for months.

"A shrug is not an answer, Em."

She shrugged again, smiling at him and flipping her bleached-blond hair behind her. Casey assumed her natural hair color was a dark brown, judging by her brows and thick lashes. Although that could be makeup, too. She wore a lot of it. She looked...brassy. Almost cheap. And though he had no intention of telling her so, she made him sweat.

"I got mad at my date," she said in her low drawl, "so I took off." Her mouth, shiny with lip gloss that a few of the guys had told him tasted like cherries, tilted up at the corners. "Why d'you care?"

Casey snorted at that lame explanation and defensive response, deciding not to question her further. At seventeen, Emma's idea of a date was to be picked up long enough to add to her already questionable reputation, then get dropped off again. He'd never understand her, but he couldn't help feeling sorry for her.

Just as he couldn't help wanting her.

"C'mon. I need to get inside." When he got out of the car, she scrambled out, too, and rushed around to him.

"You're not mad at me, are you?"

He pulled the bag of clothes from the back seat, sparing her a quick glance. "It's really none of my business, Emma."

She looked hurt for a moment, then the shirt slid off her shoulder and his gaze dropped to her scantily covered chest. He turned abruptly away.

She ran to keep up with him as he headed inside. Thankfully it had stopped raining, but the air felt too cool and still too damp. Water dripped from every tree, shrub and building. He felt a bit chilled. Or at least he had moments ago, before he'd noticed that the night air had caused her nipples to tighten.

He wouldn't look at her there again.

Once inside, he made his way to the waiting room, where he assumed he'd find his uncles. His stride was long, a little too fast, but a small smile curled his mouth as he remembered Gabe relaying the evening's events. His uncle Jordan in a fight? It sounded absurd, although he'd grown up hearing stories of the few occasions when Jordan had lost it, giving into his fierce temper. It wasn't something Casey had ever seen, but he'd believed it was possible.

Jordan was just so…intense. Especially about things he really believed in.

Or people he cared about.

Casey rounded the corner to the open waiting area and stopped short at the sight of Jordan with a little boy sound asleep in his lap. There was a chocolate mustache on the kid, and he was snoring softly. Casey grinned. Jordan had a poleaxed expression on his face, as if deep in thought.

Morgan sat on the floor opposite a tiny girl with a glass-topped coffee table between them, playing Go Fish. Casey had stopped so abruptly, Emma bumped into his back. His breath caught as he felt her soft, young body flush against his. Her hands settled low on his hips and she went on tiptoe, her warm lips touching his ear as she whispered, "Sorry."

Casey ignored her.

"Have I missed anything important?"

Jordan glanced up, then raised one finger to his mouth, cautioning Casey to be quiet. Carefully, his movements very slow, Jordan removed the bundle from his lap and put the boy on the couch. He covered him with his coat. With a wide yawn and a little squirreling around, the kid resettled himself into a rolled-up lump and dozed off again.

Morgan laid his cards down and pushed to his feet. "'Bout time you got here." He nodded to the little girl. "Lisa here is a card shark."

Lisa—long brown hair in disheveled braids— grinned at what she obviously considered a compliment. Morgan tugged on one of those braids with affection. "Maybe she'll be gentler with you, Casey."

Casey leaned in the wide door frame. "I dunno. She's got that ruthless look about her."

Lisa looked up at him, blinked, and kept on looking. Like a natural-born flirt, she batted her long eyelashes at Casey and gave him a wide, adoring grin. She even sighed.

Morgan turned to Jordan. "Would you look at that? She's only six and even she's smitten by him."

Jordan grunted. "He's worse than Gabe."

"Or better."

Casey laughed out loud, well used to their razzing. "Kids just like me."

Morgan looked at him from under his brows. "Females just like you, you mean."

Casey shrugged. It was true, as far as it went. The females did seem to like him. Since he'd first become a teenager, they'd been after him. Not that he had any intentions of getting permanently caught.

Morgan glanced around the waiting room. It looked like chaos with empty foam cups and candy wrappers and kids shoes on the floor. "You okay here now," he asked Jordan, "or do you want me to stick around?"

Jordan stretched tiredly. "We're fine. Go on home. You're starting to get worry lines."

Case walked the rest of the way into the room, keeping his voice as low as his uncles'. "And here I thought those were laugh lines caused by his sunny disposition." Morgan swatted at Casey, making him duck. "Gabe told me to tell you that Misty is sound asleep, konked out from the medicine Sawyer gave her, so you don't have to keep fretting."

Morgan's shoulders—wide as an ax handle—softened with relief. "And Amber?"

Thoughts of his little cousin, now nearing the terrible twos, which on her weren't so terrible, made Casey chuckle. "She wore herself out chasing Gabe in a pillow fight. Last I saw her, she was as zonked as the little guy there." He indicated the boy on the couch.

Jordan rubbed his chin, appearing somewhat exhausted and ultimately pleased at the same time. It was a strange expression for him. "That's Adam, Georgia's son."

"Georgia?"

Morgan leaned forward and said in a whisper, "The bar dancer who Jordan fought over."

"I did *not* fight over her."

"Shh!" Morgan gave him a severe frown for his raised voice.

Jordan glanced at Lisa, who was oblivious as she attempted to shuffle the cards, which sent them all flying to the floor. "It was a misunderstanding," he growled in a lowered voice.

Casey noticed his uncle's color was a bit high and choked back a grin. "Hey, whatever you say, Jordan."

Morgan shook his head, then looked beyond Casey with a questioning frown. Casey turned and saw that Emma had backed up until she was against the wall beside a plastic floor plant. It almost seemed she was trying to be invisible, which of course was impossible for a girl who looked like Emma.

He frowned. So brazen one minute—especially when they were alone—and so timid the next.

He held out his hand. "Emma, have you met my uncles?"

Her big brown eyes widened at the attention given to her, and she swallowed hard. For the first time that

Casey could ever remember, her face turned bright red. "I've…um, that is, I know who they are of course, but we've never actually been introduced or anything."

Since Casey still stood there with his hand out, she finally stepped forward and took it, the embarrassed heat positively pulsing in her cheeks.

He rubbed her knuckles with his thumb, trying to reassure her. Damned if he knew why. "Emma, my uncle Jordan and my uncle Morgan."

Strangely enough, she did an awkward curtsy of sorts, then looked appalled at herself. "Uh…hi."

Morgan grinned, which always made him look menacing. "You two out on a late date?"

"No." Casey turned her loose so fast, both his uncles scowled at him. He hadn't meant to hold her hand anyway. "I just picked her up."

Jordan raised both brows at that.

Emma pulled the shirt tight around her and folded her arms beneath her breasts. "Casey is just…giving me a ride. Home, I mean."

"But you live in Buckhorn," Morgan pointed out. "Isn't that right?"

"Yeah." Even her neck turned red. "I was…um, headed that way, but Casey said he needed to come here first, then he'd drop me off later."

Morgan glanced at Casey, then back at Emma. "If you're in a hurry to get home, I can drop you off on my way. I'm heading out now."

Jordan made a disgusted sound and stepped in front of Morgan. Casey knew he was trying to shield Emma, since Morgan tended to always look a bit like a marauder. "You and Casey can both head out. I think they'll probably get Georgia's mother settled in her own room soon."

Emma glanced at Casey. He took his time thinking about it, not wanting to embarrass her, but not wanting to give her the wrong impression either. "You want to call your folks first, so they won't be worrying?"

"No."

She said that far too quickly and Jordan and Morgan shared a look. It didn't surprise Casey; he'd already figured out Emma's home life wasn't exactly ideal. If it had been, no way would she have been walking home alone at this time of night. Or done half the other things her reputation suggested. He turned back to his uncles.

"You're sure you don't want me to stick around, Jordan?"

Jordan gave Casey a searching look before he shook his head. "We'll be fine."

As Casey handed him the keys to the car, Morgan took Jordan's arm. "I want to talk to Jordan for just a minute, Case. Can you keep an eye on the kids?"

Lisa looked up and sighed at him again. Casey smiled. "No problem."

"Thanks. I'll bring the Bronco around and wait out front for you both."

They were barely around the corner when Morgan asked, "What the hell is Casey doing out so late with that girl?"

Jordan shrugged. "Hell if I know. But I don't think there's anything going on between them."

"Why not?"

"She doesn't look like his usual type."

Morgan snorted. "Like Georgia is your usual type?"

Jordan almost faltered. He did frown. "Who says I'm even interested?"

Morgan came to a complete stop and turned to give Jordan an incredulous look. "Well, let's see. You can't look at her without tensing up. And that hard-on you had while arguing with her might be a good clue."

Jordan flushed. And it made him madder than hell, because not a single one of his other damned brothers would have. They'd have grinned, hell, they might've even bragged. They would not, however, have turned red. But Jordan wasn't at all pleased that all he had to do was breathe in Georgia's scent and he wanted her. Bad.

Morgan shook his head. "It's a full moon tonight, did you know that? Maybe that accounts for a few things. Like Casey showing up with a girl that I know damn good and well has a reputation that far exceeds the one Gabe had at her age. And that's saying something."

"Are you sure about that?" Jordan frowned, concern for his nephew overshadowing his embarrassment. And talking about Casey was definitely preferable to talking about himself. Or Georgia. Or him and Georgia.

"Yeah. It's a long sad story and I'm too damn tired to go into it tonight. Besides, I reckon Casey has a handle on things. Though she's not eighteen yet, so if you get the chance, warn him to be careful, okay?"

Jordan nodded. While Casey was only eighteen himself, he gave the impression of being much, much older.

"At least it's stopped raining." The doors slid open as Morgan approached them. He looked outside, giving Jordan his back as he surveyed the starless sky. With a nonchalance that didn't fool Jordan for a minute, Morgan asked, "Should we expect you back at the house tonight?"

Jordan hadn't really thought about it, but now that he did… He dropped his head forward, brooding. His muscles felt tight and he rolled his shoulders, trying to relieve some of the tension.

But there was no hope for it. "She doesn't have a car," he said, stating an obvious fact. "Hers is still at the bar."

Morgan nodded. "I know."

"It doesn't seem right to leave her and two kids at a house alone, with no transportation. What if something happened? What if she no sooner got home and her mother needed her?"

"And odds are," Morgan interjected, going right along with him, "even if her mother rests easy tonight, Georgia'll still want to check on her first thing in the morning, so she'll probably need a ride. Assuming you all get to go home tonight at all." Morgan faced him again. "I can't see you leaving her here alone."

"No, I wouldn't do that." Jordan gestured at the mostly quiet hospital. "With the kids and everything…."

"Yeah." Morgan tilted his head, his expression thoughtful. "So I guess we'll see ya sometime in the morning." He stepped into the open doorway. "Let me know tomorrow if there's something I can do to help."

"Thanks."

"Oh, and Jordan?"

Wishing his damn brother would just go away, Jordan raised a brow. "What?"

Morgan grinned. "It's going to get worse before it gets better. I just thought I should let you know that."

Jordan stiffened. "You don't know what the hell you're talking about."

"On the contrary, I married Malone, didn't I? I know

exactly what I'm talking about. And my advice would be not to fight it."

"It?"

"The whole chemistry thing."

"Oh, for the love of—"

Morgan shrugged. "You should just give up right now, and save yourself a pound of heartache. Tell her what it is you want. Be up front with her."

Tell her that he wanted to strip her naked? That he wanted to bury himself inside her and spend all night finding ways to make her climax—and the fact that she was a mother, that she danced for drunks, that she didn't appear to particularly like him, hadn't blunted his need one bit? "She has two children, Morgan."

"So? She's still sexy as hell. Any man who's seen her in that getup she's wearing tonight can damn sure vouch for that. Besides, the more you fight it, the worse it is. You're caught. You might as well accept it."

Morgan walked away before Jordan could correct him, before he could assure him that he wasn't *caught* at all! He was turned on, to where he couldn't seem to stop shaking, to stop wanting.

But that was all it was.

Hell, Morgan had taken one look at Misty Malone and started acting the fool. He'd fallen head over ass for her in a single heartbeat.

But he wasn't Morgan. Just as he wasn't Sawyer or Gabe. He wasn't looking for a wife, had no desire for home and hearth, and even if he was, Georgia wouldn't qualify as wifely material. Not for him.

Still, maybe Morgan was right. What did he have to lose if he told her flat out that he wanted her? She had reacted to him, he wasn't imagining that. Maybe that chemistry mumbo jumbo had some truth to it. Maybe she wouldn't mind an uninvolved sexual relationship.

Jordan swallowed hard at the mere thought, imagining her saying yes, imagining her peeling off that skimpy costume for him....

Oh, hell. *Her outfit.* If she came back to the waiting room before Jordan could head her off and give her the change of clothes, who knew how Casey might react. There was no doubt he'd be surprised, because who would expect a woman to be running around a hospital dressed as she was?

He didn't want Casey to accidentally hurt her feelings with his shock. And he didn't want his nephew ogling her either.

Unfortunately, Jordan reached the waiting room just in time to see Georgia stumble over her own feet. She stared toward Casey, who'd stood when she entered the room.

"Who," Georgia asked, eyeing the way her daughter clung to Casey's hand, "are you?"

"He's Casey," Lisa said.

Casey smoothed his dark blond hair out of his eyes, then held out his free hand. "I gather you're Lisa's mother?"

Georgia looked mesmerized, then gave him her hand. She tipped her head back to see Casey's face, before looking him over with awe. "Why, I wonder, did I think you'd look like an average kid?"

Casey grinned, showing off his killer smile and shaking her hand gently. "I don't know, ma'am."

"Is the whole family like you?"

Emma, who had been sitting quietly on the couch by Adam's feet, spoke up. "Yes, they are."

"Incredible."

Jordan stepped up behind her. "Casey brought you a change of clothes."

"Oh, yeah." Casey reached for the bag and offered it to her. "Honey, my stepmother, wasn't sure what size you might be, so she told me to apologize and explain that she sent things that would adjust." To Jordan, he said, "She refused to send her a man's shirt."

Georgia looked into the bag and pulled out white, elastic waist cotton slacks, a soft pink cotton T-shirt, and a long sleeved matching cardigan. There was even a pair of slip-on casual canvas shoes.

She glanced back up at Casey with a grateful smile. "Please be sure to tell her how much I appreciate this. And I promise to return the clothes right away."

Casey skipped a look toward Jordan before smiling. "You can tell her yourself. She said to invite you and your family over to the big cookout at the end of the month. Honey likes to show all our neighbors how much she appreciates them by having this huge get-together. It worked out real well last year, so she wants to make it a traditional gathering."

Jordan choked and considered stuffing Casey into the damn bag. Georgia, he noticed, looked panicked.

"But…" She sputtered, her gray eyes wide, "We're not neighbors!"

"You live in Buckhorn?"

Georgia nodded.

"Close enough." He ignored Jordan when he added, "You don't have to wait till then to visit though. Our house is pretty far off the main road without any other houses close by. Honey said to tell you she'd love the company anytime you feel up to visiting."

Lisa clapped her hands together, staring with naked adoration toward Casey. "Can we, Mommy, please, please, please?"

"But…"

Casey ruffled Lisa's hair, then turned to the couch, caught Emma's hand and pulled her to her feet. She tried to hang onto his hand, but Casey made that impossible. "We've got to go before Morgan leaves without us."

Georgia hustled after him. "Wait! Please, tell your stepmother—"

"Honey."

"Yes, well, tell Honey that I appreciate the offer, but I can't possibly come."

"Jordan'll bring you." Casey stared at Jordan, knowing exactly what he was doing. His brown eyes warmed to glittering amber as he said, "He wouldn't want to disappoint Honey."

Keeping a relationship purely sexual, Jordan thought, would be pretty damn tough if the whole family got to know her. But then he looked at Lisa, and he gave up with a sound somewhere between a growl and a sigh. "No, I don't want to disappoint Honey."

Georgia held the clothes clutched to her spectacular chest, her pale gray eyes flared with dismay, her golden brown hair practically standing on end.

And perversely, Jordan said, "I insist. It'll be fun."

"But…"

He turned away and bid Casey and Emma goodnight, noticing that Casey was staying just out of Emma's reach. He shook his head.

"What?"

Georgia stood beside him. He could smell her, warm and sweet, and he wanted to press his nose into her neck, taste her skin. "My nephew," he said in a rough voice, filled with lust, though she didn't seem to know it, "didn't even notice what you're wearing."

He hadn't quite realized it until he said it. But not once did Casey look her over. He'd kept his gaze respectfully on her face, his manner as polite and friendly as ever.

Georgia looked down at herself. "I know you think I should be embarrassed." She met his gaze, her eyes now somber, sad. "But I'm just too worried."

Jordan touched her cheek. That didn't seem like enough so he put his arm around her shoulders and led her to the chair Casey had just vacated. Luckily, there was no one else in this particular waiting room. Earlier a man had come in with a badly cut finger, and a woman had shown up with a twisted ankle. But they had each been attended to and no one had shown up since.

Once Georgia was seated, her hands twisting in the clothing Honey had sent, Jordan asked, "What did they say about your mother? How is she?"

He knelt in front of her, unable to stop touching her. This time his hands rested on her knees. Her skin was so incredibly warm, so silky, he wanted to part her thighs, wanted to tip up her face and kiss her deeply as he moved between her legs. Her thighs were strong, he'd seen that as she danced, and he could only imagine how tightly she'd hold him.

She didn't seem to notice his touch or his preoccupation, or else she didn't care.

Jordan shook himself. Adam snored nearby on the couch and Lisa was starting to get bored with the cards. She'd taken to deliberately scattering them, and the last time they'd flown everywhere, she hadn't bothered to pick them back up.

He had to get hold of himself. Lusting after a woman in front of her children wasn't something he ever would have done. He wouldn't do it now. Out of all the brothers, he was the one most circumspect, most discerning.

"Will she be all right, Georgia?"

Georgia nodded. "Mom has emphysema. My father was a big cigar smoker and they say it was his second-hand smoke that…" She looked furious for a moment, then started over. "She's never been a smoker herself. In fact she hates the things."

"Me, too." He took one of her hands, and she didn't pull away.

"They think she has bronchitis. With her lung disease, that's a big problem. They're going to keep her a few days, put her on IV antibiotics, do a breathing treatment every four hours or so. As soon as they get her settled in her room and I make sure she's got everything she needs, I'll be able to head home. I just don't want to go until I know—"

"Of course not. There's no rush."

She gave him a distracted, grateful nod.

"When was the last time you ate?"

She looked at him as if he were crazy. "I'm not hungry. But the kids…" She glanced over at the couch. Jordan looked, too. Lisa was still sitting on the floor, but she'd slumped sideways, sound asleep, her head mere inches from her brother's big toe.

Jordan grinned. "I fed them. It wasn't the most nutritional meal going. Just sub sandwiches from the vending machine with chips and hot chocolate."

She rubbed her forehead with a shaking hand. "I

should have thought of it. Thank you. It didn't even occur to me…"

"Hey." Jordan leaned lower to see her averted face. Very gently he touched her chin. "You had your hands full."

"I'll pay you back. How much was it?"

Her polite query set his teeth on edge. "I don't want your money, Georgia."

To his surprise, she came to her feet, making him quickly stand so he wouldn't be stampeded. "It's not your job to take care of my children."

Jordan crossed his arms over his chest and stared down at her, studying her set expression. "I don't mind helping out."

Her soft lips flattened into a hard line. The way she squeezed Honey's clothes, they'd be all wrinkled by the time she got them on. Not that he was in any hurry for her to change now that they were virtually alone. The kids were asleep, Casey and Morgan had left, the hospital was quiet.

She looked incredible, sexy and tousled and earthy. His breath came a little faster. "You're going to need more help, you know."

She rounded on him, nearly dropping the clothes. Her eyes, circled with smeared mascara and exhaustion, turned stormy gray. She kept her voice low, but it sounded like a growl. "We'll manage just fine."

"Georgia…"

Her chin lifted. "You can leave now. I'm sorry I kept you so long. I lost track of the time, but now that I know my mother will be all right, I can—"

Very gently, he interrupted her. "You know I'm not going to leave."

"Don't be ridiculous. It's…" She looked around for a clock.

"It's very late." Jordan kept his tone soft and easy, soothing her. He had no idea why she'd suddenly turned defensive, except that she probably hadn't eaten for a while, her mother was sick, and she'd nearly been arrested.

And he couldn't stop thinking about getting her naked and under him. Or over him. Or…

He felt like a complete bastard. "Listen to me, Georgia." He waited until her gaze lifted to his. "I'm going to drive you home after everything is taken care of here."

"Why?" She stared at him, her face flushed. "You don't even know me. And what you do know about me, you disapprove of. You certainly don't owe me anything."

"Georgia." He said her name like a caress. He didn't mean to, but he did. "No man would leave you here alone like this."

She laughed at that, a mean, bitter laugh. "You are so wrong."

It took a lot of effort not to get riled, not to react to his sudden suspicions. But she was too upset right now, too overwhelmed, for him to start interrogating her. There'd be plenty of time for him to learn more about her past later. He'd see to that. "How else would you get home?"

"We can take a cab." She drew a shuddering breath. "Since I got my money from Bill, I can easily afford—"

Jordan took her shoulders and pulled her closer to him, leaning down so that he could whisper. The very last thing he wanted to do was wake the children.

Her eyelashes fluttered at his nearness, but she didn't look into his eyes. She stared at his mouth instead.

"I'm taking you home, Georgia. Accept it. We'll get your car tomorrow and then you can check on your mother and, after all that, we'll talk about the cookout my family has planned."

She covered her ears with her hands and pulled away. "I have to change now. Will you…" She made a disgusted sound. "Will you stay here with Lisa and Adam?"

"Of course." Why was she covering her ears? It wasn't like he'd been being abusive. He'd offered her help. He'd been gentle, calm. He hadn't told her that he wanted her, that just touching her damn shoulders and bringing her close had nearly driven him to his knees and made him semierect.

He watched her walk away, and decided that he *would* tell her. Tonight.

He wasn't at all sure he could last another day this way.

Chapter 5

The car ride home was mostly silent. There wasn't a single other vehicle on the road, the kids were sound asleep and the clouds had finally cleared enough to let the moonlight dance over the wet streets. Overall, it was a sleepy, relaxing, lulling ride.

But she was far from relaxed. "Jordan... I'm sorry I lost my temper with you."

Jordan glanced at her as if surprised that she'd spoken. Aside from getting her arrested, he'd been wonderful, and she'd been a raving bitch. All because he scared her.

And when she was around him, she scared herself. The man didn't need to say anything important, not even anything seductive, and she wanted him. An intolerable situation, and she was far too tired to deal with it.

She could hear the smile in his mellow, mesmeric voice when he spoke. "No problem. You've had a rough day."

Georgia made a sound of agreement, leaned her head back and closed her eyes. Maybe if she didn't look at him, if she didn't see his wide, hard shoulders, the thickness of his muscled forearms, the way his light brown hair caught the moonlight and how deep, how seductive his green eyes were when he turned them toward her—well, maybe it would help. But she doubted it. He was a sinfully gorgeous male, tall and strong and hard, but she'd seen strong attractive men before, dealt with them every night at the bar. No, it was much more than Jordan's looks, much more than his physical attributes.

All the man had to do was mutter two syllables and she wanted to melt. Something about his voice affected her deep down inside, stripping away her defenses. It made her imagine awful, wonderful things.

She shook her head, more at herself than anything he did or said. "I appreciate the ride home. And how you carried the kids out. I could have managed, but—"

"But you've had enough to deal with." He reached across the seat and his large hand squeezed her shoulder. Even through the borrowed T-shirt, his touch was electric. She caught her breath, not wanting him to know how he affected her, how amazingly turned on she was even at this moment.

She'd had very little sleep over the past two days. She'd worked a double shift and dealt with the threat of being arrested, then the gut-wrenching fear over her mother's health. She had no idea how she was going to manage to work and take care of her mother at the hospital, with no baby-sitter. Things looked very grim.

But still she wanted him when she never wanted any guy. She'd long since considered herself immune to the normal urges most women felt. So what if Jordan was an uncommonly patient and wonderful man? She shouldn't care that he was gorgeous and as finely built as a Greek statue, or that he had a voice warm enough to melt butter.

She knew he disapproved of her, and that should have taken care of the rest. But somehow, maybe because her children seemed so taken by him, his disapproval didn't matter.

"You deserve to take a break, Georgia. And I like your kids. Adam reminds me a little of Casey when he was that age. Constant motion right up until he runs out of steam."

A distracting topic if ever there was one. She gladly accepted it. "Your nephew certainly took me by surprise."

Jordan's smile was gentle and filled with pride. "He's an amazing kid. Only eighteen, but I swear he has more common sense, more backbone and maturity than a lot of men twice his age. We pretty much raised him ourselves, you know."

She didn't know. Since she'd moved to Buckhorn, she'd kept to herself except for her work. And she certainly hadn't tried to form any friendships at the bar. She didn't have time to gossip with neighbors, or go out of her way to get to know anyone. "We, meaning you and your brothers?"

"That's right. Casey's mother couldn't deal with a newborn infant, and she took off. Sawyer, my oldest brother, the one who's a doctor? He was still in medical school when Case was born, but he brought him home from the hospital and that was that. I was…let's see, fifteen at the time. And I remember being absolutely fascinated. I looked up to Sawyer and Morgan a lot, and I'd always seen them in a one dimensional way, you know?"

"Yes." She saw most men in a one dimensional way—*selfish*. Her father, her ex, her boss, the men who threw money at her while she was on stage.... She squeezed her eyes shut at that thought, praying that none of the men were spending grocery or bill money. Some of them, she was sure, couldn't afford what they tossed at her while downing drink after drink, night after night. And if she thought about that too much, she felt miserably guilty.

But the brothers, even the nephew, had thrown her for a loop. They were unlike any men she'd ever known. Their very posture spoke of confidence and honor and respectability. She found herself intrigued.

Because she knew it had been true for her father, and true for her ex, she asked, "Things changed a lot with a baby in the picture?"

She waited for Jordan's complaints on the hardships of keeping up with an infant. Once again, he took her by surprise.

"I wouldn't say they changed, just adjusted a bit. In a good way. Sawyer was always so straight-faced, so serious. And then there he was, cuddling this little squirt and grinning all the time and looking so happy to change a diaper or give a bath."

Georgia stared at him. When she'd had Lisa, she'd always felt the same way. Everything her baby did she'd thought was magical and amazing. But she'd never considered that a man might have that outlook. "You're serious?"

Nodding, Jordan said, "I used to think nothing could pull Sawyer from his books, not even a beautiful woman. But if Casey made a noise, he was there, checking on him, smiling at him."

Jordan grinned with the memories, then shook his head. "Morgan was always the rowdiest. He fought for the fun of fighting. Everyone still jokes about him bordering on the side of savage."

"I can see that."

Jordan glanced at her quickly before returning his attention to the road. "He makes a hell of an impression, doesn't he? He's kept our town peaceful, usually with little more than a look. But whenever he touched Casey, he was so gentle. It boggled my mind. Now, with his own daughter, Amber, who's heading on two, he's the same. I swear he could wrestle buffalo with one arm and hold her close with the other, making sure not a one of her little curls got ruffled. He makes a hell of a sheriff, and an even better dad."

"You have an impressive family." Beyond impressive really. Having only met Jordan and Morgan, she should have been prepared for Casey. How could he have been anything less than spectacular, surrounded by such incredible uncles?

Jordan gave one nod. "Yeah, I think they're pretty great. Gabe, the youngest, started his own business not too long ago and already he's got more work than he can handle. He can build or repair anything, and after his marriage he decided he needed to get things a little more on track."

"On track how?"

"Before he met Elizabeth, he just worked when the mood struck him—or if someone needed something. He was always willing to help out. But Gabe preferred to spend his time in other pursuits. I doubt there was ever a day when he was without female company. Women flocked to him. It was almost uncanny. From the time he learned the difference between males and females, every girl in the area was after him, and he took advantage of it. They spoiled him rotten."

Jordan said that with a fond smile, making Georgia shake her head.

"The worse his reputation got, the more they seemed to come after him. It used to drive my mother nuts until she and Brett retired to Florida."

His poor wife, Georgia thought. A man like that never settled down, never really gave up his old ways....

Jordan touched her cheek. "Why are you frowning?"

She'd been so absorbed in her thoughts, she hadn't realized she frowned. "No reason."

"Come on, Georgia." He turned down the old road leading to her house. It was bumpy and filled with muddy puddles thanks to the rain. "I could almost see the evil thoughts going through your brain."

"Not evil. Just...realistic."

"Like?"

She didn't appreciate being pushed. She didn't appreciate having him affect her this way, either. Perhaps it would be best to tell him up front exactly how she felt so he'd leave tonight and not come back. That would be the most intelligent course to take.

So then why did the possibility make her feel so desperate?

Georgia cleared her throat, peeked at her kids to make certain they were still sleeping soundly. "Very well. If you're sure you want to hear this?"

"I do."

"I imagine," she said slowly, measuring her words,

"that any man who's used to running from one woman to the next, to indulging every sexual whim, is not likely to settle down with only one woman, just because he says a few vows. If it's in his nature to be a…sexual hedonist—"

Jordan laughed. "Gabe is that."

"—then he'll always be a hedonist."

"True. I won't argue with you there. All of my brothers are very sexual." He glanced at her and shrugged. "There's nothing wrong with that, by the way."

Georgia didn't bother to argue with him on it. She did, however, wonder if he included himself in the "very sexual" category.

No! She did not wonder. She didn't care. Refusing to look at him, she stared out her door window and watched the passing shrubbery on the side of the road. Even in the darkness, everything looked wilted by the rain.

Without her encouragement, Jordan continued. "Gabe is still a man, still very interested in sex, and I can't see that ever changing. But now he does all his overindulging with his wife."

Lord, how had she gotten onto this subject? She felt so hot, her window was beginning to steam. "If you say so," she mumbled, hoping he'd let it go.

But of course he didn't.

"You don't believe me?" When she didn't answer, he whistled. "Must have been a hell of a marriage you had."

Georgia denied that with a shake of her head. "The marriage was fine. It was the end of the marriage that was hell."

So softly she could barely hear him, Jordan asked, "Because you still loved him?"

"No." By the time the divorce was finalized, she knew she'd been living a fairy tale, created and maintained all in the fancy of her mind. She'd seen what she'd wanted to see, not what had really been there. "No, I didn't still love him. And it didn't matter that he had never really loved me. But he never loved his kids, either. And that I can't understand."

"I'm sorry."

"Why?" His voice had that low, hypnotic sound to it again, making her insides tingle, making her breasts feel too full. It pulled at her until she wanted to lean toward him, wanted to press her face into his throat and breathe in his scent, feel the warmth of his hard body. "What difference does it make to you?"

Jordan turned into her driveway and cut the engine. "Maybe I can explain it once we get inside." His gaze, glittering bright, held her. "Go unlock your front door and I'll carry the kids in."

She quickly shook her head, dispelling the trance he'd put her in with that melodic voice. "No. Thank you. You've done enough and I insist on repaying you for your—"

"I'm walking you in, Georgia." His tone was now firm and commanding. His large hand cupped her cheek, tipping up her chin. "We have a few things to say to each other."

"We have nothing to discuss!"

"Mommy?" Lisa sat up, rubbing her eyes and looking around in confusion.

With one last glare at Jordan—where she couldn't help but notice that he appeared understanding and sympathetic still—Georgia got out of the front seat, then opened her daughter's car door. "Sweetheart, we're home." She unfastened Lisa's seat belt and smoothed her tangled bangs out of her face. "Wait right here while I go unlock the door, then I'll get Adam and we'll all go in, okay?"

She'd forgotten to turn on a porch light before they left, and the path to the front door, broken and overgrown with weeds, would have been impossible if Jordan hadn't flipped the headlights back on. Her hand shook as she struggled to get the key into the lock and open the front door. But when she turned around, she almost fell over her daughter.

Jordan stood there, Adam snuggled blissfully unaware in his arms while Lisa held on to one of his belt loops. He gave her a gentle smile and said, "Move."

Like a zombie, Georgia stepped out of the way. What choice did she have? None. As a matter of fact, Jordan, with his quiet, calm ways, had been taking away her choices from the moment she first saw him.

She closed the door and started after him, hearing Lisa direct him to Adam's room at the top of the stairs. Lisa followed him, then veered off to her own bedroom. Georgia went to her first, helping her to get her nightgown on and tucking her into bed.

"I didn't brush my teeth."

Georgia smiled and pressed a kiss to Lisa's forehead. "You'll brush them twice tomorrow morning, okay?"

"Okay. I love you, Mommy."

Tears blurred her eyes for a moment. She was just so tired. And she had so very much to be thankful for. "Oh baby, I love you, too." She scooped her daughter up for a giant bear hug. "So, so much."

"Will you tell Jordan g'night for me?"

"Of course I—"

"I'm right here." Jordan stepped out of the shadows and sat on the edge of Lisa's bed, practically forcing Georgia to scamper out of his way. He was an enormously large man and took up entirely too much space. "Thanks for helping me out so much today, Lisa. I appreciate it."

Her teeth flashed in a quick smile. "It was fun. Except for grandma gettin' sick."

Jordan stroked her hair. "You were asleep, but your mother assures me that your grandma will be fine. The doctors are going to take very good care of her, and before long, she'll be back home."

Lisa nodded, then looked back at her mother. "Who's going to baby-sit us when you go to work?"

Georgia had been standing there in something of a stupor, amazed and a little appalled at how at ease Jordan seemed to be with her daughter, and how at ease her daughter was with him. There hadn't been many men in their lives, certainly not one who would smooth a blanket and stroke back a wayward curl.

Her father had never been close to her, much less his grandchildren. He'd died without ever knowing how truly wonderful Lisa and Adam were. Her ex-husband had walked away from them without a backward glance. But Jordan Sommerville had not only cared for them, he'd done so willingly, and even claimed to have enjoyed himself.

Seeing him now, she could believe him.

The lump in her throat nearly strangled her. She did not want to like him, not at all. But it was getting harder to stick to that resolve.

Forestalling her daughter from saying too much, Georgia said, "It's all taken care of, sweetie. I'll tell you about it in the morning. But for now, you need to get to sleep. The sun will be up before you know it."

Just like that, Lisa rolled to her side, snuggled her head into her pillow, and faded back to sleep.

Jordan smiled as he stood. In a low whisper that made every nerve in her body stand on end, he said, "Children are the most amazing creatures. Awake one minute, zonked out the next."

Georgia turned off the bedside lamp, throwing the room into concealing darkness. Only the dim light from the hallway intruded. She headed for the door. "My children are very sound sleepers. Once they're out, not much can wake them."

She turned to pull the door shut and found herself not two inches from Jordan. He looked down at her, his gaze lazy and relaxed. Her heartbeat jumped into double-time. She stared at his mouth—and he moved out of her way.

Georgia decided not to look at him again, but it turned out not to be a worry. He didn't follow her to Adam's room. Instead he headed back downstairs.

She found Adam still in his jeans and T-shirt, but his shoes had been pulled off and the blankets pulled over him. Her heart swelled at the sight of his teddy bear clutched in his arms. How had Jordan known to give it to him? It was a certainty her son hadn't awakened enough to ask for it. But he might have missed it in the middle of night.

She sighed, kissed him gently—which prompted a snuffled snore—and smiled. She left his room with her thoughts in a jumble, pausing in the hallway for a good three minutes while she tried to figure out how to get rid of Jordan, how to remove him without looking totally ungrateful for all he'd done.

Honesty, she decided, might be her best course. She'd simply tell him outright that she neither wanted nor needed his help—not anymore. She'd thank him for all he'd done that day, regardless of the fact that part of the trouble had been his doing.

Then she'd tell him good-night, and that would be that.

She headed into the kitchen, her back stiff with resolve, and found him making coffee. Before she could speak he turned to her and his expression was so intense, so…sensual, she caught her breath.

"We have to talk," he said, and just those simple words, muttered low and rough, made her heart pound too sharply, her body too warm. She literally trembled with need, and it made her angry and scared and frustrated. How could he affect her this way? He stepped toward her and touched her cheek. "But first, why don't you go get showered and get all this makeup off? The coffee—I found decaf so it won't keep you up—should be done by then."

With her breath coming fast and low, her stomach in knots, Georgia nodded. He was making her coffee, one of her favorite things on this earth. And it sounded heavenly. *He* sounded heavenly. Lord, what a combination.

She hadn't stood a chance.

Jordan had himself well in check. He would stop reacting like a teenager with raging hormones, where the sight of a girl's panties could put him into a frenzy of carnal greed. Hell, he could see a woman *without* her damn panties and still control himself. He would be calm. He would explain to Georgia that he wanted her, that he thought they should take advantage of the incredible chemistry…no, not incredible. Just good old chemistry. Nothing special, but there was no reason why they couldn't get together and, as mature, reasonable adults, have a brief affair.

It only made sense. There was no reason for them *not* to indulge their mutual desire. She was a divorced woman working in a bar. It wasn't like she was a prim and proper virgin.

But even as Jordan listed in his mind all the reasons that they should and could get together to take the edge off the urgent, burning hunger threatening to consume him, he worried that she'd refuse.

Damn, even looking at her sink full of dirty dishes made him want her. The whole house was a wreck, and rather than make him disdainful, it drove home to him how overwhelmed she was. He looked around again and wondered which issue he should resolve first: his lust, or the fact that he was going to give her a helping hand whether she wanted him to or not.

The old house was silent except for the creaking of the pipes as she showered. His hands shook and his vision blurred as he imagined her naked, wet and soapy and slick and…

He groaned aloud. The shower shut off and he pictured her drying her lush breasts, her flat belly, her thighs….

To distract himself, he started on the dishes. She needed a dishwasher, but there was really no place in the ancient kitchen to put one. The cabinets were a tad warped, some of them mismatched, and they'd been painted many times. They weren't very deep, but there was certainly an abundance of them. Too many, in fact.

The linoleum on the floor, besides being of a singularly ugly design, was cracked and starting to peel. The ceiling, which he guessed to be just beneath the shower judging by the noise, had water stains, indicating that at least a few of those squeaky pipes were leaking.

He was done with the dishes, all of them stacked on a dishtowel to air dry, when the coffee finished dripping. She'd be getting dressed now... Jordan forced himself to keep busy.

Right off the kitchen was a glass-enclosed patio that opened to the backyard. Vents in the floor-to-ceiling windows were opened about an inch, letting in the cool, damp night air. Jordan, who needed a little cooling off, carried his coffee into that room and looked out at the backyard. Beautiful, he thought, even with the rough grounds. There was an enormous oak tree that probably provided an abundance of shade to the room during the hottest part of the day.

A padded glider, two chairs, a few rattan tables that had seen better days, and various toys scattered about filled the room to overflowing.

Light from the kitchen slanted across the floor, mixing with the softer, gentler moonlight. The wind stroked the trees, making the shadows dance. The house, while in need of repair, was perfect. It would take only a few pets—and a man—to make it a complete home.

Jordan held his coffee cup with a barely restrained grip. What was she doing now? How would she dress? He imagined she'd look vastly different in regular clothes, with her hair freshly shampooed and all her overdone makeup gone.

And then finally he heard her.

"Jordan?"

"Right here." The words, whispered low, barely made it past the restriction in his throat. He didn't turn to face her, attempting to get himself back under control first. But damn, it was impossible. It was insane.

He could smell her, he thought with an edge of urgency, sweet and warm and so damn female. Even fresh from her shower, he detected her scent. He felt like a bull in full rut.

He cleared his throat. "There's a cup of coffee waiting for you on the counter."

Her footsteps were nearly silent as she padded to the kitchen and back. He knew she was coming out to him.

"Thank you." She, too, had lowered her voice, and there was an edge of wariness in her tone. He heard her sip, then heard the creak of the glider as she sat down. "I should have known you'd make great coffee."

It sounded like an accusation. Slowly Jordan turned to face her. Moonlight touched her in selective places— over the crown of her hair, making it glow a soft gold, across her shoulders now covered in a baggy white cotton pullover, and her knees, bare from the sloppy gray sweatshorts she wore. There were thick white ankle socks on her feet.

Not a seductive outfit, at least not deliberately. But then, nothing that she'd done to him had been deliberate. Most of her face was hidden, but he saw enough.

"My God, you're beautiful." Without the makeup, she looked young and innocent and…distressed. Because of him?

Her quiet laugh was incredulous. "Hardly that. Only

my mother, who loves me dearly, would ever call me beautiful."

Jordan heard the words, but he couldn't quite comprehend them. Not with her sitting there making him shake with the most profound emotions he'd ever experienced.

She laughed again, nervously this time as he continued to stare. "But I suppose anything is an improvement after the war paint, especially since it had all been smudged. I nearly scared myself when I looked in the mirror."

She took another drink of the coffee, then set the mug beside her on the floor. With a loose-limbed dexterity that amazed him, she twisted one leg up across her lap and began massaging her foot. "Now, about our talk."

Jordan looked at her foot, so small and feminine, less than half the size of his own. He breathed hard and felt like an idiot. How the hell could her feet raise his fevered urgency to the breaking point? He searched his beleaguered brain for an ounce of logic.

"You're going to need some help for the next few days." Damn, he hadn't meant to blurt that out.

She paused, looking up at him with a blank sort of disbelief. She forced a smile. "We'll be fine."

In for a penny, in for a pound.... "Who will watch your children," he asked, "while you visit your mother at the hospital? I assume you'll want to visit her?"

That got her frowning. "Of course I will! I'm not going to just leave her there...."

"I didn't think so." The love she felt for her mother, the closeness, was as obvious to him as her feelings for her children. It had pained him to witness her worry, her fear. All his life, he'd had his family around him, his mother, his brothers, ready to share any burdens, ready to support him in any way they could. But the one person Georgia had was now ailing, and it turned him inside out trying to imagine how the hell she could cope with that reality.

His own mother was the epitome of female strength, her love and loyalty unshakeable, unquestionable. She was fierce in her independence, and God help anyone who tried to come between her and her family.

He knew if it was his mother in the hospital right now, he'd move heaven and earth for her. But Georgia didn't have his financial or familial resources.

Georgia needed him, and his mother would be the first to have his head if he didn't insist on helping. As much as it pained him, he was going to have to put lust aside, at least for the time being.

"What will you do when you have to work?" Jordan asked. "Do you have any baby-sitters? Other than your mother, I mean."

Her head snapped up and she dropped her foot back to the floor. Jordan had a feeling she was ready to pounce on him. He quickly set his own coffee cup on the rickety rattan table and stepped close enough so that she couldn't come completely to her feet without touching him.

He waited, hoping, his breath held. But with no more than a wary look, she retreated.

He settled both hands on her shoulders and gave her his patented stern look. "Is it true, Georgia? Or do you have someone you can call to help out until your mother gets well?"

They were still speaking in hushed tones, and her

voice sounded gruff with emotion when she answered. "Of course I have people I can call."

Jordan knelt down in front of her. His long legs encased hers; he surrounded her, wanting her to know he'd protect her, that she could trust him. "Who?"

Silence filled the room. Jordan loved the way her gray eyes darkened, making her thoughts easy for him to read. Others would consider her eyes mysterious, but he understood her. He *knew* her.

Finally, after long seconds, she shook her head.

His heart swelled painfully. "There's no one, is there?" She turned away and he whispered, "Georgia?"

"No."

Without conscious decision, he began caressing her shoulders, feeling the smoothness of her, the softness. In a tone so low he could barely hear himself, he said, "Don't ever lie to me again, Georgia. It's not necessary. Whatever men you've known—"

She laughed at that, a sound without much humor.

"—I'm not like them. You can trust me."

She stared at his mouth. "Oh, I know you're different, Jordan. No doubt about it. But don't you see? That's part of the problem."

"You want to explain that?"

"Why not?" Her hand trembled when she touched his jaw, and her voice was husky with wonder. "I've found it very easy to ignore most men, even the men yelling crude suggestions from the audience when I dance. But I can't ignore you. You make me feel different. You... affect me." Then with a frown: "I don't like it."

For the first time in his life, Jordan's knees felt weak. He sucked in air, trying to fill his lungs enough, trying to dredge up just a little more calm. This was important and he wanted it resolved.

He cupped her face, pulled her forward to the edge of her seat until her breasts were soft and full against his chest, until he could feel her thundering heartbeat, meshing with his own. "You affect me, too."

And then he kissed her.

Her lush mouth softened, warmed, under his. She made a small sound of confusion and her hands settled on his shoulders, her fingers biting deep into his muscles.

He tasted her deeply, his tongue pushing gently into her mouth, making them both groan. Jordan was a hairsbreadth away from taking her completely when he forced himself to lift his mouth away. They both struggled for breath. "This is insane," he whispered.

She nodded, staring into his eyes with a mix of wonder and fear.

"Here's what we're going to do." He used the tone that made women agree with him no matter what. He considered it successful, given that she rested her head on his shoulder and her hands still held him tightly.

"I'll see to the children," he insisted, "after I've taken care of all my appointments. With a little rearranging, I think I can be done by three each day, which means you'll have plenty of time to visit with your mother, and then get into work, right?"

With an obvious effort, she pulled herself away from him. She looked dazed, but said, "Sometimes I waitress in the afternoons, too."

Jordan barely resisted the urge to kiss her again. "You work alternate shifts?"

"No. Sometimes I work both. We…that is, I need

the money. This house has a lot of repairs that have to be done and…"

It seemed the words came from her unwillingly. "Shh. I understand. When I can't make it, Casey or one of my other relatives will help out. You'll love them. They're all terrific with kids."

She didn't reply to that, either to deny or accept his offer. Jordan looked at the weariness etched into every line of her body. It was no wonder she looked so tired, so utterly defeated. "You were finishing up a double shift today, weren't you?"

"Yes."

He lifted one hand to her cheek and used his thumb to stroke her cheekbone. "How many hours do you usually work in a day?"

"However many I need to."

Her matter-of-fact answer hit him like a slap. He looked up at the ceiling, wanting to roar with frustration. Since meeting her, he'd been indulging visions of wild lechery while she was barely able to stay on her feet. He felt like a complete and total bastard, an unfeeling—

"What is it you do, Jordan? You said you have appointments?"

It wasn't easy to tamp down his anger at the thought of her working herself into the ground, especially at that sorry place. But her exhaustion was a palpable force, wearing her down, *wearing him down,* and he couldn't bring himself to add to it. He reminded himself that she needed his strength, not his temper. Not his lust.

"I'm a vet." He moved to sit beside her on the glider and as she turned toward him, he took her hand. The unusual day had brought them a closeness that might normally have taken a week or more to achieve. He'd seen her vulnerability, and her strength. But they'd had little time to actually get to know one another. He'd rectify as much of that as he could right now.

"I've always loved animals and they've always loved me. I feel gifted, because they respond to me."

"It's your voice," she said, and she smiled.

Jordan shrugged. All his life he'd heard about his mystical voice, but so far, Georgia had seemed quite capable of resisting him. "Why don't you have any pets? The yard is plenty big enough and the kids would love it."

"So would I. But pets cost money. They need food and shots and...not only would it cost too much, but I don't have much spare time left. The kids are too young to be solely responsible for a pet, and my mother does enough as it is."

Jordan decided to think on that. As isolated as she was in the big house, a dog would be ideal. He said, "I have a clinic not that far from here. That's why it'll be easy for me to help you out with the children. They like me, Georgia, so that shouldn't be a problem. And if you still have any doubts about my character, well, ask around town tomorrow. Anyone can tell you that I'm good baby-sitting material."

She looked down at their clasped hands, then tugged gently until he freed her. Scooting over a little to put some space between them, she again pulled her foot into her lap and began rubbing. In a ridiculously prim voice considering they were sitting alone in the darkness and he'd had his tongue in her mouth only moments before, she said, "I don't want to impose on you."

"I'm offering, and besides—" he tipped her face toward him "—what other options do you have?"

Her eyes closed and she sighed. "Options? I don't have many, do I? I've often wondered what my life would be like with more options."

Jordan growled out a sigh. She was the most exasperating woman he'd ever met. "I'm trying to give you some options, sweetheart."

"Don't call me that."

Jordan ignored her order. "I want you to be able to visit your mother and work without having to worry about Lisa or Adam."

Her eyes slanted his way, heavy with fatigue. "You don't approve of me."

Fighting the urge to shake her, Jordan frowned. "Wrong. I don't approve of where you work. They're two entirely different things."

She laughed at that, and focused on flexing the arch of her left foot with intense concentration.

Jordan caught her wrists. "What are you doing?"

"My feet hurt." Her tone was abrupt, as if that particular question had annoyed her more than anything else. "Try staying on your feet all damn day—in high heels no less—and your feet'll hurt, too."

He flexed his jaw. He told himself to just leave. He even cursed himself privately in the silence of his own mind. But it didn't make one whit of difference. He was already so far off track, he had no idea where he was going, but was just as intent on getting there.

"Lay down."

She reared back as if he'd struck her. *"What?"*

Jordan caught her hips and pulled her toward him so that she landed flat on her back on the flowered cushions. She was stunned for a moment, not moving, and before she could gather her wits he deftly flipped her onto her stomach. He had her feet in his lap and his gaze glued to the sight of her rounded ass in the loose shorts, by the time she started to struggle. He must have masochistic tendencies, he decided, tightening his grip on her ankles, holding her secure.

Georgia levered up on stiffened arms, gasping in outrage—until his fingers moved deeply over the arch of her left foot, then up and over her toes. She gave a long, husky, vibrating groan.

The sound of her unrestrained pleasure made Jordan break out in a sweat. Her shoulders went limp and her head dropped forward as if her neck had no strength to hold it up. "This isn't fair."

"What?"

"A voice that seduces, perfect coffee, and now a foot massage." She groaned again. "Ohmigod, that feels good."

Jordan closed his eyes and applied himself to giving her the best damn foot rub she'd ever had in her life. "Relax," he ordered, though he was so rigid a mere touch would have shattered him.

She obeyed. She dropped flat to the glider and rested her head on her folded arms. Every few seconds she moaned in bliss, stretching her toes like a cat being petted.

Jordan was so hard he hurt. He desperately wanted to slide his hands up the backs of her firm thighs, to slip his fingers beneath the loose hem of the shorts she wore. Probably, he reasoned, she'd thought the shorts to be unappealing because they were old and gray and faded. But the material hugged her curves and they were loose enough in the legs that he could now see all the way to the tops of her thighs.

He slid his hands up her warm, resilient calves. She had excellent muscle tone, and even as he stroked her, kneading her flesh, feeling her muscles relax, he admitted he was beyond pathetic when a woman's muscle tone brought him to the edge.

Feeling like a damn lecher, he lifted one of her legs and was even able to see the edge of her panties, which—contrary to all he'd been telling himself—nearly made him erupt with carnal greed.

In a rasp totally unlike his normal seductive tone, he said, "Agree to my help, damn it."

She sighed, adjusted her head more comfortably and murmured in a barely there voice, "It wouldn't be right."

Affronted, Jordan realized she was on the verge of sleep. Conflicting emotions bombarded him. Lust was there, tearing at his resolve, making his guts cramp, but there was also a throbbing explosion of tenderness, enough to expand his heart and tighten his lungs.

"I want to help you, Georgia."

She sighed, and in the next instant started to snore softly. A reluctant smile curved his mouth. Never in his benighted life had a woman fallen asleep on him. It was a novelty he could have lived without, but then it occurred to him that perhaps this was exactly what he needed to gain the upper hand.

"Georgia?" He continued working the tendons in her feet, something he knew from experience that all women seemed to enjoy. Personally, if a female was going to rub him, he could think of better places than his feet.

She didn't reply and after he gently placed her foot in his lap, he reached up and shook her shoulder.

She never stirred.

Jordan sat back with a grin. She'd said her children were very sound sleepers and now he knew that it was an inherited trait.

Beyond his feelings of triumph—because he really did have her now—it dawned on him that she was as vulnerable as a woman could be with a man, so she must trust him to some degree. And he wasn't above taking advantage of it.

He stroked her hair, silky soft and warm. He indulged his need to touch her, to learn the textures and curves of her face, her neck, her shoulder. Her spine was graceful, leading down to that superior rump that looked so damn tantalizing there before him, like an offering.

He was an honorable man, so he kept his hands on safe ground, but he looked at every inch of her, then whispered, "I've got you now, sweetheart."

And still she didn't move.

It took a lot of willpower to walk away from her, to find a blanket to cover her with and then to walk out of the room. But he managed it; he had a lot of fortitude when something really mattered.

And this mattered. Much as he hated to admit it, it mattered too damn much.

Chapter 6

Georgia woke with the sunlight bright in her face. She didn't move, at first making an attempt to orient herself. Something wasn't right. She squinted; why was there so much light?

As her eyes adjusted, she saw the huge oak in her backyard through dirty windows, stately and still, not a single leaf stirring. There must be no wind, she thought, now that the dreadful rain had obviously ended.

And then it dawned on her that she wasn't in her own bed where she should be, or she certainly wouldn't be looking at the backyard. She was, as incredible as it seemed, in the enclosed patio curled up on the glider under a quilt.

She was still putting those thoughts together in the cobwebs of her mind when she heard a faint, muffled laugh. Lisa, then Adam. They sounded happy and for

just a moment she thought everything was as it was supposed to be, as it had been the day before. Her mother,
an early riser, was probably making coffee and the kids
liked to hang next to her, waiting for cereal, chatter-
ing nonstop. Georgia always got up when she heard
the kids, even though she was still exhausted and even
though she knew her mother would complain and tell
her to sleep more—and then she heard another deeper,
more masculine laugh.

Jordan!

She jerked upright so fast the glider rolled, nearly
spilling her onto the floor. Her heart racing, she remembered everything, her near arrest, her mother's illness—that orgasmic foot rub Jordan had been giving
her late last night.

She twisted to face the kitchen behind her, and sure
enough, that was Jordan's rough-velvet voice whispering, "Shhh. We don't want your mother to wake up yet.
She had a long night."

Adam, sounding a bit blurry as if he hadn't been
awake long himself, said, "Mommy always gets up with
us, even when grandma grouches at her 'bout it."

Lisa bragged, "She won't hear anything, but she always hears us. Even when we're quiet. Grandma says
that's a mommy's sixth sense."

"You've got an excellent mommy." Jordan said that
with conviction, and Georgia wondered if he meant it.
More likely he was merely trying to appease the kids.
"But today we'll try to let her catch up on sleep."

Lisa asked, "Can I have the next pancake?"

Pancake?

"Absolutely. I can't believe you've eaten two already.

Are you sure they're in your belly? You didn't hide one behind your ear?"

Lisa laughed again and Adam joined her.

Georgia nearly choked. She'd been sleeping so soundly one minute, and jarred awake the next, that she felt nearly drunk as she staggered to her feet in righteous indignation and groped her way toward the kitchen. Jordan was feeding her children? He had invaded her kitchen? What in the world was he doing here so early? The kids knew better than to go anywhere near the doors without her or their grandmother. She'd reminded them again and again that they were never ever to open the door to anyone.

Georgia stopped in the entryway, her thoughts scattering at the sight of Jordan. He looked…*gorgeous*. Sinfully gorgeous. His light brown hair was mussed, his jaw rough with beard stubble, his sleeves rolled back over his thick forearms. And he wore an apron around his waist.

For the first time she understood the appeal of "barefoot and pregnant in the kitchen". Jordan's bare feet looked very sexy, and though he wasn't in the family way, he was being domestic—which she assumed was the point. He smiled at Lisa and it made her heart expand painfully against her rib cage. Georgia rubbed a hand under her breast, trying to ease the constriction, but it didn't help.

God, the man looked good standing at her stove. He looked good with her children, too. And he looked far, far too good in her life.

Both kids wore aprons as well, tied up under their armpits and with the hems dragging near the floor. They were huddled around the stove while Jordan used a turkey baster to put pancake batter on the griddle with complex precision.

"I'm an artist," he proclaimed, and both kids quickly agreed.

Curiosity swamped her, and when she finally got her hungry gaze off Jordan and onto the griddle she saw that he was making the most odd-shaped pancakes she'd ever seen. They were...well, they looked like faces. And fish. And...

"Mommy!"

Adam rushed to her, nearly knocking her off her feet as he barreled into her legs. Jordan looked up with a frown. Lisa ran to her and took her hand.

It was traditional for them to share kisses and hugs first thing in the morning, and this morning was no different.

It wasn't traditional, however, for a very large, very sexy man to be looking on. A man with noticeable chest hair showing through the open collar of his shirt. A man with very warm, appreciative eyes.

Maybe the kids hadn't let him in. Maybe—she gulped—he'd spent the night! She couldn't seem to remember anything after he'd started working on her feet. Nothing except how incredibly good it had felt.

Heat rushed into her face and Jordan smiled as if he knew exactly why she blushed. Georgia ignored him, holding both children close, relishing the feel of their small arms tight around her neck, their sweet, familiar smells. She could never truly regret the mistakes in her life, because it was those mistakes that had given her Lisa and Adam.

But that didn't mean she wanted to make those mistakes again. Having a male stranger invade her life so easily not only showed her irresponsibility, but her stupidity. She couldn't let it happen. She *wouldn't* let it happen.

She'd barely straightened when both kids began extolling Jordan's virtues, how funny he was, his culinary expertise, his artistic talent. He'd already promised to show them new kittens at his office, and to take them along the next time he had to treat a horse or cow.

Like a damn new puppy, they wanted to keep him. Forever.

Georgia ground her teeth together and concentrated on getting her sluggish brain in gear. Adam demanded her attention with the typical enthusiasm of a four-year-old boy.

It was an effort, but Georgia hefted his sturdy little body into her arms. He clasped her face and said, "We been cookin'!"

"So I see." Her words ended on a jaw-splitting yawn and since her hands were full holding up her tank of a son, she couldn't quite cover her mouth.

Jordan ushered Lisa away from the stove with a gentle touch. "Not too close, hon. I want to get your mother some coffee before she topples over, and you never know when a pancake might explode. So don't go near the griddle without me, okay?"

Lisa held her sides as she laughed, but she did as he asked, settling into her chair at the table.

Without her permission, Jordan relieved her of Adam's weight, holding her son as if he had the right, as if he'd known how unsteady she still felt, and to her further annoyance, Adam clung to him.

Cooking, coffee, foot massage, and now coddling her kids; the man knew his way into a woman's heart.

Jordan handed her the coffee cup as a replacement for Adam. "Here. You look like you could use this."

Fragrant steam rose from the cup, making the coffee impossible to resist. She took one long hot sip and felt her head begin to clear. "Nothing on earth," she said with relish, "tastes better than that first sip of coffee in the morning."

His eyes took on a warm glow. "Oh, I don't know about that." He looked at her mouth, and heat shot down her spine, doing more than the coffee had to revive her.

Jordan smiled at her as he deftly seated Adam at the table and put a square pancake on his plate. "Why don't you sit down, Georgia, and I'll tell you what the hospital had to say this morning."

Her brain threatened to burst. Georgia glanced at the clock and saw it was only eight. "You've called them already?"

"Yes. I thought you'd probably want to know something as soon as you woke."

He was right, of course. Not only did he excite her, he read her mind.

"They said your mother rested peacefully through the night and that she's doing much better this morning. The doctor will be in to see her sometime between eleven and one, so I thought you'd like to be there." He looked her over, taking in the rumpled clothes she'd slept in. "I'd planned to wake you in an hour or so to give you time to get ready."

Wake her? She was both relieved and slightly disappointed to have missed that happening. She couldn't remember the last time she'd been awakened by a man. Before the divorce, she was always the one up first. To have Jordan wake her…it would have been a novel experience.

Dazed, Georgia looked around the kitchen. For the first time she could remember since moving in, it was spotless. Not a dish out of place, other than the ones now loaded with the odd pancake shapes. The counters were all spotless, the floor clean, the sink polished. Even the toys that were forever under foot had all been put away. The dozens of colored pictures by Adam and Lisa were neatly organized on the front of the refrigerator.

She frowned and cast a suspicious glare at Jordan. Had he been cleaning all night to accomplish so much? And why would he do such a thing anyway? Her father and her ex-husband had considered that women's work.

"Would you like a pancake?"

Her eyes narrowed at his continued good humor and solicitousness. "No."

"I can make it in the conventional shape if the fun stuff scares you."

He knew damn good and well that it was he who scared her, not his ridiculous pancakes. She considered strangling him.

"They're the best pancakes I've ever tasted!" Lisa said with her mouth full, her lips sticky with syrup. Georgia saw the box of pancake mix—the same that they always used—sitting on the cabinet, and raised her brows at Jordan.

"It's all in the preparation," he explained. "Any chef can tell you that."

She drank the rest of her coffee, in desperate need of the caffeine if she was expected to spar with him after just rising. Last night had been the best sleep she'd had in ages, when she'd thought she'd be awake fretting all night.

With that superior gentleness that made her want to smack him, Jordan took her arm and led her to a chair. "Yes, there's more coffee," he said, saving her from having to ask.

He refilled her cup and she scowled. "Cooking, cleaning, serving. What are you? My fairy godmother?"

Leaning close to her ear, he whispered, "I'm just a man who wants you, sweetheart. And we did make that wonderful agreement last night."

She straightened so abruptly she bumped his chin with the back of her head. To his credit, he didn't curse, but he did give her a long look as he rubbed away the ache. Luckily the kids were digging into their food and not paying attention.

"What agreement?" she growled as he moved away, a man without a care in the world.

"We can go over all the details, as per your request," he said easily, "right after you get cleaned up and dressed."

"I don't remember any request!"

"Oh. Well, you were very groggy. Which was why you said it'd be better to finalize our plans—you do remember the plans?—in the morning." He turned to the stove and put three round pancakes on a plate, buttered them, and set them before her.

She had no recollection of the conversation at all. Certainly not about any plans. But those pancakes... the smells were incredible, making her stomach rumble loudly. Everyone looked at her. Lisa pointed and laughed.

Jordan pulled his own chair up close to hers. "When did you eat last?"

His gaze was too perceptive, too intrusive, demanding an honest reply. The problem was, she couldn't remember. The days tended to blur together when she worked double shifts.

He shook his head. "If you're going to burn the candle at both ends, you really need to refuel, you know."

"That's mixing your metaphors just a bit, isn't it?"

"Maybe. But the point is still valid, I swear." He watched her as she took her first bite, and smiled when she closed her eyes in bliss. "Good?"

"Very." She gave him a reluctant look, and added, "Thank you."

He touched her, stroking one long finger over her cheekbone and jaw, the side of her throat. "That wasn't so painful, now was it?"

Georgia froze for a heartbeat, mesmerized by that seductive tone and achingly tender touch. Then she shook herself and looked pointedly at her children, who were watching the byplay with an absorbed fascination. She supposed having a man at the breakfast table was even more unique for them. She doubted they remembered their father much, and what they would have remembered had nothing to do with peaceful family breakfasts together.

Jordan never missed a beat. "If you little beggars are done, why don't you go get your teeth brushed and pull on some clothes while your mother and I talk?"

"Talk about what?" Lisa wanted to know.

"Why, about you both visiting Casey again today, this time at our home. I live right near a long skinny lake. Casey can take you fishing while your mother and

I visit the hospital and fetch your car back home from where she works."

Lisa and Adam immediately started jumping up and down, squealing and begging.

"That's enough," Georgia said. The kids quieted just a bit, but their eyes were still bright and wide with hope.

She stared at Jordan, her face so frozen it hurt, and murmured, "That's low, even for you."

He looked guilty for a flash of an instant, then resolve darkened his eyes. "I'm a desperate man. And we did make that bargain—"

"Kids," she interrupted, "go ahead and get dressed. And Lisa, remember you wanted to brush your teeth twice, okay?"

"Are we going to see Casey?"

Not if she could help it. "I'll have to think about it, sweetie. There's a lot I have to get done today."

The kids trailed out, dragging their feet, their expressions despondent. Damn Jordan for putting her in this position. Her children had so few outings these days, what with her working all the time. She knew how much they'd love a visit to a lake. But the more time she spent with Jordan, the weaker her stand on independence seemed to feel. She had to make it on her own. She *had* to.

When Georgia heard their footsteps at the top of the creaky stairs, she rounded on Jordan, blasting him with all her fury. "How dare you!"

After one long, silent look, Jordan began carrying dishes to the sink. "You're just being stubborn, Georgia. Why should the kids be cooped up at the hospital while you're visiting your mother? They'll enjoy being in the fresh air, and I already spoke with Casey this morning and he agreed—"

"I didn't agree." She left her chair and faced him with her hands on her hips. "They're *my* children and I know what's best for them."

"True." Jordan leaned back on the sink and silently studied her. "I'm not questioning your parenting skills, honey. It only took me about two seconds of seeing you with them to know how much you love them, and that they're crazy about you. But you did agree." When she stared at him blankly, he added, "Last night? Don't tell me you don't remember any of it?"

Her heart lurched at his continued insistence. Last night? So much of it, once he'd touched her feet, was a blur. She'd been so tired, so stressed....

"You told me," Jordan said calmly, "that taking the kids to Casey would be fine. Sawyer is going to meet me at the hospital, and while you're visiting, he and I will fetch your car. Afterwards we'll pick up the kids and I'll take you all to dinner."

Georgia felt like a deflated balloon. Surely she hadn't discussed all that with him? But he looked so positive, so sure of himself. And she *had* been beyond weary, ready to simply cave in under the exhaustion and worry. It was conceivable that she might have said things she now couldn't remember.

She just didn't know.

Her head hurt and she rubbed her fingers through her badly tangled hair. She felt Jordan's large firm hands settle on her shoulders and pull her close. She tried to resist him and the comfort, the security that he offered. She really did. But he brought her up flush against his strong, solid body and began rubbing her back. The man's voice wasn't the only thing magical about him. His fingers were pretty amazing, too.

It had been so, so long since anyone stronger, bigger than she had held her. Her muscles turned liquid at the wondrous feel of it.

Jordan's whiskery jaw brushed her temple as he spoke. "Just stop being so defensive and think about this logically, okay? We're not bad people, sweetheart. Casey will enjoy keeping your rugrats entertained for a few hours. He adores children. We all do. And Lisa already adores Casey. He's responsible. He won't let anything happen to them."

"But—"

He tipped up her chin. "But you're still worried? Please don't be. Not now. When things get straightened out and your mother is back home, then you can give me hell, okay?"

She couldn't help but laugh. "I don't want to give you hell. It's just that... I don't understand you."

"And that worries you?"

With complete honesty, she said, "Yes."

"Well, I don't quite understand myself right now, either, so I'm afraid I can't offer any explanations. I just know I want to help out. Is that so bad?"

She searched his face, looking for answers while confusion swamped her. "We barely know each other, Jordan."

"But it doesn't seem to matter, does it?" His gaze warmed and his touch changed. Just like that, he went from comforting to being all male. All interested male. He looked at her mouth and then kept on looking. "I can't believe how you make me feel."

"Jordan?" Her lips trembled. Her entire body trembled. Nothing should feel like this, so good and so scary and so…right.

He bent toward her. His breath teased her lips as he whispered, "What you do to me should be illegal."

Oh, the way he said that! He'd turned the full power of his bewitching voice on her and, combined with the memory of that sensuous foot rub of the night before, she was a goner. "Oh, my…"

He stole her breathy exclamation with his mouth as he kissed her. Knowing that she should resist, and being able to resist, were two entirely different things. His mouth was hot, incredibly hungry, and damp. She kissed him back, unable not to. His taste was indescribable. Hot and feverish. His hands were gentle on her face, a stark contrast to the consuming carnality of the kiss, eating at her, nipping with his teeth, sucking at her tongue as he groaned low in his throat and kissed her again and again.

Her hands curved around his shoulders and the feel of him, of solid muscle, bone and sinew flexing against her palms made her insides curl with raw desire. He arched her into his body and gave her his own tongue, tasting her deeply, pressing the hard planes of his body into her softness. Her breasts throbbed and ached, their galloping heartbeats mingled, and between her thighs….

Somehow she found herself backed up to the cabinets. With no effort at all, Jordan lifted her and the second she was balanced on the edge of the counter, he stepped between her thighs. She could feel the long, hard ridge of his erection, throbbing against her. His hand curved up her side and then over her breast, and it was so wonderful she cried out.

Jordan cursed as he kissed his way to her throat, to the sensitive skin beneath her ear. "I want you."

She wanted him, too. She held on to him, unable to think beyond the need. He was between her legs, leaving her open and vulnerable and she liked it. She liked the way he moved against her, stroking her with a tantalizing touch that brought her so close to completion even though they were both completely dressed and for the most part standing. She'd never realized that such a thing was possible, but she felt her muscles tightening, felt the spiral of delicious heat curling in her belly and below.

His fingertips brushed over her aching nipple, then pinched lightly and she almost lost it, almost came right there in her kitchen with a man who was hardly more than a stranger, a man who had no compunction about taking over her life. And she simply didn't care.

The kids started to argue upstairs and Jordan lifted his mouth. He was panting hard, his body shaking. His high cheekbones were slashed with aroused color, his emerald eyes burning. Heat poured off him.

In guttural tones that turned her limbs to butter, he growled, "I'm so damn hard right now, one touch and I'd be in oblivion." He squeezed her tighter, pressed his erection hard against her. *"One touch, Georgia."*

It appeared he expected a reply to that. But she could barely think clearly enough to stay upright on the countertop, much less know what to say. She stared at his mouth, her own open in mute surprise at all she'd felt, at how incredible a kiss and a few simple touches could be. She'd been married nearly seven years, but she hadn't known, hadn't guessed....

He muttered a raw curse. "Don't look at me like that. You're killing me."

She sucked in air and tried to think.

"Say something, damn it."

Nodding, Georgia looked around her kitchen, at all he'd done, at all he still apparently expected to do. Not just to the house, but to her as well. She knew as soon as her thoughts cleared, she'd be mortified. She'd broken her own rules, she'd breached propriety. She'd shamed herself this time more than ever before.

She met his gaze and swallowed. "I'm supposed to work tonight. I... I can't go to dinner."

He shouldn't have been so angry, but his emotions had been in a whirlwind since the first moment he saw her, and he hadn't gotten a firm handle on them yet. How could he have done something so stupid as to practically take her in her own damn kitchen, with her kids upstairs? Not only was he disgusted with his own lack of restraint, but he was madder than hell at himself for upsetting her.

Once she'd really had a chance to settle down and get her wits together, she'd looked devastated. Jordan could tell she didn't blame him. No, Georgia blamed herself, and he couldn't stand it. He'd wanted to lighten her physical load, and instead, he had added to her emotional one. He could only imagine what she was thinking, but she wouldn't look at him, and that pretty much told it all.

What was between them was damn powerful, and neither of them were coming to grips with it very well. Rather than discussing it, though, she'd informed him she had to work. Again.

Jordan put up a good front for the kids, trying to shelter them from his black mood, a mood he was afraid was partially caused by jealousy. He'd never felt it before, so he couldn't be certain, but he did know that he hated it, hated the way his muscles refused to relax, the way his stomach knotted every time he pictured her on that stage. Hiding his rage wasn't easy, but he'd take a punch on the chin before deliberately upsetting her again, or making her children uncomfortable.

He must have been somewhat successful, because the kids were subdued, but far from silent. Georgia had explained to them about hospitals, so they were wide-eyed with respect for the sick people, and apparently oblivious to his turmoil.

Despite her near stomping, Georgia's soft-soled shoes made no sound as they walked the length of the long hospital corridor. He could feel her nervousness and he wanted to protect her. He wanted to devour her.

He didn't want her blaming herself for the uncontrollable chemistry between them. And he did not want her dancing on that goddamn stage again.

They rounded a corner, the silence between them a living thing, and then they both drew up short as they saw not only Sawyer standing there, but Gabe and Casey as well. Oh, hell. His entire family just had to turn out, didn't they? If Misty hadn't been sick, no doubt Morgan would have been here now, too.

They were likely enjoying his predicament. He'd always been different from them. More withdrawn. More self-contained. Though he never doubted their love, he often felt like an outsider; because of his father, there were things he'd never be able to share with them. Like the pride of their male parentage.

Knowing he'd gotten himself mired in an emotional conflict probably had them all rubbing their hands with glee. They just loved it when he fell into the same traps that grabbed them. It happened far too often for Jordan's peace of mind.

Lisa, being a natural-born flirt, smiled widely at the sight of Casey and took off at a run to see him. Casey grinned and knelt down to catch her. Adam quickly followed suit, but he was a bit more cautious, keeping one eye on Sawyer and Gabe.

Georgia had come to a complete and utter halt. She just stood there frozen, apparently as appalled as he felt. Jordan could have told her it wouldn't do her any good.

Sawyer started forward with a wide smile and a warm glint in his dark eyes. "Georgia?"

She nodded, staring up at him. Jordan heard her swallow. "Yes?"

Sawyer, damn him, hugged her. He put his arms right around her, as if she were a member of the family or something, and cradled her to his chest with a great show of affection.

Jordan saw red and had to struggle not to huff like a bull. Luckily Sawyer released her right away.

"It's so nice to meet you," Sawyer said. "Casey has told me quite a bit about you."

Her eyes were still round, her expression awed. "You're Casey's father?"

"Yes." Sawyer glowed with pride whenever he spoke of Case. "I understand he'll be doing a spot of baby-sitting today. We're all looking forward to it. Especially my wife. Now that we have our own little one-six-month-old Shohn—and with Morgan's daughter Amber, Honey's finding she really adores children. She's never had much chance to be around older children, so this'll be a real treat for her."

Jordan knew what his brother was doing, making it sound like a damn favor to him if Georgia didn't hesitate to let him take the kids. He'd told Sawyer on the phone that she hadn't quite agreed yet. But now, well... Sawyer's performance should clinch it.

He glanced at Georgia to see how she was reacting to Sawyer's long-winded introduction. He wasn't really surprised to see that her mouth was still open as she stared up at him. There was an innate compassion to Sawyer that drew women; they felt safe with him.

Then Gabe sauntered forward and Jordan thought she might faint. He cursed low even as he clasped her arm to steady her. Everyone ignored him.

"Hi, there," Gabe said, flashing her with his most engaging grin, and Georgia couldn't even blink. When Gabe waited, still smiling, she managed to lift one hand and flit her fingers in a feeble wave of greeting.

Jordan heaved a disgusted sigh. "Why are you all here?"

Sawyer shrugged. "I came because you asked me to. Gabe tagged along so you wouldn't have to leave Georgia here alone. He'll drive your car and drop me off to get Georgia's car, then we'll both be back. Casey is going to go ahead and take the kids to meet Honey, since she's practically bouncing with excitement."

Sawyer spoke as if the plans had all been finalized, attempting, no doubt, to head Georgia off at the pass, so to speak.

But at the mention of her offspring, Georgia came out of her stupor. "This is ridiculous. You're all going to so much trouble—"

"Not at all." Gabe winked at her, rendering her mute again. He had that effect on all women, it seemed. Even his wife wasn't yet immune. He'd ask Elizabeth if she'd like mashed potatoes, and the woman would blush scarlet. It was uncanny.

"It's no problem at all," Gabe assured her. "And for the record, my wife is anxious to meet the kids, too. We don't have any of our own yet. Not that I'm above trying, you understand—"

Jordan stepped in front of him. "You know, Georgia, since Sawyer is here anyway, why don't we let him take a peek at your mother? He's a damn fine doctor. And that way, if she ever has any other problems, you can just give him a call. They'll already be acquainted."

Sawyer nodded. "I still make housecalls, if you can believe the convenience of that! But in Buckhorn, we're all real neighborly that way."

Jordan shook his head at the not-so-subtle suggestion that Georgia could be more neighborly herself.

She turned her back on them all, one hand to her head. "This is incredible." She appeared to be speaking to herself.

"Where did you move from?" Gabe asked.

Distracted, she waved a hand and said, "Milwaukee."

"Ah, that explains it. We do things differently here."

She turned back around, her eyes intent. "Are there any other brothers I haven't met yet?"

They said in unison, "No."

"Thank God for small favors." They all grinned at her, making her fall back a step before she caught herself. "All right, I want to see my mother. I won't really feel reassured until I have. She's on the third floor."

Casey spoke up. "I'll go on and head out. The squirts are anxious to see the lake. That okay?"

Georgia looked harried, but she nodded. "Yes, okay." She pulled her children close. "You guys be on especially good behavior for Casey, all right?"

"We will!"

"We're always good."

Georgia smiled. "I know. I'm a very lucky mother to have you two."

The kids smothered her with hugs—quickly because they were anxious to be off—and she kissed each of them. "Jordan and I will be there soon. And be careful around that water!"

Casey put his arm around her shoulders and gave her a squeeze. "They'll be fine. Don't worry. We have a rule that no kids are allowed even on the shore without a life preserver on. I won't let them get hurt. I promise."

As Casey took both kids by the hand and walked away, Georgia got that shell-shocked look about her again.

Jordan gently maneuvered her into the elevator and pushed the third-floor button. In the crowded confines of the elevator, she stood closer to him than she had all morning. He assumed his brothers intimidated her because she was so damn small by comparison. Her curly golden brown hair would barely brush any of the male chins surrounding her, her shoulders were only half as wide as theirs.

Her petite build really emphasized her full breasts, he noticed. And once he noticed, he couldn't stop noticing. She wore a tailored yellow blouse buttoned to her throat and tucked into a long, trim denim skirt. There was nothing sexy about the outfit, and in fact, it was quite understated. But it did nothing to mask her appeal. He doubted a burlap sack could have managed that feat.

Jordan was lost in erotic fantasies better left to the privacy of his bedroom than a crowded elevator, when he felt her hand slip into his. He wanted to shout with the pleasure of it. She was warming to him, accepting him, even if reluctantly.

Then he saw that Sawyer had noticed it, too, and was whistling softly. He even nudged Gabe, who lifted both brows.

Jordan scowled at them. He could read their thoughts as clearly as if they were stamped on their foreheads. They liked it that he was exhibiting some male possessiveness. They'd reacted in a similar way when he'd had his first fight, ages ago. A few neighborhood bullies had been picking on an old dog, and when they'd thrown a rock and the dog had yelped, Jordan lost his temper. He'd been a young kid, but not too young to hate injustice and cruelty.

No one had been more shocked than he when he'd kicked butt on the older boys, but his brothers revelled in his loss of control. Since then, it had only happened a handful of times, but each and every time his brothers damn near had a celebration. It was as if they'd always known he could be ferocious, and loved seeing it firsthand.

Jordan had been disgusted with his loss of control then, just as he was now. Not that he would have done anything differently, but…

Before he could get truly annoyed with his brothers for being so smug at his predicament, the elevator doors opened.

Walking quickly now, Georgia made a beeline for her

mother's room. Once there, she turned back to them as if not quite sure what to do with them. She glanced at Sawyer and Gabe, then to Jordan. "I might be awhile."

Jordan nodded. "Take your time. I'm in no hurry."

"Me, either," Gabe said, making her frown.

"Gabe and I will be on our way shortly," Sawyer promised her, "but I am interested in checking on your mother myself, if you're not opposed to it. It's not that I doubt the good care she's getting here. But with emphysema, any number of small ailments can come up. If you're comfortable with the idea, why then, I'm a whole lot closer than the hospital."

Georgia looked so relieved by the repeated offer, Jordan wanted to kiss her. Anytime she was given genuine caring, she always seemed so surprised.

"Actually," she said, "that would be wonderful. I worry so much about her. She says she won't overdo, but then something like this happens. She's so determined not to complain, to continue mothering me even when I don't need it, even though I'm twenty-three..."

Jordan nearly choked when she gave her age. Twenty-three? That had to mean she'd gotten pregnant at sixteen. Good Lord, that was a lot to expect of someone who was little more than a child herself. Had she finished high school? Gotten any college at all?

He again thought of her stepping onto that stage, and tried to imagine how she personally felt about it. She was so damn young, so driven by hard-nosed pride. Did she enjoy the work at all or was she taking the only job she could that would pay the bills?

"Most mothers are that way," Sawyer assured her while casting quick worried glances at Jordan. "My own is as stubborn as a goat and twice as ornery."

Gabe nodded to that. When Georgia looked at Jordan, appalled by what she took as an insult to their mother, he managed to laugh to cover the emotions she'd made him feel. "You'd have to meet Mom to understand, sweetheart. We love her dearly, but—"

"But she did manage to raise the lot of you." Georgia shook her head. "I suppose that takes great fortitude."

They all laughed. "Exactly."

"Let me check on Mom and talk to her privately for a moment, to make sure she doesn't object to you coming in. I'll be right back."

Georgia slipped silently into the room and the second she was gone, Jordan began to pace. He could feel Sawyer and Gabe watching him.

"Any reason why you look so tormented?" Sawyer asked.

Jordan glared at him. "She's only twenty-three!"

"You thought she looked older?"

"No, Gabe, it's not that. It's just…damn she's young to do what she's doing."

Gabe asked, "What is it she's doing?"

Sawyer, having been apprised by Morgan, as well as Howard and Jesse who'd gotten a firsthand show, said, "I think he's talking about the dancing."

"Ah." Gabe caught Jordan's eye and gave him a wide, masculine smile. "You know, I was thinking of going to watch her act, myself. I haven't seen a live show in ages. Whadya think, Sawyer? You want to come, too?"

Chapter 7

Jordan turned so fast Gabe jumped in surprise. With his eyes blazing and his jaw locked, he growled, "Don't even think about it, little brother."

After biting his lips to keep from laughing, Gabe soothed, "All right. Don't get in a lather over it."

It took him a second, and then Jordan's eyes narrowed. He realized Gabe had just gotten him but good. And Jordan had made it disgustingly easy for him to do. Choking Gabe sounded better by the minute.

Georgia opened the door. She looked at Jordan's severe frown, then at Sawyer's exasperation and Gabe's innocent expression. Her own turned suspicious. "Am I interrupting anything?"

"Not at all." Sawyer stepped forward. "Am I allowed in?"

She didn't look convinced, but she let it go. "Yes.

Mom said she'd like to meet you." Georgia glanced once more at Jordan, then turned away. She and Sawyer walked into her mother's room, Sawyer's hand at her waist.

Jordan was still looking at the closed door when Gabe murmured, "I see Morgan was right."

Jordan rounded on his younger brother again. He felt dangerously close to losing his edge. "You wanna tell me exactly what the hell that means?"

"Ho!" Gabe backed up, pretending fear. And this time there was no way for him to hide his amusement. "Don't bite my face off over a simple observation. If you're still worried that I might go to the bar, I promise I was just yanking your chain. You can quit snarling at me now. Besides, Lizzy would have my head if I looked at another woman and you know it. She's got a mean jealous streak." Gabe sounded immensely pleased over that observation.

"If you don't stop pricking my temper," Jordan rumbled, "you won't have to worry about Elizabeth. *I'll* have your damn head."

Gabe laughed. "Honest to God, Jordan, I've never seen you in such a fury. It's kind of interesting."

"You're on thin ice, Gabe."

In his defense, Gabe said, "Hey, I'm justified. Don't think I've forgotten that you stole my wife from me!"

Georgia gasped behind them. When they both turned to her, she stammered, "Mom wanted a moment alone with Sawyer." She looked from one to the other of them. She appeared stricken, and embarrassed.

Gabe smiled as he explained. "My wife chose to work for Jordan in his clinic. Jordan knew that I wanted her with me, but he made up all these lame excuses and just swept her away."

"That," Jordan said, watching Georgia closely, "is only Gabe's side of the story. Elizabeth has a knack with animals, a special rapport. She's much better suited to being my assistant than she is playing receptionist for Gabe. That's all he was referring to."

Gabe shrugged. "Well, you did kiss her, too. Right in front of me."

He snorted over that. "A brotherly kiss and you damn well know it."

"Brotherly, huh? Well, in that case—" Gabe reached for Georgia, who quickly took two startled steps away from him. But he'd barely moved more than a foot before Jordan caught him by his collar and hauled him back.

"Not in this lifetime, Gabe." The statement was low and mean, and made Gabe chuckle.

"That's what I figured." To Georgia, he said, "Can you believe he kissed my Lizzy? Not that I blame him. She's about the most beautiful woman in these parts and pretty irresistible. You'll see what I mean when you meet her. And luckily for Jordan here, I let him live because she turned right around after kissing him and agreed to marry me."

Georgia gave a nervous smile. "I see."

"No you don't." Jordan released Gabe and propped his hands on his hips. "Elizabeth had just helped me save all the animals in the clinic from a fire. It was a kiss of gratitude, no more."

"Uh-huh." Gabe pretended to think otherwise. "And what Morgan told me is that your Georgia here has incredibly pretty gray eyes. Now that I've seen her for myself, I agree. Very pretty."

He and Georgia spoke at the same time.

"She's not *my* Georgia."

"I'm not *his* Georgia."

Gabe said, "Oh, look. There's Sawyer."

They both turned and Sawyer nodded with a smile. "She's doing fine. Incredibly well, in fact. Her doctor is a good man. I've always liked him." Sawyer pulled out a card and handed it to Georgia. "Here's my home number. Once she's released, probably by the middle of the week, feel free to give me a call if you have any questions or if she has any problems, okay?"

Georgia's eyes softened to pewter. "Thank you. That's very generous of you."

"You might want to share that number with the children, too, so that if anything like this happens again, they can give me a call if you're at work."

She nodded as she tucked the card securely into her bag. "They have my number at the bar, but Bill doesn't always answer the phone at night during the show. We've argued over that several times."

"I understand." Sawyer glanced at Jordan. "Perhaps a pager would be good?"

Jordan saw the guilt flash across Georgia's face and knew she couldn't afford one. He spoke quickly. "Gabe, don't you have an extra pager you're not using anymore?"

Gabe looked dumbfounded for only a second, then nodded. "Oh, yeah. Right." And with a grin: "Hey, it's even paid up for the next six months."

Georgia was already shaking her head, but Gabe

slung an arm around her, which caused her to still immediately. "I insist. That's what friends are for."

She might have protested further, once she regained use of her tongue, but Sawyer chose that auspicious moment to tell Jordan, "Her mother wants to see you."

"Me?"

"Yep. She was rather insistent on it."

Georgia groaned. "Oh, God. She's so overprotective…."

Jordan peered at the closed door with deep reservation. He hoped like hell this wasn't the familial interrogation. At thirty-three, he was so rusty he had no idea if he'd know how to answer or not. Especially considering he hadn't yet figured out what he felt for Georgia. Lust certainly, and compassion. But if there was more…

Georgia started to follow him in, but Sawyer gently caught her arm. "She specified that she wanted to see Jordan, and only Jordan."

Jordan groaned in dread, mustered his manly courage and headed in. He wasn't a damn coward. He could face one disgruntled mother, with or without all his thoughts in order. But when he peeked around the curtain to the bed, he found Ruth Samson half-sitting up, very clear-headed, and more than a little disgruntled.

Good heavens, the woman looked as ferocious as Morgan on his most intimidating days.

"Ms. Samson?"

Her eyes, the same blue gray as her daughter's, locked onto him and without preamble she stated, "My daughter has whisker burns this morning."

Jordan gulped, and before he could stop himself he

ran a hand over his now smooth-shaven jaw. Deciding to brazen it out, he said, "I only kissed her."

"Must have been one heck of a kiss." Ruth looked nothing like the frail, ill woman of yesterday. In truth, she appeared ready to get out of bed and whup Jordan's backside. "Georgia couldn't quite look at me without blushing."

Against his better judgment, Jordan grinned. "Georgia does seem prone to a pretty blush now and then."

Ruth sighed, and all the vinegar seemed to leave her from one second to the next. "It's incredible, but regardless of all she's been through, she's still so sweet. Not that I want her to toughen up. She's a wonderful daughter and a wonderful mother to my grandchildren." Once she said it, Ruth glared, daring him to disagree.

Jordan nodded. "She amazes me, if you want the truth."

"Yes. She's amazing." Her eyes sharpened and she asked, "Exactly how much do you know about my daughter?"

"Very little. I only just minutes ago found out she's a mere twenty-three."

"That bothers you? Well it shouldn't. Georgia is very mature for her years."

Jordan had no idea how to reply to that. "I also know that she works in a pretty disreputable bar."

Ruth laughed. "And of course, you don't approve?"

Jordan matched her stare without hesitation. "No, not at all."

"Good." She nodded in satisfaction. "Neither do I. But she has few choices."

"Georgia mentioned that to me."

Ruth looked surprised. "She did? That's interesting.

She usually won't give a man the time of day. And believe me, plenty of them are after her."

Jordan ground his teeth together. "I believe it."

"I can tell there's still a lot you don't know. Pull up a chair and I'll fill you in. But we better be quick because if I know my daughter, we maybe have about two minutes more before she barges back in."

Jordan obediently pulled up a chair. He was anxious to learn more about Georgia, to find out how she'd ended up in these circumstances. She and her mother both felt she had few options, but Jordan intended to give her several, and they all had to do with her staying off that damn stage.

Ruth's first burst of indignant anger had faded and had left her looking decidedly limp. She was now pale, her hands shaking. Jordan reminded himself that the woman had been extremely ill only the night before, and that he had to make certain she didn't overdo. He had the feeling she'd push herself, given half a chance, to defend her daughter. *Against him.*

"Ms. Samson," he said, hoping to reassure her, "you don't have to worry about me being with Georgia. I only want to help."

She sighed wearily, then started in coughing. Jordan was ready to call for a nurse when she waved him back into his seat.

She had to use her oxygen for a moment, taking slow shallow breaths, and afterward she took quite a bit of time resettling her blankets around her. Finally she said, "I seriously doubt Georgia wants your help."

"Well, no, she doesn't."

"But you're insisting?"

"Yes, ma'am."

She nodded, apparently pleased by that. "Georgia got pregnant when she was only sixteen."

Since he'd already done the math, Jordan didn't show a single sign of surprise.

"My husband was an old-fashioned man. A sour, undemonstrative man who never really understood Georgia. We had her late in life. I was nearly forty, and my husband was eleven years my senior. We'd thought we were past the stage of having children. So she took us both by surprise."

"A pleasant surprise?"

"Oh, surely. But adjusting wasn't easy. Avery was set in his ways, and part of those ways was being miserly to the point of wanting Georgia to wear secondhand clothes, and insisting we drive our old Buick forever, and that we make do with one old black-and-white television. It had never mattered much to me. But I hated seeing Georgia do without. She didn't fit in with the other kids because of how we lived, and it wasn't even necessary. We could have afforded better for her, but I'd always been a housewife, and Avery had always controlled the money."

Jordan nodded. "I understand." And he did. He knew plenty of older women like Ruth, women who'd been raised to believe that wives were meant to stay at home, to cater to their husbands. He could only imagine how a child thrown into the mix might have complicated things.

"Well, I don't. I could have done more. And I could have done it sooner." Ruth looked past Jordan's shoulder, her eyes so sad. "We argued endlessly over Georgia, which was probably harder for her than the divorce. I was a coward, and the idea of being on my own was terrifying. But I finally did it. I should have left him years earlier, but I kept thinking that I needed to keep our home intact. I didn't want Georgia to have to start over in a new school system just because I couldn't afford the area anymore. Then, when she started dating Dennis, I wished like crazy that I *had* moved."

"She got pregnant?"

"Yes. Dennis was every young girl's dream. He was good-looking, athletic, nice. He took her to all the dances and the parties, places she hadn't been before. Georgia went head over heels in love with him almost overnight.

"We were still hashing out the divorce when Georgia eloped. I couldn't believe it. But to give her her due, she made things work for awhile there."

Jordan imagined that Georgia had enough sheer will and determination to make anything work when she put her mind to it. He thought about her at that age, so young, so innocent. At sixteen, he'd been into more mischief than his mother ever guessed, but he'd been careful, with himself and the girls he'd been with.

He resolved to have another talk with Casey real soon. It wouldn't hurt to drive the point home one more time.

"Dennis wasn't too bad," Ruth said. "They lived like paupers, but then Georgia was used to that. And she seemed so happy, especially after Lisa was born. My gosh, she adored that baby. She took to mothering as natural as could be."

Jordan didn't want to hear about how happy she'd been with her husband. He was glad the man was long gone from the picture. "So what happened?"

"Her in-laws happened. They made life as tough for

Georgia as they could. While she was willing to make sacrifices for the marriage, Dennis wasn't used to living without. They coddled him something awful, and ignored Lisa—even to the point of questioning whether or not she was his. I tried to help out as much as I could, but I was dealing with the issue of my divorce and somehow Georgia ended up helping me."

Ruth looked so wretched over that admission, Jordan reached out patted her hand. "Your daughter loves you very much."

"I know." She spoke barely above a whisper. "My husband had always smoked and right after the divorce I started getting sick. I tried to find a job, but I had no experience and I'd get winded so easy. More so than most people, I'm prone to getting bronchitis and even pneumonia. That's when they found out how bad my lungs are. Only by then, I didn't have any health insurance because I'd been covered under my husband's policy. I was so, so stupid not to think of that."

Jordan wondered if Georgia was paying for insurance for her mother. He frowned with the thought, mentally adding up all her responsibilities.

"I was a burden to my daughter at a time when she needed me most."

"No." Jordan shook his head, knowing exactly what Georgia would have to say about that. "That's not true. Family helps family. Period. She was there for you, just as you're here for her now. She's told me several times how much you contribute."

Ruth tilted her head. "You sound like a man with a close family."

"Yes. Like you, my mother is divorced." His mother, however, had always been one of the strongest, most independent women he knew. Of course, she'd had a fabulous first husband who'd shown her exactly what marriage should be. And that had thankfully gotten her through her marriage to Jordan's father.

Jordan forced a smile for Ruth's benefit. "She's also happily remarried. Through it all, we've stayed a very close family."

"I like you, Jordan."

She said that as if he'd passed a test. "I like you, too."

"And you like my daughter?"

When he hesitated, not quite sure how she meant it and afraid of committing himself to her, she laughed. "That's all right. I didn't mean to pressure you. But I will tell you that it's not going to be easy."

"I already figured that out."

She laughed again. "The end of this long tale is that shortly after Georgia got pregnant with Adam—an accident, and a blessing from God—Dennis's parents convinced him that he was overburdened, that Georgia had gotten pregnant on purpose just to chain him down." Under her breath she muttered, "As if a broken condom was her fault."

That was *definitely* not an image Jordan wanted haunting his brain. He frowned.

"Dennis had always been pampered, and as their bills started to pile up and things got tougher and tougher, he got more and more distant, more willing to run home to his parents. And unfortunately, more willing to run up additional bills. Their combined incomes just weren't enough, and one day he went home to his folks and never came back."

Jordan nodded in satisfaction. "So she divorced him?"

"Yes. Georgia was really hurt. She loved him and yet

he just walked away. She agreed to a peaceful divorce, and allowed the courts to divide the bills down the middle even though many of them had been his recent purchases. She wanted to make the transition as easy on the children as she could. But the really sad part is that Dennis agreed to it all, wished Georgia well, then stole several thousand dollars from his parents and took off. Not only did he not pay his half of the bills, he's never paid a dime of child support."

"He doesn't see the kids?"

"No. No one's heard from him since he left. His parents blamed Georgia, and added to her burden—until I told them I'd have the police after their precious son for skipping out on his responsibilities."

She looked downright feral again, and Jordan nodded. "Good for you."

"No, it was an error in judgment. His parents apologized and promised to pay Dennis's share of things. Georgia argued with them. They were Dennis's bills, not his parents. But they insisted, and she believed them. She…trusted them. In the end, they were only biding their time until they could petition the court for custody of Adam and Lisa. They even tried to accuse Georgia of being an unfit mother."

Rage churned forth in Jordan, taking him by surprise. In a voice of icy rage, he said, "They obviously failed in their efforts."

"Yes. But not without a lot of cost and heartache to my daughter. And they didn't give up. They dogged her steps everywhere she went, making her lose jobs, constantly posing a threat to her peace of mind. Not once have they ever shown genuine concern or caring for the children. The few times they visited them, they tried to fill their heads with poison, bad-mouthing Georgia while making Dennis sound like a saint that she'd run off. Can you imagine? Their own blood kin, yet all they're interested in is using the kids to try to hurt Georgia."

"They're beautiful children," Jordan said with sincerity. He'd been surprised at how much he'd enjoyed making pancakes with them that morning. Lisa and Adam were lively and bright and polite. "She's done a good job with them."

"Yes, she has. And she'd die before letting anyone hurt those kids. So finally we thought it was best to simply move away. It makes me so mad, I want to spit."

Jordan could easily see where Georgia got her backbone. He patted Ruth's hand and tried to calm her. "Don't get yourself all riled up. You'll get winded again and the doctors will throw me out." He smiled. "Besides, Georgia is here now, away from them, and the kids seem very happy. I wish she hadn't gone through so much, but all in all, I admit I'm pleased with the outcome."

"Moving here was a blessing," Ruth agreed. "And you know, it was my ex-husband who made it possible."

Jordan raised a brow. He hoped the man had somehow redeemed himself, had supported his daughter and her decisions—mistakes included—after all. "How's that?"

"He died."

Not the happy ending he'd been looking for. Jordan sighed, wishing Georgia had been able to resolve things with her father before his death, but he had the feeling even that had been denied her.

"He hadn't ever gotten around to changing his will. He had money that he'd hidden during our divorce. It all came to me. Not that there was a fortune or anything.

But it was enough to finance the move and put a down payment on the house. I just hate seeing Georgia work so hard to keep it all together."

"I intend to help her with that."

Ruth shook her head. "She won't like it. Everyone she's ever relied on has let her down. Her father, her husband, her in-laws. She's determined to be totally independent this time."

"You never turned your back on her."

"No, but I made some awful mistakes."

Jordan pushed to his feet, anxious to see Georgia again now that he had a better understanding of her. "Making mistakes is the name of game. We're human, so it happens. Trying to atone for mistakes is what makes you a mother."

She grinned at that. "True. So what are you going to do?"

"I don't know yet."

"One thing, Jordan, before you leave."

"Yes?" He turned to face her.

"If you think there's any chance at all you might hurt her, it'd be better if you walked away right now."

Jordan stared down at his feet. He didn't want to hurt her. Ever. But even more than that, he didn't want to walk away. He wanted to gather her closer, much closer. He wanted to bind her to him in some undeniable way.

He made plans for the coming weeks, how he'd ingratiate not only himself, but his best selling tool—his family. They were irresistible, and once Georgia got comfortable sharing with them, relying on them and letting them rely on her, she'd soften. She had to.

Jordan shook his head. No doubt about it, he was in over his head. But damned if he wasn't starting to like it.

Chapter 8

With an outraged and appalled gasp, Georgia slapped the stage curtain back into place. "Damn him!" Her heart felt lodged in her throat, and with a lot of trepidation, she looked down at her costume.

"Oh, God." It looked worse than she'd first thought, given that Jordan was about to see her in it. Again she pulled the curtain aside and peeked out. But Jordan was still there, sitting at a front-row table as had become his preference, scowling at every other man in the room. He resembled a dog guarding a bone.

What in the world was wrong with him? She should have been able to ignore him, and in fact, when he'd first shown up as part of the audience, she hadn't even realized he was there until she'd almost finished. She made it a point not to look at the men in the audience; it was the only way she could get through putting herself on display that way. But she'd felt something different that night, something that had affected her deep inside. Against her will her gaze had sought out the source of her discomfort—and clashed with Jordan's hot green stare.

She'd missed a step and nearly fallen on her face. He'd looked as menacing as Morgan ever had. Of course, now that she knew Morgan better, she knew most of his dark countenance was bluster. Not so with Jordan. His brothers insisted on telling her—in private little whispers-that Jordan was the most even tempered one, the pacifist, the gentlest of men. Ha! Twice now, he'd almost started another fight.

Bill had threatened to ban him from the bar and Georgia had silently prayed that he'd follow through. But then Jordan had slipped her boss a twenty, and Bill had grinned and walked away. Curse him.

The music was getting louder, her cue had come and gone, and she could hear the rumble of impatient voices out front. If she didn't get going, she'd have to start the CD over.

She lifted her chin. So what if this particular costume left her stomach bare? That you could see her navel? So what that more of her backside showed than was covered? All that meant was that her tips tonight would be especially good and she'd finally be able to afford the electrical work needed on the house. If Jordan didn't like what she wore…well, too bad. She wasn't too crazy about him right now anyway.

Determination masking her churning nervousness, Georgia thrust the curtain aside and made an entrance onto the stage. She had every intention of ignoring Jordan completely.

Of course, that was before he fell off his chair.

He took one look at her, dropped his cola and toppled. Luckily no one seemed to pay him any mind as he hauled himself back up and into his seat.

Georgia deliberately turned her back on him—and heard a roar of applause along with some loud wolf whistles, likely because the bottom of her costume was no more than a thong. Embarrassment washed over her, so hot she felt light-headed and couldn't see beyond the fog of shame. She knew she was blushing. *Everywhere.* The dance steps that normally came so easily to her now felt forced and awkward; she had to concentrate hard to keep to her rhythm.

At least, she told herself as she executed a high kick, her top was more concealing. It had midlength sleeves and a V-shaped neck with lapels. The whole outfit was stark white, including the stupid little hat that Bill had insisted on. She wore white gloves, white high-heel sandals, and garters with black velvet ribbons.

It looked cheesy, like something out of a fetish catalogue. But already money landed at the front of the stage. Georgia moved farther back, being careful not to lose her footing on the scattering of bills.

By the time she finished her number, she figured there had to be a good three hundred dollars at her feet. Not bad for a night's pay. She almost smiled. *Almost.*

And then she accidentally caught Jordan's eye.

He looked livid, with his eyes sort of red and unfocused. Georgia frowned at him. How such a dominating, stubborn, pushy man could have such nice relatives was beyond her.

With one last bow, she turned and ducked behind the curtain. Her changing room was really a cleaning closet

overflowing with supplies. Next to her street clothes
hanging on a metal hook, rested a mildewy mop and
several stained rags. One bare bench, raw enough to
leave splinters in her behind if she was ever foolish
enough to sit on it, occupied the space next to the door.

Georgia tossed the foolish hat aside, then leaned
against the wall and struggled to catch her breath. Dancing, even at the bar, always left her exuberant. She loved
to dance, to feel her movements become fluid like the
music. And thanks to Jordan, she no longer had to go
on stage in a state of exhaustion. He and his family had
forced so much help on her, had been so supportive and
friendly and accepting, she'd gotten plenty of rest the
past few weeks.

But while she was grateful, she was also resentful
because it was Jordan's fault that she hesitated to answer tonight's screaming applause with an encore. She
just couldn't make herself go back out there. Not with
Jordan watching.

Bill pounded on her door. "Front and center, damn
it! They're calling for you."

Georgia stared at the closed door. She could probably convince Bill that it was better to leave them wanting more....

Then Jordan's voice intruded. "If she doesn't want
to go back out there, then leave her alone."

She gasped in outrage. How dare he confront her
boss? Was he trying to get her fired?

She answered her own question with an obvious,
resounding yes. Not once had Jordan tried to hide his
disdain of The Swine. This time, however, he'd stepped
completely over the line.

The door bounced hard against the wall when she

threw it open. Both Jordan and Bill jumped, but Georgia stomped right past them to the steps leading up on stage. It was uncanny, but she could actually feel the searing heat of Jordan's gaze on her exposed rump.

The second she opened the curtain, the men bellowed their appreciation. More money came flying her way and Georgia, with grim resolve, submitted to the attention.

After three encores she was finally left in peace.

For all of one minute.

She'd just stepped out of her high-heel sandals and started to relax when Jordan walked in without knocking. His gaze did the quick once-over, searing her from head to toes and everywhere in-between. Georgia glared at him. "What are you doing here?"

Despite his heated expression, his tone sounded mild enough. "I was already out."

She didn't buy it for a second. "Try again, Jordan."

"All right." He didn't appear the least put off by her hostile attitude. But then, she'd already realized how pigheaded he could be in his determination. "I stopped by to see your mother. She had the kids in bed, so I missed visiting with them. We took tea in the patio room, and when she started yawning, I told her that she should turn in, too. Though she's doing so much better, Sawyer says she should continue to get plenty of rest."

His words were easy and rehearsed. But his gaze burned over her, lingering in places that always felt too sensitive whenever Jordan Sommerville was in the vicinity.

Realizing she still wore the stupid gloves, she jerked them off and stuffed them into her bag. Jordan leaned against the wall, crossed his arms over his chest, and watched her every movement with an intensity that set her stomach to roiling. She couldn't very well finish changing with him standing there.

"It's rude to stare," she grumbled.

"Honey, the whole point of that getup is to make men stare."

She lost it, stepping forward and poking him hard in the chest. "Not *you!* Other men, okay, men who want to watch me dance, men who—"

Rubbing at his chest and frowning at the same time, Jordan interjected, "I came to watch you dance."

"No, you came to watch everyone else watch me dance!" Her head pounded, keeping time with her heart. She felt ready to burst into tears, to scream. He and his family were so wonderful, so giving, they made her feel terrible in comparison. All her life she'd screwed up. Having Jordan around only emphasized that, and weakened her resolve to learn independence. But she needed to know she could protect her children now, and in the future.

"You," she said in a tone nearing a snarl, "came to make sure no one did anything improper like *speak* to me."

Jordan took his own step forward. "Are you telling me you *want* to converse with these yahoos?"

"I'm telling you it's none of your damn business what I do!"

Jordan stalled, then in a voice as soft as warm velvet, he whispered, "I want it to be my business, though. Keeping my hands off you the past few weeks has been torture. Hell, Georgia…"

Her heart slammed into her ribs. He reached for her, touched her face with a gentleness she'd never known, and her knees went weak. "Jordan?"

Even to her own ears, his name sounded like a plea. The past few weeks had been hell, with the memory of his touch haunting her. She'd dreamed about that morning in the kitchen, and every night the dreams got hotter, more real.

Jordan cupped her jaw. "Don't ask me to go away, sweetheart. And don't ask me not to care."

Georgia watched his eyes darken, now so close to her own since he loomed over her. She exhaled on a trembling sigh. "You're making me crazy," she admitted. "I don't even know what I'm thinking or saying anymore."

His gaze flickered, becoming more intimate, hotter. "I don't mean to upset you."

"I know that." She almost laughed, it was so absurd. Jordan and his family had irrevocably changed her life—all for the better. Casey cut her grass, Gabe fixed her leaky pipes, they all doted on the children and on her mother. And on her.

But what if she came to depend on them, if she let her children start to love them, and then they went away? What would she do then? She'd be no better off, and she'd have the memories to torment her.

She squeezed her eyes shut, but quickly opened them again when Jordan's big thumb teased at the corner of her mouth. "Jordan," she said, hoping to make him understand, "dancing on that stage is hard enough for me. Especially in this getup. I do what I have to do, but I don't like it. When you're here, passing judgment and waiting to condemn, well…it only makes me more nervous."

Jordan shook her gently. "I'm not condemning *you*. How could you even think that?"

"You condemn all this." She'd learned so much about

him from his family. Her visits with them had started out strained, but Honey wasn't a woman who left anyone feeling uncomfortable, and his brothers were too outrageous to be kept at an emotional distance. They treated her with all the teasing irreverence normally reserved for a little sister. And she loved it.

Where Jordan tended to close up about anything personal, his brothers took delight in sharing his deepest darkest secrets. Gabe had told her that Jordan never drank. And Morgan had told her because of his father, he protested any abuse of alcohol.

Georgia shook her head. "You may not condemn me specifically, but the bar, the men here, the atmosphere... And I'm a part of it, Jordan." She hesitated, unsure how much she wanted to push him, especially in a damn closet, but she just couldn't take it anymore.

She stepped away from him and concentrated on what she had to say while putting away her high heels. "You've done so much for me. I never would have gotten through the past weeks without your help."

"Nonsense. You're about the most resourceful woman I've ever met. I have no doubt you'd have managed just fine. But you know I wanted to help."

His praise made her feel more vulnerable than ever. "And I appreciate it more than I can say. You're...well, you're wonderful."

Jordan stared at her hard. "But?"

She drew a deep breath, forcing herself to say the words. "But I want to make it on my own. It's important to me. I've made some really dumb mistakes in the past, mistakes that have hurt me, my children and my mother. I'm trying to fix all that."

"You can't fix the past, sweetheart. All you can do is make the future different."

She nodded. "I know. And that's what I'm going to do. My mother insists she's feeling as good as ever, and I've cut back on the hours I work during the day so she's not overburdened with the kids. And thanks to Bill's stupid costume choices, I'm making more money in the evenings so my budget is more sound than ever. I'm managing, Jordan, and that's what I want to concentrate on."

Jordan gave her a long, considering look. As if she hadn't just spilled her guts to him, he said, "Your mother likes me."

Georgia had no idea how to respond to that. Truth was, her mother adored him.

"Your kids are crazy about me."

She smiled. "I know. They're also crazy about your family. Honey has been promoted to honorary aunt. Morgan, that big ox, astounds me every time he manages to be so gentle with them. And Sawyer and Casey…" She shook her head. "They're incredible men."

Jordan stepped closer until his chest brushed her breasts. "We're your friends now. You can't just expect us all to go away."

"I wouldn't want that!" It was so difficult to think clearly with him this close. She wanted to wrap her arms around him, to ask him to hold her. But he hadn't touched her sexually since that morning in her kitchen, and she knew that was for the best.

"My children," she said slowly, measuring her words, "have never had enough people in their lives who cared about them. My ex-in-laws…" She shook her head, not willing to go into details. "They weren't nice people. They've never really cared about Lisa or Adam."

"They must be idiots, then, because your children are very lovable."

Anyone who loved her kids automatically got her love as well. And that fact scared her to death.

Feeling almost desperate, she put a hand on his arm and explained, "I want to keep the friendship." She wanted that so badly her stomach felt like lead whenever she thought of losing it. As a child, she'd craved friendship so badly, always watching from the sidelines as someone else got picked for tag, as other girls gathered in clusters to giggle, excluding her. As a teenager, she'd put everything into her dance, detaching herself from the hurt, telling herself that she didn't care. She'd gone from being almost totally isolated from friends, to being Dennis's wife, then to being on her own again.

Gaining friendship only to lose it once more would be unbearable. "I just... I just don't want you here at night, watching me. I don't want it to go beyond friendship."

Jordan cradled her face between his large hands. She felt helpless against the drugging pull of his nearness, the warmth of his body, his scent. Everything he'd ever made her feel came swamping back with his first gentle touch.

"I'll tell you what I think." His sensual tone made her heart race. "I think everything you've just said is bullshit."

She stared at him, appalled, wondering if he could really see through her so easily.

"I think," he growled as he pulled her into the hardness and heat of his body, "that you want me every bit as much as I want you. Friends? Hell yes, we'll be friends. And a whole lot more."

She wasn't at all surprised when he kissed her.

Jordan wanted to devour her. The need she created just by being close nearly made him crazy. It was a live thing, a teeth-gnashing hunger that he had no control over. He groaned, sucking her tongue into his mouth and stroking it with his own.

Georgia's arms slipped around his neck, her soft breasts nestling into his chest. Her costume top was skimpy and he slipped his hands beneath it to feel the warm skin of her back, then couldn't resist sliding his hands down to her sweetly curved ass. His body pulsed with need, his erection growing painfully. Her bottom was bare except for the thong and her cheeks were hot, soft. He traced the thin line of material with his fingertips as deeply as he could, and took her rough groan into his mouth.

She went on tiptoe against him, pushing into him. Her nipples were hard and he used his other hand to explore her breasts. He wanted her naked. He wanted to see her nipples, to taste them.

He kissed her neck as he brought both hands up to the lapels on her top and pulled them open. The low vee of the costume made it easy to expose her and the second her breasts were freed, pushed up by the material bunched tightly beneath them, Georgia gasped. Jordan didn't give her time to pull away. He dipped his head down and licked one dark rosy nipple.

Her fingers clenched in his hair. *"Jordan."*

"Shhh." Even with his blood roaring in his ears, Jordan cautioned himself to go slow, to tease her, to make her admit to the incredible passion between them. All the well-grounded reasons to give her more time, to avoid sexual interludes, were chased away by the sight of her.

Her nipples were large, tightly puckered. He licked again, then again, using the rough tip of his tongue to torment her. Tantalizing sounds of hunger escaped her. He caught her with his teeth and nipped gently, then not so gently. Georgia trembled. When she tried to pull him closer he sucked her deep into the heat of his mouth.

"Jordan..." she whispered on a vibrating moan.

"I know, sweetheart, I know."

He cupped her between her legs. She was so hot, and she pushed against his probing fingers, her thighs opening without his instruction. He could feel her swollen flesh, feel the dampness of her even through the material. The bottoms were tight but he insinuated his fingers beneath the right leg opening and found her wet and ready—for him. He straightened and held her tightly with his free arm.

Her hips moved with his fingers, seeking more of his touch. Jordan felt swollen and thick, achingly hard. The damn saloon could have blown up and he might not have noticed. He was only aware of the feel of her, her scent, now stronger with her excitement.

"Come on, sweetheart," he encouraged roughly, seeing that she was already climbing toward a climax. Her eyes were cloudy, unfocused, her lips parted as she panted for breath. His fingers moved more deeply, stroking, sliding insistently over her slick flesh then up to her swollen clitoris. Delicately now, he touched her, light, rhythmic touches.

Georgia groaned and squeezed her eyes closed. Jordan watched her face, saw her skin flush darkly, her lush mouth tremble. Her pulse raced in her throat, and her hands bit into his upper arms, caught between pulling him closer and pushing him away.

"Come for me, Georgia," he groaned, knowing he, too, was perilously close to the edge. "I want to see you come."

Her beautiful breasts heaved, her throat arched, and then she bit her bottom lip and groaned harsh and low and Jordan supported her, mesmerized as she jerked and shuddered and it went on and on. He felt so much a part of her that he knew nothing would ever be the same again.

Long seconds passed. Gently, he pulled his fingers from her. Her eyelashes fluttered and she looked at him, still slightly dazed. Her forehead and temples were dewy, her breathing still labored. Jordan met her gaze, held it as he lifted his fingers to his mouth and sucked them clean.

Georgia shuddered. She clung to him with a rough tenderness he'd never known before. She was pliant, accepting of his will.

He gave her a kiss of lingering need and apology. Holding her, seeing her like this, brought him back to reality. The very last thing she wanted or needed was to be taken quickly in a damn saloon closet. Not that he regretted giving her pleasure. How could he?

"We have to stop." Jordan couldn't quite believe the words came from his own mouth. Not when he wanted her so badly. But the past few weeks had been a carefully wrought campaign to win her over, and he wouldn't blow it now. If he made love to her here—and he was about a nanosecond away from doing just that—her embarrassment would drive a new wedge between them.

He took a deep breath and said, "I can't take you here, sweetheart." He kissed her damp, open mouth in quick little pecks, hoping to soften his next words. "Let's go somewhere else."

The slumberous, sated look left her eyes. Her cheeks, warmly flushed only seconds before, went pale. He knew before she answered that she'd refuse.

Georgia pushed away from him and covered her face with both hands. In a tone more startling for the lack of emotion, she whispered, "I can't believe I just did that."

Alarmed, Jordan smoothed her hair away from her face with trembling hands. "I can't believe I stopped."

She looked up at him. "You must think I'm awful."

"No." She started to say something more, but he didn't let her. "Shh. It's okay." Even with her heavy stage makeup, she looked precious to him. "Actually, it was better than okay. Much much better."

"But you didn't—" She glanced down at his very visible erection.

"Believe me, I know." Jordan ran a hand through his hair and tamped down his sexual frustration. He met her wary, shame-filled gaze, knowing his own was hot, piercing. "The thing is," he said, his voice sounding like sandpaper, "making you come was a helluva fantasy. And I wasn't disappointed."

"It was wrong."

"No. Hell, no. Nothing wrong can feel that right and you know it." He shook her gently. "Don't ask me to apologize, Georgia. We've both been on the ragged edge since first meeting and it was only a matter of time before this—and more—was bound to happen."

She attempted to turn away. "Please, don't come here again. I can't trust myself around you."

She asked the impossible. The first time he'd sat there and watched her dance, he swore he'd never come back. It ate him up to see all those men drooling over her, to know what they were thinking, that she was the center of so many drunken, lurid fantasies.

But he'd discovered that staying away was even harder. He couldn't sleep for wanting her; she occupied his thoughts both day and night. The few times he managed to get her out of his mind, he found himself thinking about the kids instead, smiling, missing them. And Ruth, too. She was such a gutsy woman, altering a lifetime of social conformity to stand up for her daughter.

"I'm not just here because of you." The second the words left his mouth, Jordan felt hemmed in by his own deceptions. He came because of Georgia, but he did have another purpose.

He truly detested the place, the smells of sour alcohol, sweat and dirt, the foul language and the overall atmosphere of depression. He considered The Swine a major nuisance, perhaps even a threat to the peace. It wasn't a quaint small-town saloon. It didn't provide lively conversation or a relaxing ambiance.

It was run-down, dirty and bred trouble because of a distinct lack of conscience on the owner's part. It didn't matter how staggering drunk the patrons might be, they could always get one more drink.

But because of Jordan's personal bias against alcohol, he'd have left others to deal with the bar if it hadn't been for Georgia. With her working at night, dressed so provocatively, he couldn't bear the thought of any of his friends or acquaintances seeing her.

Georgia looked shaken to her soul. She turned away and began pulling on her clothes over the costume. "If… if you're not here because of me, then why?"

"I'm here," he said gently, trying to ignore the demanding throb of his body, and the pleasant buzz of satisfaction despite his still raging lust, "because the Town Advisory Board had another meeting."

She turned to him with open anxiety.

"After Zenny and Walt and the others told them what they'd seen that first night, they've been outraged about the whole thing."

"Zenny and Walt?"

Jordan nodded. "I told you I was here with other men that first night? Well, they're the elders of the town, fairly set in their ways, too. When the trouble started they didn't even wait around to see how it'd turn out. They took off and by that next morning everyone in Buckhorn knew what had happened."

Her mouth opened and she breathed deeply. She stared at the far wall. "They know about me dancing?"

He nodded. "That, and the fact the police were called. I'd say folks are suffering equal parts of morbid fascination and outrage."

Georgia closed her eyes on a grimace.

He wanted to protect her from the opinions of others, but she deserved to know what was going on. Given a choice, many of the townsfolk would prefer the bar be shut down. That'd put Georgia out of a job, and into one hell of a predicament. "Sawyer and I cautioned them not to get up in arms, but then last night Morgan arrested two men who were menacing a mule."

Georgia's eyes snapped open again. "Menacing a *mule?*"

"That's right. They drove straight into a pasture, knocking down fence posts and tearing up the ground. The mule is a gentle old relic, but those bastards drove around with their horn blaring and their bright lights on, chasing her and scaring her near to death."

His fists clenched. He couldn't abide cruelty of any kind, but especially cruelty against women, children— or animals. "They're lucky Morgan found them instead of me. I'd have been tempted to teach them a better lesson than a night in jail, three-month suspension of their licenses, and a large fine."

Georgia's gray eyes were soft and sympathetic. "I thought you were the least militant one in the family."

"They were chasing a poor mule, Georgia, and they destroyed a good deal of property. Of course I'm feeling militant."

She touched his chest, her small hand gently stroking. Since his lust was unappeased, she nearly sent him into oblivion. "They had been drinking here?"

"That's right." Jordan felt far too hot. He wanted her hand on his bare skin. And he wanted it a good deal south of his chest. Just the thought of her slender fingers curling around his hard swollen flesh made him quiver like a virgin. He hurt with wanting her. "Your boss," he rasped, "knew they were drunk when they left here."

She nodded. "Bill could care less as long he's getting paid."

Jordan struggled for breath. He flattened his own hand over hers, stilling her caressing movements. "Morgan is meeting with the sheriff here. He thinks they might hit the bar with a heavy fine." Jordan braced himself against her reaction and admitted, "A lot of people are pushing for it to be shut down."

With an embarrassed little shrug, Georgia said, "I understand." Then she moved away from him. "I need to get going. It's late and I'm tired and I've got some things to do when I get home."

He hated seeing her withdrawal. "Georgia…" He was uncertain what to say. "I don't mean to hurt you."

"I know. But if I lose this job… I don't know where I'll be able to make as much money." She went about pulling on her shoes and slipping on her lightweight jacket. Jordan watched her movements with barely leashed possessiveness.

"You could work for me." He didn't really need more help, but he'd hire her in a heartbeat. In fact, he really liked the idea once he said it out loud.

Her eyes looked silver rather than gray in the dim light. "I'm sure Elizabeth will have something to say about that."

"She'd be glad for the help."

"Nonsense. You bragged to me yourself that she keeps everything running smoothly." With her purse and her bag hanging from her shoulder, Georgia clasped her hands together and silently requested that he stop blocking the door.

Even in his wildest dreams, Jordan couldn't have imagined how badly he'd dread leaving a damn closet. But he had no reason to keep her inside now that she was ready to go. He opened the door and stepped out. "I'll walk you to your car."

"I would object, but I suppose you'd start insisting?" In spite of all that had just happened, she sounded shyly teasing, and Jordan smiled in relief.

"Of course."

Because they were looking at each other rather than where they walked, they almost bumped into Honey and Elizabeth.

"Hey," Elizabeth said. "Great show, Georgia!"

Jordan gaped at them. His sisters-in-law? In The Swine? He said, "Uh…"

Honey pulled Georgia—who was speechless with astonishment—into a tight hug. "I had no idea you were so talented. And I love the costume!" In an audible whisper, she said, "No one would ever guess you'd had two kids. You looked fantastic." Then in a further confidence, she added, "Sawyer would keel over dead if I wore anything that sexy."

Elizabeth laughed. "Gabe would probably faint. *After.*"

"After?" Georgia asked, still looking bewildered.

"Yeah, after he wore himself out." She chuckled. "The man does like to—"

Jordan said again, "Uh…"

"Oh, relax, Jordan," Honey told him, patting at his chest. The touch didn't feel at all the same as when Georgia did it.

He caught Honey's hand and gathered together his wits. "What are you two doing here?"

In unison, they said, "We came to watch Georgia dance."

"I… I didn't see you," Georgia told them, glancing nervously at Jordan.

Jordan felt poleaxed. When his brothers found out, there'd be hell to pay and somehow he'd probably get blamed. "Neither did I."

"Well, we didn't just sit out in the open, silly." Honey looked at him as though he should have figured that one out on his own. "We didn't want to make Georgia nervous. We were in the back corner booth. The bouncer—what was his name, Elizabeth?"

Elizabeth smiled. "Gus."

"Yes, Gus made sure no one bothered us."

Jordan glanced at the big no-neck ape who he'd tangled with that first night, and got a sharp nod. Jordan nodded in return. Good grief.

"Anyway," Honey said, waving away the remainder of that topic, "I was positively amazed how well you dance. It's incredible. Even when Jordan fell off his chair, you barely missed a beat."

Elizabeth snickered.

His face red and his temper on the rise, Jordan asked, "Where does Sawyer think you are?"

"At the movies."

His grin wasn't nice. "Not for long."

Honey gasped. "Don't you dare tell! You know he'll have a fit."

"Rightfully so."

Elizabeth shrugged. "I don't care if you tell. Gabe's not my boss."

Honey considered that, then shrugged, too. "Well, Sawyer's not my boss, either, but he is somewhat overprotective."

"Somewhat? Ha!" Elizabeth flipped her long red hair over her shoulder then leaned toward Georgia. "Before you get too involved with this family, you should know that they're autocrats. All in different ways, of course, but they sure do like to hover, if you know what I mean."

Jordan couldn't wait to deliver Elizabeth back to Gabe. "I do *not* hover."

Elizabeth raised an auburn brow and gave a pointed look at Jordan's arm squeezing Georgia's shoulders.

Muttering to himself, he asked, "Instead of debating this now, why don't we get the hell out of here? Bill's not too happy with me tonight anyway."

"He's not?" asked Georgia.

Jordan didn't want to explain exactly what her boss had said about a drinking limit, or how Jordan had reacted to his apathy. Luckily Honey saved him.

"He's a smarmy one, isn't he?" Honey asked.

Jordan stopped dead in midstep. In lethal tones, he asked, "Did he say something to you? Did he insult you?"

Both Honey and Elizabeth rushed to reassure him, patting his chest and shaking their heads. "No, of course not. He just looks like a weasel."

Georgia laughed. She looked at each of them, saw that they had no idea what she found humorous, and laughed some more. Jordan smiled, too. The ways that she affected him were numerous. Georgia breathed and he got aroused. But what her laughter did to him was enough to cause spontaneous combustion.

Still chuckling, she said, "I really do like your family, Jordan."

Elizabeth and Honey grinned widely.

The moist night air was very refreshing after being in the stale bar. A light breeze teased through the trees, ruffling Georgia's loose curls. She lifted her face into the breeze, breathing deeply. Jordan watched her, wanting her more than ever.

When they reached the parked cars, he played the consummate gentleman. He opened car doors and kissed cheeks and when his sisters-in-law were finally ready to head home, he cautioned them to drive safely.

Elizabeth rolled her eyes. Honey told him to do the same. They waved to Georgia and drove off.

When Jordan looked down at Georgia, there was still a small, very sweet smile curving her mouth. He tipped up her chin with the side of his hand. "Do you know how badly I want to kiss you right now?"

"You're incorrigible."

"And you're breathless, which means you want me to kiss you, too. Don't you?"

"I'm breathless," she said somewhat smugly, "because Honey and Elizabeth were so complimentary. It's been a long long time since anyone praised me for my dancing skills. And no, don't you dare say anything. The way men view what I do on stage has nothing to do with my actual talent."

Jordan blinked at her. An idea bloomed in his mind, growing, gaining momentum. "Where'd you learn to dance?"

"I took lessons as a child. All the other kids made fun of me for it, but I loved it. I've always enjoyed moving to the music. By the time I was a teenager, I was helping to teach the rest of the class. It's something that's always come naturally to me."

Jordan caught her shoulders and pulled her to her tiptoes. He kissed her soundly before she could object. For the first time since meeting her he felt like he had the upper hand. He could help her while helping himself to get closer to her. He pulled Georgia into his arms and spun her around, lifting her off her feet.

Georgia laughed in surprise while clinging to his shoulders. "What are you doing?"

"Dancing with you." She started to say something more, but he stopped and asked, "You won't forget about this weekend, right? The cookout? Honey has been planning it all month and the kids are looking forward to it. Sawyer has promised to make them his famous fruit salad with melon balls—kids love melon balls—and Casey intends to take them boating."

She ducked her head and said, "We'll be there."

Tipping her chin once again, Jordan asked, "You don't sound very happy about it. What's wrong?"

She shook her head, refusing to answer. But then, he didn't really need her to. He knew she resisted their growing closeness and the need that got harder and harder to ignore. She was afraid if she relied on him, he might let her down. Jordan smiled, remembering that she wanted options.

He'd start working on that first thing in the morning.

Chapter 9

The kitchen was filled to overflowing with meddling relatives when Jordan walked in for breakfast. Even though Morgan and Misty now lived up on the hill, they often came down for breakfast. Honey insisted on it. And since Gabe and Elizabeth were still living downstairs in the renovated basement of the big house, they were always there in the mornings, too. The women generally helped each other out, cooking, watching babies, laughing and providing a nice feminine touch to what used to be a totally masculine gathering.

Casey, he noted, wallowed in all the attention. The women doted on him shamefully.

Jordan saw everyone look up when he closed the kitchen door. His own apartments were over the garage, converted years ago when he realized he was a little different than the others, that he wanted and needed more privacy than they did. "Morning."

Morgan, with his daughter Amber perched on his lap, leaned back and grinned. "I hear you're checking into property around town. You thinking of moving?"

"No!" Honey put down the spatula she'd been using to turn eggs and turned to Jordan with a horrified expression. "It's bad enough that Gabe and Elizabeth are planning to move. I *like* having you all here!"

Misty picked up the spatula and took over for her sister. "He's been looking at warehouses, not homes."

"Oh." Honey seemed so relieved that Sawyer walked up to her, put his arms around her from behind and began kissing her nape.

"You can't keep them all underfoot forever, sweetie."

She looked dreamy for a moment—a common occurrence when Sawyer kissed her or touched her—then scowled at him over her shoulder. "Don't say that. You'll have them thinking we want them to leave."

"My brothers know they're always welcome."

"And their wives."

Sawyer nodded. "I think I hear Shohn."

He left the room, oblivious to Casey's chuckles. "How the heck does he hear Shohn," Casey asked, "when no one else does? What'd the baby do? Burp?"

Everyone laughed except Honey. She, being as attuned to the baby as her husband, said matter-of-factly, "No, he yawned."

Morgan brought the conversation back around just as Jordan sprawled into his seat. "So why are you checking out warehouses?"

Jordan tried to stare him down before everyone started questioning him, but it didn't work. Amber reached up and pulled on her daddy's nose, and Jordan

had to smile. He adored kids and Amber was a real
cutie. Luckily, she looked just like her mother.

He wondered how they'd found out about his property inquiries so soon. Granted, he'd started checking into it yesterday morning, right after the idea had
come to him the night before. But he'd barely called five
places. Half the time he thought his family had radar.

Misty, long since recovered from her bout with the
flu, jumped in, saying, "According to what Honey and
Elizabeth told me about Georgia's talent, I bet he's
thinking of putting together a dance studio. Buckhorn
doesn't have anything like that, you know. A little cul-
ture wouldn't hurt anyone."

If he'd been prepared, if he'd had any forewarning at
all that Misty might guess so close to the truth, Jordan
could have blustered his way out of it. But he didn't. He
simply stared, in awe of Misty's ability.

She felt him looking at her and glanced back. "What?
Am I right?"

Morgan laughed. "Damn, you're good, sweetheart!
And Jordan, I personally think it's a helluva idea."

"Helluva idea," Amber said, and Morgan quickly
tried to hush her, but not quick enough. Misty glared at
him with one of her you're-in-trouble looks.

"Amber, sweetie," Misty said, "Daddy's got a nasty
mouth and says things he shouldn't. You can't always
copy him or people will say you have a nasty mouth,
too."

Amber pursed her cute little rosebud mouth and nodded. "Daddy's nasty."

"That's right." Misty kissed her daughter, who kissed
her nasty daddy, just to make him stop looking so guilty.

Sawyer walked back in with Shohn on his shoulder.

The baby still looked sleepy and had a soft printed blanket clutched in his chubby fist.

Honey said immediately, "Jordan is going to buy Georgia a dance studio."

Sawyer drew up short. "He's going to what?"

Jordan leaned forward, put his head on the table, and covered it with his arms. Amber patted his ear.

"A dance studio?"

"Yes." Honey took the baby and snuggled him close. "Georgia would be a wonderful dance instructor."

"How do you know?" Jordan asked, his voice muffled because he hadn't sat up yet.

A heavy pause filled the air. Everyone looked at Jordan. He sighed and propped his head up on his fist. "What makes you think she'd be a good instructor?"

Knowing his ploy, Honey lifted her chin and said, "Because I watched her dance two nights ago, as you very well know."

Jordan couldn't have been more amazed by her admission than if she'd thrown an egg at him. "You told him?"

She nodded. He glanced at Elizabeth who sat in Gabe's lap. "Of course we told."

Jordan stared at his brothers' red faces. "And neither of you are angry?"

"Damn right I'm angry," Sawyer admitted. "I told her she should have told me if she'd wanted to go and I would have taken her."

"Damn right," Amber said. When Sawyer groaned, she asked, "Unca Sawyer nasty, too?"

"Yeah," Morgan answered. "Nastier than me." He kissed Amber's belly and made her laugh.

Gabe made a face. "I had fully intended to impress

upon Elizabeth the error of her ways, but it didn't work out quite as I had intended."

Morgan covered Amber's ears and said with remorse, "I know what you mean. You plan on giving a woman a good swat, but once you've got her pants off, you forget what you're doing."

Misty pinched Morgan for that bit of impertinence. Elizabeth just laughed, knowing it was all bluster. It was the truth not a one of them would ever lay a harsh hand on a female and their wives more than understood that.

Jordan laughed. God, he loved the lot of them. They were all nuts and overbearing and intrusive, and he had no idea what he'd do without them. The phone rang so he decided to excuse himself from the chaos.

He went into the family room and when he picked up the receiver and said, "Hello," he heard a long pause before his mother asked, "What's wrong?"

Jordan stared at the phone. "Mother?"

"Of course it's your mother. Now tell me what's wrong."

Of course it's your mother? Jordan held the receiver away from his ear to stare at it. His mother and Brett now lived in Florida. She'd called last week, but he'd been at Georgia's and missed her.

Because he wasn't sure how much she knew, Jordan hedged. "What makes you think anything's wrong?" Though he'd just been entertaining softer thoughts about his family, he now considered knocking all their heads together. If one of his damn brothers had been tattling, upsetting their mother, he wouldn't be pleased.

"I can hear it in your voice," she explained. "You've always had the most betraying voice. Even when you were a baby, I could tell by your gurgles what you were thinking and feeling."

Jordan dropped onto the edge of the couch and without giving himself time to plan out his reply, he said, "I think I'm in love."

Another pause, then softly: "Will you tell me about her?"

Even as he considered his words, Jordan smiled. "She's beautiful."

"Of course."

"But that's not what got to me." He frowned. "She has two kids. Lisa, six and Adam, four. They're incredible."

There was a smug note in his mother's voice when she said, "Then obviously *she's* incredible."

"She is. And gutsy. She's made a few mistakes, I guess. And…" Jordan hesitated. "In a lot of ways, she's like you."

Another pause. "How's that?"

Jordan looked toward the doorway, saw no one was lurking, and said, "She'll do anything necessary to see that her kids are taken care of."

His mother laughed. "What in the world did I ever do to warrant that comment? You make it sound like I worked in the coal mines to feed you or something."

Jordan considered all the things she had done, the sacrifices she'd made, how hard she'd always worked to make them happy. But the one thing that really stood out in his mind, the one thing he'd always hated, slipped out without his permission. "You married my father," he said, "hoping to make a complete home for Sawyer and Morgan."

"Jordan!" She sounded incredulous that he'd come

to such a conclusion. "I married your father because I loved him!"

Jordan heard a muffled shout in the background and his mother said, "No Brett, it's not Gabe. It's Jordan." And then: "Yes, I can see how you made that assumption."

Jordan chuckled. He could just imagine what Brett, Gabe's father, was thinking right now. "Tell Brett I said 'hi.'"

"Later. Right now I have something that I want you to understand. Do you have your listening ears on, Jordan?"

"My listening ears?" She hadn't used that term on him since before he'd become a teen.

"Don't get smart, son. Just pay attention."

He grinned even as he said, "Yes, ma'am."

"I have never regretted marrying your father. How could I when I have you?"

"He was a damn drunk."

"He was human. He made mistakes and in my mind, he's paid dearly for them. He lost me, and he lost all of you. Surely there couldn't have been a worse penalty."

Jordan gripped the receiver hard. "He was irresponsible, selfish—"

"No, sweetheart, he was just an alcoholic." She sighed, then continued. "We humans are prone to screwing up our lives on occasion. Most of the time we're given the chance to make amends. Your father was a wonderful man when I met him. Things happened that he couldn't deal with, and he…well, he wasn't strong enough to cope. If you ever get to meet him, I hope you keep that in mind."

Jordan didn't want to meet him, ever. But to appease his mother, he said, "I'll think on it."

"Now tell me about this young lady you're going to marry."

He choked on his own indrawn breath. "I didn't say anything about marrying her! I haven't even known her that long. It's just…"

"It's just that you love her. So why wait?"

"Well, one good reason might be that she doesn't want to marry me. In fact, she doesn't even want to see me."

"That's ridiculous! Why wouldn't she? There's no finer man than you."

Jordan got an evil grin when he said, "I'll tell the others you said so."

Laughing, his mother replied, "You're all equally fine men. And I can tell them myself this evening."

"There's no need to call back. Everyone's here for breakfast."

"That's not what I meant. Brett and I are flying in tonight. We should make it to the house by about five."

Jordan froze. "You're coming here? Tonight?"

"Now, Jordan, if I didn't know better, I'd say you didn't want to see me."

Jordan quickly reassured her otherwise. But in his mind, he was thinking of the cookout, the fact that Georgia would be there with her kids. He'd hoped to tell her about the studio, but until he knew for certain that there was a building that'd work, he didn't want to mention it.

His mother again told him that she loved him, and Jordan reciprocated. It'd be good to see her, and the babies would love it, not to mention how Casey would feel.

But with his mother there, he didn't know if he'd be able to get a single moment alone with Georgia.

And that's what he wanted, because he was through with waiting. He'd planned to cement their relationship in the oldest way known to mankind.

Now that he'd seen firsthand how she responded to him, he knew it would be so damn good, so explosive, she'd never be able to deny him again.

Ruth was in the kitchen baking when Georgia walked in. She paused, watching her mother for a moment before announcing herself. Ruth looked pretty in a matching nightgown and robe decorated with small sprigs of yellow flowers. Her light brown hair, now slightly streaked with gray, was twisted at the back of her head in a loose knot. She was humming as she put a new sheet of cookies in the oven.

"Morning, Mom."

Ruth turned with a smile and then went to Georgia to kiss her cheek. "You're up early!"

Georgia grinned. "So are you. And baking already?" She made a beeline for the coffeepot, as usual. Now, whenever she drank a cup, she thought of Jordan—and remembered everything he'd made her feel.

"I wanted to bring something to the cookout today. I'm looking forward to it."

Georgia's heart swelled. The kids had talked about little else for the past few days and her mother's eyes glowed with just the mention of the gathering. Georgia hadn't realized how isolated, how withdrawn from society she'd kept them all. Between working so much, both at the bar and on the house, there'd been little time for playing. It seemed every day she found another way that she'd failed the ones she loved most.

"I'm sorry. I hadn't thought about how lonely you might have been."

Ruth shook her head. "Or how lonely *you've* been?"

She started to deny that, but Ruth took her coffee cup and set it aside, then clasped both of Georgia's hands and squeezed them. "Georgia, it's okay to admit it, you know." Her mother met her gaze squarely and stated, "It's also okay to want a man."

"Mother!" Georgia felt a hot blush begin creeping up her neck.

"Oh, don't give me that tone." Ruth paid no heed to her daughter's embarrassment. "I'm older, not dead. I know how it is. And Jordan is…well, he's a potent male. Personally I think you're downright foolish to keep putting him off."

Georgia thought she might fall through the floor with her mother's words. "He *is* potent, and that's what scares me." In a softer voice, she admitted, "It'd be so easy to love him."

"So?" Ruth sounded totally unconcerned with her plight. "The kids and I love him, so you might as well, too."

Georgia shook her head. "It isn't that easy, Mom. I thought I loved Dennis—"

"You did love Dennis. And I think he honestly loved you. He was just young, Georgia. Young and foolish." Ruth hesitated, then said, "Let's sit down. I want to tell you something."

Georgia agreed, but she also snatched back her coffee cup. No way could she handle all this without some caffeine. Luckily the kids were still sleeping soundly, giving them some quiet time alone.

As Georgia refilled her cup, she looked around her home. Everything was in order now. Oh, there were still plenty of repairs to be made, but nothing crucial. She could finally see the end of the tunnel. And beyond the material things, her children were more lively than they'd ever been. They'd flourished under all the added attention from Jordan and his family.

Morgan had dubbed them "official deputies" and given them both badges to wear. Casey took them swimming and boating and taught them both how to fish. Saywer had let them listen to their own heartbeats with his stethoscope. The women had praised Lisa for helping with the babies and had convinced Adam that he was the handsomest guy in Buckhorn, even more so than Gabe—which made her shy son start strutting.

And Jordan... Georgia sighed just thinking about him. It amazed her that one man could truly be so wonderful. He'd gone with them to find salamanders in the woods behind the house. One day he had even paid them to help him at his office, though Georgia knew they'd been in the way more than not. Still, he never seemed to mind. They started the day talking about him, and often wanted to call him in the evening to tell him good-night.

"Georgia?"

She hadn't realized that she'd stopped in the middle of the floor and was just standing there. She looked at her mother, saw her caring and love and acceptance, and she burst into tears.

Ruth didn't cry with her. As she got out of her seat to embrace her daughter, she gave a sympathetic chuckle. "Love is the damndest thing, isn't it?"

Georgia tried to mop her eyes and hold on to her coffee at the same time. "I don't know what I'm going to do."

"You're going to tell him." Ruth held her away so she could see her face, and nodded when Georgia shook her head. "Sweetheart, don't make the same mistakes I made. Don't waste your time being afraid. Sometimes you just have to take a few chances, and I think Jordan's worth the risk, don't you?"

With a shuddering breath, Georgia reached for a napkin off the counter and blew her nose. She whispered, "He's never said anything about loving me."

"So? Your father dutifully told me every night that he loved me. But it would have meant so much more if he'd shown me instead. If he'd cared when I was tired or sick. If he'd held me when I was upset."

Georgia stared at her mother. *If he'd given her foot rubs and held her when she was afraid and loved her children...* . Her father had never really loved her, not the way she loved Adam and Lisa.

As if she'd read her thoughts, Ruth nodded. "Jordan has shown you that he cares in more ways than I can count."

"Oh, God." Her mother was right. From the moment she'd met Jordan, she'd known he was different. True, he was pushy and arrogant and determined—but according to his family, he only behaved that way when he really cared about something. Or someone. She didn't want to rely on him, but...maybe it would be okay. Maybe depending on him to share with her, to give and let her give, too, wouldn't be so bad. If she could only balance her independence against what he made her feel....

But she knew she'd always hate herself if she didn't at least give him a chance. "I'll tell him today."

Ruth laughed out loud. "That's wonderful!" She hugged Georgia again before gently pushing her into a seat at the table. "Now, how about a cookie to celebrate?"

From the doorway, Adam and Lisa said, "I want one, too!" and as Georgia opened her arms to her children, still sleepy warm from their beds, she thought that she had to be the luckiest woman alive. Perhaps after today, she'd also be the most fulfilled.

Jordan heard her car pull up and walked around to the front of the house. People had been arriving all afternoon, and he'd been anxiously waiting for her. He'd found a studio, and he could barely wait to discover her reaction to that.

The moment they saw him, Adam and Lisa jumped out and came running, followed by Ruth. Jordan was barely able to swallow down his emotion as he embraced both children. They chatted ninety miles a minute, telling him about all the cookies their grandma had made and about the pictures they'd colored for him to decorate his office, and about a frog they'd found in the backyard.

"Jus' like you tol' us to, we played with it and then turned it loose."

Jordan stroked Adam's downy hair, warmed by the sun. "I'm sure the frog appreciates it. They're not meant to be pets."

Lisa nodded. "We remembered." Then she leaned forward to whisper, "'Sides, Grandma hates frogs."

Jordan was still chuckling when Ruth and Georgia

reached his side. Ruth gave him a hug, though Georgia
looked shyly away, prompting him to curious specula-
tion. Following the lead her mother and children had set,
Jordan pulled Georgia close for a hug. To his surprise,
she briefly nuzzled her nose into his throat and sighed.

Just that easily, he was aroused. Of course, he stayed
semiaroused around her anyway.

Trying to discern her mood, Jordan studied her and
only vaguely heard Ruth announce that she and the
kids were taking the cookies to Honey. Georgia waited
until she'd gone, then licked her lips in a show of nervousness.

Jordan touched her hair, teased by the warm afternoon breeze. He loved how the golden-brown curls
framed her face and how the sunlight glinted in them.
"Georgia?" His voice was husky, affected by more than
his sexual need of her. He wanted her, all of her. Forever. "Is something wrong?"

He took her arm and started her toward the back of
the house where everyone was gathered. He could feel
the tension emanating from her and sought to make her
more at ease by rubbing her back.

Her eyes closed and she moaned softly, then suddenly blurted, "I have something I want to tell you."

Jordan tensed. He could tell by her expression that
she wasn't completely comfortable with what she had to
say. If she thought to try pulling away from him, after
they were finally getting so close, she could damn well
think again. He took her hand in his and laced their fingers together. Jordan could hear the others chatting in
the backyard as they rounded the house, though Georgia seemed oblivious.

"I've been going over everything you said." She

peeked a look at him, then frowned in concentration. "That last night at the bar, I mean."

Jordan nodded. "I want to talk about that, too." He now had options for her, viable options. He hoped she'd be pleased.

She stared at him in sudden horror. "You've changed your mind? You don't want me anymore?"

"What?" Jordan jerked around to stare at her. "No," he said, his frown deepening. "Hell, no. Where'd you get that crazy idea?"

"I thought—" She shook her head and started walking again. "I thought maybe, because I pushed so hard, you'd decided to leave me alone now."

"Georgia." How could she possibly think such a thing? Leave her alone? He couldn't even stop thinking about her, so how would he keep away?

They had just stepped into the backyard when she drew a deep breath and said, "That's good, because… I want you, too." She looked up at him, her eyes so pale in the sunlight. "Jordan, I don't think I've ever wanted any man as much as I want you. What…what you did to me the other night? That was wonderful and I loved it. I haven't been able to think of much else. But I want more than that." She stared him right in the eyes and whispered, "I want to feel you inside me and I want to watch your face when you come, and I want to hear your voice and hold you. I want that so badly I can't stand it anymore."

Jordan sucked in a huge breath of air, but it didn't help. Just that quickly he had an erection that threatened the seams of his jeans. Every muscle in his body shook.

And then the sound of conversation intruded and he looked around, seeing himself surrounded by family and neighbors. Luckily no one was paying them any attention.

He groaned aloud. Georgia finally admitted to wanting him, and there wasn't an ounce of privacy to be found. "Sweetheart, you really know how to make a man crazy."

She stared up at him, her eyes full of questions. And invitation. "It's fair. You've certainly made me nuts." She reached up and touched his face. "Can I ask you something?"

Jordan put his arm around her and led her to the side of the yard, as far away from the others as he dared to go without drawing a lot of attention. "You can ask me anything, Georgia. Don't ever forget that."

Her smile was so sweet and gentle. He loved her mouth. Damn, how he loved her mouth.

"If," she said, looking uncertain once again, "I didn't want to be involved with you. If I made it clear that I had no feelings for you at all—"

"Then I'd respect your wishes, even if it killed me."

She went on tiptoe to give him a quick kiss. "I already knew that. You're not a man to ever force a woman in any way."

Jordan laughed at her assumptions. "I'd do my damnedest first to convince you."

"You already have. Done your damndest *and* convinced me. But you're such a seducer with that sexy voice—" she touched his mouth with one fingertip "—it wasn't that hard."

The way she touched him, how she looked at him, took him to the edge. In a rasp, he said, "Speak for yourself."

She understood his meaning and glanced down at his

fly. "Oh." Warmth colored her cheekbones, making him nuts, but when he went to kiss her, she said, "Jordan, it was something else I was going to ask."

"Tell me."

"If we had no personal relationship, would you still want to see my kids? Or would you suddenly disappear from their lives?"

Jordan didn't give a damn if everyone in Buckhorn saw him. He cupped her face in his hands and took her mouth in a kiss meant to offer reassurance and so much more. When he lifted away, she clung to him, as unconcerned with their audience as he was. "I love your kids, sweetheart. I'd never do that to them."

Tears glistened on her lashes. "That's what I thought."

Jordan knew what she was getting at. Their own father had walked away, just as his had. For whatever reason, her ex had been able to give up his own two offspring, never knowing if they were all right, if they needed him or not.

But Jordan was different. He'd never before realized exactly how different until that moment. "I used to worry about my father," he said. "Not about his well-being, but whether or not people would associate me with him. Like your ex-husband, he split after the divorce and no one has seen him since. Not a single phone call, not even a card. If I died, I'm not sure he'd know, or even care."

Jordan shrugged and admitted, "There've been times when I hated him because I felt so ashamed. Not because he wasn't here, but because my brothers had respectable, honorable, loving fathers and yet my father was a huge mistake."

His throat felt raw as he told her things he'd never

said to another living soul. "I wanted to hold myself to a higher standard, to prove to myself and to everyone else that I was better than that, better than him."

Georgia put her arms around him and rested the side of her face on his chest. He cupped the back of her neck, tangling his fingers in her soft curls.

He smiled when she said, "You're the best person I've ever met." But then she added, "You make me feel so inferior."

Jordan abruptly pushed her back so he could scowl into her face. "What the hell are you talking about?"

She lifted her shoulders in a slow shrug. "I know it probably bothers you to want me. I got pregnant at sixteen, I've already been divorced and I dance in a bar." Her smile was sad and fleeting. "I'm hardly anybody's idea of a 'higher standard.'"

Rage washed over him, making him break out in a sweat. His vision narrowed to her face, a face he loved. He gave her a quick, sharp shake. "Don't you *ever* say anything like that again!"

"Jordan!" She glanced around, reminding him that they weren't alone. "Someone will hear you."

It took all his concentration to lower his voice, to temper his fury. Tears filled her eyes again, slicing into him like the sharpest blade. It was her vulnerability that gained him some control. He pulled her into his chest and held her tight. "I never thought," he whispered against her forehead, "that I'd meet someone as beautiful as you. Do you know what I see when I look at you, Georgia?"

She shook her head.

"I see a woman who will do anything she has to in order to take care of the people who depend on her. A woman with enough strength and courage and honor to beat the odds, and still be so incredibly sweet that it breaks my heart just to look at her."

Georgia's self-conscious laugh teased along his senses. He felt her wipe her eyes on his shirt and wished he was alone with her. She filled him with lust, broke his heart with her gentleness and humbled him with her strength.

"You make me sound like a conquering Amazon," she whispered.

He put his mouth close to her ear. "From the moment I saw you," he breathed, relishing her scent and her softness, "I was so hot to have you I nearly ground my teeth into powder. That's never happened to me before. I stay so aroused I ache, but I only want you."

Her hands fisted in his shirt. "Me, too. I want you so much, it scares me."

He didn't want her to fear him, but he'd explain that to her later. "I think you're the sexiest woman I've ever met. And the more I got to know you, the worse it became, because your sexiness is earthy. It isn't just about your gorgeous body, or the way you move or how you look at me. It's you. Everything about you, Georgia. Do you understand?"

She nodded. "All right."

Jordan suddenly felt someone behind him. He jerked around and found Morgan and Gabe both breathing down his neck.

"Hey," Morgan said, as if he hadn't just intruded. "You two are embarrassing everyone, me included. Why don't you find a room somewhere?"

Gabe shoved Morgan. "You're so crude." Then to Georgia: "Put him out of his misery, sweetheart. Jordan isn't used to this kind of excitement. Sawyer says it isn't good for his heart."

Georgia covered her face and laughed. Jordan thought about tossing his brothers into the lake. But then Morgan whispered, "You know, the gazebo is real private. Everyone is getting ready to eat and I can keep the kids occupied if you two want to go...talk things over."

Jordan looped his arm around Georgia and pulled her to his side. He peered around the yard. Zenny and Walt and Newton waved to them. Georgia groaned, but waved back. Howard and Jesse were arguing—as usual.

Morgan's enormous dog, Godzilla, had the kids well occupied. Lisa, Adam and Amber were all petting him and Godzilla rested on his back in doggy bliss, his tongue hanging out of the side of his mouth. Godzilla looked more like the missing link than a pet, but he was about the sweetest creature Jordan had ever seen. Even Honey's calico cat liked the dog. She sat next to Lisa, getting her own pet every now and then and rubbing her head against Godzilla's hip.

"Will you look at my mother?" Georgia said in awe.

Jordan followed the direction of Georgia's gaze and found Ruth in animated conversation with Misty's and Honey's bachelor father. Damned if there wasn't a bright blush on her face, too. Well, well, Jordan thought. He wasn't crazy about the man, despite how he'd softened since his daughters had joined the family, but whatever he said to Ruth must have been complimentary because she hadn't stopped smiling once.

He heard a laugh and noticed Casey was sitting beneath a shade tree, surrounded by female admirers. Gabe nodded toward Casey, chuckling. "They've been after him all day. He can't get himself a cola without them all trailing behind."

Even as Gabe spoke, Emma walked up to the group. She wore another halter top that showed more than it concealed and shorts that should have been illegal. She was barefoot, carrying her sandals, and Casey made an obvious point of not looking at her, at completely ignoring her existence—until two of the girls said something obviously snide. Emma, head bowed, started to walk away and within two heartbeats Casey was at her side. They appeared to disagree on something for just a moment, then Casey shook his head, slung his arm around her shoulders, and practically dragged her off.

A lot of feminine complaints ensued as Casey and Emma disappeared around the side of the house.

Georgia sighed. "I really adore your nephew."

Morgan laughed. "We're rather fond of him, too." Under his breath he added, "But what the hell is he up to?"

"You two should get going," Gabe said. "But I'd take the long route if I was you. Casey's not the only one with disgruntled females hunting for him."

Georgia frowned over that, looking around the yard with an evil glint in her eyes. Jordan appreciated her mild show of jealousy; she'd admitted to wanting him and now she was acting possessive. All he needed was a quiet spot to show her how much he cared.

Morgan suddenly laughed. "Too late. You should have fled when you had the chance."

"What are you talking about?" Jordan demanded, not in the least amused by the possibility of yet another delay.

"She's here." Morgan tipped his head toward the

backdoor of the house. "And you know there's no way in hell she'll let you slink away."

Georgia's frown turned ferocious. "She *who?*"

Gabe, too, looked at the house, then started to laugh. "Our mother. Prepare yourself, Georgia, she's making a beeline this way."

All three brothers smiled and started forward; Jordan pulled Georgia along with him. They met Sawyer on the path and before Megan Kasper could descend off the back stoop, she was enveloped in masculine hugs that kept her completely off her feet for a good five minutes.

Chapter 10

"Your children are wonderful."

Georgia smiled at Megan as she stroked Lisa's hair. "Thank you."

Lisa sent Megan a big grin, worshiping her. Of course, she and Adam had both been amazed by this tiny woman who ruled her gigantic sons with an iron fist. The men jumped at her slightest whisper, and did so with grins on their faces.

Georgia had heard so many stories about Megan's stubbornness, her strong will, she'd certainly expected someone…bigger. But while Megan was small in stature, she had an enormous smile and an innate gentleness and she loved to laugh.

It tickled Georgia to see how her sons fawned over her. When Megan had first arrived several hours ago, she'd been passed from one strong set of arms to an-

other. How such a small woman could mother such co-
lossal men was beyond her. When one of the neighbors
had commented on it with a smile, another had said that
Megan always gravitated to the "big guys." Seeing her
husband, Georgia understood.

Brett Kasper had stood there looking pleased and
smug and adoring over everything Megan did. He resembled his son Gabe quite a bit, in that they were
both drop-dead gorgeous, they both liked to pet on
their wives, and they were both strongly built. Once
the brothers had finished with Megan, Brett had been
treated to a round of bear hugs himself, with no pref-
erences shown. He was, obviously, very well loved.

"I'm going to skin Casey when he gets here."

Georgia laughed at that, knowing Megan was anxious to see him again. Georgia leaned forward and said,
"He went off with a girl."

"I never doubted it for a moment." Megan frowned at
Jordan, sitting beside her in a lawn chair, and said, "He's
far too much like his uncles *not* to be with a female."

Lisa thought that was funny and giggled, but when
she saw Adam go by chasing the dog, she ran after
them. Georgia watched her go, feeling so incredibly
at peace.

Jordan shrugged. "He's a little like Gabe, with the
girls after him. And a little like Sawyer, being so com-
passionate. I'm just not sure what's motivating him
today." As he spoke, he lifted one of Georgia's feet,
pulled off her sandal, and started another foot rub. She
gawked at him, but Megan only smiled and Jordan
didn't even seem aware of what he was doing. "I think
Emma has him on the run."

Both Megan and Jordan ignored Georgia's struggle to retrieve her foot. *"Jordan..."*

He smiled at her, then said to his mother, "Georgia's a dancer, you know. In high heels."

"Ah." Megan did her best to hide her amusement as Jordan caught her other foot also. "I suppose that explains it."

Georgia thought she might die of embarrassment, but instead she ended up groaning. Everyone talked about Jordan's magical voice; why hadn't anyone warned her about his magical hands?

Megan stood. "I see Ruth and Misty calling the kids in. Sounds like they're going to make popcorn. I think I'll help."

Sure enough, Amber led the way with Lisa and Adam following, trailed by the dog and cat. Misty held Shohn in her arms while Ruth kept the door open for the parade. Georgia was amazed at how the kids were so accepted by everyone. They didn't deliberately take turns that she'd noticed, but somehow it worked out that way. Earlier she and Jordan had taken them all on an expedition to the lake where they'd lifted stones along the shore and found not only crawdads, but minnows and rock bass. Amber, strangely enough, had been the most daring at grabbing for the creepy-crawly creatures. But then Jordan explained that she'd been in or near the water since her birth, thanks to Gabe. Adam and Lisa professed to love it, too, so Jordan had promised to get Gabe to take them to the dam very soon.

They were all so giving and so accepting. Her children had found a family here. And that made her full to bursting with happiness.

Since Georgia couldn't stand, given that Jordan had

both her feet held firmly in his lap, Megan bent down to her instead. After a tight hug and a kiss on the cheek, she said, "I'll be in town for awhile this trip. Do you think we could get together for lunch or something? I'd love to visit more."

Georgia glanced at Jordan, saw his small smile, and agreed. "I'd enjoy that. Thank you."

Next Megan clasped Jordan's face between her hands and said, "I love seeing you so happy."

Jordan chuckled. "I'm rather fond of the situation myself."

She kissed him soundly and then took herself off. She'd barely gone ten feet when a rubber-tipped dart hit her in the backside. Megan jumped, whipped around, saw Gabe hiding behind a tree and started after him. Gabe ran for his life as Morgan and Sawyer, standing together at the back door, doubled over in laughter.

Georgia couldn't help but laugh, too. Then she looked up and locked gazes with Jordan. He looked…serious.

"Jordan?"

His fingers continued to work over her feet, only now his touch felt more sexual, more exciting. She let out a small, breathy moan, imagining those hands in other places.

"Do you know," he whispered, his eyes so hot she felt scorched, "that I'm about to die from unsated lust? I want you so bad right now I'm close to—"

"Ho!" Sawyer slapped him on the back, nearly knocking Jordan out of his lawn chair. "Hold that thought until I'm a safe distance away."

Jordan's growl was feral. "*Damn it,* will you guys stop sneaking up on me!"

Sawyer bit back a laugh. "Mom has decided to do a

sleepover, just like she used to when we were young."
In a stage whisper he added, "It's possible she's hoping
to give you a helping hand."

Then to Georgia, "Honey's already dragging the
family-room furniture around, making space for the
tent, but Mom said she wants your permission to invite
Adam and Lisa to spend the night, too."

Jordan closed his eyes and ignored Sawyer.

Georgia, a bit shaken by the interruption and her own
repressed desire, said dumbly, "A tent?"

"Yeah. Kids love making tents out of blankets and
stuff. They'll sleep on the floor and Mom and Brett
will sleep on the couch." He shrugged. "It's her way of
giving everyone a night off. Except me because Honey
is still breast-feeding, but we're claiming tomorrow afternoon." He grinned shamelessly with that admission.

Jordan came to his feet in a rush, cupped the back
of Georgia's head, and gave her a hard kiss. "Say yes."

She looked into his eyes, saw all the promise there,
and nodded. "Yes."

Jordan's eyes flared with satisfaction. "Let's see if I
can keep you in such an agreeable mood," he murmured.

Ten minutes later Georgia found herself being hustled across the yard to Jordan's apartments over the
garage. Her kids had kissed her goodbye and good-
night without a qualm. They knew she'd be close if she
was needed. Ruth had been invited to 'camp out' with
them and had accepted, especially when Mr. Malone
had done the same.

Jordan paused beside the steps leading to his front
door.

"What is it?" Georgia asked, a little breathless from
the idea of what they were about to do.

"I thought I heard something." Jordan frowned, looked around the yard, then shook his head. "Nevermind. It doesn't matter." He put his arm around her shoulders and together they practically ran up the steps. No sooner did Jordan have the door closed than Georgia found herself in his arms.

"God, I need you," he whispered and his rough velvet voice stroked over her as surely as his hands were doing. "Let me love you all night."

She would have said yes, but his mouth covered hers and his tongue thrust inside, hot and wet and hungry and all she could do was moan. Jordan must have understood; one of his large hands settled on her breast, softly kneading, and the other curved around the front of her thigh. He pressed into her, all hard, tensed muscles and trembling need. She felt his erection against her belly and rubbed herself against him.

In that instant, he lost it.

Casey chuckled as he saw the light go out in the rooms overhead. Jordan was a goner—and Casey had never seen him happier.

He was behind the garage in the darkest shadows, Emma clinging to his side. Very gently, he eased her away. "We should join the others."

"No." Her hand, so small and soft, stroked down his bare chest, but Casey caught it before she reached the fly to his jeans.

It took more control than he knew he had to turn her away. "Emma," he chided, and hopefully he was the only one who heard the shaking of his voice. He'd started out befriending her, but Emma wanted more. She was so blatant about it, so brazen, it was all he could do not to give in. But more than anything Emma needed a friend, not another conquest. And beyond that, Casey didn't share.

"Are you a virgin?" she taunted, and Casey laughed outright at her ploy.

"That," he said, flicking a finger over her soft cheek, "is none of your business."

She shook her head in wonder. "You're the only guy I know who wouldn't have denied it right away!"

"I'm not denying or confirming."

"I know, but most guys'd lie if they had to, rather than let a girl think—"

"What?" Casey cupped her face and despite his resolve, he kissed her. "I don't care what anyone thinks, Emma. You should know that by now. Besides, what I've done or with who isn't the point."

"No," she agreed, her tone sad. "It's what I've done, isn't it?"

He repeated his own thoughts out loud. "I don't share."

"What if I promised not to—"

"Shhh. Summer break is almost over and I'll be leaving for school. I won't be around, so there's no point in us even discussing this."

Big tears welled in her eyes, reflecting the moonlight, making his guts cramp. "I'm leaving too, Casey."

"And where do you think to go?"

"It doesn't matter." He could see her soft mouth trembling, could smell her sweet scent carried on the cool evening breeze. Boldly, she took his hand and pressed it to her breast. She was so damn soft.

With a muttered curse, Casey pulled her closer and kissed her again. It didn't matter, he promised himself, filling his hand with her firm breast, finding her nipple and stroking with his thumb. He was damned if he did, and damned if he didn't. And sometimes Emma was just too much temptation.

But it wouldn't change anything. He told her so in a muted whisper, and her only reply was a groan.

"I wanted to go slow," Jordan ground out as he jerked Georgia's T-shirt high, pushed her bra aside and bared one breast. He had very large hands, but even for him she was lush and full. "I wanted to make this last."

"Don't you dare go slow," she gasped, and gripped his head as he closed his mouth over one taut straining nipple. *"Jordan."*

He pulsed with incredible need, his heartbeat wild and uncontrolled. She tasted even better than he remembered, ripe and hot. With a low groan, she parted her thighs and she pushed against him, using her body to stroke his erection, her movements sinuous and graceful, making him think of all the fantasies he'd had when watching her dance.

He sucked her nipple deep, drawing on her while with his other hand he teased the crease of her behind. "Do you know what I want?" he growled, and switched to her other breast. The nipple he'd just abandoned was wet and so tight he ached just seeing it. He pinned her against the wall, knowing if he didn't slow her down he'd be gone in under three seconds.

Georgia gave a breathy, barely-there laugh. "It's obvious what you want." Her small hand pressed between them and curled around his hard-on. "This is a dead giveaway."

Jordan squeezed his eyes shut and concentrated on holding back his orgasm. "Don't do that." He stepped away, putting an arm's length of distance between them, staring at her through a haze of lust. "I'm not sure how you manage it, but you set me off and I don't want to end this too quick. Not for me and not for you."

Georgia looked at him while using the wall for support. Her chest, bared from his petting, rose and fell with deep breaths and quick pants. Her legs were still parted, her hands flat on the wall beside her hips. She looked enticing and tempting and Jordan wanted to drag her down to the carpet and bury himself inside her until they both screamed with the pleasure of it.

Slowly she gathered her wits and a small, seductive smile curled that sexier-than-sin mouth. Her eyes were dark and inviting. "Tell me what you want, Jordan."

He didn't hesitate. "I want you to ride me. Hard. I want to lie on my back and watch you while you take your pleasure. I want to see all those sensual movements you make when you dance, only I want them for me and me alone." Her lips parted, her breath came faster. He added in a whisper, "And I want it all while I'm deep inside you."

She came away from the wall in a rush, grabbing him and kissing him—his mouth, his throat, his chest. Jordan palmed her backside, lifted her and started for his bedroom. When her legs wound around him he had to stop for just a moment and kiss her deeply, but he could feel his passions on the boiling point, ready to erupt.

He tripped over a pair of slacks on his bedroom floor, stumbled to the bed and dropped there with Georgia still in his arms. "Don't move," he rasped.

She ignored him, grabbing his shirt and trying to yank it off him. He did that for her, then wrestled her own shirt over her head, leaving it and her bra twisted around her arms to try to hinder her movements just a bit.

"You're pushing me, sweetheart and I can't take it."

"Damn it, Jordan…" She struggled with the shirt and bra and by the time she had her arms free he'd already yanked her shorts and panties off.

Sitting back on his heels between her wide-spread legs, he whispered, "I could come just looking at you."

She moaned.

"Don't move now. I mean it." And before she could ignore that edict, he caught her hips in his hands, lifted her, and stroked with his tongue. She was already wet and hot and he grew voracious in his need to take as much of her as he could. "You taste so sweet."

Like a wild woman, she writhed and squirmed and cried out. Jordan loved it all, just as he loved her. His fingers bit deeply into her cheeks and he used his thumbs to open her further, stroking with his tongue and teasing with his teeth and breathing in her heady, musky scent.

His erection throbbed and strained against his fly, but he wanted her pleasure first because he wasn't at all certain how long he'd last once he got inside her. He'd meant to seduce her, but he forgot everything he knew about women and what they enjoyed. He acted solely on instinct, but it must have been enough. After several minutes of reacting to her moans and her small movements and her breathless encouragement, Jordan felt her climax start.

Her hips jerked, her thighs trembled and she groaned, long and low and real, pressing herself against his mouth to take everything he could give her. He held her closer, used his tongue to stroke her deeper, faster, and she came with all the energy she gave to her dance.

When she quieted, her harsh breathing the only sound in the room, Jordan rested his face against her thigh. Her completion, as if it had been his own, had helped to calm him. Idly, he traced his fingers over her slick flesh, her soft brown curls, making her twitch and moan.

He grinned. "This," he whispered, softly stroking her swollen folds before slowly, carefully pushing one finger deep, "was worth the wait."

She moved to his touch, lazy, sated movements. He loved seeing her spread out naked on his bed. When he pulled his fingers away, she heaved a long, shuddering sigh, and he decided he'd better not stall any longer or she was liable to fall asleep on him. And he knew first-hand how difficult it was to get her awake again.

Jordan stood beside the bed and stripped off his jeans. Georgia watched him through heavy, slumber-ous eyes—until he was naked. Then her cheekbones colored with renewed heat and her lips parted.

She took him completely off guard when she whis-pered, "I love you, Jordan."

An invisible fist squeezed his heart. Every bit of calm he'd just achieved shot out the ceiling.

He barely had the sense or patience to find a condom and put it on, especially when the second he sat on the mattress she pushed him to his back. Jordan dropped flat, more than willing to give her control. Without hes-itation she straddled his hips. For a brief moment she cradled his testicles, testing his long-lost control, her small soft hand making him crazed. Holding back be-came torture, and he told her so.

She clasped his penis in her hand and thankfully guided him into her body.

Jordan watched as she slowly slid down to envelop him, and he groaned deeply. With only that initial stroke he felt his body drawing tight in prerelease. *"Georgia."*

She seated herself completely. He held her hips and pressed her down farther; he was so deep inside her, her inner muscles gripped him and she caught her breath on a gasp. When Jordan started to lift her away, unwilling to hurt her, she shook her head and braced her hands on his chest. Her gaze was cloudy with a mix of discomfort and incredible pleasure. "I want all of you."

Jordan locked his jaw and concentrated on not coming. Georgia didn't make it easy on him. At first, she held perfectly still and Jordan, teeth clenched and thighs tensed, did all he could to keep from rushing her.

Her thumbs found his nipples beneath his chest hair. "You are, without a doubt," she murmured, "the most gorgeous, sexy man I've ever seen."

His heels pressed into the mattress and his hands fisted in the sheets.

Her small palms, cool against his burning flesh, coasted over his shoulders, down his biceps then to his abdomen. "You're all hard muscles and lean strength and I've wanted you since the first time I saw you in the audience."

Jordan felt himself jerking, knew the end was near for him. "Move, damn it. *Move.*"

With a feminine laugh of sheer power, she did as he asked, lifting with torturous slowness, then dropping hard. It took a mere three strokes, three times of watching her beautiful body slide up and then down again on his rigid shaft for Jordan to go mindless.

He cupped her breasts, arched his back, and exploded like a savage. To his immense surprise and pleasure, just as he began to regain sanity he heard Georgia sob and opened his eyes to watch her take her own pleasure. He was still hard, still buried deep inside her. She rocked her hips, her breasts bouncing, until she threw her head back and groaned out her second orgasm.

When she collapsed on his chest, Jordan put his arms around her and held her tight. He loved her so much it hurt, but when he decided to tell her, he heard her breathing even into the deep rhythm of sleep.

Pushing her hair from her face he studied her features. Her temples were damp from her exertions, her lips swollen and rosy, her cheeks still flushed. He kissed her forehead and the bridge of her nose. "I love you," he whispered, and though she didn't reply she did snuggle closer.

Smiling, Jordan eased her to his side so he could remove the used condom and find the blankets. It took him scant minutes and then he was back, pulling her onto his chest again, determined to keep her as close as possible. Forever.

Her heartbeat echoed in his chest, and with his mind at peace, Jordan dozed off.

Georgia woke the next morning to an empty bed. She automatically reached for Jordan, but he was gone. Then she heard him singing in his low, sexy voice, and with a smile, she climbed out of bed and wrapped the sheet around her.

His apartment was fabulous. Located over the three-car garage for the main house, it was open and spacious. The bedroom and private bath were the only doorways.

The kitchen, breakfast nook and wide living room all flowed into each other. Since the bedroom door was open she could see Jordan at the kitchen sink, measuring out coffee. His broad naked back made her body feel liquid and warm. He wore only a pair of faded jeans riding low on his narrow hips, and even his bare feet looked sexy. Of course he was making coffee, and she smiled.

She'd told him she loved him.

Georgia remembered her declaration with a touch of embarrassment, but decided it didn't matter. So what that he hadn't responded in kind? She knew he cared for her, and he and his family were so wonderful....

The phone rang and as Jordan turned to answer it he caught sight of her. Immediately, he forgot about the phone and started toward her with a male determination that had her blushing. "Morning," he murmured in a suggestive way.

Oh, that sexy just-up voice! Her heart picked up speed and a wave of warmth shook her. "Good morning."

His smile was so gentle. Combined with a mostly naked superior male body, Jordan Sommerville was very potent! Georgia cleared her throat. "Aren't you going to get the phone?"

"The answering machine will pick up."

No sooner did he say it than it happened. Georgia missed the beginning of the message because Jordan kissed her while slowly unwinding the sheet from her body. He held it out to her sides and looked at her in the bright morning sunlight cascading through the kitchen windows.

"You're so beautiful."

She thought to tease him about needing glasses,

since she knew her hair was tangled and her makeup smudged, but then the person on the phone said, *"So as of a few hours ago, the bar is officially shut down. Who knows how long it'll last, but I knew you'd be happy to hear it. Serving minors is a serious offense, and about the quickest way around to lose your licence. I think we can probably keep him shut down. Anyway, give me a call when you can and I'll fill you in on the rest of the details."*

They were both frozen, Jordan in what appeared to be satisfaction, Georgia with dawning horror.

She was unemployed.

She yanked the sheet away from Jordan and held it to her chin to cover her nudity. She felt lost and vulnerable and scared. What would she do now? Good God, she couldn't make the bills without that job! In a daze, Georgia swallowed hard and turned away from Jordan.

He caught her shoulder, and his voice sounded a bit harsh. "Where are you going?"

Blankly, her mind in a muddle, she stared at him. "I have to go find a job. I have to... I don't know. I have to do something." Then, before she could stop herself, she whispered, *"Jordan, what am I going to do?"*

His expression softened, and she wondered if what she saw in his eyes was pity. Details whipped through her mind with the speed of light. Scheduled dental checkups for the kids. The premium on her mother's health insurance. The gas and electric, the mortgage.... She hadn't had a chance to save up much money yet. She'd been too busy making repairs. And now...

The sheet fell to the floor, forgotten as she covered her face with her hands, knowing she'd failed yet again. "I have to find a job." She said it once more, hoping to make herself understand. But she'd already looked everywhere before accepting the work at the bar. Nowhere else had paid enough. For a high school dropout who could only work certain hours because of being a mother, she wasn't exactly prime employment material.

Jordan's hands curved around her shoulders, caressing, comforting. "It's too early to do anything right now. I'll call the sheriff back in a bit and get all the details, okay?"

The sheriff? Not his brother, so it must have been the one who'd wanted them arrested. She'd known he was watching the bar, that he was fed up with the nightly problems that seemed to erupt....

Jordan interrupted her thoughts. "I have a few solutions, sweetheart. Will you listen to me?"

Georgia realized she'd put her worries onto him; she'd come to depend on him whether she wanted to admit it or not. How had she let that happen?

He'd once offered to let her work for him, but that would be no more than charity and she didn't think she could stand it. She shook her head as she tried to pull away.

"You *will* listen," Jordan stated, and urged her toward his sofa.

"What is there to say? I won't work for you—"

"You don't have to." Jordan gently pushed her into the seat, then plucked up the sheet and handed it to her. Georgia wrapped it around herself; she had all but forgotten she was nude.

"Now just listen." He caught both her hands and held tight. "You said you wanted options, well here're two." He drew a deep breath. "You can marry me." He waited, watching her closely, and when she only stared at him in shock, his expression hardened. "Or you can teach dance at your own studio."

That was every bit as confusing as his proposal. Only…he hadn't really proposed. Not once had he ever said he loved her, only that he wanted her. And last night he'd admitted to respecting her, admiring her…

"Georgia, are you listening to me?"

She blinked. "Yes, but… I don't have a studio."

Jordan seemed to be getting angrier by the moment. "I found you one. It's in the center of town. It used to be a novelty shop, but the owner is retiring and the place is wide and airy and with a little renovation it'd be perfect."

She sat there, naked but for a sheet, confusion weighing her down. "A novelty shop?"

Jordan grabbed her chin and kissed her hard. He actually trembled he was so furious. "I already agreed to buy the building so you might as well agree." When she still hesitated, he barked, "You said you enjoy teaching dance, and Misty and Honey assure me there'll be—"

Incredulous, Georgia shot off the sofa to stare down at him. "You bought me a *building?*"

He didn't stand, but instead sprawled back in his seat and put his arms along the sofa back. Every single muscle in his arms and chest and shoulders was defined. "Yes."

"Ohmigod." She paced away, but had taken no more than ten steps when she whirled back around to face him. "How can you buy me a building? Nobody buys someone else a building!"

His eyes narrowed. "I also asked you to marry me."

"No." Wildly, she shook her head. "You told me I *could* marry you. It's not at all the same thing."

"You want all the fanfare? You want me to go down on one knee?"

"No!" Her head had started to pound and she felt queasy. It would be so easy to marry him, to let him fix everything, but she'd sworn she wouldn't do that again. She felt wetness on her cheeks and realized she was crying. Her heart ached and she said on a near wail, "I can't marry you, Jordan. Why would you even suggest such a thing?"

His eyes closed briefly; he rubbed a hand over his face. "You said you loved me."

"I do, but…you have everything. You have a wonderful supportive family and a great job, an education and respectability, a home and money and—"

He came to his feet so quickly, she yelped and nearly tripped over the trailing sheet. Jordan gripped her arms.

"So that's what you love about me?" he roared, scaring her half silly. "What I can give you?"

She'd never seen Jordan like this. She'd watched him easily subdue a man twice his size. She'd watched him face off with his brothers. She'd seen Jordan angry and frustrated and deliberately provoking, but she'd never seen him in this type of rage. Oddly enough, though he'd startled her, she wasn't afraid of him.

"No." She emphasized that with a tiny shake of her head. "I love you," she said very quietly, choking on her tears, "because of who you are."

He stepped up to her until she had to tip her head back to see his face, until his bare chest brushed her knuckles clutching the sheet and his feet were braced on either side of hers. He surrounded her and overwhelmed her and then he whispered, "That's why I love you, too."

More tears blurred her vision and she rubbed them

away, sniffing and gulping and sounding horribly like a frog. "But I—"

"You're going to really piss me off," he informed her, "if you put yourself down again." She hiccuped on a laugh. Jordan raised one hand to gently smooth her cheek. "Weren't you listening last night, baby? I love you. I'm crazy nuts about you. My whole family knows it, even my mother. Yes I have all the things you mentioned, but I don't have you. And without you, I'm not going to be happy."

"Oh Jordan." She swallowed hard. "You really love me?"

He shook his head. "What did you think? That I just enjoy giving foot rubs?"

She lost what little control she had on her emotions and dropped the sheet again to throw herself into his arms. "I love you so much."

"I do, you know," he whispered. "Enjoy rubbing on you, I mean." She laughed as he cradled her close. He slid his hands down to her backside and lifted her. "Marry me, Georgia. Let me have you. Let me make your family my own and give you mine and we can both be happy."

"It…it doesn't feel right to take that much from you."

He rocked her into his erection. "Does this feel right?" When she nodded, he kissed her gently. "And this?"

"Jordan…"

"And this?"

Georgia had known from the start that he could seduce with just a few whispered words. Now she had firsthand proof.

Epilogue

"Hey Dad!"

Jordan looked up from making salad as Lisa came barreling through the front door, followed closely by Adam and two dogs, one a mixed-breed puppy and the other an ancient dachshund. They'd all been outside playing and smelled of sunshine and fresh crisp air. Between the children laughing and the dogs barking, the house was always filled with excitement.

Jordan knelt down and caught the children to him, hugging them fiercely. Life, he thought, was pretty damn good. "Mommy's home," Lisa told him, after a loud wet kiss to his cheek.

Seconds later Georgia strolled in. Under her coat, she wore her workout clothes of leotard and tights, guaranteed to make his blood boil. Seeing the skintight outfits affected him more strongly than her stage costumes had.

Of course, nothing affected him as much as her bare, beautiful skin.

He stood, and with the kids still close to his side and the dogs jumping between them, he gave her a long, thorough kiss. "Hi," he whispered and she smiled back.

Her smiles, he decided, were downright lethal.

"What time is everyone due to arrive?"

Jordan took her coat from her and hung it on the back of an oak chair. Thanks to Gabe's handyman skills, the remodelled kitchen had become a favorite hangout for everyone. "You have time to shower, if that's what you're wondering."

"Can I do anything to help you first?"

Jordan went back to preparing his salad. "The sauce you made yesterday is already heating, and the spaghetti will go on as soon as the water starts to boil." He glanced at the kids. "My assistant chefs can wash their hands and start to work on the garlic bread."

Lisa grinned up at him. She'd lost another tooth and her words now whistled when she spoke. "Grandma said she's bringin' dessert."

Jordan shook his head. Grandma, he knew darn good and well, was smitten with Mr. Malone, who would also be in attendance. Ruth had moved into his vacated apartments over the garage. Neither he nor Georgia had wanted her to, but she'd insisted on giving them time to be alone. When Misty and Honey had begged her to stay close since the babies loved her so much, she'd agreed. She was now a paid housekeeper/sitter with her own measure of independence, which she loved.

She also loved the way Mr. Malone hung around on the pretense of visiting his daughters, though Sawyer and Morgan were both quite disgruntled by that situation. Jordan sympathized with them. He didn't understand the attraction at all. Ruth was so sweet and open and loving, but Mr. Malone—they'd known the man for ages and still called him mister—was so detached. Ruth claimed he was softening and that he wasn't at all detached when they were alone. He wasn't detached with any of the kids, either, and he was openly impressed with Casey.

Georgia touched his cheek. "You've got that protective look about you again."

Jordan grinned at her. "Do you know how many people will be here tonight?" When she shook her head, sidetracked just as he'd hoped, he said, "Fourteen, if we include all the kids. When you add the four of us, that's a lot of confusion. Are you sure you're up to this after working all day?"

Adam crossed his arms in the same pose Jordan used. "We'll need lots of garlic bread!"

Georgia laughed. "Yes, I'm up to it, and yes, we'll need lots of bread." Then to Jordan, "You know dancing doesn't tire me. Just the opposite, I always feel energized after a class."

In the two months since their small, quiet marriage, Georgia had gotten her studio set up and filled to the maximum with students. She taught not only dance classes for the fun of it, but also aerobics. She had people of all ages coming throughout the day. And true to her word, she was always bursting with energy.

Especially in the bedroom.

Jordan had to pull his thoughts away from that direction or he'd never survive the massive family gathering. Georgia left to shower and dress and a few minutes later all the relatives started to arrive.

He wasn't surprised to see Casey with yet another beautiful young lady. He seldom saw the same girl twice these days, and other than a few surprise meetings, Emma hadn't been around.

At her first bite of dinner, Georgia smiled at Jordan

and said, "Delicious. You really are perfect at everything, aren't you?"

Jordan grinned. He was used to her saying that, but obviously his family wasn't.

Morgan choked on his spaghetti, then doubled over laughing. "Maybe perfect for you," he laughed, "but I think old Jordan is plenty flawed. Now Malone, she prefers men with a little more steel, don't ya, sweetheart?"

Misty pretended she hadn't heard him, though everyone could see her trying not to smile. Amber said, "Daddy's nasty."

Sawyer shook his head. "Can't you control him, Misty? He gets more outrageous by the day."

"Look who's talking!" Morgan said.

Sawyer was trying to eat and love on his wife and son at the same time. His mother took Shohn so she and Brett could spoil him just a bit, and Honey found her chair bumping up against her husband's.

Gabe tipped Elizabeth's chair toward him and kissed her hard. She didn't even try to fight him off. Adam mimicked their smooching sounds until everyone laughed. Lisa announced to the table at large that her grandma and Mr. Malone were playing footsie beneath the table.

Casey sat back in his seat and watched them all with an indulgent smile. Things sure had changed over the past few years, and he loved it. He missed having Jordan so close, but they visited often, and it was obvious Jordan was as happy as a man could be. His father and uncles had all found the perfect women for them.

The girl beside Casey cleared her throat. She was uncomfortable in the boisterous crowd, but it didn't matter. He doubted he'd see her again anyway. She was beautiful, sexy, and anxious to please him—but she wasn't perfect for him. Though he was only eighteen and had quite a bit of college ahead of him, not to mention all his other plans, Casey couldn't help but wonder if he'd ever meet the perfect mate.

An image of big brown eyes, filled with sexual curiosity, sadness, and finally rejection, formed in his mind. With a niggling dread that wouldn't ease up, Casey wondered if he'd already found the perfect girl—but had sent her away.

Then he heard Georgia talking to his date, and pulled himself out of his reverie. No, she wasn't perfect, but she didn't keep him awake nights, either. And that was good, because no matter what, no matter how he felt now, he would not let his plans get off track. He decided to forget all about women and the future and simply enjoy the night with his family.

It was late when Casey finally got home after dropping off his date, and he'd just pulled off his shirt when a fist started pounding on the front door. He and his father met in the hall, both of them frowning. Honey pulled on her robe and hustled after them.

When Sawyer got the door open, they found themselves confronted with Emma's father. He had his daughter by the arm, and he was obviously furious.

Casey's first startled thought was that Emma wasn't gone after all. Then he got a good look at her face and he erupted in rage.

He'd been wrong. His plans would change after all. In a big way.

* * * * *

Joanne Rock credits her decision to write romance after a book she picked up during a flight delay engrossed her so thoroughly that she didn't mind at all when her flight was delayed two more times. Giving her readers the chance to escape into another world has motivated her to write over eighty books for a variety of Harlequin series.

Books by Joanne Rock

Harlequin Desire

Dynasties: Mesa Falls

The Rebel
The Rival
Rule Breaker
Heartbreaker
The Rancher
The Heir

Texas Cattleman's Club: Inheritance

Her Texas Renegade

Visit the Author Profile page at Harlequin.com for more titles.

HIS SECRETARY'S SURPRISE FIANCÉ

Joanne Rock

To Catherine Mann, my longtime critique partner, for inviting me to dream up a Harlequin Desire series with her. We've brainstormed many books together over the years, but this was a special treat, since we both got to write them! Thank you, Cathy, for being a creative inspiration and a wonderful friend.

Chapter 1

Dempsey Reynaud would have his revenge.

Leaving the football team's locker room behind after losing the final preseason game, the New Orleans Hurricanes' head coach charged toward the media reception room to give the mandatory press conference. Today's score sheet was immaterial since he'd rested his most valuable players. Not that he'd say as much in his remarks to the media. But he would make damn sure the Hurricanes took their vengeance for today's loss.

They would win the conference title at worst. A Super Bowl championship at best.

As a second-year head coach on a team owned by his half brother, Dempsey had a lot to prove. Being a Reynaud in this town came with a weight all its own. Being an illegitimate Reynaud meant he'd been on a mission to deserve the name long before he became obsessed with bringing home a Super Bowl title to the Big Easy. A championship season would effectively answer his detractors, especially the sports journalists who'd declared that hiring him was an obvious case of favoritism. The press didn't understand his relatives at all if they didn't know that his older brother, Gervais, would be the first one calling for his head if he didn't deliver results. The Reynauds hadn't gotten where they were by being soft on each other.

More important, his hometown deserved a championship. Not for the billionaire family who'd claimed him as their own when he was thirteen. He wanted it for people who hungered for any kind of victory in life. For people who struggled every day in places like the Eighth Ward, where he'd been born.

Just like his assistant, Adelaide Thibodeaux.

She stood outside the media room about five yards ahead of him, smiling politely at a local sportswriter. When she spotted Dempsey, she excused herself and walked toward him, heels clicking on the tile floor like a time clock on overdrive. She wore a black pencil skirt with gold pinstripes and a sleeveless gold blouse that echoed the Hurricanes' colors and showed off the tawny skin of her Creole heritage. Poised and efficient, she didn't look like the half-starved ragamuffin who'd been raised in one of the city's toughest neighborhoods. The one who used to stuff half her lunch in her book bag to share with him on the bus home since he wouldn't eat again until the free breakfast at school the next morning. A lot had changed for both of them since those days.

From her waist-length dark hair that she wore in a smooth ponytail to her wide hazel eyes, framed by dark brows and lashes, she was a pretty and incredibly competent woman. The only woman he considered a friend. She'd been his assistant through his rise in the coaching ranks, her salary paid by him personally. As a Reynaud, he wrote his own rules and brought all his resources to the table to make a success of coaching. He'd been only too glad to create the position for her as he'd moved from Atlanta to Tampa Bay and then—two years ago—back to their hometown after his older brother, Gervais, had purchased the New Orleans Hurricanes.

There was a long, proud tradition of nepotism in football from the Harbaughs to the Grudens, and the Reynaud family was no different. They'd made billions in the global shipping industry, but their real passion was football. An obsession with the game ran in the blood, no matter how much some local pundits liked to say they were dilettantes.

"Coach Reynaud?" Adelaide called to him down the narrow hallway draped in team banners. Her use of his title alerted him that she was annoyed, making him wonder if that sportswriter had been hassling her. "Do you have a moment to meet privately before you take the podium?"

She handed him note cards, an old-fashioned preference at media events so he could leave his phone free for updates. He planned to brief the journalists on his regular-season roster, one of the few topics that would distract sports hounds from grilling him about today's loss in a preseason contest that didn't reflect his full team weaponry.

"Any last-minute emergencies?" He frowned. Adelaide had been with him long enough to know he didn't stick around longer than necessary after a loss.

He needed to start preparing for their first regular-season game. A game that counted. But he recognized a certain stiffness in her shoulders, a tension that wouldn't come from a defeat on the field even though she hated losing, too. She'd mastered hiding her emotions better than he had.

"There is one thing." She wore an earbud in one ear, the black cord disappearing in her dark hair; she was probably listening for messages from the public relations coordinator already in the media room. "It will just take a moment."

Adelaide rarely requested his time, understanding her job and his needs so intuitively that she could prepare weeks of his work based on little more than his daily texts or CCing her on important emails. If she needed to speak with him privately—now—it had to be important.

"Sure." He waved her to walk alongside him. "What do you need?"

"Privately, please," she answered tightly, setting off alarms in his head.

Commandeering one of the smaller offices along the hallway, Dempsey flicked on a light in the barren, generic space. The facilities in the building were nothing like the team headquarters and training compound in Metairie, where the Reynauds had invested millions for a state-of-the-art home. They played here because it was downtown and easier for their fans. The tiny box where they stood now was a fraction the size of his regular work space.

"What is it?" He closed the door behind him, sealing them inside the glorified cubicle with a cheap metal desk, a corded phone from another decade and walls so thin he could hear the lockers slamming and guys shouting in the team room next door.

"Dempsey, I apologize for the timing on this, but I can't put it off any longer." She tugged the earbud free, as if she didn't want to hear whatever was going on at the other end of her connection. "I've tried to explain before that I couldn't be a part of this season but it's clear I'm not getting through to you."

He frowned. What the hell was she talking about? When had she asked for a break? If she wanted vacation time, all she had to do was put it on his calendar.

"You're going to do this now?" He prided himself on control on the field and off. But after today's loss, this topic was going to test his patience. "Text me the dates you want off, take as long as you need to recharge and we'll regroup later. You're invaluable to me. I need you at full speed. Take care of yourself, Adelaide."

He turned to leave, ready to get back to work and relieved to have that resolved. He had a press conference to attend.

She darted around him, blocking the door with her five-foot-four frame. "You aren't listening to me now. And you haven't been listening to me for months."

The team owned tackling dummies for practice that stood taller than Adelaide, but she didn't seem to notice that Dempsey was twice her size.

He sighed. "What did I not hear?"

"I want to start my own business."

"Yes. I remember that. We agreed you would draw up a business plan for me to review." He knew she wanted to start her own company. She'd mentioned it last winter. She'd said something about specializing in clothes and accessories for female fans. She hoped to grow it over time, eventually securing merchandising rights from the team with his support.

He worried about her losing the financial stability she'd fought so hard to attain and figured she would realize the folly of the venture after thinking it over. He thought he'd convinced her to reevaluate those plans when he'd persuaded her to return for the preseason. Besides, she excelled at helping him. She was an invaluable member of the administrative staff he'd spent years building, so that when he finally had the right football personnel on the field, he could ride that talent to a winning year.

That year had arrived.

"I've emailed my business plan to you multiple times." She folded her arms beneath her breasts, an unwelcome reminder that Adelaide was an attractive woman.

She was his friend. Friendships were rare, important. Sex was…sex. She was more than sex to him.

"Right." He swallowed hard and hauled his gaze upward to her hazel eyes. "I'll get right on reading that after the press conference."

"Liar," she retorted. "You're putting me off again. I can't force you to read it, any more than I can make you read the messages and emails from your former female companions."

She arched an eyebrow at him, her rigid spine still plastered to the door, blocking his exit. It had never pleased her that he'd asked her to handle things like that from his inbox. But he needed her help deflecting unhappy ex-girlfriends, preventing them from talking to the press and diverting public attention from the team to his personal life. Adelaide was good at that. At so many things. His life frayed at the edges when she wasn't around.

Plus, he was devoting every second possible to the task of building a winning team to secure his place in the Reynaud family. It wasn't enough that he bore his father's last name. As an illegitimate son, he'd always needed to work twice as hard to prove himself.

And Adelaide's efforts supported that goal. He was good at football and finances. Adelaide excelled at everything else. He'd been friends with her since he'd chased off some bullies who'd cornered her in a neighborhood cemetery when she was in second grade and he was in third. She'd been so grateful she'd insinuated herself into his world, becoming his closest friend and a fierce little protector in her own right. Even after the time when Dempsey's rich, absentee father had shown up in his life to remove him from his hardscrabble life in the Eighth Ward—and his mother—for good. His mom had given him up for a price. Adelaide hadn't.

"Then, I'll resume management of the personal emails." He knew he needed to deal with Valentina Rushnaya, a particularly persistent model he'd dated briefly. The more famous a woman, apparently, the less she appreciated being shuffled aside for football.

"You will have no choice until you hire a new assistant," Adelaide replied. Then, perhaps realizing that she'd pushed him, she gave him a placating smile. "Thank you for understanding."

Hire a new assistant? What the hell? Was she grandstanding for something, like a raise? Or was she actually serious about launching her business right now at the start of the regular season?

"I don't understand," he corrected her, trying to talk

reason into her. "You need start-up cash for your new company. Even without reading your plan, I know you'll be depleting the savings you've worked so hard for on a very long shot at success. Everyone likes an underdog but, Addy, the risk is high. You have to know that."

"That's for me to decide." Fierceness threaded through her voice.

He strove to hang on to his patience. "Half of all small businesses fail, and the ones that don't require considerable investment. Work for one more year. You can suggest a raise that you feel is equitable and I'll approve it. You'll have a financial cushion to increase your odds of growing the company large enough to secure those merchandising rights."

And he would have more time to persuade her to give up the idea. Life was good for them now. Really good. She was an integral part of his success, freeing him up to do what he did best. Manage the team.

The voices and laughter in the hallway outside grew louder as members of the media moved from the locker-room interviews to the scheduled press conference. He needed to get going, to do everything possible to keep their future locked in.

"Damn it, I don't want a raise—"

"Then, you're not thinking like a business owner," he interrupted. Yes, he admired her independence. Her stubbornness, even. But he couldn't let her start a company that would fail.

Especially when she could do a whole hell of a lot of good for her current career and for his team. For him. He didn't have time to replace her. For that matter, as his longtime friend who probably understood him better than anyone, Adelaide Thibodeaux was too good at her job to be replaced.

He reached around her for the doorknob. She slid over to block him, which put her ass right over his hand. A curvy little butt in a tight pencil skirt. Her chest rose with a deep inhale, brushing her breasts against his chest.

He. Couldn't. Breathe.

Her eyes held his for a moment and he could have sworn he saw her pupils widen with awareness. He stepped back. Fast. She blinked and the look was gone from her gaze.

"I'm grateful that working with you gave me the time to think about what I want to do with my life. I got to travel all over and make important contacts that inspired my new business." She gestured with her hands, and he made himself focus on anything other than her face, her body, the memory of how she'd felt pressed up against him.

He watched her silver bracelet glinting in the fluorescent lights. It was an old spoon from a pawnshop that he'd reshaped as a piece of jewelry and given to her as a birthday present back when he couldn't afford anything else. Why the hell did she still wear that? He tried to hear her words over the thundering pulse in his ears.

"But, Dempsey, let's be honest here. I did not attend art school to be your assistant forever, and I've been doing this far too long to feel good about it as a 'fill-in job' anymore."

He didn't miss the reference. He'd convinced her to work with him in the first place by telling her the position would just be temporary until she decided what to do with her art degree. That was before she'd made herself indispensable. Before he'd started a season that could net a championship ring and cement his place in the family as more than the half brother.

He'd worked too hard to get here, to land this chance to prove himself under the harsh media spotlight to a league that would love nothing more than to see him fail. This was his moment, and he and Adelaide had a great partnership going, one he couldn't jeopardize with wayward impulses. Winning wasn't just about securing his spot as a Reynaud. It was about proving the worth of every kid living hand-to-mouth back in the Eighth Ward, the kids who didn't have mystery fathers riding in to save the day and pluck them out of a hellish nightmare. If Dempsey couldn't use football to make a difference, what the hell had he worked so hard for all these years?

"You can't leave now." He didn't have time to hash this out. And he would damn well have his way.

"I'm going after the press conference. I told you I would come back for the preseason, and now it's done." Frowning, she twisted the bracelet round and round on her wrist. "I shouldn't have returned this year at all, especially if this ends up causing hard feelings between us. But I can send your next assistant all my files."

How kind. He clamped his mouth shut against the scathing responses that simmered, close to boiling over. He deserved better from her and she knew it.

But if she was going to see him through the press conference, he still had forty minutes to change her mind. Forty minutes to figure out a way to force her hand. A way to make her stay by his side through the season.

All he needed was the right play call.

"In that case, I appreciate the heads-up," he said,

planting his hands on her waist and shuffling her away from the door. "But I'd better get this press conference started now."

Her eyes widened as he touched her, but she stepped aside, hectic color rising in her cheeks even though they'd always been just friends. He'd protected that friendship because it was special. She was special. He'd never wanted to sacrifice that relationship to something as fickle as attraction even though there'd definitely been moments over the years when he'd been tempted. But logic and reason—and respect for Adelaide—had always won out in the past. Then again, he'd never touched her the way he had today, and it was messing with his head. Seeing that awareness on her face now, feeling the answering kick of it in his blood, made him wonder if—

"Of course we need to get to the conference." She grabbed her earpiece and shoved it into place as she bit her lip. "Let's go."

He held the door for her, watching as she hurried up the hallway ahead of him, the subtle sway of her hips making his hands itch for a better feel of her. No doubt about it, she was going to be angry with him. In time, she would see he had her best interests at heart.

But he had the perfect plan to keep her close, and the ideal venue—a captive audience full of media members—to execute it. As much as he regretted hurting a friend, he also knew she would understand at a gut level if she knew him half as well as he thought she did.

His game was on the line. And this was for the win.

That went better than expected.

Back pressed to the wall of the jam-packed media room, Adelaide Thibodeaux congratulated herself on her talk with Dempsey, a man whose name rarely appeared in the papers without the word *formidable* in front of it. She'd made her point, finally expressing herself in a way that he understood. For weeks now, she'd been procrastinating about having the conversation, really debating her timing, since there never seemed to be a convenient moment to talk to her boss about anything that wasn't directly related to Hurricane football or Reynaud family business. But the situation was delicate. She couldn't afford to alienate him, since she'd need his help to secure merchandising rights as her company grew. And while she'd like to think they'd been friends too long for her to question his support…she did.

Somewhere along the line they'd lost that feeling they had back in junior high when they'd sit on a stoop and talk for hours. Now it was all business, all the time. That didn't seem to bother Dempsey, who lived and breathed work. But she needed more out of life—and her friends—than that. So now she was counting down the minutes of her last day on the job as his assistant. Maybe, somehow, they'd recover their friendship.

She hated to leave the team. She loved the sport and excelled at her job. In fact, she'd grown to enjoy football so much she couldn't wait to start her own high-end clothing company catering to female fans. The work married her love of art with her sports savvy, and the projected designs were so popular online she'd crowd funded her first official offering last week. She was ready for this next step.

And she was very ready for a clean break from Dempsey.

Her eyes went to him in the bright spotlight on the dais where coaches and a few key players would take turns fielding questions. The sea of journalists hid behind cameras, voice recorders and lights, a wall of devices all currently aimed at Dempsey Reynaud, the hard-nosed coach and her onetime friend who'd unknowingly crushed most of her dreams for the past decade.

He was far too handsome, rich and powerful. Dempsey might not ever see himself as fully accepted into the family, but the rest of the world breathed his name with the same awe as they did the names of the other Reynaud brothers. All four of them had been college football stars, with the youngest two opting for NFL careers while the older two had stepped into front-office roles in addition to their work in the family's business empire. Each remained built like Pro Bowl players, however. Dempsey's broad shoulders tested the seams of his Hurricanes jersey, his strong biceps apparent as he leaned forward at the podium to provide his perspective on the game and give an injury report.

With his dark brown hair and eyes a bit more golden than brown, there was no mistaking Dempsey's relation to his half brothers. But the cleft in his chin and the square jaw were all his own, his features sharp, his mouth an unforgiving slash. He spoke faster, too, with his stronger Cajun accent.

Not that she'd spent an inordinate amount of time cataloging every last detail about the man she'd swooned over as a teen. There was a time she would have done backflips to make him notice her as more than just his scrawny, flat-chested pal. But the only time she'd succeeded? He'd ended up noticing her as a tool for increasing his business productivity. He had honestly once referred to her in those exact terms. He hadn't even noticed when she'd ceased being much of a friend to him—forgoing personal exchanges in favor of taking care of business.

That hurt even more than not being noticed as a woman.

"Adelaide?" The voice of the PR coordinator sounded in her earpiece, a woman who had quickly seen the benefits of a coach with a personal assistant, unlike some of the front-office personnel in other cities where she'd worked. "I'm receiving calls and messages for Dempsey from Valentina Rushnaya. She's threatened to give some unflattering interviews if she can't arrange for a private meeting with him."

Adelaide's skin chilled. Dempsey's latest supermodel. The woman had been rude to Adelaide, unwilling to accept that her affair with Dempsey was over despite the extravagant diamond bracelet he'd sent as a breakup gift. Occasionally, Adelaide felt bad for the women he dated. She understood how it hurt to be kept at a distance after experiencing what it felt like to be the center of his attention—if only briefly. But she had no such empathy for Valentina.

Stepping to the back of the room, Adelaide spoke softly into her microphone, momentarily tuning out of the press conference as Dempsey wound up his opening remarks.

"I talked to Dempsey about this and he's agreed to handle it." She didn't see any need to share her plans to vacate her position. "Anything she says would either be old news, or blatant lies."

"Should we schedule a meeting to come up with a response plan, just in case?" Carole pressed. The woman stood on the far end of the room, her arms crossed in her navy power suit that was her daily uniform, her blond bob as durable as any helmet in the league. "Dempsey's new charity has their first major fund-raiser slated for next week. I think he'll be disappointed if this woman succeeds in deflecting any attention from that."

Adelaide would be equally disappointed.

The Brighter NOLA foundation had been her idea as much as his, a youth violence prevention initiative where Dempsey could leverage his success and influence to help some of the more gang-ridden communities in New Orleans. Like where they'd grown up. Or, more accurately, where he'd lived briefly and where she'd been stuck after he got out.

She'd had her own run-ins with youth violence.

"I'll make sure that doesn't happen." She would honor those words, even if it meant communicating with Dempsey after she walked away from the Silver Dome today. "She signed a strict nondisclosure agreement before she started dating Dempsey, so going to the press will be a costly move for her."

Dempsey had communicated as much to Adelaide in a one-line email when she'd mentioned it to him two weeks ago. He'd typed, She has no legal recourse, and attached a copy of the confidentiality agreement the woman had signed as part of his megaromantic dating procedure. In Adelaide's softer-hearted moments, she recognized that the single life could be difficult for an extraordinarily wealthy and powerful man in the public eye. He had to be practical. Careful. But the nondisclosure agreement, complete with enforcement clause and confidentiality protection, seemed over-the-top.

Given the number of women who still lobbied to be in his life, however, it must not deter many.

"Valentina is wealthier than some of the ladies he's

dated," Carole pointed out. "But I hope she's just stirring trouble with us and not—" She stopped speaking suddenly and leaned forward. "Wait. Did he just say he has a personal announcement? What is he doing?"

From across the room, Adelaide noticed all of the PR coordinator's focus was on the lectern where Dempsey was facing down the media.

The audience sat in stillness, making her wonder what she'd missed. In the hushed moment, Dempsey held the room captive as always, but more anticipation than usual pinged through the crowd. She could see it in their body language, as the journalists sat straighter in their seats, all dialed in to whatever it was the Hurricanes' head coach was about to say.

"I got engaged today." He announced it as matter-of-factly as if he'd just read the latest update on a linebacker's injury report.

Murmurs of surprise rippled through the crowd of sportswriters while Adelaide reeled with shock. Engaged?

The floor seemed to shift beneath her feet. She reached behind her, searching for something to steady herself. He'd never mentioned an engagement. Her chest hurt with the weight of how little he trusted her. How little he cared about their old friendship. How much this new betrayal hurt, not to even know the most basic detail of his personal life—

"To my personal assistant," he continued, his gaze landing on her. "Adelaide Thibodeaux."

Chapter 2

Adelaide reeled back on her high heels.

Dempsey had just publicly declared an engagement. To her.

The man who was so cautious about every aspect of his personal life. The man who trusted her never to betray him even though he'd betrayed her in a million little ways over the years. How could he?

In her ear, Adelaide heard Carole squeal a congratulations. A few other members of the press who knew her—women, mostly, who were still vastly outnumbered in the football community—turned around to acknowledge her. Or maybe just study her to see what renowned bachelor Dempsey Reynaud would find appealing in the very average and wholly unknown Adelaide Thibodeaux.

Of course, the answer was obvious. She had no appeal other than the fact that Dempsey didn't want her to leave the team. And he was a man who always got his way.

She'd naively thought she could just turn her back on her job as his assistant and start a company that would rely upon good relations with the Hurricanes and the league in general for securing merchandising rights down the road. Something she couldn't afford to jeopardize if she wanted her company to be a success.

If she stood up and challenged him, she'd lose team support instantly. She didn't dare contradict him. At least not publicly. And no question, Dempsey absolutely knew that, as well.

Realization settled in her gut as smoothly and firmly as a sideline pass falling into a wide receiver's hands. She'd been outflanked and outmaneuvered by the smartest play caller in the game.

Her brand-new fiancé.

She needed time to think and regroup before she faced him and blurted out something she would regret. Adelaide darted out of the press conference just as a reporter began quizzing Dempsey about the quarterback's thumb. She didn't know what else to do. She lacked Dempsey's gift for complicated machinations that ruined other peoples' lives in the blink of an eye. Storming off was the best she could come up with to relay her displeasure and give herself time to think.

She tore off her earpiece even though Carole currently informed her she needed to stick around the building for any follow-up interviews.

Like hell.

Adelaide picked up her pace, heels grinding out a frantic rhythm on the concrete floor as she burst through a metal door leading to the stairwell. She headed down a flight to the custodial level of the dome, taking the route where she was least likely to encounter media.

The sports journalists hadn't really known what to do with the story about the Hurricanes' coach getting married. Sure—they would recognize the news value. But in that he-man room full of sports experts, no one would quiz the tersest coach in the league about his love life. They would hand that off to the social pages.

Who, in turn, would eat it up. All four of the Reynaud brothers had been in *People* magazine's Sexiest Men Alive list for two years running. The national media would be covering Dempsey's engagement, too. While she ran away.

She stumbled as her heel broke on the bottom step because her shoes were meant for work, not sprints. Hobbled, she shoved through the door on the ground level just as her phone started vibrating in her bag. She ignored it, trying to think of the most discreet way to reach her car two floors up.

A car engine rumbled nearby. It was the growl of a big SUV—a familiar SUV that slowed as it neared her. Dempsey's Land Rover, although it had probably never been operated by the owner himself.

Evan, his driver, lowered the tinted passenger window. He could have passed for a gangster with his shaved head, heavily inked chest and arms and frightening number of face piercings; his appearance gave Evan an added advantage in his dual role serving as personal security for their boss.

"Miss Adelaide," he said, even though she'd told him a half dozen times it made her feel like a kindergarten teacher when he called her that. "Do you need a ride?"

"Thanks, Evan," she huffed, out of breath more from runaway emotions than the mad dash out of the dome. "My car is on the C level, if you don't mind bringing me up there."

Relief washed through her as she limped over to the side of the vehicle. Before she could get there, Evan jumped out the passenger side and jogged around to help her, all two hundred sixty-four pounds of him. Before he blew out a knee, he'd been a top prospect on the Hurricanes' player roster, one she knew by heart.

She'd worked so hard to impress Dempsey over the years, memorizing endless facts and organizing mountains of information to help him with his job.

Only to be rewarded like this—by having him ignore her notice of resignation, refuse to discuss her concerns and announce a fake engagement to the very industry whose respect her future work depended upon.

"No problem." Evan tugged open the door and gave her a hand up into the passenger area of the vehicle specially modified to be chauffeur driven, complete with privacy screen. "Happy to help."

She waited for his knowing grin, certain he'd been listening to the press conference in the garage, but his face gave nothing away, eyes hidden behind a pair of aviator shades.

"I appreciate it." She tried to smile even though her voice sounded shaky. "I parked on the west side today. Close to the elevators."

Ticket holders had cleared out after the game, leaving the lot mostly empty now, save for a few hardcore fans that stuck around for autographs. The press parking area was separate, three floors up.

"Got it." Evan shut the door with a nod and she settled into the perforated leather seats. The bespoke interior was detailed with mother-of-pearl and outfitted with multiple viewing screens that Dempsey used to watch everything from game film to feeds from foreign stock exchanges to keep up with the Reynauds' family shipping business in the global markets.

Sadly, she knew the stats of most of the ships, too.

Her phone continued to vibrate in her bag, a hum against her hip where her purse rested, a reminder that her life had just fallen apart. Squeezing her eyes shut, she felt the Land Rover glide into motion and wished she could seize the wheel and simply keep driving far, far away from here. As if there was anywhere out of reach of the Reynauds, she thought bitterly.

Out of habit, she touched her right hand to the bracelet on her left wrist to feel the smooth metal that Dempsey had heated and shaped into a special present for Adelaide's twelfth birthday. The jewelry was worth far more than any of the identical diamond parting gifts he'd doled out to lovers over the years. Maybe she'd been foolish to see so much meaning in those years they'd spent together when his life had gone on to change so radically. She'd always thought she would do anything for him.

But not at this price. Not when he stopped being her friend and started thinking he was the boss of every aspect of her life. He couldn't dictate her career moves.

Or her choice of fiancé, for crying out loud. The funny part was, there had been a time in her life when she would have traded anything to hear him announce their engagement. But she'd grown up since the days she'd harbored those schoolgirl hopes. Once his father's limo had arrived to take him out of her world and into the rarefied air of the Reynaud family compound in Metairie, things had never been quite the same between them. Sure, he'd checked up on her now and then when the family was in Louisiana and not one of their other homes around the globe. Yet he always seemed acutely aware of the expectations of his family, and they did not include hanging out with a girl from the old neighborhood. For that matter, Dempsey had put all his considerable drive into becoming a true family heir, increasing his workload at school and throughout college. Eventually, he'd dated women in his same social circles, and Adelaide had remained just a friend.

Peering out the dark tinted windows, she noticed that Evan had exited onto the wrong floor of the parking garage. She reached for the communications panel to buzz him even as the SUV slowed by the east side elevators a floor below where she needed to be.

"Evan?" she said aloud when he didn't answer right away. "Can you hear me?"

"Yes, Miss Adelaide?" His voice sounded different. Sheepish?

Maybe he knew he'd made a mistake.

"We're in the wrong spot—"

She stopped when the elevator doors opened. Dempsey strode out, a building security guard on either side of him.

"Sorry, ma'am. The boss called."

Of course Evan hadn't made a mistake. He'd come here to pick up the man who called all the shots. Or had he been sent downstairs earlier to retrieve her? Either way, she was screwed. Her escape plan was over before she'd even gotten it off the ground.

At almost the same time, the stairwell door opened and a small throng of reporters raced out, camera lights

spearing into the parking garage gloom as they shouted
Dempsey's name and called out follow-up questions
he must not have addressed in the televised press conference.

"Coach Reynaud, have you set a wedding date?"

"How do you think this will affect your team?"

"How long have you been dating your assistant?"

The last question came from a thin woman who
reached him first, her voice recorder shoved toward
his face. One of the security guards warded her off
easily enough, opening the door of the Land Rover so
Dempsey could step up into the vehicle.

"Does Valentina know?" the skinny reporter shouted,
banging on the window of the SUV as Dempsey closed
the door and locked it behind him.

Adelaide scooted to the far end of the seat as he lowered himself beside her, the soft leather cushion shifting beneath her as the vehicle started into motion again.

"Hello, Adelaide." He made the greeting sound like
so much more than it was, his deep voice tripping along
her senses the way it sometimes did when he used her
whole name.

She hated that he could inspire those feelings even
now. It was as if he'd sucked all the air out of the small
space so she couldn't catch her breath. She watched
in silence as he tugged off his team jersey, tossing the
Hurricanes gear onto the opposite seat and leaving him
clad in a simple black silk T-shirt with his black pants.
He looked like a very hot hit man.

A hit man who'd targeted her business. Her future.
All for his own selfish ends.

"Can you call Evan and remind him my car is on
the C level?" She glared at him, reminding herself with

every breath not to get too emotional. Not to let all the anger fly, as much as she wanted to do just that.

She'd seen him in action for years, knew him well enough to understand that no one won battles with him by acting on feelings. Dempsey ran right over adversaries who couldn't negotiate with the benefit of cool reason.

"It might not be wise to drive when you're angry." He set aside his phone and stretched an arm along the back of the seat.

Almost touching her. Not quite.

Not the way he had back in that vacant office before the press conference when she'd inserted herself between him and the door. When she'd felt the warmth of his hand on her hip. Brushed up against him chest to chest in a moment that had almost caused cardiac arrest. She swallowed hard and refused to think about all that wayward attraction, which had always been one-sided.

"It might not be wise to kidnap the assistant you're dating either." She couldn't keep the bitterness out of her voice.

"We're not dating. We're engaged." He reached to tug a lock of her hair, as easily as if she still had pigtails. As if she would still follow him anywhere just because he said so. "I'll send someone back for your car later. It will be safer to stick together."

"Safer for who exactly?" She tried not to wrench away from him, would not let him see how much this cavalier treatment got under her skin. Even now, despite the anger inside, another heat simmered right along with it. "And who made you lord of what I can and can't do? Turn the damn car around."

Being trapped beside his powerful presence in the

back of a private luxury vehicle only stirred to life those other potent feelings she'd tried so hard to stamp out long ago.

"I don't think either of us wants to create a firestorm around the team right now," he reminded her.

"Seriously? Which is why you chose to announce an engagement to the press when you knew I couldn't contradict you." She clenched her fingers tight and contained her temper as Evan drove the SUV out of the parking garage and into the early-evening traffic heading west, away from her home.

Toward the Reynauds' private compound in Metairie. She didn't need to ask where they were headed, any more than Evan needed to ask. The world simply moved according to Dempsey's wishes.

"I realize you think I did this just for me. For the team. But I did it for you, too." His golden-brown eyes remained on her even when the viewing screens built into the overhead console flipped to life with game updates from around the league.

Being the focus of his undivided attention had the power to rattle any woman.

"We've been friends for too long for you to trot out that kind of BS with me." She folded her arms tight across her chest, her body reacting all kinds of erratically around him today. "Can we at least be honest with each other?"

"I am being honest." He shifted in his seat, turning toward her. Moving closer. "Adelaide, I don't want to see you fail at anything. Ever. And I promise you, if you stick this out with me—just this one more season—I will ensure that your company gets off the ground with all the benefits of my connections."

It was a lot to promise her. Worth a heck of a lot more than those diamond bracelets he passed out like consolation prizes.

"I don't want a company that is a glorified Reynaud hand-off. I want the satisfaction of developing it myself." There had been a time when he would have understood that. "Don't you remember what it feels like to want to build something that is all your own? Without the benefit of—" she waved her arm to encompass his custom-detailed world in a vehicle that cost more than most people's homes "—all this?"

His phone rang before he could answer her. And worse? He held up a hand to indicate that he needed to take it.

"Reynaud," he growled into the device.

Tuning him out, she fumed beside him. This was precisely why she needed to leave. She understood that he worked eighteen-hour days every day and that he took his business concerns as seriously as his team. But it had been too many years since he'd even pretended to make time for her or the friendship they'd once shared. He spoke to her as his assistant, not like the girl who had once been privy to all his secrets.

He had no idea about the strides she'd made in her business over the past few weeks—the way she'd pulled off funding for a short run of her first clothing item. He hadn't been there to applaud her unique efforts or otherwise acknowledge anything she did, and she was sick of it. Sick of his whole world that could never pause for one moment. Even for the conversation they'd been having.

By the time Dempsey disconnected his call, she could barely hold on to her temper.

Enough was enough.

* * *

Setting aside his phone after clearing up some problems in Singapore, where it was already Monday morning, Dempsey hoped the time-out from the confrontation with Adelaide had helped her to cool off and see his side. She sure had backed him into a corner by quitting out of the blue.

What else was he supposed to have done when she'd forced his hand like that? The engagement was simply a countermove.

"Adelaide," he began again, only to have her swing around in the seat to glower at him.

"How kind of you to remember we were in the middle of a conversation." Her clipped words suggested her temper wasn't anywhere close to cooling down. "Do you need a refresher on what we were discussing? One, our ridiculous engagement." She ticked off items on her fingers. "Two, your sneak attack of having Evan lying in wait for me in the garage so I couldn't make a clean break from the stadium today. Three, your inability to understand why I want to build my own company from the ground up, without the almighty Reynaud name behind me—"

"How can you, of all people, suggest I don't understand what it's like to want to develop your own company? To build your own team?" His voice hit a rough note even as his volume went softer. "You know why I went into coaching. Why it means everything to me to win a championship for this town."

He remembered shared rides home that weren't in the back of a Land Rover. Shared rides in a cramped bus full of bigger, stronger kids who amped up their street cred by converting new gang members or beating the living crap out of nonconverts. Of course he knew. He was giving back with his foundation. Constructing a positive environment with the Hurricanes for a community that needed an identity. Creating a team to root for that wore football jerseys instead of gang colors.

Adelaide didn't answer, though. She stared at him with a stony expression. He didn't have a clue what she was thinking. When had he lost the ability to read her? His gaze dipped to her mouth, set in a stubborn line. He read that well enough. Although, after that brush up against her before the press conference, he suddenly found himself wondering what she'd taste like. He hadn't let himself think along those lines in years, always protecting their long-standing friendship. Something had gone haywire inside him after he'd touched her today. He couldn't write it off as passing awareness of her as a woman, the way he had a few times as a teen. This attraction had been fierce, making him question if he'd ever be able to see her as just a friend again. It rattled him. He'd grown to rely on her too much to have an affair go wrong.

And it would. Adelaide was not the kind of woman to have affairs, for one thing. For another? Dempsey only conducted relationships that came with an expiration date.

With an effort, he steered himself back to his point.

"I've got controlling shares in businesses around the globe," he reminded her as they got off I-10 and headed north toward Lake Pontchartrain. "But being CEO of this or vice president of that doesn't mean as much when it's handed to you. With coaching, it's different. I earned a spot in this league. I am putting my stamp on this team, and through it—this town. I'm creating that right now, with my own two hands."

He pulled his eyes away from her, needing a moment that wasn't filled with the distracting new view of her as more than just his friend. He did not want to think about Adelaide Thibodeaux's lips.

"You're right." She reached across the seat and touched his forearm. Squeezed lightly. "I'm upset about…a lot of things. But you deserve to be proud of your efforts with the team and with Brighter NOLA." Her hand fell away, briefly grazing his thigh.

Then she pulled back fast.

He wished he could will away his reaction just as quickly.

"I understand you're angry." Maybe that was the source of all this tension pinging back and forth. Passions were running high today between the team's loss, the start of the regular season and her trying to quit. "But let's hammer out a plan to get through it. You want to build your own business, fine. Just wait until after the season is over and I'll at least help you finance it. I can offer much better terms than the bank."

The moon hung low over the lake as the SUV wound around the side streets leading to the family's waterfront acreage. The lake was shallow here, requiring boat owners to install long docks to moor their watercraft. Dempsey couldn't recall the last time he'd taken a boat out, since all his time was devoted to football and business.

"That's very generous of you. But I can't stay a whole season." Briefly, she squeezed her temples between her thumb and forefingers. "I posted a design of my first shirt and won crowd funding for the production. I need to honor that commitment after my followers made it happen for me."

And he had missed that milestone, even if it was just enough capital for a small run of shirts and not the launch of an entire business. He admired that—how she'd started off things so conservatively that her potential buyers had bought the clothes before she'd even made them. She was smart. Savvy. All the more reason he needed her. He could help her with her business after she helped him solidify his.

"Congratulations, Addy. I didn't know about that. So give me four weeks." He did not want to compromise on this. But four weeks bought him more time to convince her to stay longer. To show her that she had a place with the team. "The deal still stands. I'll help you with the startup costs. You retain full control. But you will stay with me for another month to get the season underway."

"What about the engagement? What happens to that ridiculous fiction next month?"

"You can break it off for whatever reason you choose." He trusted her to be fair. He might not have been paying much attention to her for the past few years in his intense drive to lead his team, but he knew that much about her.

When the time came to "break up," she wouldn't drag him through a scandal the way Valentina had threatened. Especially since he and Adelaide would still be working together, because no way in hell was he losing her. Four weeks was a long time to win her over now that he understood how high the stakes were. A season like this might only come around once in a lifetime. If he didn't make the most of it and secure the champion-ship now, he might never get another shot.

"And until then? What will your family think of this sudden news? Will you at least tell them the truth so we don't have to pretend around them?" She bit her lip as they drove through the gates leading to the Reynaud family acreage along the lake.

She'd never seemed at ease here, not from the first time she'd set foot on the property for his high school graduation party and spent most of the time searching for shells on the shore.

The SUV rolled past the mammoth old Greek Re-vival house where Dempsey had spent his teen years, now occupied by his older brother, Gervais. Henri and Jean-Pierre split an eleven-thousand-square-foot Itali-anate the family acquired when they'd bought out a for-mer neighbor. Neither of them stayed with the family for long, since Henri and his wife had a house in the Garden District and Jean-Pierre spent the football sea-son in New York with his team.

Dempsey's place was slightly smaller. He'd specially commissioned the design to repeat the Greek Revival style of the main house, with four white columns in the front, and a double gallery overlooking the lake in back.

Evan parked the vehicle in front, but Dempsey didn't open the door. "My family doesn't need to know the truth about our relationship." He reached for her hand to reassure her, guessing she would be bothered by the lie. "It will be simpler if we keep the details private."

Her hand closed around his for a moment, as though it was a reflex. As though they were still friends. But damned if he didn't feel that spark of awareness again.

Whatever had happened between them back at the stadium was not going away.

"Your family won't believe it." She shook her head. "We've kept things strictly platonic for too long to feel… *that* way."

She withdrew her hand from his. Either he was really losing his touch with women, or they'd both been feeling "that way" today. Was it the first time it had happened for her, or had she thought about him romantically in the past?

It bothered him how much he wanted to know.

"It's none of their business." He didn't care what anyone thought. His brothers were too caught up in their own lives to pay much attention to Dempsey outside of his work with the Hurricanes. He'd been the black-sheep brother ever since their father had shown up with him in tow as a scrawny thirteen-year-old. "The engagement is important, since Valentina threatened to cause trouble for the Brighter NOLA fund-raiser by going to the media with some story about my nondisclosure agreements. The announcement of my marriage to you trumps her ploy ten times over. No one will care about her story, let alone believe it."

"Ah. How convenient." Adelaide wrenched her purse onto her lap and started digging through it. Finding a tube of lip balm, she uncapped it, twisted the clear shiny wand upward and slicked it over her mouth until her lips glistened.

His own mouth watered. Then he recalled her words.

"It is useful." He watched her smooth her dark hair behind her ears, the primping a sure sign of nerves. "The engagement helps me to keep you close and prevents Valentina from sabotaging something you and I worked hard to develop. That foundation is too important for her to derail our efforts."

"Well, I don't find it useful. Or convenient." Adelaide's eyes flashed a brighter jade than normal, her cheeks pink with a hint of temper. "I am not an actress. I can't make an engagement believable to your family when they've hardly noticed me in all the time we've known each other."

"We can address that."

"If you think I'm going to start tossing my hair—" she exaggerated some kind of feminine hair fluffing "—or slinking around your house in skintight gowns to convince anyone that I'm the kind of female who could capture your attention…"

"You think that's what I notice in a woman?" He couldn't say if he felt more amused at her attempt to toss her hair, or dismayed that she perceived him as shallow.

Her shrug spoke volumes.

"Your challenge could not be clearer if you'd thrown a red flag on the field." Something stirred inside him— something deeper than the earlier flashes of attraction.

A bone-deep need to prove her wrong. He was not a shallow man. He'd simply dated women who could go into a romantic relationship with eyes wide-open. He refused to give any woman false expectations.

"I'm not challenging you." She bit her lip again, her shiny gloss fading as her anxiety spiked. "Simply pointing out what has historically intrigued you about the fair sex. I won't be the only one who finds our decision to marry a total farce."

She reached for her door handle as if to end the conversation on that note.

He reached for her, bracketing her with his arms. Stopping her from exiting the vehicle.

"No one is going to doubt that you have my attention." The space around them seemed to shrink. He noticed she remained very, very still. "That much is going to be highly believable."

She swallowed hard.

"Do you believe me, Adelaide?" He wanted to hear her say it. Maybe because it had been a long time since someone had questioned his word. "Or shall I prove it?"

Her eyes searched his. Her lips parted. In disbelief? Or was she already thinking about the kiss that would put an end to all doubts?

"I believe you," she said softly, her lashes lowering as her gaze slid away from his.

He had no choice but to release her then, his argument won. He should be relieved, since he didn't want to give Adelaide false expectations of their relationship. But as they exited the SUV and headed into the house, he couldn't help a twinge of disappointment that she hadn't challenged him on that last point, too.

He'd been all too ready to prove that the attraction he felt for her was one hundred percent real.

Chapter 3

Everything about this day felt off-kilter to Adelaide as she followed Dempsey up the brick steps onto the sprawling veranda of his house. Fittingly, she limped up the steps in her broken heel, unable to find her footing around him.

He'd commissioned the home when he'd first taken the head-coaching job in New Orleans, though it hadn't been completed until last spring. As if the Reynaud family complex hadn't been impressive enough before, now Dempsey's stalwart white mansion echoed the strong columns of the main house where he'd grown up. His place, just under ten thousand square feet, was only slightly less intimidating than Gervais's historic residence on the hill that had been built in the same style two centuries prior. She could see the rooftop from here, although the live oaks gave the structures considerable privacy. It helped to have the billions from Reynaud Shipping at their disposal, though the generations-old wealth was one of many reasons Adelaide had always felt out of place here.

Today, she had even more reason to feel off her game.

From the erratic pounding of her heart to the all-over tingle of awareness that lingered after their talk in the back of the Land Rover, she felt too dazed to don her usual armor of professionalism. What had he been thinking to focus that kind of sensual attention on her? She'd been so breathless when he'd bracketed her between those powerful arms, his chest just inches from her own, that she hadn't been able to think straight. Hadn't been able to question why they needed to enact this crazy charade for his family that had always intimidated her.

She slipped off her unevenly heeled shoes at the door and walked barefoot into his house. Once she shook off this fog of attraction, she would talk sense into Dempsey and leave. She'd wanted a clean break from him, and now he'd changed the playing field between them so radically she didn't know what to expect. Should she put her product launch on hold? Or should she keep fighting to end her commitment to the Hurricanes? She needed to sort through it all without the added confusion of this new sensual spark between them.

"You might remember from the blueprints that there's an extra bedroom upstairs and one downstairs." He led her through the wide foyer past a grand staircase. He used an app on his phone, she realized, to switch on lights and lower blinds as they moved through the space. "Both have en suite facilities. I can send Evan to your place to pick up some things for you when he retrieves your car."

They paused in an expansive kitchen at the back of the house, connecting to a dining area with floor-to-ceiling French doors that opened onto the yard overlooking the lake. There was another set of French doors in the family room, also accessing the back gallery and lawn. It was a perfect place for entertaining, although she would be surprised if Dempsey had hosted many people here. She certainly hadn't been invited to any private parties at his home even though she'd helped choose any number of fixtures and had spoken with his contractors more often than he had.

But in all fairness, Dempsey had always spent the majority of his time on the road or at the office. She doubted he'd spent many nights here himself.

"The house is beautiful," she said finally. "You must be pleased with how it turned out. I know I looked at the plans with you when you first approved the blueprints, but seeing the real thing... Wow."

She shook her head as she took in the ceiling medallions around matching chandeliers that were either imported antiques or had been designed by a master craftsman. The natural-stone fireplace in the kitchen gave that space warmth even when it wasn't lit, while another fireplace in the family room had a hand-carved fleur-de-lis motif that matched the ceiling medallions.

"Thank you. I haven't spent much time here, but I'm happy with it. Why don't I order some food and we can hash out a plan for the next few weeks while we eat?" He set his phone on the maple butcher-block top of the kitchen island, one of the elements of the house she'd helped choose, along with the appliances.

But when she'd been comparing kitchen options on her tablet, she'd simultaneously been investigating a wide receiver's shoulder injury and a competing team's new blitz packages. No wonder she'd all but forgotten the details until now.

"Anything is fine." She wasn't in the mood to eat, her body still humming with awareness and a sensual hunger of a more unsettling kind after those heated few moments earlier.

Even in this giant house, Dempsey's magnetic pull remained as potent as if they were separated by inches and not feet. When he walked toward her, her breath caught. Her heart skipped one beat. Then two. It had been one thing to ignore her reaction to him when he'd always treated her as a friend. But now that he'd opened that door to a different kind of relationship, teasing her with hints of the possible chemistry they might have together...her whole being seemed to spark and simmer with the possibilities. That kind of distraction would not make figuring out her professional life any easier.

First she needed to strategize a method for dealing with him and this fake engagement, then find a way out of the house as soon as possible. She couldn't survive spending twenty-four hours a day with him, especially when she wasn't sure if he genuinely felt some kind of attraction, too, or if he'd always known about the feelings she thought she'd kept well hidden. Would he be so cruel as to use that attraction now to his advantage?

"Gervais has a full-time chef at his place now that Erika is having twins." He gestured in the general direction of the house on the hill where his older brother had settled his soon-to-be wife, a beautiful foreign princess who would fit right into the Reynaud family. "It's easy to have something sent over."

"I'm too wound up to eat." She shrugged. "I would make some tea, though." She peered around the kitchen, not seeing a kettle or any other signs of basic staples.

"Tea." He typed in something on his phone and shook his head. "I'll ask for a few things." He set the device aside. "Evan will bring it over in half an hour or so. I'll show you the rooms so you can choose one. You'll be safer from the press here. You have to know that my family's security rivals that of Fort Knox."

The very last thing she wanted to do was choose a bedroom in Dempsey's house, especially when her pulse fluttered so erratically just to be near him. It didn't matter to her body that she was angry with him and his high-handed move. Some fundamental part of their relationship had shifted today; a barrier that she'd thought was firm had caved. She felt raw from having that defense ripped away.

He stalked through the family room into the western wing of the house and pushed open the door of an expansive bedroom with carpet and walls in blues and grays, a king-size modern bed with a pristine white duvet and a white love seat in front of yet another fireplace, this one with a gray granite surround.

The en suite bath on the far end of the room had a stone bathtub the size of a kiddie pool, spotlighted with an overhead pendant lamp on a dim setting. Gray cabinets and white marble were understated accents to the dominant tub.

"You didn't take this one for your room? I thought you had chosen that tub especially for you," she asked over his shoulder, realizing as she said it that she'd al-

lowed herself to stand very close to him to better see
the whole space. If she leaned forward just a little, she
could rest her cheek against his back where broad shoulders tapered to a narrow waist.

It didn't help that she'd been thinking about him
lounging in that huge custom tub, muscles glistening.

"The view is better from the suite upstairs." He
turned to face her and it was all she could do not to scut-
tle backward. She did not need to have both Dempsey
and a bed in her field of vision. "I'll show you the bedroom near mine."

"No. I mean—there's no need." She would sleep
downstairs by herself if it meant they could end this
tour faster. "I can sleep here tonight."

She wasn't committing to spending any more time
than that in this house. One night was bad enough, but
she had too much to work out with him to leave just yet.

"Are you sure you'll be all right alone down here?"
He frowned. But then, he knew when they traveled she
preferred a room close to his. Her house had been broken into as a teenager—after he'd moved away from
her. And she felt jittery at night sometimes.

"I'm certain. Your family's security rivals Fort Knox.
Remember?" She nodded, knowing she wouldn't sleep
well under Dempsey's roof for entirely different reasons
than that long-ago robbery where she'd hidden under her
bed for half an hour after the thieves had left. "But you
mentioned discussing a plan for the next few weeks?"
She backed up a step now, out into the hallway away
from the warmth of his broad shoulders. "I'll rest easier
once we talk through this. Actually, if we can come up
with a plan, I'll say good-night and leave you to watch
your game film."

She knew his habits well. Understood how he spent most nights after a day on the field, watching the action on the big screen where he could replay mistakes over and over again, making notes for the next day's meetings so the team could begin implementing adjustments.

"Come upstairs first." He turned off the light and headed back toward the front of the house, where she remembered seeing the main staircase. "I want you to see my favorite part of this place."

Something in his voice—his eyes—made her curious. Maybe it was a hint of mischief, the same kind that had once led them into a haunted house, which turned out to be the coolest spot in their neighborhood after she got over being scared of the so-called voodoo curse on the place. Besides, she needed to see hints of her old friend—or even her boss—inside the very hot, very sexy male she kept seeing instead. So she focused on that "I dare you" light he'd had in his eyes as she padded up the dark mahogany stairs behind him, the two-story foyer a deep crimson all around them.

He'd come a long way from the apartment on St. Roch Avenue where he'd battled river rats as often as his mother's stream of live-in boyfriends, each one more of a substance abuser than the last. His mom had been a local beauty when she'd had an anonymous one-night stand with Dempsey's father after meeting at the restaurant where she'd waitressed. She hadn't read the papers enough to recognize Theo Reynaud, but when she'd seen him on television over a decade later, she'd remembered that one night and contacted him.

Adelaide hadn't been at all surprised when Dempsey's real father had shown up to claim him. She'd known as soon as she'd met Dempsey—way back when he'd saved her from a beat down in a cemetery where she'd gone to play—that he was destined for more than the Eighth Ward. In her fanciful moments, she'd imagined him as a prince and the pauper character like the fairy tale. He had the kind of noble spirit that his poor birth couldn't hide.

And even though she wanted to think she was destined for more than her tiny studio still a stone's throw from St. Roch Avenue, she was determined to make it happen because of her hard work and talents. Not because of all the wealth and might of Dempsey Reynaud.

"Through here." He waved her past the open door to another bedroom, the floor plan coming back to her now that she'd walked through the finished house. She recalled the two huge bedrooms upstairs and, down another hall, the in-law suite with a separate entrance accessible from outside above the three-car garage.

She didn't remember the den where he brought her now. But he didn't seem to be showing her the den so much as leading her through it to another doorway that opened onto the upstairs gallery. As he pushed open the door, moonlight spilled in, drawing her out onto the deep balcony with a woven mat on the painted wooden floor. A flame burst to life in the outdoor fireplace built into the exterior wall of the house, a feature he must have been controlling with the app on his phone. An outdoor couch and chairs surrounded the fireplace, but he led her past those to the railing, where he stopped. In front of them, Lake Pontchartrain shone like glass in the moonlight, a few trees swaying in a nighttime breeze making a soft swishing sound.

"I haven't spent much time here, but this is my favorite spot." He rested his phone and his elbows on the wooden railing, staring out over the water.

"If this was my house, I don't think I'd ever leave it."

There was so much to take in. Lights from Metairie and a few casino boats glittered at the water's edge. Long docks were visible like shadowy fingers reaching out into the lake, while the causeway spanned the water as far as she could see, disappearing to the north.

"I wish I had more free time to spend here, too." He turned to face her, his expression inscrutable in the moonlight. "But someone might as well make use of it. Move in for the next few weeks, Adelaide. Stay here."

Normally, Dempsey wouldn't have appreciated an interruption of a crucial conversation. But Evan's announcement of dinner had probably prevented another refusal from Adelaide, so he counted the disruption as a fortuitous break in the action.

Now they ate dinner in high-backed leather chairs in the den, watching highlights from around the league. They attempted to name the flavors in the naturalistic Nordic cuisine with ingredients specially flown in to appease Gervais's fiancée's pregnancy cravings. The white asparagus flavored with pine had been interesting, but Dempsey found himself reaching for the cayenne pepper to bring the flavor of Cajun country to the salmon. You could take the man out of the bayou, but apparently his palate stayed there. Dempsey's birth mother may have been hell on wheels, but before she'd spiraled downward from her addictions, she'd cooked like nobody's business.

"I can't believe you have Gervais's chef making meals like this for you." Adelaide took more asparagus, finding her appetite once she'd glimpsed the kind of food prepared by the culinary talent being underutilized by Gervais and his future wife. "That is another reason I could never live in this house. I'd weigh two tons if I could have dishes arrive at my doorstep with a phone call. What a far cry from takeout pizza."

"I think you're safe with asparagus." He'd always thought she'd eaten too little, even before he started training with athletes who calculated protein versus carb intake with scientific precision to maximize their workout goals.

His plan for dinner had been to keep things friendly. No more toying with the sexual tension in the air, in spite of how much that might tempt him. He needed Adelaide committed to his plan, not devising ways to escape him, so he would try to keep a lid on the attraction simmering between them.

For now.

If she moved into his house, he would spend more time here, too. He'd keep an eye on her over the next few weeks, solidify their friendship and learn to read her again. He'd taken her friendship for granted and he regretted that, but it wasn't too late to fix it. He'd find time to help her with her future business plans, all while convincing her to stick out the rest of the season.

"You don't understand." She pointed her fork at him. She'd put on one of his old Hurricanes T-shirts about six sizes too large for her, her dark hair twisted into a knot and held in place with a pencil she'd snagged off his desk. She still wore her black pencil skirt, but he could only see a thin strip of it beneath the shirt hem. "I peeked in the dessert containers while you were finding a shirt for me and I already gained twelve pounds just looking at the sweets. There is a crème brûlée in there that is…" She trailed off. "Indescribable."

"This you know just from looking?" He remembered how much she loved sweets. When they were growing up, he'd given her the annual candy bar he'd won each June for a year's worth of good grades. Now that he could have bought her her own Belgian chocolate house, though, he couldn't recall the last time he'd given her candy.

"I may have sampled some." She grinned unrepentantly. Then, as if she recalled whom she was talking to, her smile faded. "Dempsey, I can't stay here."

"Can't, or won't?"

"I've already told you that I don't want to pretend we are engaged in front of your family, and this puts me in close proximity to them every day," she reminded him. Then she pointed wordlessly to a screen showing a catch worthy of a highlight reel from one of the players they'd be facing in next Sunday's game. It was a play that he'd already heard about in the Hurricanes' locker room.

He admired how seamlessly Adelaide fit into his world. He'd had a tough time bridging the gap between life as a Reynaud and his underprivileged past, acting out as a teen and choosing to work his way up in the ranks as a coach rather than devote all his attention to the family business. But Adelaide never acted out.

Or at least, not until today.

"I saw that catch," he said, acknowledging her. "We'll definitely keep an eye on that receiver." Then, needing to focus on Adelaide, he shoved aside his empty plate. "But regarding staying in the house, you don't need to worry about my family. I will spend more time here, too, so I'll be the one to deal with any questions that come up."

"Can you afford to do that? I know you often sleep at the training facility."

The schedule during the season was insane. He was in meetings all day, every day. He talked to his defensive coordinator, his offensive coordinator, and addressed player concerns. And through it all, he watched film endlessly, studying other teams' plays and tailoring his game plan to best counter each week's opponent. Yet he couldn't regret that time, since it was finally going to pay off this year in the recognition he craved, not just for himself but for the people he'd brought up with him. People who had believed in him.

"You are important to me. I will make time."

He'd surprised her, he could tell. For the first time, he was seeing how much he'd let her down in recent years, focused solely on his own goals. His own friend was surprised to hear how valuable she was to him.

"That's kind of you, but I know you're busy." She frowned. "It's no trouble to simply enjoy the comfort of my own home."

He made an exaggerated effort to look around the room.

"Is this place lacking? Hell, Addy. Upgrade my sheets if they're not to your liking."

"I'm sure your sheets are fine." She set aside her plate and made a grab for her water, taking a long swallow.

He watched the narrow column of her throat and wondered how he'd ever look at her in a purely friendly way again. Just thinking about her under his sheets was enough to spike the temperature in the room. To distract himself from thoughts of her wrapped in Egyptian cotton, he stood, stalking around the table to sit on the ottoman right in front of her, turning his back on the game.

"But?" he prompted, an edge in his voice from the pent-up frustration of this day with her.

"But no matter how lovely your home is, I'd rather be close to my own things. I don't see the benefit of being here."

"The benefit is the complete privacy as well as safety, since the family compound is absolutely secure. No media gets through the front gate." He knew she valued privacy as much as he did. This angle would be more effective than telling her the truth—that he wanted her close at all times so that he would never miss an opportunity to push his agenda over the next four weeks. "You know as well as I do that public interest in our engagement will be high, especially after how thoroughly the press covered my split with Valentina."

"So I hide out here because of a manipulative exlover?" Her expression went stony. "I have business to conduct."

"Use my office," he offered, hitting the button to mute the sound on the television. "The facilities are excellent."

She frowned. "I do not like being put in this position."

He hoped that meant she was done arguing. He couldn't remember ever arguing with Adelaide before today—or at least not since she'd worked for him. "I don't like you leaving, but I'm trying to find a workable solution."

She opened her mouth to speak and then closed it again.

"What?" he prodded her, wanting to know what was going on in her head.

"I'm not looking forward to being in the public spotlight with you."

"You've been there a million times." He knew because he usually met her gaze a few times during his press conferences, her hazel eyes wordlessly communicating to him if he was staying on track or not.

"Not in a romantic way." She shook her head, a few tendrils of dark hair sliding loose from the haphazard knot she'd created. "We've got the Brighter NOLA fund-raiser coming up, and no matter what you say about how convincing I'll be as your fiancée, I definitely don't look the part."

"Because of all the hair tossing and slinky gowns." That comment of hers still burned. He didn't care for that view of himself. "I believe we've covered that. And if you're correct that I've become too predictable in my dating choices, I'm glad for the chance to shake up public perceptions."

"I didn't mean to suggest you only dated women for their looks." She bit her lip. "The sad truth of the matter is a far more practical concern. I have the wardrobe of an assistant. Not a fiancée."

He tried to hide his grin and failed. "So you're saying we actually need the slinky gowns to pull this off?"

"You don't have to look so damn smug about it," she fired back, making him realize how much he'd missed their friendship.

He held up both hands to show his surrender. "No smugness intended. But I sure don't have time to dress shop this week, Addy, what with our first opponent being the defending National Conference champions and all."

"Wiseass," she chided, shaking her head so that the

pencil holding the knot in her hair slipped. She reached up to grab it as the dark mass fell around her shoulders.

He'd seen that move before in private moments with her. Never had it made his mouth water. Or kicked his lust into a full-throttle roar.

Some of what he was feeling must have shown on his face because the hint of a smile she'd been wearing suddenly fled. Pupils dilating, she stood up fast, letting go of her hair and setting aside the pencil.

"I'll figure something out." She stared down at him, her face bathed in the blue glow from the television playing silently in the background, her delicate curves visible through the thin fabric of his too-big T-shirt. "With the wardrobe and with my business. I'll use your office and stay here. It's just for four weeks anyway."

She'd just conceded to everything he'd been angling for, but the reminder of the four-week time limit on their arrangement sure stole any sense of victory he might have felt. Slowly, he got to his feet before she bolted.

"Thank you." He wanted to seal the deal with a handshake. A kiss. A night in his bed. But putting his hands on her now might shatter the tenuous agreement they'd come to in the past few hours.

She deserved so much better from him.

She nodded, the big T-shirt slipping off one shoulder to reveal her golden skin. "I'm going to let you watch your film now."

Edging back a step, she moved away from him, and it took all his willpower not to haul her back.

"For whatever it's worth—I'm proud to call you my fiancée. To my family, the media. The whole damn world." He thought she deserved to know that much.

Today had shown him that he'd taken her friendship for granted too often.

He hadn't paid attention to her—really paid attention—in far too long.

He paid attention now, though. Enough to see the mix of emotions he couldn't read cross her face in quick succession.

"Good night," she said softly, her cheeks pink with confusion.

Watching her retreat, Dempsey turned on the television even as he knew the game film wasn't going to come close to holding his attention the way Adelaide did.

Chapter 4

"Sweetheart, stop fidgeting," Adelaide's mother rebuked her, a mouthful of pins muffling the words.

"I'm just nervous." Adelaide stood on a worn vinyl hassock in the one-bedroom apartment on St. Roch Avenue where she'd grown up.

With less than an hour before her first official public appearance with Dempsey, she had realized the gown she'd chosen for the Brighter NOLA foundation fundraiser was too long despite her four-and-a-half-inch heels. She could have phoned the exclusive shop where Dempsey had given her carte blanche, but the price tag had nearly given her heart failure the first time around. She couldn't bring herself to request an emergency tailor visit simply because she'd forgotten her shoes the day she'd chosen the dress.

So instead, she brought the pink lace designer confection to her mother's apartment for a last-minute fix. And perhaps she also craved seeing her mom when she was incredibly nervous. She hadn't been home since her "engagement" had become front-page news in the New Orleans paper and she hated that she couldn't confide the truth to her mother. But she could at least soak up some of her mom's love while she got the hem adjusted—with Evan waiting for her out front in the Land Rover.

"Addy." Her mother straightened, tugging the pins out of her mouth and setting them in the upside-down top of the plastic candy dish on the coffee table. "You're engaged to one of the richest, most powerful men in the state. You could have a dozen seamstresses fixing this gorgeous dress instead of your half-blind mama. You know better than to trust a woman who needs bifocals to do this job."

Guilt pinched Adelaide more than her silver-and-pink stilettos.

"You're not half-blind," she argued, leaning down to kiss her mother's cheek and breathing in the scent of lemon verbena. "And you could sew stitches around anyone working on Magazine Street. But I'm sorry to foist off the job on you last minute. I just missed you and I didn't want a snippy tailor frowning at my choice of shoes or thinking how my breasts don't suit the elegant lines of the gown."

Her mother gave her a narrow look. Taller than Adelaide, her mother was a commanding woman who had worked hard to raise Adelaide after her father died in a boating accident when she was just a toddler. Della Thibodeaux had given Adelaide her backbone, but there were days when Addy wished she'd gotten more of that particular trait. Her creativity and her dreamy nature were qualities she'd inherited from her father, apparently. But it was her mother's unflinching work ethic that had helped Adelaide excel at being Dempsey's assistant.

"Bite your tongue," Della said. "How will you survive your future mother-in-law if you can't put an uppity dress-shop girl in her place?"

"I know. I'm being ridiculous." She blinked fast, trying to control her emotions. It had been a crazy week fulfilling her duties as Dempsey's assistant while maintaining her commitments to her new business. And now she had a role to play as his fiancée, all the while fighting off waves of nostalgia for what she'd felt for him in the past. "Living the Reynaud life with Dempsey has put my emotions on a roller-coaster ride. I'm not used to the way the Reynauds can just…order the world to their liking."

From personal chefs to chauffeurs, there was no service that wasn't available to Dempsey around the clock. And now to her, too. While she'd witnessed that degree of luxury from a business standpoint for years, she hadn't really appreciated the way there were no limits in his personal life. He'd offered to have designers send samples from Paris for tonight's gown, for crying out loud.

And the ring he'd ordered for her… She'd nearly fainted when she'd opened the package hand delivered by a courier who'd arrived at the house with a security escort earlier in the day. The massive yellow diamond surrounded by smaller white ones had literally taken her breath away.

Between the ring—temporarily stashed in her purse,

since it seemed over-the-top for her mother's house—
and the dress, she'd started to understand how closely
scrutinized she would be as Dempsey's fiancée. It increased the pressure for tonight tenfold.

"My sweet girl." Her mom spared a moment to put
a hand to Adelaide's cheek. "If you *are* emotional, is
there any chance you could be pregnant?"

"Mom!" Embarrassed, she fluffed the hem to see how
the length was coming. "There is no chance of that."

Her mom studied her for an extra second before
bending to her task again. Della took up the needle and
continued to make long stitches to anchor the hemline.

"Well, you must admit the engagement came a bit
out of the blue. People are bound to talk." Her mother
straightened, still wearing purple scrubs from her shift
at the hospital where she'd worked for as long as Adelaide could remember.

She hadn't thought about that. "Well, it's not true,
and the world will know soon enough when I don't start
showing. I just want tonight to go well." She kicked
out the sagging hem of her gorgeous dress. "I feel as
if I'm off to a bad start already since I lost time to do
my makeup and my hair when I realized I had a wardrobe malfunction."

Her mother frowned. "Addy, you just got engaged.
You should be glowing with joy, not running to your
mother and fretting about your makeup. Are you going
to tell me what's wrong?"

Closing her eyes, she realized her mistake in coming
here. Her mother didn't suffer fools lightly. And Adelaide was taking the most foolish risk of her life to put
herself in close proximity to Dempsey every day and
night. What if her old crush on him returned?

Actually…what if it already had? Remembering the way her thoughts short-circuited whenever they had spent time alone together this week, she had to wonder.

"You know I've always liked Dempsey," she began, unwilling to lie to her mother.

She could at least confide a little piece of her heart to the woman who knew her best.

"I would have to have been blind not to see the adoration in your face from the time you were a girl." Her mother went back to sewing, taking a seat on the chair next to the hassock. "Yes, honey. I recall you've always liked him."

"Well, his proposal caught me by surprise," she admitted, her gaze rising over the sofa and settling on the wooden shelves containing her mother's treasures— photos of Adelaide, mostly. "And I want to be sure—" she cleared her throat "—that he asked me to marry him for the right reasons. I don't want to just be convenient."

Her mother paused and then resumed her sewing. Adelaide waited for her mom's verdict, all the while focusing on a chipped pink teacup Adelaide had painted for her for Mother's Day in grade school.

"Damn straight you don't," her mother said finally. "That boy's whole life has been *convenient* ever since he was whisked out of town in a limo." She knotted the thread once. Twice. And snapped it off. "Maybe you should ruffle his feathers a little? Catch *him* by surprise."

"You think so?" Adelaide worried her lip, remembering she'd better start her makeup if she didn't want to be late.

Evan had made her promise she'd be finished in time to meet Dempsey outside the event promptly at 7:00 p.m.

so they could walk in together. A shiver of nerves—and undeniable excitement—raced up her spine.

"Honey, I know so." Her mother held out a hand to help Adelaide down to the floor. "You've made yourself very available to that man—"

"He's my boss," she reminded her.

"Even so." She shook her finger in Adelaide's face. "He's not going to be the boss in the marriage, is he? No. Marriage should be a partnership. So don't let him think you're going to be the same woman as a bride that you are as his assistant."

Easy enough advice if her engagement were real. But for the next few weeks, she was still more an employee than a fiancée. Then again, he had looked at her with decided heat in his eyes ever since that accidental touch in the stadium last weekend. And truth be told, it stung that he thought he could boss her into an engagement when they were supposed to be friends.

"Maybe I will surprise him." She picked up her makeup and went to work on her eyes, hoping to look more like an exotic beauty and less like an efficient, capable assistant.

Mascara helped. Besides, she'd gone to art school. If she couldn't create a good smoky eye, she ought to turn in her degree.

"No maybe about it." Her mother went to work on Adelaide's hair, her fingers brushing through the long caramel-colored strands. "This dress is a good start." She winked at Adelaide's reflection in the hallway mirror. "You don't look like anyone's assistant tonight."

"How close are you?" Dempsey shifted the phone against his ear as his hired driver pulled up to the venue in Jackson Square.

He'd left the Land Rover and Evan with Adelaide this week, trusting his regular driver to keep her safe. By safe, Dempsey had meant keeping reporters away. He'd never imagined his temporary fiancée would have a sudden desire to visit the old neighborhood.

A tic started behind his eye as he thought about her there without him. She'd moved to an apartment closer to the French Quarter after college, but her mom had never left the place on St. Roch. Even Dempsey's mother had found greener pastures nearer the lake.

But then, his mother had the financial cushion of whatever his father had paid her to keep clear of Dempsey.

"Two minutes, max," Evan assured him. "I'm right behind the building, just crawling with the traffic."

"I'll walk toward you." Dempsey exited the vehicle close to Muriel's, the historic restaurant chosen for the event. Then he sent the driver on his way.

He would have preferred to pick up Adelaide personally tonight, but practice had run long and the meetings afterward had been longer still. There was unrest among some of the younger guys on the offensive line, but Dempsey was leaving the peacekeeping to his brother Henri, their starting quarterback. Henri had mastered the art of letting things roll off him, which was key for a player who operated under a microscope every week.

But the same quality could tick off other guys in the locker room, the players who took every setback like a personal affront, the athletes who were competitive to the point of obsessive. The media loved to key in on crap like that.

And with the press hinting at marital trouble in Henri's private life, the team's front man wasn't exactly feeling friendly toward the local sports journalists. Dempsey just hoped he would get through the fund-raiser tonight. No matter what was going on in Henri's personal world, he trusted the guy to lead them to a win Sunday.

"I see you." Evan's voice in his ear brought him back to the present, where he damn well needed to stay. "I'm going to pull right up to the curb for the sake of Miss Adelaide's shoes."

Looking up the street, Dempsey spied the Land Rover headed his way. He pocketed the phone and moved toward the red carpet that had been laid on the sidewalk. Players were already arriving along with prominent local politicians, artists and philanthropists. A lone trumpeter in a white suit serenaded the guests on their way into the Jackson Square landmark venue.

A staffer from the Brighter NOLA foundation hurried toward Dempsey to pin a flower to his jacket and update him on the guest list so far. He thanked her and waved the woman off as the Land Rover arrived in front of the carpet.

He didn't care about protocol, so he didn't wait for Evan to open Adelaide's door. Dempsey tugged open the handle himself and extended a hand to…

Wow.

All thoughts of guests, players and philanthropy vanished at the sight of Adelaide. She wore a pink dress that might possibly be described as "lace," but it was a far cry from a granny's doily. Beaded and shimmering, the gown hugged her curves all over. It wasn't low cut. It was long-sleeved and it fell to her toes. Yet the lace effect made strategic portions of her honey-toned skin visible right through the rosy-toned mesh. Her thighs, for example. The indentations above her hips.

Intellectually, he'd always known she was an attractive woman. Of course he had. He wasn't blind. But maybe her workday wardrobe had helped minimize an appeal that damn near staggered him now. With an effort, he dragged his attention away from her body to meet her gaze.

Only to find a simmering heat there that matched his own.

This engagement charade of his was feeling far too real. And if he wasn't careful, he would end up following that heat where it led and hurting Adelaide in the process. That was the last thing he wanted.

The very last thing he could afford.

"You look beautiful." He tugged her closer, wrapping an arm around her waist to escort her inside.

She smelled fantastic. Like night-blooming roses. Her hair was gathered at the back of her head, some of it coiled and braided, with strands left loose to curl around her face. She wore her waist-length hair up most days, wound into a simple knot. The soft curls trailing to the middle of her back made him wonder when was the last time he'd seen her with her hair let down.

"Thank you." She kept a tight hold on a beaded pink purse, the engagement ring he'd produced for her glinting on her left hand. "And thank you for the ring," she added softly, for his ears only as they walked toward the entrance behind slow-moving attendees meeting and greeting one another. "I've never seen anything so gorgeous."

He'd ordered it immediately after announcing the engagement to ensure the custom design would be crafted in time for tonight's party. He hated that he'd had to have it shipped to her at the house instead of giving it to her in person, however.

Then again, with their roles feeling a little too real, it was probably for the best he hadn't personally slipped that big yellow diamond onto her finger.

"Adelaide!" someone on the street called out to her, and she halted. Turned.

A camera flash popped nearby as a woman snapped a photo of them.

"Are you aware that Valentina Rushnaya will be attending tonight's event?" the photographer shouted over the trumpet music and din of nearby conversation.

Dempsey tensed, ready to respond. Addy beat him to it.

"How kind of her to support a Brighter NOLA future." Adelaide smiled as she lifted a hand to his chest and tipped her head to his shoulder as if they were a couple in love.

Was she simply posing for another photo? Or showing off the ring?

He followed her lead, kissing the top of her head possessively before ushering her toward the door.

"Nicely done." He wished he could pull her into a dark corner and talk to her. Make sure she was solid going into this event if Valentina truly put in an appearance. But there was no time now as people were already headed their way. "Let's stick together for the first half hour."

"Of course." She smiled her public smile, already waving to one of their biggest donors. "But you're dancing with me tonight," she warned him. "It's the perk of being your fiancée."

Normally, Dempsey worked the floor of a fund-raiser

with precision, glad-handing the necessary parties and then leaving, never giving in to Adelaide's invitations to stay longer and have fun. But this was his foundation and he was here for the long haul.

"The perk is all mine." The words fell out of his mouth before they were surrounded by well-wishers, potential patrons and community bigwigs.

Dempsey noticed Adelaide went into work mode as quickly as he did, but his focus was nowhere near his usual level. Even as he made conversation, his thoughts went back to those moments on the red carpet with Adelaide. The way she'd looked when she stepped from the Land Rover and every soul in Jackson Square had let out a collective breath. The way she'd curled against him when that photographer wanted a picture, as though she'd been born to be in his arms.

The idea bothered him.

There was no doubt in his mind that Adelaide looked different tonight, from how she wore her hair to that dress of hers that was killing him. And as the night wore on, he couldn't take his eyes off her. He wondered who she was talking to and if they noticed that she looked like a walking fantasy. Part of him wanted confirmation that something about her had changed, but another part of him wanted to make sure every other man in the building wasn't looking at her, because he didn't want anyone else thinking about her thighs.

Maybe he really had been blind all those years they'd just been friends.

Two hours into the event, the night seemed to be running smoothly enough. Casino tables had opened around the rooms blocked off for the party. The red walls and decadent furnishings of Muriel's legendary

Séance Lounge made an appealing backdrop for black-jack as the crowd loosened up. The gaming was strictly to raise money for Brighter NOLA. It was so packed that guests stood out on the balconies in the heat, snapping photos of themselves with Jackson Square in the background. The dance floor was filled and the band—as always in this town—sounded fantastic.

He was about to seek out Adelaide when a feminine voice purred in his right ear.

"My lone wolf looks on edge tonight." The low tone and soft consonants of Valentina's Russian accent made him tense.

Turning, he avoided her attempt to kiss his cheek.

"If I'm on edge, it's only because you've taken up the valuable time of my staff with empty threats and games." He gave her a level look, noting that her barely there silver gown was completely over-the-top for a charity event that raised funds for underprivileged and at-risk youths.

"Your staff? Or your fiancée?" She tossed her head in a dismissive gesture meant to be insulting.

Dempsey had to smother a mirthless laugh because—damn it to hell—Adelaide had been correct about him dating theatrical women in slinky gowns. When had he become such a cliché?

"Both." He was grateful they stood in the shadows, since he didn't need photos of them together showing up in the paper. "And I trust the only reason you're here is to write a big, fat check to the foundation, since we specifically agreed to go our separate ways."

"Agreed? There was no agreement!" She pulled a glass of champagne off a passing waiter's tray and helped herself to a long sip. "You dictated every detail of our time together, and then disappeared before my bed even had time to cool down—"

"Ms. Rushnaya, how beautiful you look." Adelaide appeared at his side, slipping an arm through his. "I'm so sorry to interrupt, but, Dempsey, we did promise a quick word with the representative from *Town and Country* before they leave."

She nodded meaningfully toward the other side of the room.

"Of course." He had always counted on Addy for well-timed interruptions, and she delivered yet again. Still, he didn't like that she'd overheard the bit about running out of Valentina's bed. He didn't treat women that way. "Please excuse us."

"Yes, do take your turn with *Town and Country*." Valentina emptied her glass and set it on a nearby table, her movements unsteady. "I have my own press to speak with, Dempsey."

She turned on her heel to march away, right toward a woman who had a camera aimed at them. Again.

"Dempsey." Adelaide laid her hand on his cheek and turned his face toward her, commanding his attention before the camera flashed. "There isn't actually an interview," she confided. "I was just trying to give you some breathing room."

The look in her hazel eyes stole all his focus. Or maybe it was the gentle press of her breasts as she arched closer.

"Thank you." How many times had she served as a buffer for him with the media or with football insiders he didn't particularly like? She ran interference like a pro.

"Dance with me?" she asked, a hint of uncertainty in her gaze.

Had he put that vulnerability there? He hadn't spent much time with her this evening, handling the room with the same "divide and conquer" approach they'd used in the past at events he'd needed to attend. But tonight was different. Or at least, it should be. If he'd had Adelaide by his side earlier, Valentina might not have tried to ambush him in a dark corner.

"With pleasure." He lifted Adelaide's hand to his mouth and brushed a kiss along her knuckles. Her skin smelled like roses.

He'd done it to reassure her that he wanted to be with her. To thank her for sending Valentina on her way.

At least, the kiss started out with good intentions. But as the slow blues tune hit a long, sultry note, Dempsey couldn't seem to let her go. Adelaide was getting under his skin tonight, and it wasn't just that damnable dress. So he flipped her hand over and placed a kiss in her palm, where he felt her pulse flutter under his lips. Which made him think about all the other ways he could send her heart racing. All the pulse points he could cover with his mouth. In turn, his own heart slugged harder inside his chest.

Every damn thing got harder.

"My song will be over by the time we get out there," she whispered, though she didn't sound terribly disappointed.

Her pupils dilated so wide there was just a hint of color around the edges.

"It's less crowded right here." He wanted her to himself, he realized. Craved her, in fact. "Plenty of room to dance."

"Really?" She peered around them. "I guess it's the kind of thing an engaged couple would do."

"Exactly." He pulled her into his arms, fitting her curves against him, close enough to catch her scent, but not nearly as close as he'd like. "No sense letting anyone think Valentina caused any drama."

At the mention of the woman's name, Addy's gaze dropped. He cursed himself for being an idiot as he backed them closer to the open doors leading out to the balcony.

"Is that what this whole charade is about?" she asked when she looked up at him again. "Have I been promoted to your round-the-clock protection from the she-wolves of the world?"

She couldn't be jealous. Yet the thought nearly made him miss a step.

"No." He lowered his voice, knowing how the walls had ears at events like this. "You and I have a whole lot more at stake between us and I think you know it."

"If there's more at stake, you might want to up your game while we're in public, since newly engaged men don't tend to prowl the perimeters of parties alone." She practically vibrated in his arms as he drew her out onto the balcony and into the farthest deserted corner.

He couldn't remember the last time she'd spoken to him with so much fire in her eyes.

"You're jealous." He tested the idea by saying it out loud as he studied her in the moonlight. The song came to an end.

He didn't let go of her.

"And you're *mine* for four weeks, Dempsey Reynaud." She tipped her chin up at him. "I suggest you act like it if you want to pull off this ruse of your own making."

Heat rushed up his spine in a molten blast. The need to offer her what she'd asked for made him grip her tighter, pulling her hip to hip, chest to breasts.

And if that was a little too much PDA for a charity event, too damn bad. It wasn't anywhere near enough for what he wanted to do with her. She felt even better up close than he'd imagined, and his head had been full of inventive scenarios all week.

"Careful what you wish for, Addy," he warned her, grateful for the night shadows that kept them hidden.

He'd been a gentleman for her sake. At least now she would know exactly how much he was feeling like her fiancé. Her hips cradled the hard length he couldn't begin to hide.

And that was when things got crazy. Because instead of storming off like his affronted best friend, Adelaide gripped the lapels of his tuxedo and pressed a kiss to his lips.

Chapter 5

Adelaide saw stars.

Clutching Dempsey's jacket, she fulfilled a secret dream as her lips brushed along his. They stood under the night sky, his back shielding her from view. Behind her, the iron bars of the balcony pressed against her spine. In front of her, warm male muscle was equally unyielding but oh-so-enticing.

She'd seen a chance to surprise him—just as her mother had suggested—and she'd taken it. She knew better than to think this fake engagement was going anywhere. But she could use this time to indulge herself and her long-standing fantasies about Dempsey. Because in less than four weeks, things were going to change between them forever when she left her job with the Hurricanes.

Her senses reeling, she broke the kiss, needing to

put some distance between them. He didn't move far
from her, though. It took another long moment before
he released her.

"Let's go," he urged, threading his fingers through
hers and claiming a hand.

Blinking through the fog of desire, Adelaide followed him, her steps smaller and quicker by necessity
due to the fitted gown. Her lips tingled pleasantly, her
nerve endings humming with awareness of the man
beside her.

"Are you sure we should leave?" She glanced around
the private rooms at the full dance floor, the crammed
gaming tables, the busy bar stations. "As hosts of the
event—"

"We've done our part," he assured her. "The event
planner will take it from here. And I'm dying to get
you alone."

To explore what she'd started? She hadn't missed
the indication of attraction when she'd been pressed up
against him. But she couldn't afford to trade her heart
for a night in his bed, and she knew herself well enough
to know that was a very real possibility. Her feelings for
Dempsey had always been strong. Complicated. And
this engagement wasn't exactly simplifying matters.

"I didn't mean to send mixed signals." She hated to
have this conversation here, in a quiet corridor as they
waited for an elevator. But it was too important to wait.
"I got caught up in the moment—" She bit her lip to
refrain from telling him about her mother's suggestion
that she surprise him.

She'd taken the gamble, but she wasn't sure she was
ready for the payout he had in mind.

"Will you promise me something?" His eyes searched

hers, as if he could see straight through to her heart. "Will you think about how rewarding it could be to get caught up in another moment? Not tonight, maybe. But we've got a lot of days to spend together and I think there's something worth exploring in that kiss."

Her heart did a little flip that made her feel woozy and breathless at the same time. She settled for a nod, unable to articulate an answer just now.

He pressed a button for the elevator and stepped into the cabin behind her when it arrived. His grandfather, family patriarch Leon Reynaud, stood against one wall inside the elevator. Adelaide didn't know him well, but he attended all of the Hurricanes home games and she'd seen him in the owner's suite on the fifty-yard line a few times.

He'd been a big man in another era, playing football and becoming a successful team owner of a Texas franchise until he'd sold it to be closer to his grandsons in Louisiana. But the years had bowed his back and he'd grown much thinner. Dempsey had told her once that Leon had never considered himself a good parent to his own sons and because of that, he tried harder to be a presence for his grandsons. Adelaide knew for a fact the older man held far more of Dempsey's respect than his philandering father, Theo.

"Hello, Mr. Reynaud," she greeted him while Dempsey clapped him on the shoulder.

"We're heading home, Grand-père. Do you need a ride?" Dempsey asked.

"No need. I want to try my hand at blackjack and see if the Reynaud luck holds." He gave Adelaide a rakish grin and straightened his already perfect tie. "My dear, did you know my own grandfather won his first boat in a game of cards? From there, he grew the Zephyr Shipping empire."

It was a much-loved bit of Reynaud lore.

"Adelaide probably knows the family history as well as I do." Dempsey met her gaze for a moment and she drank in the compliment.

He rarely handed out praise, especially publicly. The elevator bell chimed, and the door opened to the first floor. She stepped out into the crowd while Dempsey held the door for his grandfather.

"Adelaide, you say?" Leon frowned as he moved slowly toward the bar, his expression blank for a moment before his gray brows furrowed. "Be careful with the ladies, son. You wouldn't want your wife to find out."

"But, Grand-père—" Dempsey called after him as the older man disappeared into the crowd. Turning toward her, Dempsey pulled out his phone. "He's been getting more confused lately."

"Should we stay with him?" Adelaide hadn't heard about Leon having any moments of confusion, but then, Dempsey didn't share much about his family outside of business concerns.

Some of the magic of their kiss evaporated with the reminder of how removed she was from his private life. Even as his so-called fiancée.

"I'm texting Evan. He has a friend here tonight providing extra security. I'll have him keep an eye on Leon and make sure he gets home safely."

"One of your brothers might still be here." She peered back into the party. "I saw Henri with some of the other players—"

"It's handled." He tucked his phone in his pocket and pressed a hand to her lower back.

A perfunctory touch. A social nicety. She could feel that his attention had drifted from her. From them.

Ha. Who was she kidding? There was no *them*. Dempsey maneuvered her now the same way he orchestrated the rest of his world. He wasn't the kind of man to be carried away by a kiss, and right now he clearly had other things on his mind.

Forcing her thoughts from the chemistry that had simmered between them, Adelaide promised herself not to act on any more impulsive longings. She'd wanted to shake things up a bit between them and she had. But his silence on the ride home told her all she needed to know about the gamble she'd taken with the kiss.

It hadn't paid off.

From now on, she would take her cues from Dempsey. If he wanted their relationship to be focused on business, she only had three and a half more weeks to pretend that old crush of hers hadn't fired to life all over again.

The next day, she balanced two coffees in a tray and a box of pastries from Dempsey's favorite bakery as she strode through the training facility toward his office. She reminded herself she'd done the same thing for him plenty of other times in her years as his assistant. When they'd been in Atlanta together and Dempsey had still been an assistant coach, they'd shared a secret addiction to apple fritters and she'd grown skilled at sneaking them into the training complex so the health-minded nutritionists wouldn't discover them.

Now that they were back in New Orleans, Adelaide knew to pick up beignets on game days when they were downtown. But in Metairie, for an occasional treat, she bought raspberry scones. Technically, procuring pastries wasn't on her formal list of duties. And maybe it was her sweet tooth that had driven this one shared pleasure. But after last night's awkward end to the evening, she found herself wanting to put their relationship back on familiar ground.

It wasn't as if she was offended that her kiss hadn't made him realize he'd always loved her from afar or had some other fairy-tale outcome. But maybe she'd dreamed once or twice that such a thing could really happen if they ever kissed. That Dempsey would see her with new eyes and forget about the Valentinas of the world.

Right. He'd made it clear she would be welcome in his bed, but he hadn't seemed inclined to consider what that would mean for them—their friendship, their work together or even this farce of an engagement. How could she knowingly walk into an intimate relationship with him when she'd seen the devastation he left in his wake?

The sun hadn't even risen that morning when she'd awoken to an empty house, and she'd known that Dempsey had left for work. He'd been restless when they'd arrived home after the charity fund-raiser, excusing himself to call his brother Jean-Pierre in New York. She'd thought then that maybe he was more upset about his grandfather's mistake than he'd let on. Why else would he call Jean-Pierre when it would have been after midnight in Manhattan?

Unless he'd been fighting the riot of yearning that had plagued her.

She backed into the double doors leading to the front offices and nearly ran into Pat Tyrell, the Hurricanes' defensive coordinator.

"Well, good morning, Miss Adelaide." He tipped his team hat to her since, even at seventy years old, the grizzled old coach was still a flirt. "Those wouldn't happen to be illicit treats in that white pastry box of yours?"

The older man knew her well. He held the door open for her.

"I figured I didn't have to hide them at this hour since the trainers won't be in until at least nine o'clock." She lifted the box toward him. "Want a raspberry scone?"

"You speak an old man's language." His black-and-gold windbreaker crinkled as he reached into the box to help himself. "Dempsey ought to be ready for breakfast soon. I came in this morning to find him running up and down the bleachers like a kid in training camp."

Her mouth went dry as she envisioned Dempsey in his workout routine. He was as fit as any of his players, even if she did manage to tempt him into an occasional scone.

"Maybe he's getting ready to run a few plays himself on Sunday." She sidestepped Pat to head into her office. "He's always saying we need more discipline on the field."

"Damn shame that boy didn't have a shot to play in the NFL. When you get that kind of football mind combined with talent, it's a beautiful thing to watch." He raised his pastry in salute. "Thanks for the sweets, Addy."

Settling into her small office next door to Dempsey's massive suite, Adelaide set down the coffees and dropped her purse on the floor beside the desk. She'd only been joking about Dempsey getting ready to run plays. Maybe because she wasn't a football player she hadn't given much thought to the fact that Dempsey's decorated college career as a tight end had never gone to the next level. He'd told her once that he'd chosen to coach because he could bring more to the game that way, and she believed him.

But she also knew from articles in the media that an injury in his youth had never mended properly and that another hit to his spine could paralyze him—something that his college coaches hadn't known about, but had been quickly discovered in a physical by the team that had drafted him. Dempsey had been on a plane back to Louisiana the next day and, Adelaide recalled, Leon Reynaud had threatened to sue the college where he'd played.

At the time, she'd been busy finishing up her fine arts degree and debating whether to apply to a master's program. She'd also been in recovery mode from her crush on Dempsey and had been trying to ignore the stories about him.

The knock on her office door startled her from her thoughts. Dempsey appeared in the doorway in cargo shorts and a black team polo shirt that fit him to perfection. His hair, still wet from the shower, was even darker than usual. He hadn't shaved either. The jaw that had been well groomed just twelve hours ago for the charity ball was already heavily shadowed.

"Morning." He strode past her desk to stand by the window overlooking the training field, where a few players were loosening up even though official warm-ups wouldn't start for another hour or more. "I didn't expect you today."

She'd worked overtime this week, as she did most weeks. But he seemed to understand her desire to devote some hours to her own business because he'd told her last night that she should take the day off.

She watched him now, struck anew by his masculine appeal. After all the years she'd known him, she would have hoped to have been used to him. Some days, when they were embroiled in work, she managed to forget that he was an incredibly magnetic male. Other times, the raw virility of him made her a little light-headed, like now.

"You seemed so distracted last night, I wasn't even sure you would remember saying that." She handed him his coffee and joined him at the window. She tracked the movements of two new receivers racing each other down the field.

Every day she encountered virile, handsome men. Men that other women swooned over on game days. What was it about Dempsey alone that drew her eye?

"I meant it." He sipped his coffee and stared at her until her skin grew warm with awareness. "I'm worried about Leon."

That shifted her focus in a hurry. She couldn't remember the last time he'd shared a personal concern with her.

"He thought he was speaking to Theo last night when he told you to be careful your wife didn't find out about me." She knew that Theo Reynaud had a notorious reputation, dating back to his years as a college athlete and straight through his time as a pro.

His wife had left him shortly after Dempsey—the son of an extramarital affair—arrived in her household. She'd told Dempsey that he was her "last straw."

"Right." He shook his head. "We've known that he has episodes of confusion, but he claimed he saw a doctor who diagnosed it as a thyroid problem. I looked it up, because I wasn't sure if we could believe him, but that is a possibility."

"So either he's not taking the right medicines for it—"

"Or he's been BSing us the whole time and he's never seen a doctor. He's as hardheaded as they come and he doesn't put much faith in the health-care system."

"He is always telling the trainers not to coddle the players." She'd heard him bark at the medical staff often enough, imparting a "tough it out" mentality.

"Exactly." Dempsey frowned. "I asked Jean-Pierre to try to spend some time down here this season so we can present a united front to get Leon evaluated and, if necessary, into more aggressive medical treatment."

Reaching toward her desk, she pulled the box of scones closer.

"Jean-Pierre will have to come home for Gervais's wedding." She'd tracked the wedding talk on social media as part of her duties managing Dempsey's profile pages online. With the Hurricanes' owner marrying a foreign princess, the topic had more traction than any other team news.

The fact that there'd been no official announcement only fueled the rumor mill until speculating on the whens and hows of the nuptials filled page after page of gossip blogs.

"That's still six weeks away." He relinquished his coffee to grab a couple of paper plates from her stash near the minifridge. "I think we need to act soon. I don't want something to happen to Leon because we're all too damn busy to pay attention to the warning signs. We owe him better, even though he's not going to be happy about us strong-arming him."

"Will you invite your dad to be there?" She took a plate and a scone and passed him the box. "Or any of the rest of the family?"

Leon had another son who lived in Texas, and one out on the West Coast, and there were cousins as well, but the relationships had been strained for a long time.

"No. If Theo happens to be in town, fine." His jaw flexed at the mention of his father, a tic shared by all of Theo's sons. "But I'm not going to seek him out for a family event that will be stressful enough as it is." He set aside his breakfast.

Then slipped hers from her hands and set it on the desk.

"Is that a hint?" she asked, her gaze following the bit of raspberry heaven now out of reach. "Am I indulging my sweet tooth too often?"

"Of course not. I wanted to apologize for last night." He took her hand between his and gave her his undivided attention.

Making her whole body go on full alert.

"You don't owe me any apologies." She hadn't expected a discussion about what happened and, consequently, was completely unprepared.

"I do. I didn't pick you up last night to bring you to the event. I didn't deliver your engagement ring personally. And then the episode with my grandfather distracted me from one of the most shockingly provocative kisses of my life."

"Oh." Completely. Unprepared. "I—"

"Can I ask you a personal question?"

Her heart hammered so loudly in her ears she wasn't entirely sure she'd hear it, but she nodded. The warmth of his palm on the back of her hand sent sparks of pleasure pinging around her insides.

"Have you thought about us that way before? Or is this a whole new experience, feeling all that chemistry?" His golden-brown gaze captured hers.

Her cheeks heated and she cursed the reaction bitterly even as she shrugged like an inarticulate teenager. But answering the question felt like a "damned if she did, damned if she didn't" proposition.

"Right." He let go of her hand. "Maybe I have no business asking you that. But I'll admit I'm having a tough time concentrating today. I came in early just to hit the gym and try to work off some steam because I damn well couldn't sleep."

That got her attention.

"Because of me?" Her voice sounded as though she'd been sucking down helium. She grabbed her coffee and took a healthy swig.

"Things got heated last night, wouldn't you agree?" His voice lowered. Deepened.

The words felt like a stroke along her skin, they were so damn seductive. But she needed to proceed with extreme caution. She'd heard Valentina's accusation the night before. Dempsey had left her bed before the sheets cooled, according to her.

"That's what happens when you play games and pretend things you don't feel." She kept her cool, needing to make herself heard before she did something foolish, like respond to all that simmering heat she felt when he touched her. "You can't tell where the game ends and reality begins."

For one heart-stopping moment, she imagined what would happen if he kissed her this time. If he laid her on her desk and told her the games ended here and now. She could almost taste the moment, it felt so real.

"Why does it have to be a game?" He edged back from her, his gaze level. "We've always been good together. We respect each other. Why not enjoy the benefits of this attraction now that it's becoming a distraction?"

She could hear the influence of his Reynaud roots in his word choices. It took a superhuman effort not to roll her eyes.

"Maybe because I don't think of relationships in terms of benefits. We're talking about intimacy, not some contractual arrangement. And I definitely don't want to be pursued for the sake of a distraction."

"I wouldn't be so quick to write off the advantages." He took a step closer. Crowding her. "Perhaps we should make a list of all the ways you would directly benefit."

Her heart galloped. Her skin seemed to shrink, creating the sensation of being too tight to fit. She didn't think she'd make it through a discussion of the ways having Dempsey in her bed would reward her.

"Maybe some other time." She tossed her empty coffee cup in the trash and stood. "Now that I know you were serious about that day off, maybe I'll just head back to the house and do some work on my designs." She would preserve some dignity, damn it.

Although she did take the box of scones.

The light in his eyes told her that he was on to her. That he understood why she needed to beat a hasty retreat.

"Good. I'm coming home early tonight. I'll take you out for dinner."

Alone?

Her mouth went dry.

"Maybe," she hedged, backing toward the door. "I've got a meeting with a fabric company downtown later. But I'll text you afterward."

She didn't wait for his response as she walked out into the corridor. Her skin hummed with awareness from being around him and from the knowledge that he wanted her. Her kiss—practically a chaste brush of lips—had shifted the dynamic between them more than she'd imagined possible.

Dempsey wanted her.

And maybe, for now, that ought to be enough. She couldn't expect him to fall head over heels for her when he'd hardly seen her as a woman up until earlier in the week. Was she a fool to run away from the firestorm she'd created?

Part of her wanted to march back into her office and strip off all his clothes. Request that detailed list of relationship benefits after all.

Except, of course, she had little experience with men. And baiting a Reynaud was a dangerous business when she wasn't a man-eating Valentina type who could deal with the fallout. She was just Adelaide Thibodeaux and she had a feeling she might never recover from a night in Dempsey's bed. Knowing her overinflated sense of loyalty, she'd probably be lovesick for life, stuck in a job as his assistant in the hope he'd one day crook his finger in her direction so she could repeat the mind-blowing experience.

No, thank you.

Dempsey might have started this game on his terms, but she planned to finish it. On hers.

Chapter 6

Dempsey made no claim to being an intuitive man.

But even he could sense that he'd made some headway with Adelaide earlier in the day. Sure, he understood her reluctance to jeopardize their friendship. And he meant what he'd said about respecting her. Caring about her.

Yet the flame that burned between them now wouldn't go away just because they ignored it. She might not be ready to address it, but he sure as hell would. So now he found himself driving around downtown New Orleans in search of the fabric supplier she was using as a pretext for not meeting him for dinner.

He'd rearranged his day and moved his nonnegotiable meetings earlier in the afternoon. His practice had gone well. His game plan for Sunday was solid. Nothing was going to stand in the way of spending time with her tonight. He would make a case for exploring this attraction in a way he hadn't been prepared to do last night after that unsettling talk with Leon.

He needed to get to know her better—a damn sorry thing to admit when he ought to know her as well as anyone. But he'd been too caught up in his own career the past few years to pay attention to Addy. If he wanted to persuade her to let her guard down and give him a chance, he needed to understand what made her happy. What pleased her.

Spotting the storefront of the warehouse, Dempsey steered his BMW sedan into a spot on the street. Evan had driven Adelaide to this location, so Dempsey had it on good authority she was still inside.

The least he could do was show an interest in the business she wanted to start. He'd looked over her business plan briefly before driving out here and he'd been both impressed and worried. Her goals were sound, but fulfilling them would mean a lot of hands-on involvement to get it up and running. Maybe if he discussed the clothing company with her in detail, he'd see a way for her to hand off some of the less important tasks. There had to be a way to free her up enough to keep working with him.

He needed Adelaide.

In the ten steps it took to hit the front door he was already sweating, the heat still wet as a dishcloth even though it was six o'clock. The man seated at the desk out front pointed Dempsey in the right direction, and he went into the warehouse to look for Adelaide.

He found her in front of a display of laces, draping an intricate gray pattern over her calf as if to see what the material looked like up against bare skin. Making him wonder what kinds of garments she had in mind for her next design project.

A vision of her high, full breasts covered in nothing but lace and his hands blasted to the forefront of his brain, making him hotter than the late-afternoon sun had. She wore different clothes from the ones she'd had on at the training facility, trading dark pants and a Hurricanes T-shirt for the yellow-and-blue floral sundress she now wore. Wide-set straps and a square neckline framed her feminine curves. Her hair was rolled into some kind of updo that exposed her neck and made him want to lick it. So much for keeping his thoughts friendly.

"Dempsey?" She straightened, a smile lighting up her face for a moment before a wary look chased after it. "What a surprise to see you here." She gestured to the soaring shelves of fabric samples on miniature hangers, sorted by color and material. "Are you here to redesign the Hurricanes jerseys?"

He scanned a section of striped and polka-dotted cotton.

"I think the guys will stick with what we have." He peered around the warehouse to gauge their level of privacy. He'd seen one other shopper on his way in, but other than that, the space appeared empty. "I'm here for you."

The lace dropped from her fingers. "Is there a problem with our opening day? I checked my phone—"

He caught her hand before she could dig in her purse for the device.

"No problems. Things are running just as they should for the regular-season opener."

He couldn't even touch her anymore without images of that tentative kiss of hers heating him from the inside out. He didn't know how he'd found the willpower to let her retreat to her own room last night when the need for a better taste of her rode his back like a tackle he couldn't break.

"Then, what did you need?" She slid her hand away from his, making him wonder what she felt when they touched.

"What do I need? To see you." He huffed out a breath and braced an elbow on one of the nearby shelves. "I came here to insist on that dinner I offered since it seemed as though you're being elusive today, and it's bugging me that I don't know why."

She busied herself with returning the lace to its small hanger and finding the proper place to reshelve it. When she didn't respond, he continued, "But now that I'm here, it occurs to me that the bigger reason I needed to see you is that I can't seem to think about anything else."

He watched as her busy movements slowed. Stopped. Color washed her cheeks, confirming his suspicion that she suffered from the same madness as he did. And yes, it gave him tremendous amounts of male satisfaction to think he wasn't the only one feeling it.

She clutched a handful of indigo-colored silk and squeezed.

"You made it clear that I've become a *distraction*," she reminded him, a hint of bitterness creeping into the words.

"Is that why you're avoiding me? Because I didn't make a more romantic gesture?" His hands were on her before he'd thought through the wisdom of touching her again.

Spinning her away from the fabric display, he turned her to face him, his palms settling into the indent of her waist. Hidden from view, he wrestled with the urge to feel more of her, to mold her to him and put an end to the damnable simmering distraction.

If she'd been anyone else, the next move would have already been made. But this was Addy.

"No. Thinking about romance will not help get us through the next few weeks," she told him evenly. "I'm not one of your girlfriends with a legal agreement you can keep renegotiating, okay? You laid out the terms when you put me on the spot with this engagement. I'm not sure why you think you can keep rewriting those terms to give you more *benefits*."

The bitterness in her voice had vanished. Taking its place was a trace of hurt.

An emotional one-two punch that he'd never intended.

His hands tightened on her waist. His throat dried up.

"You're right." Closing his eyes, he dragged in a deep breath and only succeeded in inhaling a hint of night-blooming roses. "I haven't thought about how this is affecting you. That day you told me you were quitting, I was completely focused on making sure that didn't happen. I came up with the only short-term solution I could."

Dempsey became aware of the sound of a woman's high heels clicking on the concrete floor behind him. She was heading their way.

"Ms. Thibodeaux, do you have any questions—" A tall blonde woman in a dark suit rounded the corner and came into view. "Oh. Hello there." She blushed at the sight of them together, making Dempsey realize how close he'd gotten to Adelaide during this discussion.

How much closer he still wanted to be.

"I put the last sample back," Adelaide told her, edging around Dempsey and straightening. "I'll give you a call once I have a better idea of what I might need."

The woman was already backing away. "Of course! No problem. And congratulations on your engagement."

As soon as the sales clerk disappeared from view, Adelaide swung around to face him.

"So now that you've acknowledged this engagement was a mistake, are you ready to call it off and maybe life can go back to normal?" Her hazel eyes seemed greener in this light. Or maybe it was the combination of anger and challenge firing through them.

"Not until I have a better short-term solution." He understood they needed to have this discussion since this attraction was proving far too distracting at a time when he needed absolute focus. "But you can help me brainstorm alternatives. Over dinner."

Two hours later, Adelaide sat cross-legged on a wooden Adirondack chair behind Dempsey's house overlooking Lake Pontchartrain. A blaze burned in the round fire pit in front of them as they finished a meal of Cajun specialties obtained by Evan from a local restaurant. Adelaide hadn't wanted to risk a public outing, unwilling to smile and lie politely about her engagement to Dempsey when the man was hell-bent on taking their relationship into intimate terrain.

And that's a problem...why? some snide voice in her head kept asking.

Sure, she wanted him. Desperately. But since a corner of her heart had always belonged to him, she feared this new development could have devastating consequences when the time came to return to their regular lives. And the time would come. She'd witnessed Dempsey's parting gifts to his exes enough times to know that relationships came with an expiration date for him. Still, she simmered with thwarted desire. While she finished her meal, she tormented herself with fantasies about touching him. Agreeing to his offer of sensual benefits. Bringing this heat to the boiling point. Even now she wanted to cross over to his chair and take a seat on his lap just to see what would happen.

From her vantage point, his thighs appeared plenty strong enough to bear her weight. Those workouts of his seemed to keep him in optimal shape.

Was she really ready for him to relegate her to friendship for life when she had this opportunity of living with him for the next few weeks? When he'd admitted he couldn't stop thinking about her? She'd nearly melted in her shoes when he'd confessed it at the fabric warehouse.

"Remember when you stole a crawfish for me and I was too afraid to eat it?" she asked, deliberately putting off the more serious conversation he'd promised over dinner.

She wasn't ready to help him brainstorm solutions to their dilemma. And right now she wanted a happy memory to remind her why she put up with him and all that driven, relentless ambition, which kept him from getting too close to anyone. She blamed that and his need to prove himself to his family for his unwillingness to take a risk with the relationship.

Although maybe she just needed to tell herself that to protect her heart from the more obvious explanation— that he saw any attraction as a fleeting response doomed not to last.

"I didn't steal it." He sounded as incensed about it now as he'd been when he was twelve years old. "If a crawfish happened to walk over to me, it was exercising its free will."

Laughing, she set aside the jambalaya that had made

her think of that day. They'd walked to a nearby crawfish festival. When one of the restaurants selling food at the event refilled its tank of crawfish, a few escapees had headed toward Dempsey and Adelaide, who'd been drooling over the food from a spot on the pavement nearby.

"I don't know what made you think I would eat a raw mudbug." She shivered. "Sometimes I still can't believe I eat them when they're cooked."

"A hungry kid doesn't turn his nose up at much," he observed. "And I figured it was only polite to offer them to you before I helped myself."

Adelaide had never gone hungry the way Dempsey sometimes had. His mother could be kind when she was drug-free, but even then the woman had never had any extra money thanks to her habit. When she'd been using more, she'd even forgotten about Dempsey for days on end.

"You were very good to me." When Adelaide looked back on those days, she could almost forget about how much he'd shut her out of his personal life since then.

He stared into the flames dancing in the fire pit.

"I still try to be good to you, Addy."

She bit back the sharp retort that came to mind, purposely focusing on the friendship they used to have so as not to bad-mouth the turn things had taken over the past five years.

"I take it you don't agree?" he asked.

"We've had a strict work-only relationship for years." She traced patterns in the condensation on her iced tea glass. "You convinced me to take this job that furthered your career while delaying mine. You've ignored our friendship for years at a time, going so far as referring to me as a 'tool for greater productivity.'" She wanted to stop there. But now that the brakes were off, she found it difficult to put them back on. "Or maybe you think it's *kind* of you to toy with the chemistry between us, pretending to feel the same heat that I do and using it to your own ends to convince me to stay?"

She knew she'd admitted too much, but sitting in the dark under the bayou stars seemed to coax the truth from her. Besides, if she didn't put herself on the line with him now when he'd admitted to being "distracted" by her, she might never have another chance to find out where all that simmering attraction could lead.

"Damn, Addy." He whistled low and sat up straighter in his chair, his elbows on his knees. Firelight cast stark shadows on his face. "You must think I'm some kind of arrogant, selfish ass. Do you really think that's how I perceive things? That I created a position for you just to benefit me?"

"You're putting words in my mouth."

"Nothing you didn't imply." He rose to his feet, his agitation apparent as he paced a circle around his vacated chair. "And I can assure you that you were not the most obvious choice to work with me in this capacity. There aren't many assistant coaches who bring an administrative aide with them when they take a new job, but I did it just the same because you needed a job at the time. And I'm the only coach in the league with a female personal assistant, so I'm breaking all kinds of ground there."

"You can't honestly suggest that you created the job for me to further my career. I wanted to be an artist."

"Yes. An artist. And your work led you to a studio in an even worse part of town than where we grew up. A place I warned you not to take. I offered to rent another space for you. But then—"

"The break-in." She didn't want to think about that night when gang members, high on heaven knew what, had broken into the studio and threatened her.

They'd destroyed her paintings when they'd realized there was nothing of value in the place to steal. Then they'd casually discussed the merits of physically assaulting her before one of them got a text that they needed to be elsewhere. The three of them had disappeared into the night while she'd remained paralyzed with fear long afterward.

"Those bastards threatened you. And I suggested every plan under the sun to help you, Addy, but you were too stubborn and proud to let me do anything."

Crickets chirped in the silence that followed. A log shifted in the fire pit, sending sparks flying.

"You wanted to build me a studio in the country." She recalled a fax from an architect with the plans for such a building, including a state-of-the-art security system. "How on earth could I have ever repaid you for such a thing? I was barely out of college."

"Like I said. Too stubborn." He spread his hands wide. "I was just a few years out of college myself and I was dealing with a lot of family expectations. The studio would have been easy for me to give you and I was happy to do it, but you wouldn't hear of it."

"I'd never take something for nothing. And don't you blame me for that, because you wouldn't either if our positions were reversed." Maybe she hadn't let herself remember that time in detail because it had taken a long time to recover from the emotional trauma of that night.

Seeing her canvases hacked to bits had been different than having her computer stolen or her phone smashed. Her art was an extension of her, a place where she poured her heart.

"So I gave you a job. That, you would accept."

"And now, years after the fact, I'm still supposed to kiss your feet for the opportunity?" She shot out of her chair, a restless energy taking hold as she closed the distance between them.

"Absolutely not."

His quick agreement didn't come close to satisfying her.

"I worked hard in an industry I knew nothing about," she pressed. "I left my home and everything I knew to go to Atlanta with you." Her first task had been finding housing for them.

Relocating to a new city had been so simple with Dempsey's seemingly limitless resources and connections.

Unlike starting over in New Orleans, which had seemed impossible after her sense of safety had been shredded and her body of work reduced to scraps.

"Yes. And you proved yourself invaluable almost right away. My work was easier with your help. You never needed direction and understood me even on days I was so terse and exhausted I could only snap out a few words of instructions for you."

"I had a long history of interpreting you." A wry grin tugged at her lips, but she wasn't going to let nostalgia cloud her vision of him. Of them.

"But we'd scarcely seen each other for a decade." He reached toward her, as if to stroke her cheek, but he must have thought better of it when his hand fell to his side. "I was surprised how well we got back into sync."

"You might be more surprised to know how much more in sync we could be." The words leaped from her mouth.

One moment they were in her head. The next they were in the air, with no way to recapture them.

She saw the instant that full understanding hit him. The instant he heard the proposition underlying those words. His gaze shifted to her mouth, the heat in his eyes like a laser in its intensity.

"Of course it would *not* surprise me. That's exactly what I've been trying to tell you." He focused all his attention on her. "You've occupied every second of my thoughts today. You've got me so damn distracted, I can hardly think about football."

Still he didn't move toward her. Didn't give in to the current that leaped back and forth between them. Her cells practically strained toward the sound of his voice.

"Then, maybe you ought to call off this engagement charade before you tank a season that means everything to you." She wouldn't make the first move again. Being impulsive with him the night before had only complicated things between them.

"I don't think so." He reached behind her and tugged a pin from the knot at the back of her head. Then, sifting through the half-fallen mass, he found two more and pulled them free.

Her hair tumbled to her bare shoulders and covered her arms. She shivered despite the warmth of the night, awareness flooding through her like high tide.

"Why not?" Her voice rasped low from the effort of not stepping closer. She wanted him to touch her the way he had the night before. Craved the feel of his body against hers.

"Because I have a better solution for all this distraction you're causing." He combed his fingers through the ends of her hair, smoothing it along her back.

Sensation shimmered over her skin, nerve endings

dancing to life. Desire pooled in her belly as her gaze roamed over his powerful arms and shoulders, the solid wall of his chest that would be warm to her touch.

"A way to stop all this distraction?" She needed to know what he was thinking before her thoughts smoldered away in the blaze erupting between them.

"I'm beginning to think that's a lost cause after last night." His hands moved to her hips as he stepped into her space, crowding her in the most delicious possible way. "That dress you wore last night flipped some kind of switch in my head and I can't stop thinking about this spot." He palmed the front of her thigh. "Right here."

Her breath caught on a hard gasp. Pleasure spiked. Her breasts beaded under the bodice of her dress.

"Do you remember where I mean?" His eyes were dark and lit by firelight, reflecting the bright orange flames beside them. He traced a pattern on the front of her leg, fingering gently. "There was a sheer place in the lace. Here."

He increased the pressure of his touch and she couldn't swallow a strangled sound in the back of her throat. He hadn't even kissed her yet and she was utterly mesmerized.

"I remember." Her words were a breathless whisper as she steadied herself against his shoulders, anchoring her quivering body with his strength.

"If I'm a bad friend to you, Addy, you only have that dress to blame." He shifted his hold on her to align their hips, allowing her to feel how much he wanted her. "But I damn well can't resist any longer."

Chapter 7

Dempsey's control had snapped the second she'd suggested they could be even more in sync. He'd been hanging on by a thread before that moment, willing himself not to think about the tender brush of her lips on his the night before. Not to think about that damn siren's dress she'd worn or the way she'd melted in his arms.

So by the time she'd made that one coy, flirtatious taunt, his restraint had simply incinerated.

From that moment on, he'd been plagued with sweaty visions of them moving together in perfect sensual accord. Now that he had his hands on her, molding her sweet, curvy body to his, he didn't have a prayer of putting a lid back on this combustible attraction.

He kissed her. Hard. With deliberate purpose. Need. Seeking entrance, he explored every nuance of her mouth, claiming it with a hunger and thoroughness he couldn't hold back. The way she opened for him, swayed into him, encouraged him all the more.

Unleashed, his emotions fired through the kiss until he all but devoured her. She clutched his shoulders, her nails biting ever so slightly into his skin through his shirt. He wished he could torch their clothes so he could feel the sting of that touch without barrier.

He bent to nuzzle her neck, tasting the skin all along her throat and under her ear until he found the source of her fragrance. The scent of roses made him throb with teeth-jarring need. He nipped and licked his way down her collarbone along the strap of her dress and peeled the fabric free. He had to feel more of her.

But right before he helped himself to one of her breasts, he remembered they were still outdoors. And even though it was nighttime, the fire might make them visible to one of the houses dotting the lake if someone was so inclined to spy. The porches of plenty of coastal homes were furnished with telescopes.

"I want to take you inside." He nudged the strap of her dress back up her shoulder, his hand unsteady and his breath uneven. The ache from wanting her still heated his veins.

"I want to take you anywhere I can have you." She loosened her hold on him as she edged back a step. "So that's definitely fine with me."

Her words fanned the flames hotter inside him. Aching to have her, he swept her up in his arms and charged over the lawn toward the house.

"Your room is closer." He said it to himself as much as her, directing his steps toward the downstairs bedroom. "But the condoms are all upstairs." He changed direction, cursing himself for the mansion's extravagant square footage when it delayed having Adelaide.

She nipped at his neck while he covered the distance, those delectable breasts of hers pressed tight to his chest as she clutched him. She made a luscious armful, her thighs draped over one arm while her hip grazed the erection that had hounded him the better part of the day.

"I can't wait to feel you without the barrier of clothes," she murmured against his ear, her breath puffing a silken caress along his skin.

"That's good." He ground the words out between clenched teeth as he finally reached the door to his suite. "Because I don't think we're going to leave this room until the game on Sunday."

He needed to wear himself out with her. To excise this hunger spilling over into every aspect of his life until all he could think about was Adelaide.

Setting her on her feet, he backed her into the nearest wall, yearning to feel more of her. Light spilled into the room from low-wattage sconces on either side of the bed that came on automatically at sunset. He toed the door shut behind them and took another valuable second to flip the lock into place. Then all of his focus returned to Adelaide.

Immersing his hands in all that long, caramel-colored hair of hers, he shifted the length of it over one shoulder in a silky veil. His body pinned hers in place, hips sinking into hers where they fit best.

He was dying to have her. It was as if he'd been holding back for years instead of days, and maybe subconsciously he had been. That friendship wall could be a strong one. Mistresses were plentiful. Friends, true friends, were few. But the time for restraint was long gone as he tugged the straps of her thin sundress down and exposed a pretty turquoise-colored bra that wouldn't be nearly as enticing as what was underneath. Applying his hands to the hooks, he swept that aside, too, so he could get his mouth around the tight buds of dark pink nipples he'd felt right through her clothes.

Her back arched to give him better access, her body straining toward his while he laved and licked at one and then the other. She made soft sexy sounds that told him how much she liked what he was doing, and her hands worked the buttons on his shirt until she was touching bare skin. He hauled the shirt off his shoulders and let it slide to the floor, his eyes never leaving her. With her dress tugged down and all that goddess hair draped over her shoulders, she made one hell of a vision.

Lifting her against him, he slid a hand up her skirt to wrap her leg around his waist. Positioned that way, the vulnerable, hot core of her came up against his rock-hard erection. She shuddered against him, a subtle vibration he felt right there, a sensation so damn good he cupped her hips and moved her against him again and again. A sensual ride he wanted to give her for real.

"That feels…" Her words broke on a small cry of pleasure as she braced herself on his shoulders.

"Tell me." He wanted to know everything she liked. Exactly how she liked it.

While he'd always striven to pleasure the women in his bed, this was different. He needed this night to be perfect because this was Adelaide and *she* was different. So much more important to him.

And he wasn't ready to think about what that meant or all the ways that was going to complicate things for them.

"It feels so good." Her eyes flipped open long enough

for him to see the haze of desire there, her gaze unfocused. "I'm so close. Already."

Knowing that only cranked him higher. He kept up the friction beginning to torment him and fastened his lips back on one breast. He drew on it. Hard. Then, finding the edge of her panties with one hand, he slid beneath the satin to stroke the drenched feminine folds. Once. Twice.

She came apart with a high cry she muffled against his shoulder. The force of it, combined with the way she went boneless in his arms, made him sway back on his feet a little.

Damn. He used that moment to watch her, to soak up the vision she made with her cheeks suffused with color and her chest heaving with all that sensation.

Giving her a moment—giving himself one, too—he tried to catch his breath before he carried her over to the bed and deposited her there. His own release was close and he hadn't even taken off his pants. Leaving her just long enough to retrieve a box of condoms from the bathroom cabinet, he dropped it on the nightstand.

Then he went to work on his belt while he watched her slide off her heels. He dropped his pants while she wriggled out of her dress. He was left wearing only his boxers at the same time she wore nothing but turquoise-colored satin panties.

"I'll show you mine if you show me yours," she dared him, hooking a finger in the lace waistband about as substantial as a shoelace.

He slid off the boxers.

"I'm going to see yours, all right," he warned her, edging a knee onto the bed and stretching out over her. "Up close and personal."

She let go of the panties, her hand moving to his chest as he shifted closer.

"Oh?" Her breathless question told him exactly how much she liked that idea. "Well, I'm going to revisit on you all the same pleasure that you give me." She arched an eyebrow at the sensual promise.

Laying a hand on her hip, he slipped the satin down her thighs and off.

"Not a chance. This isn't like a favor where you can keep an accounting. In this bed, I get to give and give and give all that I want." He stroked the soft curls just above her sex, sliding touches lower and lower while she drew in a breath between her teeth.

"Dempsey." She arched her hips toward him, a silent plea.

One he was powerless to resist.

Parting her thighs, he made room for himself there. She watched him with wide eyes, biting the soft fullness of her lower lip while he found a condom and opened the packet. She stole it away from him, rolling it into place herself and positioning him where she wanted.

Where they both wanted.

When he entered her, she tightened her grip on him. Her arms wrapped around his shoulders. Legs tightened around his waist. And her inner muscles squeezed him with sensual pulls that had him gritting his teeth against the sweetly erotic feel of one hundred percent Adelaide.

For a long moment, he held himself still, breathing in the scent of her hair and giving her time to adjust to him. When he thought he could move again without unmanning himself, he levered up on his arms and began a slow, steady rhythm. Addy held herself still for a moment, and then, as if she'd just been waiting for the right time to join him, she swiveled her hips in a way that rocked him.

Heat blazed up his spine as she undulated beneath him, meeting his thrusts and making him see stars. She locked her ankles behind him, her heat, her softness and her scent surrounding him. He wanted to draw this out, to make the pleasure go on and on, to explore every facet of what she liked. But not this time. Not now when just being inside her was enough to send him hurtling over the edge.

Next time, he'd find some self-control. Some way to make the pleasure last. Right now the need to come inside her was the most primal urge he'd ever felt. He closed his eyes, cued in on her breathing and synced his movements, causing her to gasp and arch. He moved faster, needing to focus solely on her. On pleasuring her.

He wouldn't let himself go until then.

She called his name with a hoarse cry as her whole body went taut. Her release pulsated through her and freed his. He kissed her to silence, the shout poised in his throat as wave after wave of pleasure pounded through him. The moment went on and on until they were both spent and lying side by side, their breathing erratic and heartbeats pounding crazy rhythms. He knew because one of his hands rested on her throat, where he could feel her pulse hammer.

She must know, too, because her hand lay on his chest, where his heart thrummed so hard it felt as though it wanted out.

Long minutes passed before their skin began to cool and Dempsey thought he could move again. He drew her into his arms and stroked her hair, smoothing tangles and skimming it to one side of her beautiful body.

"I'm speechless," she murmured, her breath a soft huff on his chest.

"We could make talking optional for the next few hours," he suggested, already wanting her again.

She peered up at him through long lashes. "Save all our energy for the important things?"

"Exactly." He cupped her cheek and tilted her face to kiss her. "You can practically read my mind anyhow. You can probably guess what I'd like to do next."

She sidled closer, her hips stirring him to life with a speed he hadn't experienced since his teens.

"I have an excellent idea. But I stopped being your dutiful assistant when you gave me the day off. So I won't be fulfilling your every need tonight." She ran a lazy hand up his biceps and onto his chest. Then trailed her nails lightly down the center of his sternum.

"No?" His voice rasped on a dry note.

"I might give a few orders of my own," she teased.

"Is that what I do? Order you around?" He found a ticklish spot on her side and made her laugh.

"Definitely." She gripped his wrists and pinned them to the bed. Climbing on top of him, she let all that glorious hair fall around him. "Now it's my turn."

Adelaide couldn't resist teasing him. She stared down into Dempsey's impossibly handsome face and wondered how long he would let her play this game.

Judging from the impressive erection resting on his abs, he was liking it well enough so far.

"I can't imagine what you'd ask me to do when I've already put so much thought into pleasing you, Ms. Thibodeaux." His dark eyes wandered over her in the most flattering way.

"I already like your deferential tone." She kissed his cheek and brushed her breasts against it. "Why don't you tell me about this effort you say you've put into pleasing me? I'd love to hear all about that."

Kissing her way down his chest, she paused now and again to look up at him. Make sure he was still watching. Still liking what she was doing. Because honestly, she had little enough experience with men, and none with a man like Dempsey. She could only trust her instincts to guide her and have fun with him in this rare moment to play and tease.

And enjoy his sinfully delicious body.

"I've taken all my cues from you tonight," he informed her, his muscles flexing under her as she slid down him to kiss his abs.

"How do you mean?" She peered up to find him shoving a pillow under his head.

Making himself comfortable? Or getting ready to watch the show? Nerves danced along her skin, mingling with anticipation. When he put his hands behind his head, it was a devastating look for a man with his build, emphasizing the way his upper body tapered to narrow hips.

"You get a sexy look in your eyes when you're thinking wicked thoughts, Addy. I know that's when to make my move."

"A sexy look?" She stroked a light touch up the hard length of him.

He hissed a breath between his teeth. "Definitely." He shifted under her, his whole body tensing.

She climbed back up him to whisper in his ear, "I've never done this before. Feel free to offer instruction." She paused to kiss his lips and wander her way down his body again, taking his incoherent groan as a good sign that he was on board with her plan.

She listened to every intake of his breath, repeating the things he liked best. When she traced the indents between his abs with her tongue, he almost came off the bed.

That was when she experimented with how she touched him, discovering it was easy to know what he liked. Tasting him received wholehearted approval. In fact, the more of him that she took into her mouth, the more encouraging his reaction.

"Addy." His tone warned her more than his words. And he would have hauled her up to kiss him if she hadn't paused to remind him who was in charge.

"Let go," she commanded, meeting his gaze one last time before she returned to the kisses he liked so well.

When his release came, she savored it, loving that rare moment of seeing him lose control. Of knowing she'd given him that pleasure.

But when the hot pulses halted and a final groan ripped from his throat, Dempsey reached for her and dragged her back up his body. His golden-brown gaze seared her. As if he'd taken her game as a personal challenge, he settled between her thighs and kissed her.

The sharp jolt of sensual pleasure was like an electric shock, rippling through every part of her. He dipped one shoulder beneath her thigh and then the other, finding just the right angle to slowly drive her to the edge of madness. Each stroke of his tongue sent quivery ribbons of pleasure to her belly. Fingers twisting in the sheets, she held on as he nipped and licked, making her fly apart in hard spasms that went on and on.

She wanted to say something about that, the intensity of the orgasm unlike anything she'd ever felt. But the hungry look still lurked in his eyes as he stretched out over her, kissing her mouth while he found another condom and seated himself deep inside her.

Any words she'd been about to speak dried up in her throat. All she could do was hold on and trust him to take care of her body, which was in the grip of a hunger that seemed bigger than both of them. Tucking her cheek against his chest, she closed her eyes and got lost in the feel of him inside her.

Dempsey. Reynaud.

She felt as if all her life had led to this moment. This joining. This wild heat that shook her to her core. And when at last he found his release, taking her with him yet again, Adelaide kissed him hard in a tangle of tongues and pleasure.

Afterward, she could barely move, but she didn't need to. Every part of her felt sated. Happy. And—at least in the physical sense—well loved. She knew they'd taken an irreparable step away from friendship toward something potentially more dangerous. But with the heavy feeling in her limbs and Dempsey's naked body wrapped around hers, she refused to have any regrets tonight. They would come, she guessed, as sure as the sunrise.

For now, however, she was going to squeeze every moment of pleasure she could out of this fake engagement and their time together. There was always a chance Dempsey could learn to care about her as more than a friend before their four weeks were up.

If sex was a way to make that happen, she would just have to sacrifice her body for the greater good.

And if her gamble didn't pay off? Adelaide would

have some incredible memories to keep her warm at night. She told herself it was a good plan. The only plan she had. But a little voice in her head kept reminding her that Dempsey didn't have affairs without an expiration date. How many times had Adelaide shipped off one of those extravagant tennis bracelets to a former lover?

She ought to know better than anyone. The only reason Dempsey had initiated this unwise relationship was because she was quitting soon. Yet knowing how their affair would end before it happened wasn't going to make it any easier when Dempsey walked away.

Chapter 8

When Dempsey's alarm chimed before dawn, he slammed the off button and hoped it hadn't woken Adelaide. They hadn't slept much with the fever for each other burning in their blood. He didn't want to wear her out, but the last time they'd been together had been her idea after they'd headed into the kitchen to refuel after midnight. She'd made crepes from scratch and they'd been amazing. Including the part when she'd taunted him to find the hint of raspberry sauce she'd dabbed on her bare skin while he wasn't looking.

That game had ended deliciously, but it had required a shower, where he'd gotten to wash her long hair himself. He'd wanted her then, too, when he'd carried her damp, freshly washed body back to his bed. But he hadn't wanted to exhaust her.

Studying her face in the shadows cast from the

bathroom light—they'd fallen asleep without shutting it off—Dempsey wondered what it would be like to work side by side now that they'd shared this incredible night. He'd never touched a woman he did business with. It was a rule he'd kept all through the years as he'd learned about the Reynauds' shipping empire from his grandfather, unwilling to have anyone draw a comparison between Dempsey's personal ethics and his parents.

"I can hear you thinking," Adelaide whispered, her eyes still closed.

"Maybe I'm thinking about how good you taste." He stroked her hair, still damp in places from their late-night shower. In other spots, strands had turned kinky, a phenomenon he remembered from when they were kids and she'd let it run wild.

He kissed her bare shoulder, breathing in the scent of roses that lingered even now that it mixed with his soap.

"My female intuition suggests there's more going on in your brain than that." She captured his hand where he touched her and threaded her fingers between his. "Do you really need to go to work already?"

"No. But I received a text last night from Evan that one of the players I cut in training camp—Marcus Wheelan—was picked up by the cops for getting into a fight in a local bar. I need to talk to him. See if I can get through to him before he heads down a path that he can't recover from." Dempsey had been saved from choosing that kind of life by a fluke of birth, a lucky chance. But if Theo Reynaud hadn't shown up to pluck Dempsey out of his old life, what were the chances that it would be Dempsey who spent the occasional Friday night in jail?

Or worse.

"Won't that attract the kind of publicity you don't want around the team?" Adelaide shifted, turning to meet his gaze.

"I'll get a lawyer to look at the bail situation and pull Marcus out of there so I can speak to him privately." Dempsey wasn't clear on the charges yet, but hoped they were no more serious than disorderly conduct or resisting arrest—the kinds of things police leveled at drunken, noisy athletes.

But according to Evan, who kept in touch with a lot of the players who'd been invited to training camp, Marcus had been out with a rough group. He'd taken it hard when he hadn't made the Hurricanes' regular-season roster after getting cut by a West Coast team last spring.

"That's good of you." She feathered a light touch along his cheek, her expression troubled. "I hope he listens."

"Me, too." He kissed her forehead and waged an inner battle not to slide his hands beneath the sheets and lose himself in her one more time. "And I hope you can get some more sleep."

She ignored his efforts at restraint, sidling over to him and slipping a slender thigh between his.

"I'll sleep better knowing you left the house happy." Her whispered words were like a drug, finding their way into his bloodstream and sending a fresh wave of heat through him.

"I could get used to this in a hurry." He gripped her hips and molded her curves to his, her breasts flattening against his chest.

He needed to be inside her, exploring her heat and hearing her soft moans in his ear. He'd never felt this way about a woman before, when every time with her made him want her even more. Again and again. He'd barely be able to walk by tomorrow at this rate.

But he didn't even care.

She pressed kisses along his shoulder and skimmed a hand down his chest. Lower.

"Good. Because I want you thinking about me at work today. And I want you to rush home early because you need to be with me all over again."

They both knew that was exactly what would happen, too. Already he couldn't imagine spending hours away from her. For a moment, he felt a pang of conscience that he was allowing this kind of relationship to grow unchecked, the kind where they could lose themselves in each other completely. He wondered how he would handle it once that heat finally burned itself out, but far more important, he should be thinking about Adelaide.

What would it do to her?

Not ready to consider that right now when they were only just beginning to discover all the ways they could drive one another to new heights of pleasure, Dempsey shut down his thoughts. He let the magic of Adelaide's touch carry him into a sensual world that was all their own.

Afterward, Adelaide walked along the lakeshore at sunrise as Dempsey showered and prepared to drive into the training facility. The grounds all around the Reynaud homes were breathtaking, the landscaping exotic and a little wild. She'd never gardened much herself, but she knew well how fast things grew in this kind of weather, and that it would take a whole fleet of full-time gardeners to meticulously maintain all of the dense plantings around the low-rock retaining walls and fountains, or the vines crawling up some of the outbuildings.

And, to her way of thinking, the rich greenery and abundance of flowers looked more natural than precisely trimmed boxwoods or well-spaced English gardens. Turning her attention back to her path along the lake, she spied a feminine figure walking toward her.

Princess Erika Mitras was engaged to Dempsey's older brother, Gervais, and she'd recently moved into his home near Dempsey's place. Adelaide had met her a few weeks ago when she'd first arrived and been thoroughly dazzled. Refined, royal and incredibly lovely, Erika was the kind of woman who would always draw stares, but there was much more to her than that. She'd served in her country's military, defying her parents' wishes to fulfill a call to civic duty.

Smiling, the princess navigated the walking path in glittery gold sandals and a gauzy white sundress. Her cool Nordic looks and platinum blond hair were shielded by a wide-brimmed hat.

"Good morning," Adelaide greeted her. "Did you happen to see the sunrise?"

Even now, the sky streaked with bright pink light.

"I was awake and waiting for it." She covered a yawn. "It is the curse of pregnancy that I can only sleep when I do not want to."

Adelaide turned to walk in the same direction as the other woman. In the distance, she saw a shirtless Gervais running toward them.

"Well, you look fantastic for someone who didn't sleep well."

"Maybe it is the pregnancy glow," Erika said wryly. "Or else just plain happiness. I cannot believe how lucky

I am to have Gervais in my life. I told him how beignets settle my stomach in the morning, and now he has fresh, warm beignets for me every day."

"How thoughtful. And romantic." Adelaide wondered if Dempsey would do things like that for the mother of his child one day. She paused to pick up a piece of driftwood with an interesting shape, thinking she might find a spot for it in one of the gardens.

"True. Although that is why I have taken to walking in the mornings. I will need the exercise to bear the many, many pounds I plan to gain over the next months."

Adelaide laughed. "You must have so many plans to make to prepare for your baby."

"Babies, actually. Did you not hear that I am having twins?" Erika rested a hand on Adelaide's forearm, a friendly touch that made her realize how few close female friends she had in her life.

Of course, she'd been living and breathing work and football these past four years.

"Oh, Erika." Adelaide's chest ached with a longing for the kind of happiness this woman had found. "How incredible. Congratulations." She hugged her gently. "Please, please let me know if there's anything I can do to help."

"Gervais already treats me as though I am carrying the weight of the world on my shoulders." Her good humor was contagious. "I have to tell him I am a healthy, strong woman. I do not need to put my feet up every moment of the day." She leaned close to lower her voice. "I am telling him that an active sex life will lead to happier babies."

"Well, it must have worked." She pointed to where

Gervais had paused to do a cycle of push-ups along the path. "He looks as if he's in training for a marathon."

"As I said, I am a lucky woman." Erika winked and shared her plans for decorating a nursery as they walked.

Adelaide listened attentively, all the while wondering what it would be like to be expecting a first child. She had never stopped to think much about babies, since she had never come close to finding a lasting love relationship and, of course, that needed to happen first.

But all the talk of babies and parenting tugged at her heart. She couldn't help but wonder what would happen if she were to become pregnant. Would Dempsey be excited? More likely he would not be pleased. He'd made it clear their relationship would have boundaries. For years, they had just been friends. Then, she'd been his assistant.

Now she was his lover.

After that? She feared she would be very much alone.

When Dempsey left the house that morning, he spotted Adelaide down by lake, walking with Gervais's future wife. For all that Adelaide had resisted getting close with his family, she looked comfortable enough, pausing in her walk to give the other woman a hug.

The sight did something peculiar to his insides. She was so naturally warmhearted and caring. Of course she would befriend the pregnant foreign princess who must be struggling to adjust to life in New Orleans as she prepared to be a mother.

Dempsey crossed the driveway to reach the detached garage when he caught sight of a familiar figure jogging toward him, his only neighbor right now while

Henri spent the season in the Garden District house with his wife.

"Gervais." Dempsey lifted a hand in greeting.

The eldest Reynaud brother, like Dempsey, had walked away from football after college because of injuries. He still ran every day, though, and Dempsey had caught sight of him in the players' gym after-hours some nights, working out to the point of exhaustion. Dempsey had never fully understood his brother's demons, since Gervais had always been the heir to a billion-dollar corporation and he'd been born with the innate business sense to run it well. But then, Gervais had always been the most coolly controlled one of them.

"Congratulations on your engagement." Sweating and shirtless, he slowed his pace to run in place. "Sorry I haven't been by to welcome Adelaide to the family. It's been a busy week in the front office while we prepare for the regular season to start."

"I wouldn't have chosen the week of our home opener for the engagement announcement if it hadn't been necessary." If Addy hadn't decided to quit on him, that is. Although it was tough to regret her decision now, knowing it had led to the most incredible night of his life.

Gervais raised a brow. "Necessary? As in, I won't be the only one trying to navigate the challenges of fatherhood next spring?"

"No." Dempsey hit the remote to raise the door to the farthest right bay in the garage. "You're on your own with that—double dose. Adelaide and I got engaged for different reasons, but the timing was unavoidable."

"Spoken like the romantic soul you've always been," Gervais said drily, clapping him on the shoulder. "But at least Adelaide understands you well. You two want to come up to the house for dinner tonight? Erika is used to having her sisters around. I know she would be glad to get to know her future sister-in-law."

"I'll check with Adelaide, but given how they seem to be enjoying their conversation on the beach now, I think that'll be a good plan." Surprised at the invitation— they'd never extended such invites to one another as bachelors—Dempsey wondered for a split second how family dynamics would change with women around. But then, that wasn't really a concern for now, since Adelaide wouldn't be under his roof for long. He would return to his usual role as the Reynaud black sheep then.

"Good. We can sneak away to watch some game film after dessert." Gervais started jogging again, backward. "You can let me in on the highlights of Sunday's game plan."

"Of course." So it would be a working dinner. Still, he appreciated the offer. "I'll text you once I speak to Adelaide."

Since the four Reynaud brothers had gone off to college, they hadn't spent much time together outside of family gatherings that their grandfather insisted on. Even now, Leon was the most likely to bring them together. Dempsey hated to think that their grandfather's decline in health would be the next thing to put Gervais, Dempsey, Henri and Jean-Pierre in the same room together.

Maybe tonight would be a step toward having a stronger relationship with Gervais—they had a working partnership to protect in the Hurricanes if nothing else. The only drawback would be that Dempsey would have to share Adelaide for a few hours, and with their time together limited, he didn't like the idea of giving up any of it.

They'd been together intimately for less than twenty-four hours and already Adelaide had gotten under his skin deeper than any other woman he'd ever known.

"I love your earrings." Erika lifted a hand toward Adelaide's ear as they sat outside by the pool behind Gervais's breathtaking home that evening. "May I?"

They were sipping virgin margaritas under a pergola heavy with bright pink bougainvillea. Adelaide had mixed feelings about the evening, since getting closer to Dempsey's family would only make their breakup more difficult when it happened. But visiting with Gervais's fiancée this morning and this evening had been surprisingly fun. There was nothing pretentious about this Vikingesque princess who, apparently, was one of five daughters in a family of deposed royalty from a tiny kingdom near Norway.

Their casual outdoor dinner had made Adelaide all the more committed to building a business and a life for herself outside the male-dominated world of football. She craved more girl time.

"Of course." She scooted closer on the massive side-by-side lounger they shared, since Erika had wanted to put her feet up and insisted Adelaide should, too. "These are a sample from an accessory collection I hope to design for female sports fans."

"Sports fans?" Erika frowned, a pout that didn't come close to diminishing her stunning good looks. "They do not look like sports paraphernalia."

Close up, Adelaide marveled at the other woman's skin tone. But then, maybe living so far north the sun couldn't wreak the same kind of havoc. She'd rather take the freckles, she decided, than live for months in the cold.

"That's because they are intended to offset other team-oriented clothes. Most women don't want to dress in head-to-toe gear like a player. So I have some pieces that are very focused on team logos, and some accessories that pick up the colors or motifs in a more subtle way so that fans can be coordinated without being cartoonish."

"So when I buy Henri's jersey to wear—just to tease Gervais, of course—" she gave Adelaide a conspiratorial grin as she released the jewelry "—I can wear gorgeous black-and-gold earrings with it."

"Exactly." Sipping her icy-cold cocktail that made good use of fresh oranges and limes, Adelaide winked at her new friend. "And how can your future husband argue when the jersey has the Reynaud name on it?"

"There is a bit of competition among them. Have you noticed this?"

Adelaide nearly choked on her drink after the unexpected laugh. "I've noticed. You'd be surprised to know it was even worse when they were teenagers."

"Tell me." Erika peered over her shoulder where the brothers had sat a few minutes before. "It is safe. They are watching their games on television."

"When I first met Dempsey's brothers, I was thirteen." It was a year after he'd been living with the Reynauds and she'd been so excited that he'd invited her to his fourteenth birthday party. The day had been a disaster for many reasons, mostly because she'd realized that her friend had become someone else since leaving St. Roch Avenue. "And they knew I was Dempsey's friend, so they decided to vie for my attention."

"Because when you have a sibling, you enjoy ir-
ritating them. Trust me, I understand that part a little
too well."

As an only child, Adelaide hadn't. She wished she'd
understood because she'd handled the attention all
wrong.

"One of them decided they should have a race to see
who was fastest. On that particular day, fastest was syn-
onymous with best."

"I would bet Gervais won because he was eldest."
Erika sipped her drink, adjusting her blue-and-white
sundress around her legs as she shifted to her side.

"Well, he would have, except Dempsey tripped him."
She'd been so disappointed he'd cheated that she'd failed
to see the significance of him needing to win for her. At
least, that was what she'd decided it meant later.

"Of course he did. You were *his* friend." She stirred
the ice in her glass with the red straw and waved over
a maid who had emerged from the house to pick up the
dishes from their dessert. "May we have some waters?"
she asked the server, passing off her glass. "And the
men are in Gervais's study. I believe he keeps brandy
in there, but will you see if they need anything?"

The woman nodded before disappearing into the
house.

"I didn't really understand how competitive they
were at the time. I just thought it meant Dempsey had
turned into a bully and I spent the party being kind to
Gervais."

Erika laughed. "So he won after all." Her blue eyes
sparkled. "What a clever clan we are marrying into,
Adelaide." She reached to squeeze her hand. "I'm so
glad I will have a new sister here."

Adelaide swallowed, her throat and eyes suddenly burning. Tricking nice people did not sit well with her. She blinked fast.

"I've never had a sister." She cleared her throat, grateful for the maid's return so she could accept a fresh glass of sparkling water with lime. "Let's not be competitive, though," she added.

"Deal." Erika clinked her water glass with Adelaide's. "Now, will you order me some of your earrings? And whatever else I need to be a stylish sports fan?"

"Of course." Flattered, Adelaide wondered if she would still want the items once her engagement was broken. "Thank you."

"But I'll need some things in blue and white, too, in addition to the Hurricanes gear."

"Blue and white?" Puzzled, she turned to see Gervais and Dempsey headed down the steps from an outdoor deck on an upper story.

"Some days I'll have to root for Jean-Pierre's team, of course. He *is* family." She pantomimed zipping her lips and throwing away the key.

The princess was a firecracker in couture clothes. It made Adelaide happy for Gervais, who seemed as if he could use more fun in his life. But as they said their good-nights and walked back across the landscaped properties separating their homes, she couldn't help a hollow feeling in her chest.

"Thank you for spending time with my family." Dempsey slid an arm around her waist as they passed a line of Italian cypress trees and rounded a courtyard with a fountain at the center.

"You don't have to thank me. I had fun." She held her

hand out as they neared the fountain so she could feel a hint of the cool spray drifting on the breeze.

"Did you?" He halted their steps on the gray cobblestones and tipped her chin up. "You look troubled."

She took comfort in his concern. "Erika was so kind to me. It feels wrong to deceive them about us." She searched his expression for clues to what he was thinking.

"An unfortunate necessity," he admitted, his handsome face revealing nothing while his hands smoothed down her back in a reassuring rub. "What do you think of Erika?"

"I like her. She's witty and sharp. I think she will liven up Gervais's world, and I bet she'll be a fabulous mother."

"That's good. He deserves to be happy." Palming the small of her back, he turned her toward his house again.

"Why? What do *you* think of her?" She knew Dempsey well enough to understand when he wasn't saying everything on his mind.

"I didn't get to speak with her one-on-one the way you did, but I trust your judgment. I researched her when Gervais announced the engagement, and her family—for all that she's royalty—has come close to bankruptcy in the past. So I wondered—"

"That's a horrible thought." Defensiveness surged at the insult to their lovely hostess. "And incredibly cynical."

"My grandfather taught us to be wary of fortune hunters from an early age." He kept to the cobblestone path until they reached his driveway. "Said he worked too hard building the company to have it torn apart by that kind of infighting."

"So is it safe to assume your brothers and grandfather are all reviewing my financial information this week?" She didn't like the idea of being held up to scrutiny for a fake engagement. She quickened her step as they neared the front door. "Because if a foreign princess rouses suspicion of gold digging, I can only imagine what the Reynauds think of a struggling artist from your old neighborhood."

"No one questions our relationship when we've been friends for more than half my lifetime." He circled around so he could hold the door open for her. "Every single member of my family knows you're important to me."

Some of the frustration eased out of her at the reassurance. She was important to him. But would she remain that way once she was no longer his fiancée?

A ball of panic bounced through her at the thought, but now they were inside and Dempsey's golden-brown eyes were already alight with desire as he stared down at her in the foyer.

"All through dinner, I was thinking about the moment when that door would close behind us." He crossed the polished Italian marble floor to eliminate the distance between them. "You know what else I was thinking about?"

"No." Her heartbeat did a crazy dance, and she was all too willing to let go of her doubts and worries about the future. This time with Dempsey was precious. A chance she'd been awaiting for half a lifetime.

Oh, what this man could do to her. With his hands. His sinful lips. The powerful thrust of his hips. He was better than any fantasy she'd dreamed up in the days when she'd had a crush on him.

"I was obsessed with this." Reaching behind her, he hooked a finger in the loop of the tie for her dress's halter top. "Do you have any idea how provocative it is to wear an outfit that allows a man to get you naked with a single tug on a lace?"

Her skin tightened like shrink-wrap.

"I hadn't known." Her neck tingled where his knuckles grazed it. "But now that I do, I will put the knowledge to work the next time I want you thinking about me."

Keeping his finger threaded through the loop, he didn't pull it free, but simply palmed her bare back and drew her closer.

"I'm thinking about you lately, no matter what you're wearing." He breathed the words in the hollow under her ear, right before he kissed her and then licked a trail across her most vulnerable places as he headed lower toward her shoulder.

The rasp of his jaw was a gentle abrasion on her skin, a sexy contrast to the wet heat of his lips and his tongue. She liked knowing that she was on his mind as much as he lingered in hers. Against all reason, she wanted to stay there.

"Are we alone in the house?" she asked, an idea coming to mind to help her stay in Dempsey's thoughts.

With only three more weeks of working as his assistant remaining, she wanted to fill his home with memories of her. Of them.

"Absolutely." He lifted his head from his task, eyes flaming with heat. "Why? Afraid of being an exhibitionist?" He tugged on the tie to the halter top of her dress.

"I'd prefer tonight to be for your eyes only," she admitted, clutching the dress to her breasts before it could fall. "And actually, the reason I wore this dress was just in case dinner by the pool turned into a pool party."

She let go of the fabric, and it fell away. She wore a simple strapless red bikini beneath.

If Dempsey was disappointed she wasn't naked under her clothes, he sure didn't show it. In fact, he stared at her body in a way that felt deliciously flattering.

"Damn." He whistled softly as he slid a finger beneath the tie in the center of the bandeau top. "You mean I could have been watching you cavort around the pool in this?"

"It's not too late for a swim." She backed up a step and then another. "We could head outside—" she clutched the knot between her breasts and tugged it "—and skinny-dip."

Dempsey made a strangled sound as he came after her. She pivoted on her toes and raced through the kitchen and toward the back door with the hottest man she'd ever met on her heels.

Sprinting through the rear of the house, she found one of the French doors leading out to the pool. Only the underwater light illuminated the surface, although the grounds were decorated with low-wattage bulbs around the trees and bushes. The pool was well hidden from any prying eyes on the other side of the lake, the landscaping planted to provide natural privacy.

Adelaide slipped off her shoes and jumped in wearing only her bikini bottoms. Dempsey surprised her by diving in a moment after her wearing…nothing.

Her breath caught as the low lights reflected off his impressive frame. Strong thighs. Powerful shoulders. A butt that had no business being so appealing. And then a splash engulfed her and she had no more time to admire the man swimming across the pool toward her.

She made a halfhearted effort to get away because, of course, she couldn't wait to be captured.

When she felt a hand wrap around her ankle and drag her back through the water she welcomed the heat of his touch.

"That's not skinny-dipping," he accused, seizing her hips and dragging her bikini bottoms off before she could protest.

He flung them onto the deck with a wet splash, then backed her against a wall in the shallow end. Despite the slight chill of the water, his body was like an inferno against hers. He wrapped her in his arms, warming her, his erection trapped against her belly as he kissed her deeply. Thoroughly.

She got so lost in him she didn't know how long they stayed there, hands gliding over slick skin, tongues tangling as they moved together. She watched, fascinated with the way their bodies looked beside one another, his muscles so impressive in the moonlight.

"I want you inside me." She shifted her hips to stroke him with one hand as she circled his waist with her leg. "Please."

"I don't have any protection out here," he said in her ear, nibbling her earlobe and driving her mad with need.

She bit her lip against the hunger, already so close to release. She could just let go and enjoy the sensations he could pull from her so easily with his talented hands. But she wanted to hold out for having him deep inside her.

"Let's go in," she pleaded, the hollow ache almost painful.

Dempsey lifted her into his arms and climbed the built-in stairs while water sluiced off them. He must look like Poseidon, rising from the depths, but she was too busy kissing him to see for herself. He paused near a deck box and withdrew two prewarmed towels, laying both of them on her as he carried her against his chest.

"I can walk." She pulled back as he edged sideways through the open French door. "You can let me down."

"And risk having you run?" He nipped her ear. "I already caught my prize. I'm not letting go now."

He bypassed the main staircase for the narrow steps up from a butler's kitchen, probably because the thick rubber treads provided traction when they were still dripping wet.

"You're crazy if you think I'd run now." She delved her fingers into his wet hair and brought his lips to hers. "I keep thinking that I must have been dreaming last night and that sex couldn't have been as incredible as I remember. I want to see for myself. Again."

"I like a challenge." He angled into his bedroom and fell onto the bed with her, taking her weight on him as they rolled. Together. "Why don't you keep track of how many times I make you scream my name tonight?"

She might have laughed or teased him about that, but his hand was already between her legs, the heel of his palm pressing where she needed him most.

Desire shot through her like a Roman candle, a bright burst that fired again and again. She clung to him, calling out his name just as he'd promised she would. It was only the beginning, she knew. She hadn't imagined how thoroughly Dempsey would dominate her world, her thoughts, her nights.

She had gladly given him her body. But as tender feelings crowded her chest for this man, Adelaide feared she was giving him much, much more.

Chapter 9

Dempsey awoke to the scent of coffee just how he liked it, thick and strong. Still half-asleep, he reached for Adelaide, only to find her side of the bed cold.

Coming more awake, he realized she must be responsible for making the coffee. He would have to tell her that he would far rather wake up to her in his arms, but he did appreciate the gesture on a game day. It was still dark out, but he needed to get to the stadium for their home opener—a banner moment in a career-making season. He could feel it in his bones.

And damn, but he would have liked to share that good feeling with Adelaide.

Shoving out of bed, he shrugged on a clean T-shirt and boxers, thinking he could coax her back upstairs. Then again, the kitchen table would do just fine. Last night had been so wild. So unexpected. He picked up his pace to find her.

When he reached the kitchen, he found her making breakfast in his shirt, her legs bare and her hair restrained in a messy braid that rested on her shoulder. But as he got closer, he could tell something was off by the way she moved. She fried eggs at the stove, her movements jerky and fast.

"Everything okay?" he asked as he passed the walk-in pantry. He might have lost his ability to read her more subtle emotions, but he'd have to be blind not to correctly interpret anger.

"No." She pulled down two plates from a cupboard and slid the eggs onto them. "I got up early because of a notification on my phone. I keep alerts on various buzzwords in the media as they pertain to you and the team." She pointed toward the kitchen table. "Have a seat and check out the morning paper."

Worry stabbed him hard in the gut as he headed toward the table.

"Is Marcus back in trouble?" He'd sprung the kid from jail on good faith, offering him a job helping Evan with some work for the Brighter NOLA foundation. Dempsey needed extra hands for a renovation project on a building that would house a local recreation center for the kids.

"No. Not this week anyway." Her clipped response gave nothing away as she retrieved silverware and linen napkins from a sideboard near the breakfast bar.

"Hurricanes Coach Muzzles Stormy Girlfriends." He read the headline aloud from the social section's front page. "Old news, right? Did she offer anything different than the rumors that have been around for years—that I rely on confidentiality agreements for some of my personal relationships?"

Was this what had Adelaide so riled? They'd seen worse and weathered it in the past.

"No." She put his eggs down on the table and tugged out a chair to sit across from him. "But nice timing on a game day, isn't it?"

"Whoa." He reached for her, bracketing her shoulders with his hands. "What am I missing? Why is this so upsetting?"

"Why?" Adelaide's eyes widened. "Because for all she knows we really *are* getting married. And what kind of evil witch does that to someone who is newly engaged?"

She blinked fast, emotions swirling through her eyes quicker than he could register them.

"Someone selfish." He shrugged, still not sure he saw what the big deal was, although he knew better than to say as much. "Someone who doesn't give any thought to who she hurts to get her own way. I'll bet you any money she wants to tout a new contract or sponsor or has some kind of promotional angle—"

He let go of her to turn the paper toward him so he could read the story.

"She has a part in a new action-adventure film," Addy admitted. "She mentions it toward the end."

"You see? Self-centered and trying to scam off the Hurricanes' publicity when a lot of people are paying attention to the team." He kissed Adelaide's cheek and pulled her to him again, holding her close, savoring the feel of her wearing precious little under that T-shirt. "C'mon. Let's have this breakfast you made. It smells fantastic."

"It's just eggs," she grumbled. Then her lips curled upward a bit. "Although I did make use of the cayenne pepper, which is why you like the scent, you crazy Cajun."

She hadn't called him that in a long time. Memories of their past—her friendship and unswerving loyalty—stirred along with it. Reminding him he didn't want to hurt her. She'd made him breakfast long ago when there'd been no food at his place. Eggs were a cheap meal, and even though he had access to the most exotic foods in the world, there was nothing he'd rather share with her right now than the eggs she'd cooked for him herself.

Taking care of him.

"Some spice in life is a good thing." He tugged her back and kissed her harder, more comfortable thinking about the chemistry they shared than that other, deeper connection. "And speaking of which, last night was incredible."

"I had fun, too." She shot him a flirtatious look as she took her seat at the table. "I'm glad you're not upset about the article in the paper—even if I'm still steaming a little."

He flipped it over and shoved it away.

"Not at all." He tucked her chair in and then sat beside her. "Valentina is annoying but predictable. I'm only upset for you."

He took a few bites before he noticed Addy had gone quiet. Glancing up, he noticed her studying him.

"Is that a plus when you're dating?" she asked, carefully cutting a piece of her egg and sliding it onto her toast. "Predictability trumps selfish and annoying?"

And just like that, he stood alone in a minefield with no foreseeable path out.

"You must know that I've deliberately simplified my

personal life these past few years in order to focus on my career." He set down his fork, realizing he should have paid more attention to the nuances of this conversation.

It wasn't about the article in the paper. Or about a potential distraction for him on his season opener.

Adelaide was more than a *little* angry about Valentina.

"You want simple *and* predictable." She tapped the heavy band of her engagement ring on the table. "It's strange that you opted to stage a relationship with me right now since it's both complicated and unexpected."

Didn't she understand that she was nothing like other women he'd been with? He wouldn't trade this time with her for anything.

"But you're not like other women, Addy. I trust you not to turn our private affairs into a three-ring circus for your own ends." He wanted to salvage a good day. He wanted to get back to where they were yesterday, when they'd had dinner with family and then driven each other wild all night long.

"You trust me to keep this simple and be predictable, too." She shook her head, a smile that was the opposite of happy twisting her lips. She shot out of her chair. "Unbelievable how the Reynaud arrogance has no bounds."

"Wait a minute." He stood as well, scrambling to follow her, to understand how he'd hurt her when that was the last thing he'd intended.

"No." The word was sharp. A short warning that her emotions were seething close to the surface.

He could see it in her face. In her eyes.

"Addy, please. Let me explain."

"No." She shook her head, her braid unraveling as

she moved, since she hadn't bothered to wrap a tie around the end. "I'm going to drive separately to the stadium. And when I get there, I will be an excellent assistant, as I've always been. I'll even keep the ring on my finger. But don't ask me to pretend with you, Dempsey. Not today."

For a moment, he felt stunned, as if she'd kicked him in the solar plexus.

"What do you mean? You can't end our agreement—"

"Please." She held a hand up to stop that line of discussion. "I'm not ending anything except this conversation. But I'm asking you—don't put me on the spot today, okay? I might not be as predictable as you'd like to think."

Members of the media rushed onto the field after the Hurricanes won 21–17 in their home opener against the defending Super Bowl champs. Adelaide watched from the sidelines, a rare spot for her, since her duties were more behind-the-scenes. But after her exchange with Dempsey over breakfast that morning, she had been reminded that in three more weeks, she would no longer have a role on the team. She might never have the chance to witness a game from this vantage point again.

Rap music blared from the speakers in the stands, adding to the celebratory mood. Fans whooped it up with one another. While some headed out to the parking lots to party or drive home, many hardcore followers remained in the stands, getting as close to the field as ushers would allow.

A photographer with a camera and a big plastic sound shield shuffled past her, his lens trained on Dempsey where he shook hands with the opposing team's coach.

A coach who did not look happy. The guy's face was still red after a screaming match with a ref about a pass-interference call that had not happened.

But the Hurricanes' game one was in the books. Dempsey and his team were off to the start he'd wanted for this season, the start that meant so much to him. Logically, she understood why. He'd always felt like an outsider in the Reynaud family, working relentlessly to prove he belonged, that his father had not made a mistake in plucking him out of that crappy apartment down the street from hers.

Yet, she couldn't help but think that if St. Roch Avenue wasn't good enough for him, then she wasn't good enough for him either. He'd dated one beautiful woman after another for years, never looking at Adelaide twice until she tried to quit. Hearing his easy defense of Valentina this morning had brought that hurt to the surface. When Adelaide's time with Dempsey was through, he'd go right back to women who were simple, predictable and from a much different world than hers.

She had no illusions about his ability to move on. She'd seen him do that plenty of times. But she seriously doubted hers.

Heading for the door that led into the medical staff's offices and bypassed the locker-room area, Adelaide picked up her pace when she saw a female reporter charging toward her, a cameraman in tow. Seriously?

The press on the field were normally big-time sports reporters, not from the social pages.

"Adelaide!" the woman called. "Excuse—"

Arriving at the door, Adelaide hauled it open and risked a glance back to see what had happened to her follower.

Henri Reynaud, the Hurricanes' quarterback and Dempsey's younger brother, had planted himself between Adelaide and the woman. Addy's heart fluttered a bit. Not that she thought Henri was Mr. Dreamy the way the rest of the female fans did. But because Dempsey's brothers had made her feel as though she mattered this week. Gervais by inviting her to dinner. Henri by running interference.

Seeing how she might have been accepted into their world made her chest ache for the things she wasn't going to have with Dempsey. She would be walking away from so much more than a job in three weeks. So why was she spending this window of time second-guessing herself—and Dempsey—every time she turned around? Why couldn't she just enjoy the moment?

Maybe she needed to stop worrying about the future. Starting tonight, she wasn't going to look beyond three weeks from now.

She would save up her memories of being the woman who got to be on his arm and in his bed. The memories of being part of a family. They wouldn't be enough, but if they were all she would ever have of him, she would make each moment count.

Dempsey drove the fastest street-legal BMW produced to date, but it didn't get him out of downtown any quicker after the game.

Had he ever felt so uneasy after a win?

He switched lanes to pass a slow-moving car, his G-Power M5 Beemer more than ready to launch into overdrive at the earliest opportunity. Too bad the ribbon of brake lights ahead meant he only succeeded in hurtling headlong from one stop-and-go lane to the next.

He'd asked the public relations coordinator if she'd seen Adelaide, but Carole didn't know where his fiancée had gone after the game. Now he gave in and phoned Evan. Hitting the speed-dial icon on the dashboard, he listened to Evan's line ring via Bluetooth.

"Hey, Coach. What's up?" Evan had lost his roster spot due to injury, but unlike most guys who'd been in the league for any length of time, he hadn't been in a hurry to rehab and look for a new team in the spring. He understood well the hazards of being a player and had been content to simply stick around the team.

Dempsey had asked him about returning to school for sports medicine and coming aboard as a trainer, but Evan called himself a "simple guy with simple needs," insisting he liked driving the Land Rover.

"Just checking to see if you're taking good care of my future wife." The comment didn't roll off his tongue the way he thought it would.

His wife.

The idea made his chest go tight and he wasn't quite sure why.

"She's teaching me about the garment business at the moment. Just a sec." Clearly holding his hand over the phone, Evan spoke to someone else—Adelaide, presumably. But a man's voice came through in the background, too. Then Evan came back on the line. "We're just finishing up a tour of a manufacturing facility. She's hoping that with some customization it might work out for producing her apparel line."

Her apparel line. Dempsey ground his teeth together, biting back a retort.

Apparently he hadn't made any headway yet convincing her to stay with the Hurricanes—with him—for the rest of the season. But then, he'd spent all his time romancing her after being surprised by an attraction he hadn't accounted for.

He needed to get their relationship back on track.

"I'd like to surprise her with dinner," he improvised, although maybe that wasn't a bad idea. "Are you bringing her home soon?"

Dinner aside, he just wanted to know when he would see Adelaide. She hadn't picked up her phone or answered his text after the game.

But then, she obviously took her start-up business more seriously than him.

"Definitely," Evan returned. "I think she's finishing up her meeting with the Realtor now. We're about half an hour away."

"Good deal. Thanks." Disconnecting the call, Dempsey pulled into the driveway of his house.

The outdoor lights were on, along with a few indoor ones. He had everything on timers, and he'd increased the periods when the grounds were lit, wanting to make the place as hospitable as he could for Adelaide.

Had her decision to tour a manufacturing facility been made this morning, spurred by her frustration regarding Valentina? Or had Addy been quietly taking care of her own business concerns all week, in spite of their agreement that she'd devote her time to the Hurricanes?

To him. This upset him far more than it should have.

His phone rang after he'd parked the BMW and headed into the house. Juggling his keys in one hand, he didn't check the caller ID before he thumbed the answer switch.

"Reynaud." He didn't need team problems. He had enough personal ones, since Addy was giving him the runaround.

"Hey, bro." The voice of his youngest brother came through the airwaves. "Congrats on the win."

"You, too, Jean-Pierre. I saw you put up some hellacious stats today." Dempsey hadn't been able to watch any film highlights on the way home, since he'd had to drive himself, but he'd checked for updates on the other one o'clock games before he left the stadium.

"Perfect football weather in New York. The ball sailed right where I wanted it to all day." The youngest Reynaud was the starting quarterback for the New York Gladiators and currently the only member of the family who wasn't a part of the Hurricanes organization. "Tomorrow's practice is light. I could head down there afterward if you think we need a powwow about Gramps."

"That'd be good. I think it's going to take all four of us to figure out how to approach him." Dempsey stepped inside the house, which was too quiet without Adelaide there.

Already, all his best memories in this place were with her.

Undressing her in the foyer. Chasing her out to the pool. Carrying her up to his bed.

"He's getting worse?" Jean-Pierre asked, pulling Dempsey's thoughts away from Addy.

"He thought I was Dad at a fund-raiser event the other night. Implied I needed to be careful my wife didn't find out about the woman on my arm."

On the other end, Jean-Pierre let loose a string of soft curses.

"That sucks," he finally said, summing it up well. "I'll be off the practice field by noon. I can probably be at the house by four." A perk of being in New York was that private planes were plentiful. Jean-Pierre didn't come home often, but he could make the trip in a hurry when he needed to.

"Sounds good. We practice at noon, but I'll make sure we finish up in time. See you then." Disconnecting the call, he knew he'd have to go in early to meet with his assistant coaches and watch game film.

Hell, he'd be watching game film tonight, too. But first, he would order dinner for him and Adelaide. Do something nice for her to make up for all the things he'd said wrong over breakfast. Maybe then he would be able to confront her about that trip to see a potential manufacturing facility. The capital investment for a start-up business would compromise her operating costs. She had to know that.

Her role with the Hurricanes aside, it was too soon for her business to launch in that kind of direction. Small growth was wiser. Subcontracting the manufacturing would give her more cushion for expenditures. As much as he understood she didn't want him interfering with this company she wanted to build, he simply couldn't let her fail.

Ah, hell, who was he kidding? He might be a selfish bastard, but he couldn't ignore the truth.

He didn't want her to leave.

Chapter 10

"No one could hold a grudge after that dinner." Adelaide swirled a strawberry through a warm chocolate sauce served in a melting pot over an open flame. "I might have to pick fights with you more often if this is the aftermath."

Dempsey had ordered an exquisite meal to be catered for them, and considering it must have been on short notice, the food was outrageously delicious. Her scallops had been prepared in a kind of sauce that took them from good to transcendent. The grilled vegetables were hot and tender, perfectly seasoned. But the dessert of exotic fondues was inspired.

She couldn't get enough of the chocolate sauce with a hint of raspberry liqueur.

"Are you sure?" Dempsey asked her, reaching under the mammoth dining room table to skim a touch along her knee. "I know you were upset this morning."

They were seated diagonally from one another—he was at the head of the table and she was to his right. The table was a chunky dark wood handcrafted in Mexico, the coarse finish making the piece all the more masculine and right for the house. Adelaide liked all the decor even if—in her fanciful imaginings—she pictured what she would do if she lived here. She'd put a vase of birds of paradise on the table, for one thing. Bright splashes of color to warm up this cool, controlled world.

"I was upset," she admitted. "But as I stood on the sidelines today, it occurred to me that I don't want to spoil this time with you. Working for you has been an incredible opportunity and I will miss it... I have to confess I will miss working with you, as well. Seeing you."

"Tell me what else you'll miss." He pulled her bare foot into his lap and massaged the arch.

"That feels amazing." She settled deeper into the red leather cushion on her high-backed wooden chair. Popping a raspberry into her mouth, she told herself she could have one more chocolate treat if she ate two plain berries.

Those were actually delicious as well, the juicy fruit almost tart after the sweetness of the chocolate.

"Turn your chair and I can do both feet." He nodded toward the side that needed shifting. And sure enough, pivoting toward him made it more comfortable to give him her other foot, too.

His thumbs stroked up the centers, over and over.

"What else will I miss?" She repeated the question to remind herself what he'd asked her before she slipped into a foot-massage-induced trance. "Always having a seat for the big games. The scent of barbecue in the parking lot from the tailgaters before home games. Seeing the young players at training camp and watching them horseplay because they're overgrown kids."

He was quiet for so long she wondered what he was thinking.

But hadn't she promised herself to simply enjoy this time with him? To make the most of every day of these next few weeks?

"I'll bet chocolate sauce would taste good on you," she observed lightly, dragging the warm pot closer.

That captured Dempsey's attention completely. He slowed the foot massage.

"The catering staff is still here," he reminded her, peering over his shoulder toward the kitchen.

They hadn't seen anyone since dessert was brought out, but two servers waited behind the scenes to clear their dishes and put away the leftovers.

"I'll bet they won't mind billing you for a fondue pot if I bring it upstairs with me."

Releasing her feet, he pushed back from the table in a hurry. He took the sauce from her, securing it under one arm, and then pulled out her chair to give her more room to stand.

A gentleman.

"No." He put a hand on her back and guided her away from the staircase. "Your room this time. You've got that big tub for afterward, and I think we're going to need it."

A thrill shot through her. Something about this new pact she'd made with herself—to live in the moment and store up these memories—made her bolder. More willing to take chances with him and see what happened.

He was already prepared to walk away from their

engagement in three more weeks, so why not at least ask for the things she wanted in a way she never had before? Chocolate sauce all over Dempsey… It was the stuff of fantasies.

Except once they closed the door to her bedroom, he set her decadent treat on the glass top of a double dresser, and then spun her in his arms. A whirlwind of raw masculinity, he hauled her up in his arms and carried her toward the large bathroom, his eyes blazing with undeniable heat.

"Dessert?" she asked, walking her fingers up his chest, her breathing unsteady at the feel of his arms around her.

"It's going to have to wait," he growled. "If you wanted slow and sweet, you shouldn't have looked at me like that over the dinner table."

A laugh burst free, but it turned into a moan as he settled her on the vanity countertop and stepped between her legs.

"I have no idea what you're talking about," she teased, her mouth going dry as he bunched up the fabric of her skirt and snapped the band on her panties with a quick tug.

Fire roared over her skin.

"The look you gave me?" He passed her a condom a second before he dropped his pants. "It said you wanted me right here." He slid a finger inside her.

The condom fell from her fingers. She wound her arms around his neck, needing more of him. All of him. Her heartbeat pounded so fiercely she felt light-headed. She pressed her breasts to his chest, doing her best to shrug out of the bodice. He must have retrieved the condom because she could feel the graze of his knuckles against her while he rolled it into place.

And then he was deep inside her.

His thrusts were hard, fast, and she loved every second of being with him. She held on tight, meeting his movements with her own as she caught glimpses of them moving together reflected in the mirrors all around. His powerful shoulders all but hid her from view from the back. But from the side, she saw her head thrown back, her spine arched to lift her breasts high. He ravished them thoroughly, one hand palming the back of her scalp while the other guided her hip to his.

Again and again.

"Let me watch you, Addy," he whispered in her ear, his breath harsh. "Come for me."

And she did.

Pleasure burst through her with fiery sparks, one after the other. He followed her, muscles flexing everywhere as he joined her in that hurtle over the edge.

His hand swept over her back, holding her close, his forehead falling against hers. She clutched at the fabric of his shirt, amazed that he was still half-dressed.

When she caught her breath, she pulled back, looking up at him. She wasn't sure what she expected—a smile, perhaps, for the crazy bathroom sink encounter. But she hadn't expected the seriousness in his eyes. Or the tenderness.

There was a connection there. A moment of recognition that sex hadn't been just about fun and pleasure. Something bigger was happening. She felt it, as much as she didn't want to. Did he?

Maybe he did. Because just then he blinked. But the

moment had passed. The look had vanished. His expression was now carefully shuttered.

She knew it would be wisest, safest, to pretend that moment had never happened. To keep things light and happy and work on stockpiling those memories before she left to start over—a new career, a new life.

But it took every ounce of willpower she possessed to simply call up a smile.

"Where did that come from?" She walked her hands down the front of his chest, admiring his strength.

His beautiful body.

"I missed you today," he said simply. "It didn't feel right, starting our day off arguing." He shifted positions and helped her down from the counter.

They cleaned up and she followed him into the bedroom. She sprawled on the California king–size mattress beside him, pulling pins out of her hair and setting them on the carved wood nightstand.

"Well, I sure don't feel like arguing after that amazing meal and the…rest." She laid her head on his chest and listened to his heartbeat.

In some ways, she would miss these moments even more than the torrid, tear-your-clothes-off encounters. A swell of emotions filled her, and she couldn't resist kissing the hard, muscular plane.

This, right now, was her best memory so far. Being cradled in his arms and breathing in the pine scent of his soap.

"All day it was on my mind, how much I wanted to get home and fix things with you." He stroked fingers through her hair.

That moment of connection in the bathroom? Could he feel it even now?

But she knew him well. Knew that he'd pushed away his other lovers once they started to get too close. Expect more from him. As his friend, she wouldn't follow that same path. There had to be some way to salvage at least their friendship when this was all over.

"I have the perfect stress reliever that will make you feel better about your day." She sat up on the bed, letting her hair fall over her shoulder now that she'd taken it all down.

Light spilled in from the bathroom, casting them in shadows. They'd eaten dinner late after the game and she knew he'd have to watch his game film soon.

"My stress faded as soon as I got you alone." His wicked grin made her heart do somersaults.

"Take off your shirt and turn over," she commanded, already plunging her fingers under the hem of his T-shirt.

"Yes, ma'am," he drawled, his eyes lighting with warmth again as he dragged the cotton up and over his head.

"You know how they say chocolate is good for the soul?" She retrieved the dessert sauce and dipped a finger in the warm liquid.

"I think it's books that are good for the soul." He propped his head on a pillow, his elbows out.

"Well, chocolate is good for mine." She traced the center of his spine with her finger, painting a line of deliciousness and then following it with her tongue. "But I think you're going to like this, too."

An hour later, she'd proved chocolate was good for everyone. Dempsey had bathed her afterward, whispering sweet words in her ear while he washed her hair.

She felt sated and boneless by the time he slipped from her bed to put in the necessary hours at his job.

She hated that he couldn't sleep with her all night, but in some ways, she wondered if it was for the best. She could tell herself that he had to work to do, and maybe that would make the hole he'd left in her heart a little more bearable.

Dempsey was still thinking about Adelaide the next day when he arrived at Gervais's house to meet with his brothers. Physically, he stood outside the downstairs media room and made himself a drink at the small liquor cabinet in the den. But mentally, his brain still played over and over the events of the night before.

Mostly, he thought back to that electric shock he'd felt when he'd looked into her eyes and the earth shifted. He couldn't write off that moment when he'd never experienced if before with any other woman. He had feelings for Adelaide. And that was going to complicate things in more ways than he could imagine.

"Dude." Jean-Pierre strode into the den behind him. "You're getting old when that passes for a drink. I come to town once in a blue moon. You can do better than—" he held up the bottle to read it "—coconut water? You'd better turn in your man card."

"I get the last laugh when I live longer." Dempsey set down his drink to give his brother a light punch in the stomach, a favored family greeting that their grandfather had started when they were kids.

Jean-Pierre returned with a one-two combination that—while still mostly for show—made Dempsey grateful he maintained a rigorous ab workout. Of all his brothers, he was closest to Jean-Pierre, making him the only one in the family he still punched.

"You'll be a hundred and five and wishing you'd

had more fun in your life," Jean-Pierre joked, going straight for the scotch decanted into cut crystal. "I've got transportation home tonight, so I don't mind if I crack open the stash Gervais likes to hide at the back of the cabinet."

"You have no idea where I hide my real stash." Gervais stalked out of the media room, where game film seemed to run on a continuous loop during the regular season. "I leave the swill out when I know the hard drinkers are coming."

Gervais hugged their brother.

"Did someone say swill?" Henri ambled out of the media room, where he must have been already watching film with Gervais. "Sounds like my kind of night—as long as I don't have to drink with any holier-than-thou New York players."

Even as he said it, he one-arm hugged Jean-Pierre. The two of them were more competitive with the rest of the world than each other. It had always made Dempsey a little sick inside to see them go up against one another on the field, since he genuinely wanted both of them to win. They were incredibly gifted athletes who, in a league full of gifted athletes, walked on a whole different plane.

"Sit," Gervais ordered them. "You are busy and it's rare we're all together. I'd like to deal with the issue at hand first so we can relax over dinner."

"Relax?" Jean-Pierre lounged sideways in one of the big leather club chairs arranged around the fireplace in the den. "Who can relax while Gramps is struggling to remember his own grandsons?"

The mood shifted as they each gravitated toward the spots they'd always taken in the room from the time they were kids and Theo would call them in for talks. Or, more often, when they had run of the house because their father was on an extended "business trip" that was code for a vacation with his latest woman.

When the house had still belonged to Theo and Alessandra, most of the rooms had been fussy and full of interior-decorator additions—elaborate crystal light fixtures that hung so low the brothers broke something every time they threw a ball in the house. Or three-dimensional wall art that spanned whole walls and would scrape the skin off an arm if they tackled and pushed each other into it.

The den had always been male terrain.

Now Dempsey got them up to speed on his exchange with Leon at the Brighter NOLA fund-raiser.

Silence followed, each one of them ruminating on the possibility that Leon was in the early stages of dementia.

"You do take after Dad the most," Henri offered from his seat behind the desk, Italian leather shoes planted on the old blotter. He lifted a finger from his glass to point at Dempsey.

His shoulders tensed. Every muscle group in his arms and back contracted.

"Henri," Gervais warned.

"Seriously, he looks more like Dad. He has his walk, too. Grand-père might have been—"

"I am nothing like our father." He had to loosen his hold on the cut-crystal glass before he shattered it.

He'd done everything to distance himself from Theo from the moment he'd arrived in this house as a teen. He could count the number of drinks he took in a year on one hand. As for women? He'd had contractual arrangements with every single one but Adelaide, and the time frames had never overlapped. There would never be a surprise child of his who would be raised alone. Separated from family.

"I know, man. But you've got the whole drama with the model going on the same week you get engaged. Maybe Leon just got a little muddled and—"

Dempsey was across the floor and knocking Henri's feet off the desk before the sentence was done.

"Not. The. Same." Fury heated the words.

"Seriously?" Henri put his drink down. "Are we going there? Because I'm not getting bounced off the team for some bullshit argument in the den, but if I have to pound you, I will."

Dempsey had more to say to that, since any pounding that needed doing would be meted out by him. But Gervais clapped him on the shoulder.

"Henri just doesn't want to face the fact that Leon isn't indestructible. Maybe give him a pass today." Gervais spoke calmly. Rationally.

And, probably, correctly.

No one wanted to think about their grandfather going downhill. They all loved the old man.

"I would never cut you for an argument in the den." Dempsey extended the olive branch. "But just so we're clear, I could still kick your ass."

"Not responding." Henri returned his feet to the desk. "So no one else thinks it could have been a momentary lapse for Leon? One mistake and he's an Alzheimer's patient?"

"It's not just one. There were signs this summer, too," Gervais reminded them. "He was going to see his doctor about it and he said it was a thyroid condition. If that's the case, he needs to get his meds checked. But at this point, we might need to consider the idea that he's not really taking care of himself."

Dempsey drained his water, trying to focus on the conversation and let go of the dig about his overlapping affairs. Not that Henri had worded it that way, but damn. He'd worked so hard to distance himself from his father's philandering ways. Did his brothers still see him as some kind of playboy type?

Clearly they had no idea how far gone he was over Adelaide. He couldn't even imagine letting her go at the end of their engagement. By now he wasn't even as concerned about replacing her as his assistant.

He couldn't replace her in his bed. Or if he was honest with himself, his heart. She made him laugh. She understood his lifestyle and the huge demands of his job. She even made it easier for him to be around his family. That dinner with Gervais and Erika had been one of the most stress-free times he'd ever had with one of his brothers as an adult, perhaps because he wasn't reading slights into the conversation the way he did today with Henri.

"Dempsey?" Jean-Pierre's voice knifed through his thoughts. "What do you think we should do?"

"Spend as much time with him as we can." It was all he knew how to do with people who weren't staying in his life forever. He knew it was a crap plan even as he proposed it, but he hadn't figured out anything better for keeping Addy around either.

Throughout the meal he shared with his brothers, he kept coming back to that point. He had no plan for convincing Adelaide to stay. He respected her for wanting to build her own business and he couldn't in good conscience prevent it from happening for his own selfish ends. He had to find a way to help her that would be an offer she couldn't refuse. A way to help her that wouldn't make her feel as if he was taking the power out of her hands.

He understood that much about her.

But their time shared as a newly engaged couple had shown him how good they could be together, and he refused to walk away from that without giving the relationship more time. Every day he couldn't wait to be with her. Even sitting around with his brothers in a rare meal where they were all in the same place, Dempsey was still picturing that moment when he would head home and see Addy.

She made sense in his life and she always had.

He would make a case for extending their engagement. No, damn it. He would propose to her for real. They had been friends. They'd worked together. He counted on her.

Now? Their chemistry was off the charts and they brought each other a level of fulfillment that he'd never experienced before. Adelaide was a smart woman. She would understand why they worked together.

She had to.

Chapter 11

"I think it's a great space, Adelaide." Her mother walked through the riverside manufacturing facility that Adelaide could use for mass-producing knitwear. Della's purple flip-flops slapped along the concrete floor.

"The square footage for offices is nice, too." She headed toward the back of the building to show her mother. Her Realtor had opened the door for them as long as Adelaide would lock up behind them.

She was already subcontracting out a short run of shirts after her success with crowd funding, but the time had come to think bigger. And this space would be ideal, already containing a few machines she would refit for the kind of textile production she needed. She'd been approved for a small-business loan that would cover the cost of the building and her biggest start-up expenses, but it was still a big step and she wanted her mother's opinion.

Lately, it felt as though her life was on fast-forward, and while it was exciting to have so many new options open to her, a part of her wished she could just stop for a minute and be sure she was making the best decisions. Dempsey jumbled all her thoughts lately, the passion they shared so much different from her old crush. She wasn't sure if she trusted herself to move forward in any direction.

"What does Dempsey think about it?" Della asked, examining the floor-to-ceiling windows overlooking the Mississippi in the largest of the offices.

"He hasn't seen it yet." She hated to admit as much, but he'd been so dismissive of her dreams before, so ready to leap in and save her from her own mistakes, that she wasn't ready to share this with him.

Then again, maybe moving ahead with her business simply signaled an end to her time as Dempsey's fiancée and she wasn't sure if she was ready for it to be over.

Della's brows arched. "Too busy to make time for my girl's work?"

"No. Nothing like that." She closed her eyes, hating the lies. And would it really matter if she told her mother the truth? Della Thibodeaux didn't exactly have a history of running to the press with gossip. "He didn't want me to tell anyone, but the engagement is just for show. I did it to help him."

Or because he'd put her in a ridiculously awkward position, take your pick.

But she couldn't regret it after how close they'd grown. The only problem was, now that she'd seen how amazing it was to be with him—even better than she'd ever imagined—she had no idea how she'd ever go back to their old friendship.

"Just for show?" Della folded her arms, leaning into the window frame as she studied her daughter, deep concern in her eyes.

Sunlight spilled in all around her, catching the grays in her dark hair. Her mother was a beautiful woman and so wise, too. Addy couldn't deny being curious to hear her mother's opinion on the fake engagement. Would she tell Adelaide she was the most foolish woman ever?

"He announced it in public and made it difficult for me to argue it without humiliating him."

"Of course you didn't argue, because you've always wanted to make him happy." She strode closer and put her hands on Adelaide's shoulders, her heavy silver bracelets settling against Adelaide's collarbone. "And is it still for show now, after you've been living with him for almost two weeks?"

Her cheeks heated, which was silly because she was a grown-up and could live with whomever she wanted.

"I think I'm in love with him," she admitted, the words torn from her heart, since she knew that level of emotion was not reciprocated.

"Oh, sweetheart." Her mother opened her arms, gathered her close and squeezed tight. "Of course you do. At least one of you has admitted it."

Adelaide's eyes burned. Tears fell as she rested her head on her mother's shoulder. She didn't want her mother's pity for loving a man who didn't—

Wait. She stopped crying, her mother's words sinking in.

"What did you say?" Her thoughts caught up with her ears and she pulled back to look into her mom's hazel eyes, which were lighter than Adelaide's.

"You heard me." Della kissed her cheek and stepped

back. "You two were meant to be. You just needed the right time to come along. Why do you think he's thirty-one years old and dating fluff-headed women with more boobs than brains?"

Adelaide choked on a much-needed laugh. "Mom. That's not fair."

Even if, in her meaner moments, Adelaide might have been equally unkind in her thoughts. Mostly about Valentina.

"All I mean, daughter dear, is that he has never dated a woman seriously. I think it's because he's been waiting for the right woman. He's been waiting for you, my girl." She looped her arm around Adelaide's waist as they headed for the exit and shut off the lights.

Adelaide's yellow-diamond engagement ring caught the sun's rays, sending sparkles in every direction.

"That's such a mom thing to say." Still, it warmed her heart even if she knew Dempsey far better than her mother. "Does parenting come with a handbook of mom sayings to cheer up dejected daughters?"

She wanted to trust in her mother's words but she was scared to believe that Dempsey could care about her like that.

"Mothers know." She tipped her temple to Addy's, the scent of lemon verbena drifting up from her hair.

"Well, I'm not sure about the engagement or where that's going, but I'll tell him about this manufacturing space tonight. The Hurricanes play in Atlanta tomorrow and I'm going with him. After the game, we'll have some time together to talk and I'll see what he thinks." Or she hoped they would have time together.

Last Sunday, after their home opener, they'd had a nice dinner. But Dempsey had seemed distracted this week, ever since his dinner with his brothers. She knew he was worried about his grandfather, but it seemed as if he'd been busy every night since, only falling into bed with her at midnight and sleeping for a few hours.

He also made hot, toe-curling love to her until she couldn't see straight. She couldn't complain about that part. But she did wish she had more time with him, since it felt as though the clock was ticking down on their arrangement.

And no matter what her mother said to cheer her, Adelaide had seen no sign from Dempsey that he'd fallen in love.

"I'm dying to know where you're taking me." Adelaide glanced over at Dempsey sitting beside her in the limo he'd booked after the game. "I've never known you to be so mysterious."

When she'd checked into the hotel where the team was staying the night before, the concierge had given her a card from Dempsey, who had on-site duties at the Atlanta stadium when they'd landed. The card had invited her on a date to an undisclosed location after Sunday's one-o'clock game against Atlanta. A jaw-dropping Versace gown awaited her in their suite, burgundy lace with a plunging neckline that kept everything covered but—wow. The Louboutin sky-high heels that accompanied it were the most exotic footwear she'd ever slid on, the signature red sole dazzling her almost as much as the satin toes with hand-crafted embellishments.

If she looked down her crossed legs now, she could see the pretty toes peeping out from the handkerchief hem of the tulle skirting.

He folded her hand in his, the crisp white collar of his

shirt emphasizing his deep tan gained from spending every day on the practice field. "I owed you a date night. You were kind enough to be my date for the Brighter NOLA ball, so it seemed like you ought to have a night that was just for you."

His Tom Ford tuxedo was obviously custom tailored, since off-the-rack sizes never fit an athlete's body, and the black fabric skimmed his physique perfectly. The black silk-peaked lapels made her itch to run her hand up and down the material.

Later.

For now she just wanted to know where they were headed. She'd never seen Dempsey race out of a stadium so early. She hadn't even attended the game, taking her time to dress in the hotel, then taking the limo to the VIP pickup outside the stadium. Traffic had been slow at first, but it wasn't even six o'clock yet. Almost two hours before sunset.

"I'd be surprised if there are many restaurants out this way," she observed, peering out the windows as they drove toward Stone Mountain, winding through quieter roads.

It was early yet, but her invitation had mentioned a special "sunset dinner."

A mysterious smile played around his mouth. A mouth that had brought her such pleasure.

"There's a surprise first. I hope you're not too hungry."

"I think I'm too excited to be hungry." She felt the first flutter of nerves, because Dempsey looked so serious for a date night.

She wanted to ask him about that. About his grandfather's health. Maybe that was what had been bothering him all week. But just then, the limo came to a clearing in the trees and a flash of rainbow-colored silk fluttered through the sky.

"How beautiful!" She clutched his arm, pointing to a hot-air balloon being inflated on a nearby field.

At the same moment, the limo slowed and turned into the field, heading right toward the balloon.

She stilled.

"Don't tell me…" She turned toward him, and saw the first hint of a smile on his face. "Is this the surprise?"

"Only if you'd like it to be." He squeezed her hand.

She squealed, scarcely able to take her eyes off the huge balloon that looked as if it would burst into flames any moment from the blazing blasts that shot into the bottom, filling it with air. Or helium. Or whatever did that magic trick that made it go from half on the ground to a big ball in the sky.

"Yes!" She risked her lipstick by kissing him through a shocked laugh. "It's amazing! I've never seen anything like it."

"Here." He produced a satin drawstring bag as the car rolled to a stop and their driver came around to open the door. "Better wear these for now and save your pretty shoes for later."

Opening the sack, she pulled out a pair of silver ballet slippers. Just her size.

"You thought of everything." She had to have him help her because she fumbled the shoes twice, distracted by the sight of yellow, blue, red and orange silk rising higher just outside the car.

"I would have tried to get us here earlier if I'd known you wanted to see this part." His warm hands tugged her shoes into place before he helped her out of the car. He reached back in the limo and withdrew a length of fuzzy mohair and cashmere that at first she thought was a blanket, but he unfurled it and laid it around her shoulders. A burgundy-colored pashmina fell around her. "The pilot said it will be cooler once we're up there."

A red carpet lined her path from the car door to the balloon basket. While the limo driver exchanged words with the crew that operated the balloon, Adelaide had a moment to catch her breath and take in the full extent of her surprise. Blasts of heat passed her shoulders in rhythmic waves each time the pilot pulled the cord to unleash flames into the air that kept the balloon filled.

"I just can't believe how huge it is up close." She'd seen hot-air balloons in the sky before and admired their beauty, but she'd never dreamed of riding in one. "And I can't imagine what made you think to do this tonight, but I'm so excited I feel…breathless."

He tucked her close to his side as they walked the carpeted path together. "The best part hasn't started. I hear it's incredible to go up in one of these things."

"You've never done this either?" That made it feel all the more special, that she could share a first with him. She felt like a medieval princess, traipsing through the countryside in her designer gown, the layers of handkerchief hem blowing gently against her calves as they walked.

"No. This is just for you, Adelaide." He stopped as they reached the balloon basket, his eyes serious. Intense.

"Any special occasion?" Curious, she wasn't sure why he'd put so much effort into a special night for them now.

As much as she wanted to believe that he'd planned a fairy-tale date just to romance her, a cynical part of her couldn't help but wonder why.

"I'm sorry I put you on the spot when I announced our engagement. Consider this my apology, since that's not how I should have treated a friend." He lifted her hand to his lips and kissed the back of it.

Her heart melted. Just turned to gooey mush. She would have swooned into his arms if the pilot hadn't turned to them right then and introduced himself.

While the pilot—Jim—went over a few safety precautions and briefly outlined the plan for their hour-long flight, Adelaide stared at Dempsey and felt herself falling faster. She'd tried to keep herself so safe with him, from him. But her mother was right, and this man had always had a piece of her heart. How on earth could she maintain her defenses around a man who bought her a Versace gown to take her on a hot-air balloon ride?

She hadn't heard any of Jim's speech by the time Dempsey lifted Adelaide in his arms and set her on her feet inside the basket. He vaulted in behind her, their portion of the basket separated from Jim's by a waist-high wall. Moments later, the ground crew let go of their tethers and the balloon lifted them into the air so smoothly and silently it felt like magic.

Her heart soared along with the rest of her.

Impulsively, she slid her arms around Dempsey's waist and tucked her head against his shoulder. He'd said he wanted to apologize for not being a better friend. Could that mean he wanted to be…more?

"Do you like it?" His hand gripped her shoulder through the pashmina, a warm weight connecting them.

They stared out their side of the basket while Jim took care of maneuvering the balloon from his own side. It felt private enough, especially with all the open air around them.

"I love it." She peered up at him as the world fell away beneath them. "I've never had anyone do something so special for me."

"Good." He kissed her temple while the limo below them became a toy-size plaything. "Because the past two weeks have been something special for me. I wanted you to know that, even if this engagement got off to an awkward beginning, it's been…eye-opening."

She reached for the edge of the basket and gripped it, feeling as though she needed an anchor in a world suddenly off-kilter. What was he saying? Had her mother guessed correctly that Dempsey cared more than she'd realized?

"How so?" Her voice was a thin crack of sound in the cool air, and she tugged the pashmina closer around her. The landscape spread out below them like a patchwork quilt of green squares dotted with gray rocky patches and splashes of blue.

"We make a great team, for one thing." He turned her toward him, his hands on her shoulders. "You have to know that. And you've spent years helping me to be more successful, always giving me far more help than what I could ever pay you for. I want you to know that teamwork goes both ways, and I can help you, too."

He withdrew a piece of paper from the breast pocket of his tuxedo. It fluttered a little in the breeze as the temperature cooled.

"What is it?" She didn't take it, afraid it would blow away.

"The deed to the manufacturing facility you looked at with Evan last week." He tucked the paper into her beaded satin purse that sat on the floor of the balloon basket and straightened.

"You bought it?" She wasn't sure what to say, since she'd told him she didn't want this to be a Reynaud enterprise. "You haven't even seen it. I was going to ask you what you thought when we got back home—"

"I toured it Thursday before practice. It's a good investment."

The balloon dipped, jarring her, but no more than his words.

He'd toured it and bought it without speaking to her. She didn't want to ruin their balloon ride by complaining about what he'd obviously meant as a generous gesture. But she couldn't help the frustration bubbling up that he hadn't at least spoken to her about it.

"I hadn't even run the numbers on the operating costs yet." She didn't want to feel tears burning the backs of her eyes. She understood him well enough to know his heart was in the right place. But how could he be friends with her for so long and not understand how important it was for her to make her own decisions regarding her business? "I hadn't decided for sure yet—"

"You showed me the business plan, remember? I ran the numbers. You can afford the expenses easily now."

Except she needed to make those decisions, not him. Didn't he have any faith in her business judgment?

"Perhaps." She watched an eagle soaring nearby, the sight so incredible, but more difficult to enjoy when her world felt as if it was fracturing. "But I can't accept a gift—"

"I know you don't want anything handed to you, Addy, but this is no more of a gift than all the ways you've anticipated my every need for years. How many times have you worked more than forty hours in a week without compensation?"

"I'm a salaried employee," she reminded him, still feeling off balance.

"In a job that you took to help me. Don't try to make the deed mean more than it does, Adelaide. You've worked hard for me and I'm finally in a position to achieve everything I've always wanted with the Hurricanes this year. Let me be a small part of your dream, too."

Some of her defensiveness eased. She had to admit, it was a thoughtful gesture. A generous one, too, even if a bit high-handed. And the way he'd worded it made her feel a teeny bit more entitled to the gift, even though it far surpassed the monetary value of what she'd done for him. Still, the gift left her feeling a little hollow inside when she'd just convinced herself that he'd taken her on a balloon ride because he'd realized some deeper affection for her.

"Can I think about it before I accept it?" She cleared her throat, trying not to reveal the letdown she felt. The wind whipped a piece of her hair free from her updo, the long strand twining around her neck.

"No. You can sell it if you don't want to use the facility. But it's yours, Addy. That's done." He reached to sweep aside the hair and tucked it into one of the tiny rhinestone butterflies that held spare strands. "I have one other gift for you, and I want you to really consider it."

That seriousness in his eyes again. The look that had made her nervous all week. What on earth was on the man's mind?

When he reached into his breast pocket again, her heart about stopped. He pulled out a ring box.

Her heartbeat stuttered. Her gaze flew back to his.

"Adelaide, these two weeks have shown me how perfect we are together." He opened the box to reveal a stunningly rare blue garnet set in...of all things...a tiny spoon ring design that replicated the spoon bracelet he'd given her all those years ago when he'd had to forge a gift for her with his own hands.

"Dempsey?" Her fingers trembled as she reached to touch it, hardly daring to believe what she was seeing. What she was hearing.

"It's not meant to replace your engagement ring. But I wanted to give you something special."

"I don't understand." She shook her head, overwhelmed by the generosity of the gift.

"We're best friends. We're even better lovers. And we're stronger together." He tugged the ring from the velvet backing for her and slid the box into his pocket. "This ring is my way of asking you to make our engagement a real one. Will you marry me?"

Her emotions tumbled over each other: hope, joy, love and— Wait. Had he even mentioned that part? Of course he must have. She just hadn't heard it in the same way she'd missed the pilot's preliftoff speech because she'd been marveling at how perfect a date this was. She hadn't been paying attention.

Her hands hovered beside the ring.

"Did you...?" She felt embarrassed. Flustered. She should leap into his arms and say yes. Any other woman would. But Adelaide had waited most of her life to hear those words and she didn't want to miss any of it. "I'm sorry. I was so mesmerized by the ring and the setting and—" She gestured to the balloon above them and the scenery below. "It's all so overwhelming. But are you saying you want to get married? For real?" Happy tears pooled in her eyes already. "I love you so much."

And then she did fling herself into his arms, tears spilling onto the beautiful silk collar of his tuxedo. But she was just so happy.

Only…he still hadn't said he loved her. Her declaration of love hung suspended like a balloon between them. In fact, Dempsey patted her back awkwardly now, as if that was his reply.

She hadn't missed the words in his proposal, she realized with a heart sinking like lead. He simply hadn't said them. She knew, even before she edged back and saw the expression on his face. Not bewildered, exactly. More…unsure.

It wasn't an expression she'd seen on his face in many years. Her Reynaud fiancé was used to getting what he wanted, and while he might want Adelaide for a bride, it wasn't for the same reason that she would have liked to be his wife.

"Adelaide. Think about the future we can have together. All the things we can achieve." He must have seen her expression shifting from joy to whatever it was she was feeling now.

Deflation.

"Marriage isn't about being a team or working well together." She wrapped a hand around one of the ropes tying the basket to the balloon, needing something to steady her without the solid strength of Dempsey Reynaud beside her.

"There are far more reasons than that."

"There's only one reason that I would marry. Just one." She stared out at the world coming closer to them now. Dempsey must have signaled Jim to take them back down.

Their date was over.

"The ring is one of a kind, Adelaide. Like you." His words reminded her of all she was giving up. All she would be turning her back on if she refused him now.

But she'd waited too long for love to accept half measures now. She owed herself better.

"We both deserve to be loved," she told him softly, not able to meet his gaze and feel the raw connection that was still mostly one-sided. "You're my friend, Dempsey. And I want that for you as much as I want it for me."

When the balloon touched down, it jarred her. Sent her tumbling into his arms before the basket righted itself.

She didn't linger there, though.

Her fairy tale had come to an end.

Chapter 12

Three days later, back home at the Hurricanes' training facility, Dempsey envied the guys on the practice field. After the knife in the gut that had been Adelaide's rejection, he would trade his job for the chance to pull on shoulder pads and hit the living hell out of a practice dummy. Or to pound out the frustration through his feet with wind sprints—one set after another.

Instead, he roamed the steaming-hot practice field and nitpicked performances while sweat beaded on his forehead. He blew his whistle a lot and made everyone else work their asses off. Fair or not, teams were built through sweat, and he'd played on enough teams himself to know you balanced the good times—the wins—with the challenges. And if the challenges didn't come on the field on Sunday, a good coach handed them up in practice.

"Again!" he barked at the receivers running long patterns in the heat. Normally, Dempsey focused on the full team as they practiced plays. But today he had taken over the receiver coach's job.

In a minute, he'd move on to the running backs, since he'd already been through all the defensive positions.

Adelaide had not publicly broken their engagement yet, but she had moved out of his house. Which shouldn't have surprised him after the epic fail of his proposal. He'd planned for the moment all week. Spent every spare second that he wasn't with his team figuring out how to make the night special. Yet it had fallen short of the mark for her.

Of course, they hadn't gotten to half of it. He'd ordered an outdoor dinner set up in the mountains with a perfect view of the sunset. He'd had a classical guitarist in place, for crying out loud, so they could dance under the stars.

And she hadn't even taken her ring.

Of all the things that had gone wrong that night, that bothered him the most, given how much thought he'd put into the design. Sure, he was to blame for not understanding that he could have scrapped the balloon, the limo and the guitarist to simply say, "I love you." Except, in all his planning, that had never occurred to him. He'd known what he felt for Addy was big. But was it love? He'd shut down that emotional part of himself long ago, probably on one of the nights his mother had locked him out of the house, claiming some irrational fault on his part, but mostly because she was high.

Love wasn't part of his vernacular.

That had worked out fine for him in the Reynaud house full of men. Caring was demonstrated through externals. A one-two punch for a greeting like what he and Jean-Pierre still exchanged. Covering up for Henri when his younger brother had broken a priceless antique. His first well-executed corporate raid had won the admiration of Gervais and Leon alike.

Dempsey understood that world. It was his world, and he'd handed it to Adelaide on a silver platter, but it hadn't been enough.

And now he'd lost her in every way possible. As his friend. His lover. His future wife.

Stalking away from the receivers, he was about to put the running backs to work when his brother Henri jogged over to match his steps.

"Got a second, Coach?" Henri used the deferential speech of a player, a sign of respect Dempsey had never had to ask for, but which had always been freely given even though Henri thought nothing of busting his chops off the field.

"I probably have one." He kept walking.

Henri kept pace.

"Privately?" he urged in a tone that bordered on less deferential. "Practice was supposed to end an hour ago."

Surprised, Dempsey checked his watch.

"Shit. Fine." He blew his whistle loud enough for the whole field to hear. "Thanks for the hard work today. Same time tomorrow."

A chorus of relieved groans echoed across the field. Dempsey changed course toward the offices. Henri still kept pace.

"You're killing the guys," Henri observed, his helmet tucked under one arm, his practice jersey drenched with sweat. "Any particular reason?"

They were back to being brothers now that practice was done and no one would overhear.

"We have a tough game on Sunday and our first two wins have not been as decisive as I would have liked." He halted his steps and folded his arms, waiting for Henri to spit out whatever was on his mind. "You have a problem with that?"

"I'm all about team building." Henri planted a cleat on the first row of bleachers. "But you've run them long every day this week. Morale is low. The guys are confused in the locker room. I know that's not what you're going for."

"Since when do you snitch on locker-room talk about me?" Dempsey shooed away one of the field personnel who came by to pick up a water cooler. He didn't need an audience for this talk.

"Only since you started acting like a coach with a chip on his shoulder instead of the supremely capable leader you've been the whole rest of my tenure with this team."

The rare compliment surprised him. The complaint really didn't. There was a chance Henri was correct.

"I'll take that under advisement." He accepted the input with a nod and tucked his clipboard under one arm to head inside.

"So where's Adelaide?" Henri asked, stopping Dempsey in his tracks.

"Running her own business. Having a life outside the Hurricanes." Without him.

The knowledge still gutted him.

"Since I'm on a real roll with advice today, can I offer a second piece?" Henri brushed some dirt off his helmet.

"Definitely not." Pivoting away from his brother, he noticed some of his players were lying on the field.

Were they that tired? Had he run them that hard?

The idea bothered him. A lot.

"Dude, I'm not claiming to be an expert on women." Henri hovered at his shoulder, carrying the water cooler inside. "Far from it with the way my marriage is going these days."

The dark tone in Henri's voice revealed a truth the guy had probably tried hard to keep quiet.

"Sorry to hear it." Because even though Dempsey was waist high in self-pity right now, he felt bad for his brother.

"My point is, I know enough about women to know you're going about it all wrong."

"Tell me something I don't know."

Henri laughed, a loud, abrupt cackle. "How much time do you have, old man?" Then, tossing his helmet and the water cooler on the ground, he pantomimed a quick right hook to Dempsey's gut. "Seriously. Don't let Adelaide go."

And then he was gone, scooping up the helmet and shouldering the cooler to go hassle the slackers left on the field. No doubt reinstalling the team morale that Dempsey had single-handedly shredded.

He wasn't sure what had shocked him more. He'd never been particularly close with Henri, sensing that the guy had resented Dempsey more than the others as kids because Henri had been close with their mother. The mother who'd left as soon as Dempsey had set foot in the Reynaud house. But that was a long time ago, and maybe he needed to shake off the idea that he was a black sheep brother. Figure out how to be a better brother.

How to show he cared about people beyond stilted words about being good teammates.

Henri was right. It was time for Dempsey to stop expecting Adelaide to read between the lines with him. Just because she understood him better than anyone didn't excuse him from spelling out his feelings for her. She deserved that and much, much more.

So damn much more.

But he was going to lay it on the line for her again, without any distractions or big gestures. And hope like hell he got it right this time. Because the truth of the matter was he couldn't live without her. His championship season didn't mean anything if he couldn't share it with her.

The woman he loved.

Adelaide dug to the bottom of her pint of strawberry gelato while seated on her kitchen counter in the middle of the afternoon, wishing strawberry tasted half as good as chocolate ice cream.

Except everything chocolate reminded her of Dempsey after their chocolate-sauce encounter, and if she thought about Dempsey, she would cry. And after three days back home alone in her crappy apartment, she did not feel like crying anymore.

Okay, she did a little. Especially if she thought about how much effort he'd put into romancing her on Sunday after the game. How many other women would trade anything to be treated the way Dempsey treated her? Yet she'd discounted all his efforts in the hope of hearing he loved her.

Dumb. Dumb. Dumb.

Except that she'd do it all over again because she was one of those romantic girls who believed the right guy would hand her his whole heart forever and ever. She didn't think she could go through life if that turned out to be a myth. Then again, she wasn't sure she could go another day without Dempsey.

But she could probably go through a few more single-serving-size gelatos. She'd bought every flavor that didn't contain chocolate, determined to find some new taste to love.

Her doorbell rang as she was on her way back to the freezer.

No doubt her mother on a mission of mercy to lift her spirits. Little did Della know that Adelaide was only going to stuff her with gelato to avoid hearing any kind platitudes about waiting for the right one to come along.

She yanked open the door, only to have the safety chain catch, and remembered too late she was supposed to look through the peephole. She didn't live in Dempsey's ultrasafe mansion anymore.

He stood on her welcome mat.

The man who hadn't left her thoughts in days wore black running shorts and a black-and-gold Hurricanes sideline T-shirt like the ones the players wore. He must have come straight from practice, because he made a point not to wander around town in team gear that made him all the more recognizable. He looked good enough to eat, reminding her why all the gelato in the world was not going to satisfy her craving.

"May I come in?" he asked, making her realize she'd stood there gawking without saying anything.

"Of course. Just a sec." She closed the door partway

to remove the chain, then opened it again, more than a little wary.

She told herself it was just as well he'd stopped by, since she had wanted to give him that damn deed back to the manufacturing facility. Except he looked as tired as she felt, the circles under his eyes even darker than the ones she knew were on her face. The rest of him looked as good as ever, however, his thighs so deliciously delineated as he walked that she thought about all the times she'd seen them naked. Against her own.

"How'd practice go?" Her voice was dry and she cleared it. She'd continued to work for the team from home, not wanting to leave him in the lurch.

He hadn't said anything about her absence at the training facility, acknowledging her work-related emails with curt "thanks" that had been typical of him long before now.

"Poorly. I haven't been myself this week and I've been pushing the guys too hard. Henri called me on it today. I'm going to do better." He wandered around her living room, touching her things, looking at her paintings over the ancient nonfunctional fireplace.

She was surprised that he'd admitted to screwing up. No, that wasn't true. She was more surprised that he'd screwed up in the first place. He normally put so much effort into thinking how to best coach a team, he didn't make the type of mistakes he had described.

"I'm glad. That you're going to be better with the team, that is." Nervous, she wandered over to the refrigerator that was so old that modern retro styles copied the design. "Would you like a gelato?"

She pulled out a coconut-lime flavor and cracked open the top.

"No, thank you." He set down a statue of a cat that she used to display Mardi Gras beads. "I came here to bring you this. You left it behind when you moved out your things."

He set a familiar ring box on the breakfast bar dividing the living area from the kitchen. Her on one side. Him on the other. A ring in between.

As if her heart wasn't battered enough already.

"That stone is worth a fortune." She hadn't taken the yellow diamond either, of course. That one, she'd left on his bathroom vanity.

"And you're worth everything to me, so you can see you are well suited." He opened the box and took out the ring. "It's not an engagement ring. I'd already given you one of those. Adelaide, this one is the grown-up version of that bracelet I made you. Something you've worn every day of your life since I gave it to you."

"Friendship is forever," she reminded him, something he'd told her the day he gave it to her.

He came into the kitchen and eased her grip on the coconut-lime gelato, then set it on the linoleum countertop.

"I'm glad you remember that." He held the ring close to her bracelet. "Look and see how the patterns match."

"I see." She blinked hard, not sure what he was getting at. But she couldn't wear that beautiful ring on her finger every day without her heart breaking more.

"The spoon part is supposed to remind you that you're still my best friend. Forever." He slipped his hand around hers. "The rare blue garnet is there to tell you how rare it is to find love and friendship in the same place. And how beautiful it is when it happens."

Her gaze flipped up to his as she tried to gauge his expression. To gauge his heart.

"That's not what you said when you gave it to me." She shook her head. "It's not fair to say things you don't mean—"

"I do, Adelaide." He took both her hands in his. Squeezed. "Please let me try to explain. I got it all wrong before, I know. But it was not for lack of effort."

"It was a beautiful date," she acknowledged, knowing she'd never recover from loving him. There would never be a man in her life like this one.

And it broke her heart into tiny pieces if he thought he could win her back by trotting out the right phrases.

"I spent so much time thinking about how to make the proposal perfect—how to make you stay—I never gave any thought to what *you* might want. What was important to *you*." He shook his head. "It's like spending all my time shoring up the defense and ignoring the fact that I had no offense."

She tried not to mind the sports metaphor. And, heaven help her, she did understand exactly what he meant.

"So I was just caught off guard at how much I missed the mark that day. It must tell you something that a mention of love threw me so far off my game I didn't even know what to say in return."

"You would know what to say if you felt it, too." She stepped back, needing to protect herself from the hurt this conversation was inevitably going to bring.

"No. Just the opposite. I didn't understand what I felt because I don't say those words, Addy." He looked at her as if he was perfectly serious.

And beneath the trappings of the wealthy, powerful man who was the CEO of international companies and would one day coach a team to the Super Bowl, Adelaide saw the wounded gaze of her old friend. The boy who hadn't been given enough love as a child yet still found enough kindness in his heart to rescue a little girl from a trouncing because he was an innately fair and honorable person.

He blinked and the look vanished as though it had never been, but she was left with an understanding that should have been there all along. She, who thought she knew him so well, hadn't seen the most obvious answer.

Dempsey Reynaud had never been in love. Had probably never spoken the words in his life to anyone. There was certainly never a mention of love in those notes she'd written to accompany the parting gifts to his old girlfriends.

"I understand." She nodded, the full weight of his explanation settling on her, yet still not quelling her concerns about the future, the ache of her heart. "But you can see why I'd want to feel loved and to hear that I'm loved if I was going to be your wife?"

She edged closer to him again, understanding now that she didn't need to worry about protecting her heart. If anything, she ought to think about his.

"I understand now. But it took three days of hell—not sleeping, not eating, missing you every second and damn near killing every guy on a fifty-three-man roster—to get it through my head." He swallowed hard. Tipped his forehead to hers. "So please, Adelaide, let me slide this ring on your right hand. And I want you to wear it forever because our friendship is even more beautiful now than when I gave you that bracelet so long ago."

She took a moment to think, to look in his eyes and see the truth. That they were bound together through years of love and friendship, tied together in a way that was strong. Lasting.

"Yes." She nodded. Kissed his rough cheek and liked it so much she kissed the other one, too. "But it's going to be hard being just friends after—"

He produced the second ring.

She made an unintelligible sound that might have been a cry of relief, hope or pure joy. She wasn't sure. She could feel her legs going unsteady beneath her, though.

"I brought this back with me, too." He held it between them, their foreheads still tipped together.

"It hurt leaving it behind." A few of her tears splashed down on it.

"It tore my heart from my chest to find it." He leaned back to kiss her forehead. Her temples. "But since I didn't get to personally put it on your finger the first time, I'm looking at this as my chance to do something right."

He got down on one knee in her tiny, ancient kitchen, his handsome face so intent on her that her heart did backflips.

"Adelaide Thibodeaux," he continued. "You are my heart and I am not whole without you. I love you more than anything. Will you do me the honor of being my wife?"

Speechless because her heart was in her throat, she nodded. But as the beautiful yellow diamond slid into place on her left hand, Adelaide recovered enough to fling her arms around him.

"I love you more than anything, too. And that was my favorite proposal yet." Her voice was all wobbly, along with the rest of her.

Her big, strong future husband lifted her off her feet and pressed his lips to hers, his arms banded around her waist. He took his time with the kiss, making up for the days and nights they'd missed each other. Heat tingled over her skin, awakening every part of her. She was breathless and a little light-headed by the time he broke contact.

"I meant it as a compliment that I wanted you to be on my team." He smiled up at her and she laughed.

"I am complimented." Her heart swelled with love for him. She bracketed his face in her hands while he carried her into her bedroom. "But thank you for letting me be more than that."

"I'm going to be the best husband you can imagine," he promised, his golden-brown eyes dazzling her more than either of the rings on her fingers.

"I'm going to remind you every day that I love you," she promised him in return, her body sinking into the bed as Dempsey laid her down.

He stretched out next to her, his muscular frame filling her small bed so that he crowded her in the most delicious ways.

"I'd like to start now, by adoring every inch of you." His words were warm on her neck as he kissed that vulnerable spot.

"That's perfect, because every inch of me has missed you." She trailed a hand through his dark hair, knowing she was the luckiest woman on earth.

Her fairy tale hadn't ended. The best part was just beginning.

* * * * *

*Attorney Alexandra Lattimore isn't looking for love.
She's home to help her family—and escape problems
at work. But sparks with former rival Jackson Strom
are too hot to resist. Will her secrets keep them from
rewriting their past?*

Read on for a sneak peek at
Rivalry at Play
by Nadine Gonzalez.

"Mornin'," Jackson said, as jovial at 6:00 a.m. as he was at noon.
He loaded Alexa's bag into the trunk and held open the passenger
door for her. "Let's get out of here."

Alexa hesitated. Within the blink of an eye, she'd slipped back
in time. She was seventeen and Jackson was her prom date, holding
open the door to a tacky rental limo. There he was, the object of her
every teenage dream. She went over and touched him, just to make
sure he was real.

"Are you okay?" he asked.

"No," she said. "I was thinking… If things were different back
in high school—"

"Different how?"

"If I were nicer."

"Nicer?"

"Or just plain nice," she said. "Do you think you might have
asked me to prom or homecoming or whatever?"

Jackson went still, but something moved in his eyes. Alexa
panicked. What was she doing stirring things up at dawn?

"Forget it!" She backed away from him. "I don't know why I

said that. It's early and I haven't had coffee. Do you mind stopping for coffee along the way?"

He reached out and caught her by the waist. He pulled her close. The air between them was charged. "I didn't want *nice*. I wanted Alexandra Lattimore, the one girl who was anything but nice and who ran circles around me."

"Why didn't you say anything?"

"I was scared."

"You thought I'd reject you?"

"If I had asked you to prom or whatever, would you have said yes?"

"I don't know," she admitted. "Maybe not…or I could have changed my mind. Only it would have been too late. You would have found yourself a less complicated date."

"And end up having a forgettable night?"

"That's not so bad," she said. "I would have ended up hating myself."

Alexa wanted to be that person he'd imagined, imperious and unimpressed by her peers or her surroundings, but she wasn't. She never had been. She'd lived her whole life in a self-protective mode, rejecting others before they could reject or dismiss her. She now saw it for what it was: a coward's device.

His hand fell from her waist. He stepped back and held open the car door even wider. "Aren't you happy we're not those foolish kids anymore?"

Alexa leaned forward and kissed him lightly on the lips. "You have no idea," she whispered and slid into the waiting seat.

Don't miss what happens next in…
Rivalry at Play *by Nadine Gonzalez,*
the next book in the Texas Cattleman's Club:
Ranchers and Rivals *series!*

Available July 2022 wherever
Harlequin Desire books and ebooks are sold.

Harlequin.com

Love Harlequin romance?

DISCOVER.

Be the first to find out about promotions,
news and exclusive content!

Facebook.com/HarlequinBooks

Twitter.com/HarlequinBooks

Instagram.com/HarlequinBooks

Pinterest.com/HarlequinBooks

YouTube.com/HarlequinBooks

ReaderService.com

EXPLORE.

Sign up for the Harlequin e-newsletter and
download a free book from any series at
TryHarlequin.com

CONNECT.

Join our Harlequin community to
share your thoughts and connect
with other romance readers!
Facebook.com/groups/HarlequinConnection

HARLEQUIN

Heartfelt or thrilling, passionate or uplifting—Harlequin is more than just happily-ever-after.

With twelve different series to choose from and new books available every month, you are sure to find stories that will move you, uplift you, inspire and delight you.

SIGN UP FOR THE HARLEQUIN NEWSLETTER

Be the first to hear about great new reads and exciting offers!

Harlequin.com/newsletters